HISTORY OF THE RAIN

Four Letters of Love

As It Is In Heaven

The Fall of Light

Only Say the Word

The Unrequited

Boy in the World

Boy and Man

John

HISTORY OF THE RAIN

A Novel

Niall Williams

B L O O M S B U R Y

NEW YORK • LONDON • NEW DELHI • SYDNEY

Published by Bloomsbury USA, New York
Bloomsbury is a trademark of Bloomsbury Publishing Plc

All papers used by Bloomsbury USA are natural, recyclable products made from
wood grown in well-managed forests. The manufacturing processes conform
to the environmental regulations of the country of origin.

LIBRARY OF CONGRESS CATALOGING-IN-PUBLICATION DATA HAS BEEN APPLIED FOR

ISBN: 978-1-62040-647-2

First published in Great Britain in 2014
First U.S. edition 2014

1 3 5 7 9 10 8 6 4 2

Typeset by Hewer Text UK Ltd, Edinburgh
Printed and bound in the U.S.A. by Thomson-Shore Inc., Dexter, Michigan

Bloomsbury books may be purchased for business or promotional use.
For information on bulk purchases please contact Macmillan Corporate and
Premium Sales Department at specialmarkets@macmillan.com.

For Chris, in the rain

Everything is on its way to the river.

Ted Hughes

ONE

The Salmon in Ireland

I

The longer my father lived in this world the more he knew there was another to come. It was not that he thought this world beyond saving, although in darkness I suppose there was some of that, but rather that he imagined there must be a finer one where God corrected His mistakes and men and women lived in the second draft of Creation and did not know despair. My father bore a burden of impossible ambition. He wanted all things to be better than they were, beginning with himself and ending with this world. Maybe this was because he was a poet. Maybe all poets are doomed to disappointment. Maybe it comes from too much dazzlement. I don't know yet. I don't know if time tarnishes or polishes a human soul or if it's true that it's better to look down than up.

We are our stories. We tell them to stay alive or keep alive those who only live now in the telling. That's how it seems to me, being alive for a little while, the teller and the told.

In Faha everyone is a long story.

You anything to the MacCarrolls over in Labasheeda?

To begin you must be traced into the landscape, your people and your place found. Until they are you are in the wrong story.

My mother is MacCarroll.

I was thinking that. But you are . . . ?

Swain. Ruth Swain.

Swain?

We are our stories. The River Shannon passes below our house on its journey to the sea.

Come here, Ruthie, feel the pulse of the water, my father said, kneeling on the bank and dipping his hand, palm to current, then reaching up to take my hand in his. He put our arm into the cold river and at once it was pulled seaward like an oar. I was seven years old. I had a blue dress for summertime.

Here, Ruthie, feel.

His sleeve darkened and he rowed our arm back and let us be taken again, a little eddy of low sounds gargling as the throat of the river laughed realising what a peculiar thing was a father and his daughter.

When it comes to Clare, when it passes our house, the river knows it is nearly free.

I am plain Ruth Swain. See me, nineteen, narrow face, MacCarroll eyes, thin lips, dull hazelnut hair, gleamy Swain skin, pale untannable oddment, bony, book-lover, reader of so many nineteenth-century novels before the age of fifteen that I became exactly too clever by half, sufferer of Smart Girl Syndrome, possessor of opinions and good marks, student of pure English, Fresher, Trinity College Dublin, the poet's daughter.

My History in College: I came, collapsed, came home again. Home – hospital, home – hospital, the dingdong of me. I have had Something Amiss, Something Puzzling, and We're Not Sure Yet. I was Fine except for Falling Down. I have been Gone for Tests, Not Coming Right, Terrible Weak, Not Herself, and just A Bit Off, depending on the teller and whether loud or whisper, in Nolan's shop or on the windowsill of Prendergast's post office after Mass. For the record, I have never been Turning Yellow, never been complaining of the bowels, intestines or kidneys, never been

4

spotted, swollen, palsied, never wetting, bleeding, oozing, nor, God-forgive-me, Bitch of the Brouders, raving. Mine is not the story. I am plain Ruth Swain, bedbound, here, attic room beneath the rain, in the margin, where the narrator should be, between this world and the next.

This is my father's story. I am writing it to find him. But to get to where you're going you have to first go backwards. That's directions in Ireland, it's also T. S. Eliot.

My father was named Virgil by his father who was named Abraham by his father who once upon a time was the Reverend Absalom Swain in Salisbury, Wiltshire. Who the Reverend's father was I have no clue, but sometimes when I'm on the blue tablets I take off into a game of extreme Who Do You Think You Are? and go Swain-centuries deep. I follow the trail in reverse, Reverends and Bishops, past the pulpit-thumpers, the bible-wavers, the side-burn and eyebrow-growers. I keep going, pass long-ago knights, crusaders and other assorted do-lallies, eventually going as far back as The Flood. Then in the final segment, ad-breaks over and voiceover dropped to a whisper, I trace all the way back to God Himself and say *Who Do You Think You Are?*

We are Swains. I read an essay once where the critic complained there was a distance from reality in Dickens's characters' names. He didn't know Dickens couldn't sleep. That he walked the graveyards at night. He didn't know Moses Pickwick was a coach-owner in Bath, or the church register at Chatham lists the Sowerberry family, undertakers, or that one Oliver Twiste was born in Salford, and a Mr Dorrett was confined in the Marshalsea prison when Dickens senior was there. I know, weird that I know that. But if you lie in bed all day with nothing but books you won't be Class One Normal yourself, and anyway Swains don't do Normal. Open the phonebook for County Clare. Turn to S. Run your finger down past Patrick Swabb the hurling chemist in Clarecastle and Fionnuala Swan who lives by the vanishing lake in Tubber, and before you get to Sweeney there we are. Between Sweeney and Swan we're the only entry, between the Bird King and the last daughter of Lir: Swain. The world is more outlandish than some people's imaginations.

My actual great-grandfather I never met, but because of him the Swain side of the family are what Nan Nonie calls Queer Fish. Out of the mists of my night-time unsleeping I sometimes see him, the Reverend. He too cannot sleep and walks away from a shadow church at marching pace, striking out past a graveyard where the headstones tilt like giant teeth and the stars are bared. He cannot get where he is going. His burden is an intense restlessness that will not let him lie down, and so while his lamb-wife Agnes sleeps on the very edge of their bed the Reverend walks the night. He walks twenty miles without pause. From him escapes a low murmuring hum that may be prayers. Hands behind his back, he is like a man with Business Elsewhere, and none of those he passes, lost souls, rumpled shades, dare delay him. He has the Swain jaw, the sharp up-jut, the grey beard-line that though he shaves twice daily remains like a half-mask he cannot take off. I see him, pacing out past the yew tree in the churchyard. What his business is, where he goes to meet it and how exactly it is transacted are all enfolded in the mystery of ancestors. He can only be followed so far. Above the tree I sometimes throw a fistful of stars, hang a crescent moon, but for my moon and stars the Reverend does not pause; he paces on into the dark, and then is gone.

Just a brief shiver of great-grandfather.

*

What the Reverend bequeaths to our story is the Swain Philosophy of Impossible Standard. In the year eighteen hundred and ninety-five he leaves it to his son at the christening, dipping the boy into the large cold name *Abraham*, and stepping back from the wailing, jutting the jaw. He wants his son to aspire. He wants him to outreach the ordinary and be a proof to God of the excellence of His Creation. That is how I think of it. The basis of the Philosophy of Impossible Standard is that no matter how hard you try you can't ever be good enough. The Standard raises as you do. You have to keep polishing your soul ahead of Entering the Presence. Something like that.

And Grandfather Abraham began polishing straight away. By age twelve, nineteen hundred and seven, he was a medal magnet. For Running, One Hundred Yards, Two Hundred Yards, Long Jump, Hop Step and Jump, Grandfather was your man.

Then he discovered the Pole-vault.

In St Bartholemew's School for Boys (established 1778, Headmaster, Thomas Tupping, a man notable for nothing but having eight too many teeth and lips that never touched) Abraham took the Reverend's restlessness to new heights, tearing down the runway with his lance and firing himself into the sky.

And that's where he arrives in my imagination, my mad grand-father, a blur-boy of white singlet and shorts, short sharp hair, blue eyes, charging like a knight towards an invisible enemy. There's no one watching. It's just him after school on a grey afternoon. Blackbirds have settled on the playing fields. The bounce of his stride echoes in the pole. It's not fibreglass but wood. The wind must think it's a mast and he a sail too small for lifting.

His pace quickens, his knees lift, the blackbirds turn. Down the cinderway he comes, crisp *crunch-crunch-crunch*, man on the end of a stick. Mouth pursed out and open he blows a wind-note with

7

each step, *whuu-whuu-whuu*, announcing himself, warning the air that he is coming. His eyes are locked on the concrete trap. It's his entranceway. The pole lowers, wavers slightly. A hard clack is the last sound Grandfather hears on earth.

And here he is, Abraham in lift-off, his soul bubbling as he climbs, entering the upper air with perfect propulsion and ascension both. An instant and he no longer needs the pole. Hands it off. It falls to ground, a distant double-bounce off the solid world below. The blackbirds take fright, rise and glide to the goalmouth. Amazement blues my grandfather's eyes. He's at the apex of a triangle, a pale angular man-bird. His legs air-walk, his everything unearthed as he crosses the bar above us all. There is a giddy gulp of the Impossible and he sort of rolls over in the sky, pressed up against the iron clouds where God must be watching. His mind whites out. His body believes it is winged, has vaulted into some other way of being. Abraham Swain is Up There and Away, paddling the air above the ordinary and just for a moment praying: *let me never fall to earth.*

Mrs Quinty says I have Superabundance of Style and must trim back. She was once my English teacher and comes now Tuesdays and Thursdays from the Tech after she finishes. I'm on her rounds. I'm her Tuesdays with Ruth (and Thursdays). Because of me Mrs Quinty will be taking the bypass around Purgatory and shooting straight on into Heaven.

She predicts a Brilliant Career for me if I will only Trim Back.

I will also need to stay alive.

Before she comes upstairs to my room she has a few words with my mother about My Condition.

Mrs Quinty is a small tight bow. I mean, *tight*. Everything is to be kept neat and precise. But since the departure of Mr Quinty, a lorry driver with black curls who left our narrative some time previous, she now fears something secretly loosening in her all the time. To address this she frequently gives herself a little pull in, a little sharp tug on her blouse or jacket that goes unremarked in these parts because people know her circumstances and allow for oddities. If Mr Quinty had Passed On it would have been better. If he had Gone to His Reward. Mrs Quinty would cope; she suited widowhood, and had the wardrobe. But as it was, despite Tommy Quinty being heavily pregnant with eighteen years of Victoria Sponge, Lemon Drizzle, Apple Upside Down, Rhubarb Custard Tart and Caramel Eclairs, a brazen long-legged hairdresser called Sylvia in Swansea

Wales managed to overlook the Collected Cakes and see only the black curls of the same Tommy.

He stopped in for a Do, Nan says, and he's not Done yet.

Although everyone in the parish knows this since Martin Conway took the Under-Sixteen-and-a-Halfs over to a match, stopped in Swansea for chips and toilets and saw Tommy in an outrageous quiff, powder-blue blazer and *white* shoes, no one lets on to Mrs Quinty. As if by secret agreement it was decided Tommy Quinty would drop out of all conversation. Sometimes he's in a whisper down in Ryan's or a joke out at the Crossroads on the night of a forty-five drive when the tarts are served, but for the most part he has Left the Narrative.

But in doing so he left Mrs Quinty a chill. Also migraine attacks, tinnitus, inflammation of the ear, Eustachian catarrh, occasional left-sided deafness caused she will tell you by retracted membrana tympani, swelling of glands, lacunar tonsillitis, dizziness, disorders of the digestive system – All Sorts – and what she herself diagnosed as cheese-breath.

Mrs Quinty suffers. Of illnesses she has whatever is going. Her only hope is to keep the little bow of herself tight and teach on. The teaching keeps her going. When I was her pupil a hundred years ago her classes were notable for being the only ones in which absolute silence reigned. Even though her frame was diminutive and her dress sense very Costume Drama, everyone knew: you don't mess with Mrs Quinty. She came in and the first thing she did was open the windows. It could be hail and gale outside. Mrs Quinty opened the windows. Then she took out these little wipes and wiped down the surface of the desk. That lady brought with her her own *environment*.

Still, the Tech was the last place you'd think she should be. The native population of that school was at no point under the control of Mr Cuddy. Perplexity at managing teenagers had given him a face like the letter Z and he kept it largely in his office where he pursued more available consolations by solving crossword puzzles. From school-life, one example: one Christmas week the crib was set up in the Assembly Hall, a life-size alabaster Baby Jesus, Mary and Joseph, two not-life-size camels, two lambs, one cow, one donkey, and three very Islamic-looking Magi. They were laid out on a bed of genuine hay (used) that Jacinta Dineen brought in her bag. Then, while Mrs Murphy in Room 7 was synthesising 'O Come All Ye Faithful', Baby Jesus was kidnapped. A ransom note was left in the hay. It said: 'We have Jesus.'

Mr Cuddy called in every student for questioning – *Have you seen Jesus?* – and eventually announced that unless Jesus was returned immediately there would be no Christmas Mass.

Baby Jesus did not return. He had not been seen on any of the school buses heading in the general direction of Kilrush or Kildysart or Ennis and so it was concluded: Our Lord was still in the Tech.

The First Years were recruited to help look for Jesus. Every desk, cupboard, locker was opened. But nobody could find Him.

Another note appeared in the hay. It said: 'Stop serching'.

By this stage the whole school was on the side of the kidnappers and false sightings were announced hourly. Jesus was in the Chemistry Lab. He was in the Girls' Changing Room before Games. He was taking French Oral with the Sub Miss Trigot.

That lad is everywhere, Thomas Halvey said.

Mr Cuddy decided to call the kidnappers' bluff; he reversed himself and said Christmas Mass was going ahead anyway. He figured when the parents came in Baby Jesus would be back in his crib. The Mass would shame the kidnappers into surrendering their hostage.

It didn't.

We all attended that Mass with the crib on the altar and, in the place of the Infant, a lamb on whose forehead someone had taped the word 'Jesus'.

No, the Tech is the last place you'd expect to find Mrs Quinty. But somehow the teaching saves her from herself. In the classroom she's invincible. It's ordinary life she finds hard.

When Doctor Mahon asks her why she doesn't retire from teaching on Medical Grounds her answer is: I have My Cross.

When she comes in downstairs Mrs Quinty rests her cross and asks my mother what I am on. Like Synge on Aran I hear the world through a neat knothole in my floor.

'Is her mouth very dry? Mine was terribly dry.'

'Did you bring any cake?' Nan calls from her seat by the fire. Nan is Mam's mam, she's a Talty, ninety-seven or ninety-nine, is shrunk to a doll-sized grandmother with large hands and feet. She has what Margaret Crowe calls the All-Simons, which is basically a refutation of the invention of time; all time is the same to Nan, she has that most remarkable of skills, the habit of living, and has it so perfected now that death has given up and gone away. In her Foxford blanket and ancient pampooties Nan is part-Cherokee, part-Mrs Markleham in *David Copperfield*. Mrs Markleham was the one who was nick-named The Old Soldier, a little sharp-eyed woman who always wore the one unchangeable hat. Mrs Markleham's was ornamented with artificial flowers and two hovering butterflies; Nan has the same sharp eyes and hers is a man's tweed cap. It's flat and old and faded, but plays a part later on.

'How is she doing today?'

'No change, really,' Mam says.

As politeness dictates, the conversation goes on, but we have no time for it. Mrs Quinty tightens up and brings herself up the stairs. Thirteen steep steps, more a ladder than a stairs proper, rising from the up-slope of the flagstones across from the fire and up over the dresser. For a woman with so many illnesses she has a firm step, even carrying her cross. Here she comes.

'Now,' she says when she enters the room. She says it as though she's bringing herself into focus, or as if to herself she's announcing her own landing in this bedroom with the big rough handmade bed, the skylight and the three thousand nine hundred and fifty-eight books.

It allows her to regain her breath, to consider the racing of her heart, some murmurous inner pulsing – *gall bladder?* – and to adjust her eyes to entering the sky.

'Now.'

There's the pale gleam you have to get used to up here, especially because of the rain. The rain streams down the skylight so it looks like we're under a river. In the sky.

'Now, Ruth.'

'Hello, Mrs Quinty.'

And while she gets her breath, Dear Reader, get acquainted. See how compact she is. See her pinched face, tight to the chin, as if Life was a very narrow thing you had to get through. Pointed, sharp-looking knees, charcoal skirt to shins, grey tights, shoes size six, laced, polished but puddle-dulled by the weathers of west Clare and by crossing our yard, mouse-coloured blouse with top button concertinaing together some flaccid cords in her throat and lending her voice that tendency towards – *Sorry, Mrs Quinty* – squeak, black cardigan with general dusting of chalk, tiny linen handkerchief in the sleeve at the ready. Her hair is a bun – sad reminder of Tommy the Cake-man who took all her Sweetness – her lips, where are her lips? There's the faintest remnant of them, a trace-line of not quite pink, her cheeks powdered, an all-over De Valera Comely Aged look that was very popular when it first appeared behind the yellow cellophane in the window of

MacMahon's Drapery in Faha. Glasses of round rims make huge her eyes and in them you see fear and goodness. People here are *good*. They're so good it takes your breath away. It's the kind of goodness that shows best when something goes wrong. That's when they shine. They're mad and odd as cats on bicycles but they've been shining around our family now since Aeney. And none more so than Mrs Quinty.

Mrs Quinty, meet the Reader.

Mrs Quinty needs reading glasses but has not brought them. Instead she takes off her regular glasses to look at you.

While she does I sit pillow-propped and wonder about her surname. I wonder if they were Quincy not Quinty once, and some relation, say in 1776, say boarding a ship for the New World, hurried his handwriting, blotted his C to a T, or maybe he lost an eye, was nicknamed Squinty, and dropped the S on his return to Proper Life, *Call me Quinty*, or maybe was someone grand and founded Quincy Massachusetts but was later driven out in scandal, or maybe they were people called Quin and there was one signed himself T who . . .

Less, Ruth. Less.

Mrs Quinty hands me back the most recent pages of my book. I only give her the ones in which she doesn't feature. I write like a man and I'm a bit Extreme, she has told me previously. I am that anachronism, a book-reader, and from this my writing has developed Eccentric Superabundance of Style, Alarming Borrowings, Erratic Fluctuations, and I must Must lose my tendency to Capitalisation.

Once when I answered that Emily Dickinson capitalised, Mrs Quinty told me Emily Dickinson was not A Good Example, that she was a Peculiar Case, and the way she said it you knew she regretted it right away because there was a little flinching around her mouth and you could tell she had already joined the dots and

14

remembered Swains are pretty much the definition of peculiar. And so I never did ask her about what it meant to write like a man.

Two-handed, Mrs Quinty lifts the glasses free of the minor parsnip of her nose, holds them just in front of her and scrutinises the dust gathered there. Rain makes bars of light and dark down her face and mine, as if we're inside the jail of it.

Mrs Quinty draws out her handkerchief, polishes, scrutinises again, finds more of the dust or smears school-life produces and cleans further. 'What have you been reading, Ruth?'

I have already eaten all of Dickens – Pickwick to Drood. I can tell you why Charles Dickens is the greatest novelist there ever was or will be and why all great novelists since are in debt to *Great Expectations*. I can remember things you've forgotten, like when Pip drank so much tar-water he went around *smelling of new fence*, or when Mr Pumblechook was proud to be in the company of the chicken that had the honour of being eaten by the new gentleman Pip. I read that book first in the class of Miss Brady over in Faha N.S. where there was this wire-rack library with rag-eared paperbacks donated by parents, along with a full set of *Guinness Book of Records* 1970–80. But it wasn't until Mr Mason when I was fourteen that I understood it was the Best Book Ever.

I've read all the usuals, Austen, Brontë, Eliot, Hardy, but Dickens is like this different country where the people are brighter, more vivid, more comic, more tragic, and in their company you feel the world is richer, more fantastic than you imagined.

But right now I'm reading RLS. He's my new favourite. I like writers who were sick. I like it that my father's first book was *Treasure Island*, a small red hardcover Regent Classics (Book 1, Purnell & Sons Ltd, Paulton, Somerset) with the stamp on the inside page: *Highfield School, First Prize*.

I like it that Robert Louis Stevenson said that to forget oneself is to be happy, that his imagination sailed him away into adventures while his body was lying in his bed with the first stages of consumption. I like it that he called himself an inland castaway, and that as a young man he decided he wanted to go walking around some of France, sleep out à la belle étoile *with a donkey* he christened Modestine and who, he wrote, 'had a faint semblance to a lady of my acquaintance' (Book 846, *Travels with a Donkey*, Wadsworth Classics). I know that lady too.

I myself am going to write *Travels with a Salmon* when I get further downriver.

I want to tell Mrs Quinty all this, but just say: 'Robert Louis Stevenson.' And then, by way of passing comment, add, 'I want to read all these books.'

'*All?*' She looks around at them, in proper terms my father's library, but really just the enormous collection of books he accumulated which has now been brought up to my room and stacked from the floor to where the angle of the skylight cuts them off.

'They were my father's. I'm going to read them all before I die.'

Mrs Quinty doesn't approve of any mention of dying. From her sleeve she takes the handkerchief and applies it with a light brushing to beneath her nose where the deadly word may be lingering. She catches what must once have been her lower lip in her top teeth. There is a little pinking, a flush of feeling that the powder on her cheeks cannot camouflage. She looks at the wild stacks, the ones that rise behind the others, so it seems we are in a sea and there are waves of books coming towards the boat-bed and somewhere in there my father has gone.

She doesn't quite know what to say.

'I don't quite know what to say,' she says.

'That's all right, Mrs Quinty.'

Against the cresting of emotion she tightens herself a bit more.

She pulls in her narrow shoulders and presses her knees together and she actually seems to go *in* a little. I am sorry for upsetting her, and allow a time when we both just sit here, me in the bed and she beside it, and we let the sounds of the rain take the conversation away.

'Well now,' Mrs Quinty says, giving herself a little tug. 'That is a lot of rain.'

And neither of us speaks again for some moments, we just sit up here in this sky-room flowing with rain. Then I turn to Mrs Quinty and nod towards the books that all smell of fire and rain and I tell her, 'I am going to read them all because that is where I will find him.'

3

I left my boy-blur in the air.

Always, you'll be glad to know, from his vaults Grandfather landed; but always with an unsayable disappointment.

He excelled at the school of Mr Tupping and so was quickly moved to another. The Standard rose. He was moved ahead a year, and still excelled. He came home on holidays with glowing reports but the Reverend was in his church or out seeking the few roads in Wiltshire he hadn't foot-stamped yet. The Philosophy allows for only one result: we fail the Standard. We suck small hard-boiled stones of disappointment in everything. The Swain face is narrow and, in the case of my aunts, seems to chew its own cheeks.

Abraham went to Oxford to Prepare for Life, which was the Reverend's term for what Abraham was to do while waiting to get The Call. He was to go up to Oxford and read Classics – which were not in fact the red hard-covered James Fenimore Cooper's *The Last of the Mohicans* (Book 7, Regent Classics, Somerset), the fat full water-swollen *Oliver Twist* (Book 12, Penguin Classics, London) that has come unglued at Chapter the Forty-Fifth, 'Fatal Consequences', and smells amazingly like toast, or even Tolstoy's *Master and Man* (Book 745, Everyman edition, New York) which belonged once to someone who left no further mark on this world other than the peculiarly rigid handwriting with which he wrote *belongs to Tobias Greaves* on the flyleaf of that stiff paperback. It turns out that Classics meant none of these but a lot of Greek and

Latin in slim matching volumes in red or green hardcovers with glossy cream pages intent on sticking together and sealing themselves for good.

Read and wait; that was the plan.

God had a good few clients in those days and He hadn't had anyone invent mobiles or texting yet so it took time to get around to calling them each individually at whatever they were doing, so you just had to wait. The Vocation would come in due course; the Reverend was sure. Abraham was going into the Ministry. After all, Soul-polishing was the family business.

So my grandfather waited. He read his load of Latin. He found one of the venerable poles they had there in Oxford and with it he reached New Heights.

You'd think that with him being so often that bit nearer the sky, and having that big-hint name, *Abraham*, he'd have gotten The Call right away. It was like he was knocking at the door. I suppose God might have thought it was a bit forward of him. He might have thought Abraham had a case of the Mickey Nolans who Nan says thinks three fingers of hair gel and pointy shoes makes him The Chosen One. Ever since it worked on Pauline Frawley, hoisting her skirt up four inches in the Ladies in Ryan's before going out to shake her altogether in front of him to TJ Mooney's version of Neil Diamond, he's convinced he's God's Gift.

Well, anyway, turns out God had enough gifts right then, and didn't have any great need for Abraham Swain. There was Grandfather sitting in the library all morning reading his lyric verse in Latin, his Catullus and Horace and getting on first-name basis with the Hendecasyllabic, the Lesser and Greater Asclepiad, the Glyconic, those boys, and in the late afternoon vaulting himself like an offering up against the damp skies of Oxford, as if he was shouting *Helloooo Lord*.

But no, The Call didn't come. The Almighty Fisher wasn't fishing.

I suppose the son of a different Reverend might have faked it, might have gone home and said *yes Dad, He hooked me Wednesday*, but my grandfather was a Swain, and he expected perfectly clear and personal communication because the whole Philosophy is based on the notion that one thing alone is for certain: God meets the Standard.

When He calls you you're Called.

And so my grandfather couldn't lie. He thought maybe The Call would come in a church and so he spent a fair bit of time in the evening candles. And from his kneeling intensity some soul-absorption must have happened, genetically unmodified, because our family has paid a small fortune to chandeliers Rathbone & Sons, Dublin, and we have the only house in Faha whose curtains smell of candle wax.

(I thought I should call our village something else. I spent a whole week writing names in the back pages of an Aisling copy. Musical ones like Shreen, Glaun, Sheeda, mysterious ones like Scrapul, meaningful ones like Easky, which is fishy, or Killbeg, which is basically Small Church. I was going to use Lisnabrawshkeen which is the village in the skinny white paperback of *The Poor Mouth* (Book 980, Flann O'Brien, Seaver Books, New York) and has the opening line 'I am noting down the matters which are in this document because the next life is approaching me swiftly' but every time I said Lisnabrawshkeen I felt I was spraying a little speech impediment at the reader. *Lisnabrawshkeen.* I was afraid of using Faha because if these pages get out in the world there'll be right roolaboola, not because of scandal, not because of outrage, but because everyone will try to find out if they're In It. In these parts to be in a book is still something.

'Will I get a mention?' Father Tipp asked me, sitting in beside the bed, tugging both knees of his trousers to protect the crease and, in the Good Cause of Less Ironing, giving display to the scariest three inches of white shin you ever saw. That priest is a lovely man, but his skin is seriously *white*.

To be Left Out of the Narrative is catastrophe altogether.

What did you do to her to be Left Out? I can imagine the long faces, like the man in Pickwick who found fly buttons in his sausage.

Irish people will read anything as long as it's about them. That's what I think. We are our own greatest subject and though we've gone and looked elsewhere about the world we have found that there are just no people, no subject as fascinating as We Ourselves. We are simply amazing. So, even while I'm writing these words in my copy, there's a whole throng, Allens Barrys Breens Considines Cartys Corrys Dooleys Dempseys Dunnes Egans Flynns Finucanes Hayes Hogans and – don't even begin the Macs and Os – all angling over my shoulder in the bed here to see if they're In.

The Ark.

Sit back. Leave room. If I live I'll get to you all.)

God couldn't get to Abraham Swain, but He sent a message. He sent it queerways through a nineteen-year-old called Gavrilo Princip who was waiting by the bridge over the innocent River Miljacka in the city of Sarajevo. The message went loudly from Gavrilo's gun into the passing head of Archduke Ferdinand and from there out through the mouth of Lord Kitchener in England. It was a fairly blunt system actually, download speed slower than Faha dial-up, but one hundred thousand men a month got the message and signed up to fight For King and Country. My grandfather heard it in a crowded room in Oriel College where pale young men with no practical knowledge of the world but the gleaming white foreheads of those who handled beautiful ideals voted en masse to join the Oxfordshire & Buckinghamshire Light Infantry. They poured out into the night afterwards, the starlight, the spires, Mr Alexander Morrow, Mr Sydney Eacrett, Mr Matthew Cheatley, Mr Clive Paul (these and all The Fallen listed in the index of Book 547, *The Gleaming Days: History of the Ox & Bucks*, Oxford), all of them feeling like jumping, like dancing, as if for each a weight had been replaced by a lightness, as if that's what it meant, *Light Infantry*. You signed your name on the line and you felt a little lighter, a little *ascension*. Life was not so heavy after all. Now you only had to go and tell your parents.

Abraham prepared his speech on the train. He wrote out separate Key Phrases on different pieces of paper and laid them on the table. The problem was The Swain Way allowed for no vanity. He couldn't say: *I have to Save My Country*. He couldn't say: *God wants me to do this more than that*. It couldn't be that becoming a soldier was in any way better than becoming a Reverend.

A sticky wicket, Alexander Morrow said.

Abraham decided he'd go with Not Yet. God didn't want him to go into the Church just yet, first there was this war business, Father, and it would be vain and self-serving if he thought himself better than others.

He'd use The Swain Way against itself.

He got off the train and walked up past the graveyard and the tilting tombstones with that look of Elsewhere. This is the thing about the men in this family; they all look like they are on some Secret Mission. They're here with you and doing the ordinary everyday but secretly all the time some part of them is away, is thinking of their mission. It's the thing women fall in love with, the elusive bit that they think they can fish back out of the deep

Swain pool. But that's for later. I'll get to Women & Swains later.

Abraham told his mother Agnes and she excused herself from the room the way ladies did those days so she could go and Have a Moment while a wolf ate her heart.

The Reverend came in and jutted his jaw.

'Abraham?'

'Father.'

Maybe the Reverend knew right then. Maybe that was all it took. The Swain men aren't great for talk. What I imagine is the darkening of the Reverend's shave-mask, the cold fish-glitter of his eye, narrow-nosed inhale as he realises this is his punishment for imagining Abraham would be The Next Big Thing in Holy World. He turns away to the long window, clasps one hand in the other, feels the chill of the Presence and begins to pray that his son will leap to a glorious death.

THE SALMON IN IRELAND

*With Seventy-eight Illustrations from
Photographs and Two Maps*

by

'The Fisher's Friend'

London
Kegan Paul, Trench, Trübner & Co. Ltd.
Broadway House, 68–74 Carter Lane, E.C.

PREFACE

Let me begin by stating what, although perhaps evident to even the most inexperienced of anglers on their first day in this country, nonetheless deserves repetition here: Ireland is a paradise for the salmon-fisher. The plenitude of her rivers, the particular clarity of her waters and the undiminished beauty of her topography all combine towards the creation of the fisherman's idyll. Indeed in certain weather it may seem that every part of this country is lake and stream and the angler can hardly journey a few miles without encountering waters teeming with salmon or sea trout. In times of flood from numerous miniature rivers fish freely ascend. Wet weather, which is usually plentiful, suits most rivers best and if the angler is properly attired and of sturdy character there is no reason why salmon-fishing in Ireland should not provide him with an experience as close to angling paradise as can be found anywhere.

It is the intention of the author that herein shall be a complete description, drawn from personal experience, of all of the salmon rivers of Ireland. We shall provide detail of the most noteworthy runs, annual close times, dates when netting may be plied, rods plied, as well as the best Irish salmon flies, tacklemakers, etc etc. While this alone would constitute all that is required of an angler's guidebook it is the author's belief that it would be remiss if this were all when writing of salmon in Ireland. For in this country to the salmon is attributed a magical character. Here it is not forgotten that he is in a figure of two worlds, both fresh and salt water, mystical, mythic, and in many eyes no less than an alternate God. It is not only that the salmon strives after the impossible, not only that he seeks to be a creature of air as well as water, but that in moments of startling beauty and transcendence he achieves just this. Nor is such appreciation confined only to salmon-fishers. The Irish admire the heroic and all who endeavour against outrageous odds. To give but a flavour, a small boy in Galway or Limerick or Sligo will tell you the story of Fionn MacCumhaill as if it were yesterday's news. Fionn speared the Salmon of Knowledge, he will tell you, at the falls at Assaroe on the Erne. The salmon had derived its knowledge from eating the hazelnuts that dropped in the stream and now from the salmon Fionn learned that to make a poet you need: Fire of Song, Light of Knowledge and the Art of Recitation, thereby for ever sealing salmon and poetry in the Irish mind. All of which the author believes can only serve to enrich the salmon-fisher's experience in Ireland. There shall therefore be occasional anecdotes, fragments of lore, superstition and belief, all of which in this country are inextricably entangled, not least because in Ireland Saints and Salmon have for a long time been on first-name basis.

Now, having followed the advice of Richard Penn, Esq. whose twin-volume *Maxims & Hints for an Angler* and *Miseries of Fishing* (John Murray, Albemarle St., London, 1833) have long been indispensable to the present author, namely 'when you commence your acquaintance with a salmon, allow a brief period for introductions', it is time to delay no more but take a steady stance, survey the river, breathe, and cast.

4

People are odd creations, this is my theme. None odder than Swains.

On the fourteenth of August 1914 the 2nd Battalion of the Oxfordshire & Buckinghamshire Light Infantry landed at Boulogne, France.

What happened next I imagine sometimes when I am brought out of the county by ambulance. When the Minister redrew the map of hospitals in Ireland, calling them Centres for Excellence, she forgot about Clare. It's often done. We're neither one thing nor the other, neither South nor West; we're between the blowsy tramp of Kerry and the barrel-chested Galwegians, both of them dolling up, dyeing their hair and pushing to the front. So, if in Clare you have *Something*, as I have, you have to be brought out.

Timmy and Packy come for me. Timmy has flaming orange hair and the Hurling bug and if you give him the slightest encouragement he'll let you enjoy samples of his throat-singing. Packy's mother has done the impossible and made him think he's good-looking, but they're lovely really. We go without the siren but there's still that smell that is the opposite of sickness but makes you think of it anyway. And there I imagine him, Grandfather Swain in France.

Nobody now living was there. That's the thing. But a lot of them are in the pages of books. My grandfather is inside the skinny smoky copy of *All Quiet on the Western Front* by Erich Maria

Remarque (Book 672, Fawcett paperback, New York), in the stern stiff-feeling pages of *The Guns of August* (Book 1,023, Barbara Tuchman, Macmillan, London) and the buckled second-hand *Eye-Deep in Hell: Trench Warfare in World War One* (Book 1,024, John Ellis, Johns Hopkins University Press, Baltimore), books my father read to see if he could find his father.

Here is the long tall stretch of Abraham. He's in a trench, cold rat-run muck-puddle, suck and splash, cigarette smoke and then stillness. He believes he is there for a purpose, that he was called for this and he waits in the line for the word to come. The waiting is the worst for someone like him. He's got all that mind, all that inner country he keeps going around in, mines and craters, caverns and dead ends. Mind has Mountains, that's in Gerard Manley Hopkins (Book 1,555, *Poems & Prose*, Penguin, London). Or, put another way, there's a man, Gerry Quinn, lives under the shadow of Croagh Patrick in Mayo and says he goes up the mountain most days and when they asked him on the radio why he does it he said at this stage that mountain's part of me. In Maurice Sendak's *In the Night Kitchen* it comes out as 'I'm in the milk and the milk's in me.'

There in the trenches our Abraham goes up and down those inner mountains bigtime.

What am I supposed to do with this life? is a common Swainism. It's just about embedded under the skin and the way the hook is you can't pull it out, it just makes things worse. So Grandfather Abraham wriggles on the question and waits for the word. When the command comes, when Captain John Weynsley Burke appears in the trench looking all dry-cleaned and Dad's Armyish and says, 'Cigarettes out, chaps. Today I'm going to get you medals,' Abraham does not hesitate. He doesn't think there's German guns waiting to fire on him or that the next moment might be his last. He trusts that *This Is It, O boy*, he trusts that there is a purpose, however blind and mysterious, and it's pulling him in now. He can hardly breathe with the swift tow, the sense of the Great Fisher getting him on the line, and the free feeling of just going, of release. He's filled with a sudden bright-red bloom of elation. He tosses his ciggy, shouts out, and into the air already streaming with German gunfire he leaps.

Zip zip zip the bullets fly into him.

He sees the tears in his uniform and thinks: *that's interesting.*

But he keeps going.

Then he sees the blood coming. *Why is that?*

Because there's no pain yet. There's too much adrenalin and rhetoric in his bloodstream. There's whole chunky paragraphs of What it Means to King and Country. Never mind God. There's fine speeches still pumping up along his arteries, principal and subordinate clauses, the adjectival, the adverbial, in gorgeous Latinate construction and hot breath. It's the Age of Speeches. There's exclamation marks doing needle dancing in his brain, and so he gets twenty yards into the war.

Zip zip zip. Splash muck-puddle splash.

He looks sideways and sees Haynes, Harrison, Benchley, spinning backwards like they've been hooked, invisible lines whipping them off their feet and into the Next Life. It's very Spielberg. Only without the John Williams soundtrack.

Grandfather's running on. God bless him, Auntie D says when she tells it, as if she's still not sure he'll make it through her narrative and any of us will ever be born. The way she tells it, sitting bolt upright in Windermere Nursing Home, Blackrock, room at maybe thirty degrees which is the way the Filipino nurses like it, I'm not sure I will be.

Abraham's leaking now, a sticky slather of blood gathered at his belt, but he's still running and getting ready to fire his First Shot of the War. His rifle is wavering, they haven't really explained this bit, that running & shooting is quite different to standing & shooting and that running & shooting *while being shot at* is for obvious reasons, chaps, not taught at all. It'll come to you; don't worry, men.

Grandfather doesn't see any Germans. Germans being Germans, they've taken a practical approach and decided to keep their heads down and their guns up. It's more technik than the valiant British method of running at bullets.

So, as Abraham is about to fire in the general direction of where there might be Germans, zip! another rip comes in his uniform just below the heart and instantly whop down he goes.

And that's it for Grandfather.

There's a Gap.

A white space in which he's gone from the world.

I know what that's like too, when the last thing you feel is the pinch in your arm and *this might hurt just a little* and you're off into the wherever depending on the length and breadth of your imagination. My father has a whole section of his library just for this. Here's Thomas Traherne (1637–74), poet, mystic, entering Paradise (Book 1,569, *The Faber Book of Utopias*, John Carey, Faber & Faber, London): 'The corn was orient and immortal wheat which never should be reaped nor was ever sown . . . the dust and stones of the street were as precious as gold. The Gates were at first the end of the world. The green trees, when I saw them first through the gates, transported and ravished me . . . The men! O what venerable and reverend creatures did the aged seem! Immortal Cherubims! And the young men glittering and sparkling angels; and maids, strange and seraphic pieces of life and beauty! Boys and girls tumbling in the street and playing were moving jewels.'

Paradise has actual *gates*?

Thank you, Thomas. We're back: Grandfather's dead in a hole in the ground.

It's a bomb crater. The artillery boys have had fun blowing holes in France and some of the holes like this one are deep. He's down there on his side, his mind doing last-minute preparations for the Afterlife, when the whole attack above retreats and the Germans take their turn to advance.

It's like Dancing in Jane Austen, Advance and Retreat, only with guns and mud. The German attack passes Grandfather's Hole.

But one German sees Grandfather move below and he jumps down. He does. He jumps down into the hole. And he whips out his bayonet.

It's in this thin little protective scabbard that keeps the blade clean. What Grandfather sees is a flash of light. He pulls out his pistol.

Only his arm isn't working so that doesn't actually happen.

He tries again, thinking *pull out your pistol*, but there's only this torso-wriggle in the mud, and now the German is closing in on him. Grandfather's looking at his arms telling them to wake up but he sees his whole chest is this tacky darkness and he realises the bayonet is the least of his worries.

The German is standing over him, full sky behind his head, and knife in his hand.

And then, flat German face perspiring, eyes intelligent and calm, he leans down to Grandfather and does the most remarkable thing; he taps Grandfather twice on the shoulder.

'Tommy okay,' he says. 'Tommy okay.'

Then he takes the bayonet and cuts a strip of cloth and with swift efficiency ties a tourniquet round Grandfather's arm. He opens his pack of Whatever-To-Use-if-Shot that the Germans have given their soldiers and he splashes some on Grandfather's chest wound.

He looks at his handiwork a moment. Being German there are no loose bits. He nods. Grandfather sees the eyes he is to remember all his life.

'Tommy okay,' he says.

Then the German soldier goes back to War.

He climbs up the side of the crater, into Round Two of Advance Retreat, and is shot clean through the centre of his forehead.

Next thing Grandfather knows he's on a stretcher. He's not in Paradise; there are no gold streets, no immortal wheat, not a single Cherub. Instead he's in that bounce that I know too, when you're tied into the stretcher and they carry you along and all you can see is the sky above moving backwards like you're floating downriver and thinking how peculiar it is to be on your back moving through the world.

On good days it can be a bit Michelangelo, like you've drunk Heaven-Up I told Timmy and he liked that and said you're a poet like your dad. On good days before a treatment when the sky is that blue and deep and you're being borne along you feel you never saw it before, you feel it's not a roof but a door and it's actually quite open if you just take the time. That's my revelation anyhow. No angels though. I've never gone the whole Sistine.

German-bandaged, Grandfather was carried back to British Lines. The red bloom soaked out from his chest like the Overdone Imagery Mrs Quinty says I use all the time.

I don't give a Figroll, I should have said.

The thing is, it wasn't what he was expecting. So the first phase is just this enormous surprise, this O that this is how the plot is twisting. Along he goes in the stretcher and he's all the time

34

expecting that he's done, that if the pain would lessen he could just close his eyes and wake up in Thomas Traherneland. Because he does believe in a next life, his version is one of those blue-sky kinds with the light coming from behind huge white-puff clouds and saints kind of standing on them like very serene superheroes who've decided long wavy hair in the seventies was *the* look and a peach or apricot robe was quite comfortable in the weather up there. That kind of afterlife. Anyway, what with all the Latin and kneeling and candles Abraham's pretty much got the passport. So there he is, blood crisping, eyelids kind of butterfly-fluttering, *Kyrie eleison, Christe eleison* on his lips, and here are the hands of the angels coming to lift him up.

Only they're a little rough.

That's because they belong not to an angel but to a young medic called Oliver Cissley. Oliver's so ardent it's given him glossy eyes and fierce neck acne but he has come to war to save lives.

Grandfather is delivered to Cissley right there on a plate and so bingo! Young Oliver gets to work just as Grandfather is in that place between Living and Dying, between Fish and Fisherman, my father says, and Oliver thinks this is what he came for and starts whipping the bullets out – one, two, and actually yes, there, three – and hauling Abraham back from the Hereafter.

Grandfather is a Near Thing.

Which is no fun. Believe me.

Because for Grandfather then there was only Falling Back Down to Earth, which is not great and just plain awful for a pole-vaulting salmon.

5

Sorry, I couldn't resist.

That's pure MacCarroll. We have mixed metaphors and outland-ish similes for breakfast.

When you transplant a little English language into a Clare Bog this is what happens, Miss Quinty.

Ruth Ruth Ruth.

It's just so fecund.

Ruth Swain!

Grandfather survives. The War moves away and he stays behind. They give him a little time to recover and see if he can Take up Arms again but he can't even Take up Hands. The holes in his chest and the soul-thick air of the battlefields of Boulogne join forces to give him pneumonia and next thing he's on his way back to England without Messrs. Morrow, Eacrett, Cheatley & Paul, all of whom are growing poppies in France, and he's moved into a Home called Wheaton in Wolverhampton.

Years later my father tried to find him there, first by reading everything he could of World War One, then by leaving us one October and going by train, ferry and bus to Wolverhampton long after Abraham was dead and Wheaton Home had been turned into fifty-six apartments for people who didn't see ghosts. I don't think he found him, but when he came back Mam said he smelled of smoke.

Great-Grandmother Agnes is dead when Abraham returns. In those days you could die beautifully of Failure of the Heart, and that's what she did, prayers said, palms together, close your eyes and bumps-a-daisy, another one for Greener Pastures, My Lord.

When the authorities ask Abraham of any living relatives he says he has none. A caustic shame is the natural by-product of the Impossible Standard.

So, at this stage in Our Narrative it doesn't look great for my chances. (See Book 777, *The Life and Opinions of Tristram Shandy, Gentleman*, Laurence Sterne, Penguin Classics, London.)

(Has its advantages I suppose. For one thing, I won't die at the end.)

Abraham has had his soul burned. That's what I've decided. He's had an Icarus moment, only English Protestant-style. Like all of England he has fallen the long distance from Rudyard Kipling to T. S. Eliot, which is a long way, and it left him with ashes on his soul. He was not worthy. He's a Veteran at age twenty. So he sits in a fusty room with a narrow bed and a small window that gives a view of the fumy skies of Wolverhampton and starts smoking himself to death. He can't believe he's still alive. He's God's Oversight. He should have been the hasty three-and-a-half feet under the sunny sweet-scented fields of France where they put Morrow, Eacrett, Cheatley & Paul together so they could get on with enjoying the hurdy-gurdy of the afterlife. Instead, Abraham Swain has been caught halfway, between worlds, and this is where he's to stay the rest of his days.

He's failed the Philosophy of Impossible Standard and so he lets his father believe he's dead. He lives one of those quiet little lives no one notices, wearing brown trousers, walking to the shop, 'Daily Mail *today, sir?*', chainsmoking through the horse-racing in the long dull afternoons.

And, Dear Reader, years pass.

*

37

But there's always a Twist.

Remember Oliver? Well, here comes a fine old lady, handsome, stately, wonderfully neat, who knocks with no nonsense on the door of Abraham Swain and sweeps into his room very much like Mrs Rouncewell in *Bleak House* (page 84, Book 179, Penguin Classics, London) from whom I have borrowed some of her character.

Mrs Rouncewell has had two sons, of whom the younger ran wild, and went for a soldier, and never came back. Even to this hour, Mrs Rouncewell's calm hands lose their composure when she speaks of him and, unfolding themselves from her stomacher, hover about her in an agitated manner, as she says, 'What a likely lad, What a fine lad, What a gay, good-humoured, clever lad he was!'

Only her name here is not Mrs Rouncewell, but Mrs Cissley. Her Oliver the very one that saved Abraham and who wrote letters to his mother from the Front – What a likely lad, What a fine lad – the poor woman's hands fluttering about at the near mention of his name. And in these letters – 'Look, I have them here' – and indeed she does and dips in and takes from her large black bag a pale wing of pages smelling of peppermints.

'This one,' she says. 'This one tells how he saved you. Abraham Swan.'

'Swain.'

She lays the letter before him. Freed of it, her hands catch each other in mid-air and pull themselves down on to her lap into a moment's peace. Then, while Grandfather reads of himself as the miracle Swan, head turned and squinting one-eyed to inhale, Mrs Cissley says: 'His brother died young. Oliver was Our Hope.'

Slowly rises the Swain brow.

Mrs Cissley's hands rise up off her stomach, catch each other, wring, twist, interlock, fly free and fall once more to her lap, leaving in the air an old-soap scent of despair that won't wash away. Her face cannot accommodate the population of emotions. Some of them are pushed down on to her neck where they get together to set off a poppy bloom in the shape of France.

'You see, he'd want it to be you,' she says, her hands clasped back-to-back in a reverse of praying, an exhale of peppermint into his smoke.

Grandfather's face is white, as if he has an instant's foreknowledge, as if the announcement that is coming has already reached him, like the little shudder in the phone before a text comes proper.

Mrs Cissley can hardly bear to say it, can hardly bear to let out the words because with them will go the last remnant of the long-dreamt future of her Oliver. The hands clasp a moment longer, holding to hope in Wolverhampton. 'My husband,' she says, and her tongue touches some bitterness on her lower lip. 'My husband owned the Falkirk Iron Works.' The bitterness is also inside her right cheek. The tongue presses there, the lips tighten and whiten. 'Two million Mills grenade bombs. He made a fortune from the war.'

Mrs Cissley makes no movement but her eyes widen.

'There are lands in Ireland,' she says at last, 'a house and lands. They were . . .' She can't say it. She just can't. Then she shakes her head and the name falls out, '. . . for Oliver.' And at that her hand-clasp is undone, the hands open, and the soul of her son flies away.

6

'Rain today, Ruthie!' Nan shouts up through my floor from her place by the hearth downstairs.

She knows I know. She knows I am up in the rain here and watching it weep down the skylight.

'Rain today, Nan!' I call back. She cannot come up to my room any more. If she came up she'd never get down. 'When I go up the next time, I'm staying Up,' she says, and we know what she means.

Days like today the whole house is in the river. The fields are wrapped in soft grey tissues of weather. You can't see anything but you hear the water flowing and flowing as if the whole country is washing away out past us. I used think our house would float away out of the mouth of the County Clare. Maybe it still will.

But to keep it in place today I'll write it here.

Come west out of Ennis. Take the road that rises past the old tuberculosis hospital that Nellie Hayes was in once for months and seventy years later said she remembered seeing blue butterflies there. Drive up the hill, get caught behind Noel O'Shea's bus as it drags ahead and what Matthew Fitz calls the Scholars are waving back at you and making demented faces that recall their grandfathers.

Turn down left, pass the big Boom houses, seven-bathroom monuments to that time, take a sort of right and suddenly the road is narrow and the hedgerows high since the Council stopped cutting them, and you're in a green tunnel, winding down and away all the time. That's what you'll feel, *away*, and your wipers will be going because the rain that is coming is not hard or driving but a kind you can't quite see falling but is there all the same. It started raining here in the sixteenth century and hasn't stopped. But we don't notice, and people still say *Not a Bad Day* though the drizzle is beaded on the top of their hair or in the furrows of their brows. It's a mist like the old no-reception on the black-and-white television Danny Carmody had and didn't rightly tune in because he didn't want to pay the licence, kept just a Going Blind Channel he watched up close in which the figures moved like black dots in white and the licence man said was still television so Danny took the TV out into the garden and said he didn't have a TV in the house. Well that's what we live in, that's what you can see, mouse-grey air seeping, so already you're thinking this is some other world, this place in the half-light that isn't even half, not really, not even quarter.

You head along and you know the river is somewhere down here. You'll feel you're descending towards it, river in a green underworld. And the drizzle kind of sticks to the windows so the wipers don't really take it and the fields seem lumpish and bunched together the way you imagine green dancers might if they fell under a spell and lay down. That's how I think of it, the slopes and slants, the green dips and hills on either side of you.

But keep coming. Keep coming. Stay with the river fields. Where you see the estuary wide and thickly flowing you'll have a sense of things being sucked out to sea, and you won't be wrong. There's a bend called The Yanks because three different sets of them crashed there looking sideways in river-awe. Mind yourself. But keep coming. You're in the Parish now, about which nothing is more eloquent than the first sentence in Charles Dickens's first book: 'How much is conveyed in those two short words – "The Parish!" (*Sketches by Boz*, Book 2,448, Penguin Classics, London). This is Faha parish, not *fada*, meaning long, or *fado*, meaning long ago, though both are true, not *fat-ha*, an over-eaters stand-up place, or *fadda*, as in Our Fadda who Art in Boston, though far and father are in it too, Faha, which one half of the parish politely calls Fa-Ha, and the other, who don't have time for syllables, make of it a kind of elongated bleat of the note that follows do-re-me, *Fa*.

There are no signposts to Faha. When the Bust came and Ciaran, the first of the Crowes, had to emigrate he took the signpost out by The Yanks with him. His brother, Tom the tiler, took the one on the road from Killimer. After that it became a custom. Faha went elsewhere. There are signposts to it all over the world, but none in Ireland.

You'll come to the village first. The Church lets you know someone got there before you and said *Jesus*, but that's what you'll be thinking. (*Gee*, if you're reading the American edition.) You'll be looking at the crooked twist of the main street, the only street, and the way church and street both tilt down towards the Shannon. It's a street falling into a river. The church is heading sideways. None of the shops are in a line. They've all half-turned their backs on each other, as if centuries ago each one was built out of a fierce independence, shouldering its way in and setting up overnight. Each one tries to take the best view so that the street which is Main, Shop and Church Streets all rolled into one is a ragged westward-facing curve hugging the river. It wasn't until after the village was built that the shop-owners realised they would all be annually flooded.

Next to the church there's Carty's, the funeral parlour. They're the one with the brass handles on the door, the opaque glass with the Celtic crosses in it, and, inspired touch, the plate of Milky Mints inside the door. Jesus Mary and Joseph Carty is a barrel-chested man with Popeye-arms he keeps crooked as he walks. Looks like a Lego-man, only rounder. He got his name from calling down the Holy Family on all occasions. Jesus Mary and Joseph at the Minor matches against the hairy-legged Kilmurry

Ibrickanes, Jesus Mary and Joseph at the price of petrol, at the bankers, the developers, at everything ever proposed by the Green Party, Jesus Mary and Joseph. But don't worry he's sweet and has big-man gentleness and restrains himself during the service.

Somewhere standing at a doorway will be John Paul Eustace. He's the fulltime Life Assurance man, part-time Epistle reader, Eucharistic Minister. Long and skinny, green eyes, narrow nose, oval face that can't be shaved cleanly, topped with a cowlick of brown hair he tried to dye blonde the time he thought girls would go for it. He has thin lips he keeps wetting and the whitest hands in the county. He'll note you passing. That fellow couldn't be fattened, Nan says, which is a curse in Nan language. Navy suit, clipboard in hand, Mr Eustace – *Oh call me John Paul, please* – stands three inches shorter than his height as he stoops in your doorway. He goes round the houses and drives out the townlands collecting five euros a week *for the unforeseen*. He has perfected an apologetic air. He's sorry to be calling, it's that time again. He never used to call to us, then Dad must have signed us up and he started coming. He's a threshold man, a door-stepper, who commiserates, lets slip who has taken ill, who has Not Long Left, and who has Nothing to Leave Behind, God help us. *Is Mr Swain at home at all?*

In case you've fallen out with Carty, at the other end of the village is Lynch's funeral parlour. There you can exit the world through Toby Lynch's sitting-room-turned-undertakers. Toby turns off the television and lays a doily over it when he has a corpse, except that time during the World Cup. In my mind he's played by Vincent Crummles, Theatrical Impressario in *Nicholas Nickleby* (Book 681, Penguin Classics, London). A lovely man, as they say hereabouts. *A lovely man.* Toby does the make-up for the Drama Group during Festival season and so Lynch's is a good choice if you like a little Red Number Seven and Brown Number

43

Four on your cheeks or are planning on making a Good Entrance in the next life.

If you get past Death and enter the village proper you'll pass Culligan's Hardware that's no longer a hardware shop and MacMahon's Drapery that's no longer a drapery since Lidl came to Kilrush and started selling Latvian wellingtons for nothing and blue one-piece overalls that make the farmers look like they're Nuclear Waste inspectors. The shops still have the names over the doors though and Monica Mac still has some leftover stock in her front sitting room which she sells to select clients who can't countenance living without being *à la Mode MacMahon*, which basically means 'Washes like a hanky' Mam says.

Hanway's Butchers is an actual shop. Martin Hanway too is a lovely man, huge hands, he's one of those farmer-butchers who have their own animals in the fields out back and on warm wet fly-buzzing days in June he leaves the back door open and you can see next month's chops looking cow-eyed at the stall. I turned vegetarian when I was ten. Nolan's Shop doesn't say Nolan's over it, it says SPAR in garish green, but no one calls it that. You ask someone where Spar is you'll get blankety blank, as Tommy Fitz says. Despite the Boom and despite the Bust, Nolan's are hanging on. They survive on selling sweets to the scholars and *Clare Champions* to the pensioners. Sometimes they have out-of-date cornflakes and Weetabix on Special and get a run on customers who don't believe in time. Since we decided to impress the Germans and save the world by abolishing plastic bags in Ireland there'll be any number of customers trying to balance eggs milk carrots turnips cabbage and bread loaves in their arms coming out the door.

The village has three pubs, all of which the Minister for Fixing Things Not Broken wiped out when the drink-driving laws changed and petrol stations started selling Polish beer. Clohessy's,

Kenny's and Cullen's are all ghost pubs now. They have about seven customers between them, some of whom are still living. Seamus Clohessy says one roll of toilet paper does for a month.

At the end of the village there's the Post Office which is no longer a Post Office since the Rationalisation, but following the edict Mrs Prendergast refused to surrender her stamps. Back in the day when Mina Prendergast first got the position from the Department of Posts and Telegraphs and moved into High Office as Postmistress of Faha, she felt a little ascension. She was officially lifted just a few inches above everyone. She started wearing open-toed shoes and hats to Mass, Nan says. And, as Mrs Nickleby said of Miss Biffin, that lady was very proud of her toes. To which there was nothing more that needed saying. The Prendergasts were The Quality, and even though they were living in the rainy forgotten back-end of the country they proved what Edith Wharton said about a defeated people who are without confidence in their own nature, they will cling to the manner and morality of their conquerors. So the Prendergasts had the doilies and the little embroidered napkins and proper teacups and saucers and these tiny teaspoons that you'd need about five scoops with to stop the Earl Grey tasting of ladies' bathwater. They had the BBC. For Mina the Post Office was proof that she was just that little bit Upper. So taking the stamps from her was out-and-out devastation. She wouldn't countenance it. And she didn't. So now the shoes coat and hat ensemble goes to Kilrush weekly and buys stamps, comes back, lays them on the counter and opens for business regardless. Let the Minister run the rest of the country, Mina Prendergast is running Faha PO until the end of this life.

Next to the Post unOffice is Father Tipp's, the dilapidated Parochial House that was once Grimble the land agent's, a big imposing two-storey, ten empty rooms commanding the river view where Father Tipp dilutes the pain of exile in Clare by indulging in buttered Marietta biscuits and horse-racing, lives with a fine collection of mahogany, an almighty congregation of mice.

Last house out the road, with footpath, flowerbed, pedestrian crossing and streetlight in front, is the wrought-iron and stone-fronted magnificence of our Councillor, whom pretty much everyone calls Saddam after he went on the trade mission to Iraq. As I live and breathe, Barney Cussen said when the Councillor came into Ryan's, if it isn't Saddam. The Councillor didn't object. A vote is a vote. And it was better than Leatherballs. He had a bald head by twenty-two which gave him a passing impression of intelligence and resulted in him being consulted on all manner of things. Some people become what others think of them, that's what I've decided. So, once the Councillor started getting asked his opinion, fatally he became convinced of the existence of his own intelligence. You ask him a question you get a paragraph. He is focused intently on fulfilling his mandate, he'll tell you, nodding slow and shrewd and narrowing his eyes to the distance behind you, as if his mandate is all the time trying to escape his focus.

End of the village is the graveyard; it's crooked and dark and slopes to the river which is always trying to rise and take it, but it's convenient for the church and means that dead parishioners never have to leave the parish, can enter the next world without having to learn new customs.

You're out the end of the village now. Take a right and bear left at the Y and you'll come to a cross. A right at the cross and a left that doesn't look like a proper left but is more broken-down rough cut by the place Martin Neylon with six pints in him singing 'Low lie the fields' climbed the ditch in his Massey Ferguson the time of the ice, widening the road at no charge and leaving his own mark on history in the name Neylon's Bend.

You'll feel lost, which is all right, and you're the only car now which is good because the road is only that wide and you have to slow down anyway behind Mikey who in his turned-down wellies is walking his Ladies, eighteen milking cows, along in front of you. He'll know you're behind him and in a salute he'll sort of raise the bit of black pipe he uses to welt the backsides of those same ladies but he doesn't turn around or turn the cows in to the side because they're walking bags of milk those girls and it's their road too and they graze the bits of grass that grow along the ditches but on the dung-slathered sight of their hanging udders you'll swear you'll never drink milk again.

So you travel along at cowspeed and you've time between the wipers coming and going to see the houses near the road and the ragged fields that fall down the valley to your left and because it's summer when you come there's the yellow gorse bushes that we call furze and when I was small used think was *furs*. It sort of glows in the fields and because you're not a farmer you'll think it's lovely and not that it shows how poor the land is. You'll think those patches of rushes are just shading or some other kind of grass they grow here and because you're driving at cowspeed behind Mikey you'll have time to look across and now you'll see this gleam that is the River Shannon and you'll feel the sense of an ending.

But be careful, the river can take you. It has its own mesmerism, and Mikey is turning the cows into the shed ahead of you and he's raising his black pipe again that is thanks and apology and acknowledgement that you're here with us, in our time in our rain.

Drive on a bit further now, stay with the river on your left and follow it towards the sea. Feel the quickening. Look across at the Kingdom looking over at you with a kind of Kerry contentment, and you're in our townland now. Watch out for various figures bundled in coats and hats, ditch-trawlers in early senescence out trying to gather sticks for the range since the cutbacks came to pay the bankers.

47

Pass the house of the Saints Murphy, Tommy and Breda, they do our praying for us. Both of them are in the Premier Division of praying and sometimes because we're such heathens – well, except for Nan who's a kind of Pagan-Catholic – Mam goes down to them and asks them to say a few Our Fathers or Glory Be's for us and they do. Tommy and Breda are in their seventies and they have this lovely manner that's Old Ireland, and you feel sort of quiet in their company like when the choir is singing at Christmas. Tommy is a gentle man and he loves Breda with a kind of folklore love. She's losing her hair now and bits of it land in the dinners she cooks and the scones she bakes, but Tommy doesn't object, he sees the hairs and eats away. He loves her too much to say a thing. They sit evenings sipping tea with their high-visibility vests on, kind of glowing neon yellow the way saints should. Tommy and Breda weren't blessed with children but they have nine laying pullets and any amount of free-range eggs. They'll give you half a dozen if you stop. But you can't right now.

Pass the Major Ryan's and Sam his suicidal dog who's running out and trying to get under your wheels. The Major's name derives not from any military career but from the quantity of Majors cigarettes he smoked, right-hand fingers tuberous gold, chest a mazy fibrous mass, and his voice that low husk that caused every audience to crane forward as one in Faha the time of the amateur-drama productions. The dog has been trying to kill himself for seven years, hasn't managed it yet.

That figure ahead of you is Eamon Egan, fattest man in the parish and proud of it, wouldn't walk the length of himself, Nan says. Posterboy for the anti-famine look, in the county's largest navy suit he sits propped on his front wall. Give him a nod, he'll scowl back because he doesn't know you and for the rest of the evening he'll be demented tracking around in his big head playing a game of: *who's the stranger?*

You'll pass the young Maguires who were both in the bank and both lost their jobs in the Bust and are now living in Egan's mother's place trying to grow vegetables in puddles. Next door is McInerney's, smiling Jimmy who's no oil painting Nan says and never heard of dentistry but discovered the secret to successful marriage was not teeth but Quality Street because he's fathered fourteen children on Moira and keeps the National School going. Like Matthew Bagnet in *Bleak House*, Jimmy will tell you he leaves control of everything to his wife. Where Mrs Bagnet was always washing greens, Moira McInerney is doing the same only with underpants. Those'll be McInerneys under the hedge, or on the ditch, or kicking a ball over your car, some of them pushing the prams of others or flying around on buck-wheeled bikes, and not one of them with a care in the world or even noticing it's raining.

You pass on and you think that's the end of the houses. The road nearly touches the river.

Then look, a last house. You're here.

According to Assumpta Elliott, our house is no great shakes. She was one of the Rural Resettled who came down from Dublin to populate us but then discovered what wind coming up the river off the Atlantic felt like, couldn't get used to walking slantways or being rain-washed and, Great Shakes herself, Unsettled back again. I like our house. It's a long low farmhouse with four windows looking over a small garden of Mam's drowned flowers. Out back are the three muck fields where our cows paddle in the memory of actual grass.

The house faces south, as if its first MacCarroll builders had the stubborn optimism of my Mam and believed there would maybe be some sunlight sometime. Or maybe they wanted it to have its back to the village, which is about three miles away. Maybe they were making a point, or had that little distance in them that used get me into trouble in school when The Witches Mulvey made out I thought I was better than everyone, that I was Snoot Ruth, which to tell the truth I didn't mind so much, and anyway it was only because I had vocabulary.

You come in the front door and within three feet you're facing a wall – the MacCarrolls weren't the best at planning. You have to turn right or left. Right brings you to The Parlour.

Once The Parlour was the Good Room, preserved for the possible visit of His Holiness or John Francis Kennedy, whoever made it first, complete with The Good Armchairs set at angles appropriate for polite conversation before the tiled fireplace, upon which sit Chester and Lester, china dogs that came one Christmas from my Swain aunts and which in my daydreams often scampered alongside me when I went off with The Famous Five for ginger beer – second-hand Enid Blytons were a speciality at Spellissey's in Ennis, they were your First Books once and you were to graduate from Enid into Agatha, Blytons to Christies, because books were Mysteries, the whole of life a Whodunit, which is kind of MacCarroll Deep if you think about it.

But don't, because Look, there's a glass case with assorted other ceramics, tiny cream Belleek bell with tinier shamrocks, brass Celtic cross, miniature Virgin Mary who, First Miracle of Faha, transformed herself into a plastic bottle with blue cap-crown, a Waterford Crystal clock without battery, never had a battery because it was beautiful and didn't need to also tell you that beauty and everything else passes – thank you, Mr Keats – and to the left of this a glass-topped table with embroidered doily and tile coaster of Lourdes should His Holiness wish to put down his pint. Once, this room was the sanctum saculorum, the fiddly-dee fiddly-dorum, the Havisham Headquarters of our house, the great untouched – and often undusted – that was kept for special occasions which, like good fortune, to our family never arrived. Then

Nan Nonie moved in and a bed was put in one corner of the room – His Holiness would understand – and a belted trunk of her clothes which was always open and because she preferred Flung to Folded lent an air of lewd display that might have challenged His Holiness a little, to say nothing of her Po.

Eventually The Parlour became Nan's Parlour then just Nan's. There she keeps her Complete Collection of *Clare Champions*, an ever-expanding series of yellow mountains of newspaper in which is recorded the full entire life of the county, which means that if you had the time you could start upstairs here reading the exploits of some lads in Troy and work your way through all recorded civilisation right up to the savage blow-by-blow of the Saint Senan's Under-14s two days ago. The *Champions* are an inexhaustible chronicle of everything that happened here in Nan's lifetime. She never goes back to reread it, never does any old-style finger and blackened-wet-thumb googling, flicking the pages to find something. It's enough that the papers passed through her hands once, that once she lived through that particular week. Now their physical presence filling up the room is a kind of testament to her enduring, to the River of Time and her unsinking through it. That's how I've come to think of it anyhow. No one pays it any mind, or thinks it the least bit odd. That's the thing about Faha. When Lizzie Frawley was pregnant with an imaginary child, and for fifteen months sat sideways in Mass to accommodate an invisible bulk which she'd sometimes tap gently, no one said a word.

Isn't Odd nearly God, as Margaret Crowe says.

Because the house is four rooms, each the depth of the building, Mam and Dad had to cross Nan's to get to their end room. Their room is basically a cave. The entrance is four feet thick by five feet high, a little stone passageway Dad had to duck through to get inside. It was years before he stopped banging his head.

51

I still call it Mam and Dad's room.

We are not Well-Off, we've never been Well-To-Do, never Upwardly Mobile or Going Places. A poet is upwardly mobile in a different sense, but it doesn't butter your bread as Tommy Devlin says. Without explanation, I've always understood there was a reason Dad never ever bought new clothes, why he wore shoes with oval-shaped holes in the soles, why Mam cut his hair, why she cut mine, why there was a jar on the kitchen window where coins were kept and why the stock of them went up and down depending. I understood that my father only bought second-hand books, that he could go to Ennis in a tweed jacket of Grandfather's and come back without it but with the *Collected Poems* of Auden (Book 1,556, Vintage, London), Grandfather's jacket now in the front window of the Ugandan Relief Shop on Parnell Street. I understood there was a story inside the story, understood that once Grandfather Swain's money was gone there was literally nowhere else for money to come from. My father would never accept Government Grants, Headage payments for cattle, or Unemployment. *I am not unemployed.* So as you go forward it won't be money you'll be seeing. It'll be the unsung genius of Mam who performed the Second Miracle of Faha and kept the family afloat and this roof over our heads.

Go back to the front door now, turn left, and enter The Room. The floor slopes down towards you to let the mop-water flow out the front door — a feature the MacCarrolls should have trademarked and sold to IKEA, the Crooked Floor, not only for the convenience of cleaning, ladies and gentlemen, but because once you stand up the tilt takes you towards the door; the house encourages you to leave, to go out in the world. There is the wide hearth on your right, maybe ten feet for those who need particulars, with the dresser across from it. The fire is on the grate on the floor and there's turf burning. In our chimney there's always smoke rising. Mam never lets it go out.

When she goes to bed at night she lifts the last sods with the tongs and places them under the grate where the fire sleeps until she knocks it glowing awake in the morning. It's an old MacCarroll tale I think. Some pisheog or lore I may have once been told. Something to do with spirit in the house and not letting the hearth cool completely. Mam is a horde of such things, wild bits of MacCarrollisms; for most of the time she has learned to keep them under cover, but if you stay long enough and watch her carefully, watch this beautiful Clarewoman with the brown eyes and the loose long tussle of her wavy brown hair, the indomitableness in her bearing, simple country pride and courage, you will see them sometimes, things about magpies, about blackbirds, about going in front doors and going out back doors, about May blossom or hearing the cuckoo out of which ear or picking foxgloves or cutting holly bushes.

Nan's chair with cushion consisting of recent back issues of the *Clare Champion* is right inside the hearth. Nan waits for the *Champion* on Thursday and when the Simons aren't in full swing she goes straight to Deaths and Planning, which is basically a super-condensed version of Life's Plot, 'Johnny Flanagan's building' and 'Johnny Flanagan's dead' only breaths apart.

The Room uses the dresser as a bookcase. Top shelf has these leatherbound editions of classics that came gifted from the Aunts. I smelled them long before I read them. I think they must have been my first soothers, me raw-cheeked and teething and crying and Aeney teething too and not crying, Mam looking around the Room for something to quieten me, grabbing Marcus Aurelias and plunging him up to my red cheeks. Hardy, Dickens, Brontë, Austen, St Augustine, Lewis Carroll, Samuel Butler, I gummed and smelled my way into Literature.

Below this shelf are these big dinner plates on display, they're wedding china that came from Aunts Penelope and Daphne some years before Lester and Chester. They were very china-giving aunts, which was of course secret warfare because the more they gave the more you had to find some place to display the stuff. We had china in boxes in the cabins that we couldn't sell because it had to be taken out when The Aunts arrived. There isn't much else in the room, a couple of armchairs and some wooden seats and what in Faha they call a form pronouncing it *fur-um* but which in the rest of the world is a bench.

At the back of The Room there's the New Kitchen, just fridge and cooker and things all in the one small space with a galvanised-iron roof that is rusting orange on the inside and sings when it rains. It's been New now for twenty years.

There's a narrow stairs that rises from the front of The Room up and over the dresser. At the top is my room. You come in and the ceiling slants – MacCarrolls are all angles, angels if you're dyslexic – so if you're above five foot one and a half you stand at a tilt till you reach the skylight and then you can straighten a bit.

My bed and Aeney's had to be built up here. One day Dad went out and came back with the timber. It had large dark holes in it where bolts had been removed. I think it came from Michael Honan who knew Dad didn't have the money and to whom Dad promised to give Two Days when Michael was doing silage. That's trade, Faha style. My father leased himself out and we got beds. He came home with these big heavy beams and brought them up the narrow stairs. Dad wasn't a carpenter, but because of the Swain Philosophy he believed it shouldn't be beyond him to make beds, and so he sawed and banged and sawed and banged for three days above our heads, letting little snows of sawdust down through the floorboards into our tea below. Aeney and I were forbidden to go see until the bed was done, but from the noise of the effort you could imagine that up there Dad was in mortal combat with his own limitations. It wouldn't come right for him.

How hard could it be to join up four pieces of wood?

Well, if you didn't want wobble, pretty hard it seemed.

He kept putting longer and longer screws in. The legs were the worst. Four legs wouldn't support the weight evenly so he made two spare ones and added these but still the bed rocked and he was still falling short of Impossible Standard until Mam told him I was hoping it wasn't going to be too solid but would still have a little give because I liked to rock myself to sleep.

This was always Mam's role, to show Dad he was all right, to redeem him from the place he kept pawning himself into. So at last we went up the narrow stairs and saw: what he had made were more boats than beds, but I loved it, this big heavy sky-boat I still sail.

When I'm gone, when I've sailed away, it will have to be sawed apart to get it out. If you've been to Yeats Tower in Gort, restored by Mary Hanley (Hail Mary full of Yeats's Martin McGrath said on our school tour), you'll see his is the same, made at the top of the winding stair, too big to ever bring down again. They haven't sawed it up. Not even the minister who's driving the artists out of Ireland would dare saw up WBY's bed, my father said. There's no mattress though, just this big empty frame so it's the best ghost-bed you've ever seen. WBY sleeps there sometimes still, probably September to May when the river rises and the tower is closed to poetry tourists and he needs a little more soul-polishing from the sleety winds of Gort.

Well, anyway, here you are, that's the setting. That's the way Balzac does it in *Eugénie Grandet* (Book 2,017, Penguin Classics, London).

7

Lands, a house, some money, Mrs Cissley said. She wore the cheapest perfume but compensated by wearing an enormous quantity.

Which, Dear Reader, is stifling.

There follows a small gap in our narrative.

Do a little work here yourself, I'm on medication. Pick up from that scene in Wheaton, ash on his trousers, grey light, cramped little setting for a resurrection. You go ahead.

Doctor Mahon is here to see me.

As they say on RTE, there may be interruptions to service due to Ongoing Works.

Abraham arrived in Ireland.

I think maybe it was because there were no Swains here. This was a tabula rasa. I think he came to Meath and took over the farm because he decided it was a calling of some kind and he had come around to believing in Out of the Blue. Impulsiveness and Swains are close cousins, not removed. We head off in a burst in some direction thinking *this is it* only to find ourselves nowhere.

Vision and blindness, that's us in the Short Version.

Contrariness too. Grandfather came to Ireland just as anyone remotely Anglo went in the opposite direction.

That just raised the Standard. Grandfather decided that in Meath he would out-Wiltshire Wiltshire. He would make a better place to show his father and then one day invite the old Reverend over and say *Behold*. It's a Paradise Complex. (I was going to do Psychology in college but then I read that Freud said Psychology was no use for Irish people, we're either Too Deep or Not Deep at all.)

The Paradise Complex means you keep trying to make heaven on earth. You're never satisfied. And that's the crux, as the Philosopher Donie Downes says. See also: The Jerusalem Syndrome.

Grandfather couldn't take the easy option. He couldn't close his eyes and come up with one of those imaginary paradises of which there are so many accounts in my father's library. Here's Lucian in his *True History of the Isles of the Blessed* (Book 1,989, *Utopias of the Mind*, Crick & Howard, Bristol) who said he'd seen a town made of gold and streets paved with ivory and the whole encircled with 'a river of superior perfume'. It never got dark there, and it never got light, but was in perpetual twilight and permanent springtime. Vines in paradise fruited once a month according to Lucian. There were 365 waterwells, 365 honeysprings, 7 rivers of milk, 8 rivers of wine (sorry, Charlie, no chocolate factory) and the people wore clothes of cobwebs *because their bodies were so insubstantial*. Look in Virgil's *Aeneid*, Book VI (Book 1,000, trans. J. W. Mackail, Macmillan, London) where he talks about the Elysian Fields. What about heading there, Granda?

There are any number of imaginary gardens, most of which though were pooh-poohed by Sir Walter Raleigh, who after all that voyaging probably had what Mina Prendergast channelling Shakespeare called an unbuttoned scent, but whose ego was capacious enough to write *The History of the World*. Sir Walter pointed out that Homer's description of the garden came from Moses's description, and that in fact Pindar, Hesiod, Ovid, Pythagoras, Plato and all those chaps were actually a bunch of plagiarists who added to Old Moses their own Poetic Adornments. The real heavenly garden was copyrighted to Moses, and that was that. The rest was poppycock, Your Majesty.

Thank you, Walter, have a cigarette.

No. Grandfather wasn't taking any route into the Imaginary. It was too easy. This was going to have to be actual grass-and-stones Paradise.

So Abraham laid Meath up against the Impossible Standard and began moulding the place into the dream version. He was going to do the So-Like-Paradise-You-Won't- Believe-it's-Not-Paradise kind of thing. Maybe there was already Something There to Work With, as that witch with the yellow highlights Miss Donnelly said to my mother at a parent–teacher meeting. Even so it can't have been easy.

First of all he was, you know, an Englishman.

And as I said there weren't exactly a whole load of those coming one-way to Ireland those days. The first Tourist Board was still meeting in some little room in Merrion Square and working on the posters and slogans. *Civil War Over, Come Visit. We won't kill you. Promise.* Second, he was, *sshssh*, Not Belonging to Our Church (O Divine Lord) and third, after his Oxford education he didn't know one side of a cow from the other. (Reader, there *are* sides. When I was five Nan showed me. She carried a three-legged stool and plonked it down next to Rosie, head-butting in against Rosie's side and reaching in for the udder. You go from the opposite side and Rosie will break your wrist. Such a cow.)

The thing is, the Philosophy has a No Complaint clause. You can't cry out and you can't say *this was a dreadful mistake.*

You have to just do better.

And so that's what he did.

It took years, but eventually Grandfather got Ashcroft House & Lands into a condition of Absolute Immaculacy, and sent his invitation to the Reverend.

I am alive. Come on over and visit, only in fancier English.

Then he waited.

The Reverend was already Old Testament ancient by now. In my mind he blends into Herbert Pocket's father in *Great Expectations*, Old Gruffandgrim, banging with his stick on the floor for attention. The Reverend had already used up whatever life was in his body by putting up the big mileage of hurrying Elsewhere and so by this stage he was mostly parched paper over thin little struts. He couldn't believe Our Lord hadn't taken him Up yet. Honest to God. He was all prayed up and confessed, boarding pass printed, and waiting in the priority queue. *Sweet Jesus come on*, as Marty Finucane shouts in Cusack Park whenever the hurlers are feeling the effects of forbidden Saturday-night Guinness and firing the sliothers wide into the Tesco carpark.

But no Sweet Jesus showed up.

(If you went to the Tech, you'll spot a theme.)

The Reverend lived on, thought a little more deeply about life being purgatory, and banged on the floor with his stick.

When at last he got the letter he lifted old Up-Jut and did some nostril-narrowing. It wasn't attractive. He squinted through the snowy dust of his spectacles to read his son's name and when he saw *your son Abraham* he had to squint harder.

There it was: your son Abraham.

He thought all this time his son was in Heaven interceding for him.

He thought Abraham had gone there in the first rank of Dead Heroes from The Great War and by now probably had the skintone of those creamy alabaster plaques they have in the big Protestant churches.

But no, he was *in Ireland*.

Sweet Jesus come on.

Now, I'm not going to say it was because the Reverend thought mucky Irish ground would give him foot rot, nor that it was because he couldn't say the word *Ireland* without distaste, though both were probably true. Despite the efforts of the Tourist Board, Ireland in those days was not in Top Ten Countries to Visit, and for English people it was all but *verboten* as the Pope would say. *Ireland?* Catholics and murderers, the Reverend would have thought. Ungrateful blackguards, we had not the slightest appreciation for the eight hundred years of civilised rule of His Majesty and to show our true colours once the English had departed we'd set about killing each other with hatchets, slash hooks and hedge shears.

Ireland? Better that Abraham was in Hell.

Pursuing the image, the Reverend posted the letter through the grille of the fire and began some shallow breathing. The damp boggy idea, *Ireland*, sat on his chest.

Within a week he was dead.

Amen to him.

Awomen also, as Denis Fitz said half a second after the congregation at midnight Mass before in Faha we moved midnight to half nine.

Grandfather's response to the Reverend's refusal to visit and subsequent death took an original form; he stopped believing in God, and started believing in salmon. Plans in this world were pointless. Pointless to have imagined he could ever have fulfilled his father's dreams or achieved the Impossible Standard.

Grandfather forsook the world for fishing.

In fairness, perhaps there was a deeper point; perhaps secretly it was to out-Christian the Reverend by going back to basics: to Peter the Fish, to Paul the Church, is that how it goes? I'm not great on the Bible, though we have a nice one (Book 1,001, King James Edition), black and soft with the kind of feather-light pages they only use in bibles, as if paper for bibles can only come from this one place, and the pages are thinned down to a fineness that feels holy somehow so that even turning them is kind of sanctifying. Either way, whatever

60

the reason, the Salmon it was. Grandfather stopped all work on Ashcroft House & Lands, walked out the French doors, went down across the lawn, called the workers together and to the collected jawdrops and head scratches told them stop, stop trimming the hedges boys, no more mowing the hay, pack up, go home.

There's a photograph of Grandfather when he's about thirty-five. He's in a white shirt buttoned to his chin and his face has an expression of wild impatience. His lips are so tight you'd think he was afraid he'd dribble out some awful medicine if he cracked them. He resents the moment of the pose, he wants to escape it, that Elsewhere business again, and already in his chin you can see the Reverend coming. You can see the angle of the nose, the furrow between the dark eyes, and you know the old man is arriving in his skin. There's going to be no way to escape him.

But Grandfather is going to try. Yes sir. He's going to apply the What-would-my-father-do to everything, and then choose the opposite. So, instead of settling down into the dull acceptance of midlife, instead of comfortable complacence and respectability, he takes his rods and strides out the gates of Ashcroft accompanied by two bounding wolfhounds. He leaves the house to its own devices, which means weeds, mould, mushrooms in the basement, broken panes in the upstairs bedrooms, flies, snails, mice and a family of trapped rooks.

He begins on the two Black Castle sections of the Boyne River. In the notebooks he kept of his catch there are brackets beneath the salmon he caught and the name Mr R. R. Fitzherbert.

For duties to His Majesty I suppose, maybe for going away and getting Him something nice, the Virgin Islands or something, The King had given Mr Fitzherbert all the fish that passed there – To you the fish, to you the chips, same as the Bible only English-style – and my grandfather was scrupulous enough to record which of Mr Fitzherbert's salmon he took, and with which flies.

I have his Salmon Journals, which were the workbooks for his book. They are here in my father's library, pressed flattish between *Don Quixote* (Book 1,605, Vintage Classics, London), a kind of genius Spanish miracle, and *Salar the Salmon* (Book 1,606, Henry Williamson, Faber & Faber, London), a book so good that reading it you feel you're in a river. Each journal is carefully kept, blue marbling inside and blackly leatherbound like a Lesser Bible. The first time I opened one I felt indecent. I love the feel of a book. I love the touch and smell and sound of the pages. I love the *handling*. A book is a sensual thing. You sit curled in a chair with it or like me you take it to bed and it's, well, enveloping. Weird I am. I know. What the Hell? as Bobby Bowe says to everything. You either get it or you don't. When my father first took me to Ennis Library I went down among the shelves and felt *company*, not only the company of the writers, but the readers too, because they had lifted and opened and read these books. The books were *worn* in a way they can only get worn by hands and eyes and minds; these were the literal original Facebooks, the books where faces had been, and I just loved it, the whole strange sense of being aboard a readership.

I know, I know. I'm not an e-person or an iPerson. Maybe I would be if we weren't in the five per cent. The Minister says the whole country is Broadband now, except for maybe five per cent. Hello? We're not even Narrowband. And what with having a predilection, as Thomas Halvey says, for the nineteenth century, I'm older than old-fashioned, I know. No, whatever way they built Faha down in a hole beside the river, we can't get Broadband. We still get calls from somebody in the Philippines offering us Best Internet Deals ever. We let them talk to Nan. She can keep them on for an hour. It's a sort of granny-sitting.

But look, here is one of my grandfather's Salmon Journals. Feel that. Smell that. The pages have a water warp, a buckled edge like a river wave. The paper is a heavy old stock smooth under your hand. Some pages clump together as if the recording was made in rain. The handwriting is neat and done in blue ink that is now faded lavender.

SALMON

Week of June 12th, 1929

18lbs 6oz (Jock Scot)

19lbs 4oz (Blue Jock)

15lbs 11oz (Collie)

14lbs 8oz (Collie)

21lbs 3oz (Gudgeon)

It goes on, pounds and pounds of fish, page after page of pale ink. I wondered what Mr R. R. Fitzherbert thought of Abraham taking all his salmon. Maybe he didn't know. He lived in Nottinghamshire. I have wondered if my grandfather ate them all, if the Swain jaw was partly a fish-face, and I've pouted at the mirror for half an hour one afternoon when I first became sick just to see if I could see the salmon leaping out in me.

For how long can a man go fishing? I asked Mrs Quinty, but she thought it was some cloaked reference to Tommy and the Hairdresser, that once Tommy had caught Sylvia he'd get tired or bored or not be able to sustain himself as Phyllis Lillis says, you know, in what Hamlet calls Country Matters. But what I was actually asking was: fishing. How long could my grandfather be happy getting up in the morning heading out with his rod to go fishing?

Because, Dear Reader, that's all he did.

He fished for salmon.

He pretty much let the house and grounds go Rackrent (Book 778, *Castle Rackrent*, Maria Edgeworth, Penguin Classics, London). From the first salmon of the season to the last weary fish returning

63

upriver in the autumn Abraham Swain was there, standing thigh-deep in the river proper, a little swirl of broken water in his wake and his line laying soft swished question marks in the air overhead.

Even the wolfhounds became bored. When they saw him lift his rods they would trot back across the front hall and flop down, their great hair and bone masses immovable and hearts conflicted in the classic dog dilemma of loyalty to their master and knowing he was do-lally. Grandfather let them be, and the hounds commenced what was to be the business of the remainder of their lifetimes, chewing to straggling ropes the various oriental carpets and, when these proved too fibrous a diet, laying sideways and gnawing jag-toothed the pitch-pine floorboards.

Grandfather didn't give two flying figaries. He had lost all care for this life which he believed random and meaningless, a constant proof but small comfort he found in those salmon that passed and those that were caught.

In our family history there are few stories told of this time.

Grandfather Fished just about sums it up.

He chose fecklessness as a first response. Let God or the Devil show up if they existed. He was away fishing. Nothing of the struggles then of our emerging nation, nothing of Old Roundrims, Old Gimlet-eyes, our Spanish-American First Irishman who was shaping His Country, nothing of the darkening politics of Europe touches Grandfather's life. He lives his own solitary unconfine-ment until April 19th 1939 when there is the last entry midway through Salmon Journal XIX.

It reads:

26lbs (worm)

The Salmon in Ireland

because here the confluence of fact, story and legend make for cloudy waters. Salmon derives from the Latin *salire*, to leap. It was Cattalus of course who likened the leaping salmon to an erect phallus, a version of which survives in Ireland in a story told to me by an ancient fisherman in the County Westmeath. In this story the mother of Saint Finan Cam is said to have been prompted by a bodiless voice to go swimming in a river after dark. While swimming in mid current, apparently unawares, she became impregnated by a salmon.

One imagines the surprise.

How the salmon achieves the leap has down the centuries been variously explained. By holding his tail in his mouth according to the seventeenth-century poem 'Poly-Olbion' by Michael Drayton.

> . . . his taile takes in his teeth, and bending like a bowe
> That's to the compasse drawn, aloft himself doth throwe.

That the height of the leap may be linked to a female presence is not perhaps as fanciful as might first appear when we consider that in 1922 Georgina Ballintine landed a 64lb salmon out of the River Tay. The local fishermen, who had been labouring without success on the very same run, attributed the catch to the fact that female essence, as it were, had rubbed off on the bait and this had brought the salmon erect and leaping to her.

All of this by way of getting to my point that it is a fact drawn from the author's experience in Ireland that with temperature rising salmon become distinctly more active,

8

That worm had a lot to answer for, Nan says.

In our house we have videos and a video player and a collection of fairly ancient big cassettes of old films recorded off the TV in the time when that was the coolest thing ever. So, in the movie version of Grandfather & the Worm, black-and-white, William Wyler directing, Sam Goldwyn producing, Grandfather is played by Laurence Olivier aged thirty-five. It's September 1st, 1939. There's a big grey sky with dark clouds moving to the Oscar-winning orchestral arrangements of Alfred Newman. The river is fast and there's a storm coming. We see other fishermen in the minor cast shake their heads and go home. But Laurence walks past them. He's drawn to it – the sudden pulsing of Arnold Kisch's bass lets you know A Big Moment is coming.

Laurence steps off the bank into the river.

Close-up of the water curving up over the top of his boot, a little unsteadiness as the river floor shifts underfoot, but he wades further out and casts.

Boom goes the thunder.

Boom boom goes the score. It's as if somebody knows that elsewhere Germany's just starting to invade Poland.

And then the rain comes lashing down.

Close-up of Laurence's face, rainwashed and fierce, equal parts concentration and looneytunes.

He's to his waist in the river. We know now he's probably

thinking about Merle Oberon, he wanted Vivien Leigh but she was turned down and is Gone with the Wind, so he's got Oberon which isn't a great name for romance seeing as how he's thinking Oberon was King of the Fairies (Book 349, *A Midsummer Night's Dream*, W. Shakespeare, Oxford Classics) and I'm going to have to kiss the King of the Fairies, which is a problem until he remembers fortunately he has played that role and so it'll sort of be himself he's loving and, well, he can manage that.

The sky is that big angry grey-black that's MGM's speciality and which they can somehow make look blacker and broodier still. And whoa those violins are playing faster now and look! he's got a salmon on the line. The rod tenses and bows and the rain-machine guy is told *give it your almighty best,* or whatever that is in MGM-ese, and you can picture Mervin Olbacher, conductor, leaping up and whipping that baton at those violinists. He's not a big man but boy he's put elbow into it. He's put hair-toss and sweat into it. So it's rain-music-river, all Full On and up to ten, up to eleven as Margaret Crowe says, when Laurence pulls and sways and hauls this great silver salmon up into the air. Bass drum, bass drum, batons, Mervin. More, more.

Sweet Jesus, shouts Marty Finucane. You've never seen the like.

Jesus Mary and Joseph, says Jesus Mary and Joseph Carty.

MGM Props have outdone themselves this time.

Boys o boys. That's a Big Fish.

('Big enough, Mr Goldwyn?' 'No such thing as too big.')

And it lands, splash.

Sorry, take that again.

It lands SPLASH back down in the river and the whole of Laurence is tugged forward and he's in this battle of strength now, both hands on the rod as it gets pulled horizontal, forearms quivering and mouth that twisted grimace Laurence does brilliantly when he's daring God and man and William Wyler to say he's not the finest actor that ever was.

There's more, there's a whole tugging and groaning, there's flashes of lightning and Laurence giving it the full welly, but the studio decided that was enough, and cuts to the salmon being reeled in.

It's hard to tell in the film just how big it is though. The assistant director thought maybe there should be other fish he'd caught earlier and Laurence could lay this alongside for comparison, but nobody listened and it was decided you'd just believe this was the Big One if the score and the lighting and the sound effects and Laurence's acting told you so.

Anyway, here he is getting to the riverbank. He climbs up, falls down, the rain still beating, and he unhooks the fish, holds it for its weight. Crikey, look at that. It's Number One Salmon, that's what Props has been told, and they've had three rejected and to make their point that this was ridiculous they've brought this outlandish one and that got the Thumbs-Up.

So there it is. Man and Salmon. And whatever knowledge is in the fish somehow transfers to him. Whatever secrets of the world, what mysteries of chance and concurrence, of power and force and ultimate surrender, enter him, and Grandfather lets the salmon back into the river. He lets it back and lies flat and exhausted and he's sort of crying for all that has failed in his life and for the failure of God to show up, and the rain pours down into his face; the Lighting Gaffer throws a switch and Mervin sweetens the score so even if you're looking into your popcorn you know that up there on the screen your man's in the throes of something like revelation.

Next shot he's walking across the fields.

He's walking into town. It's Trim in the County Meath, but this being Hollywood it's not even going to look like the Ealing Studios version, especially because to spare the make-up the rain has stopped.

Anyway your eyes are on my grandfather played by our man Laurence. He walks into town and up to this big house where Merle is just about done with Make-Up and Costumes. We can't have her say any of the lines here because of copyright infringement but if imagination fails and you're not in the Five Per Cent you go ahead and download them.

Fizz. Bang. Sizzle.

That's not Germany entering Poland. That's Grandfather & Grandmother in Trim Manor the evening of the Big Catch, September of 1939.

(Unfortunately the Censor cut the love scene. At that time there were no love scenes in Ireland. Most people thought kissing was sex. Tongues were penises. Only allowed out for communion. Which, unsurprisingly, proved very popular.

You don't believe me look up the Irish Committee on Evil Literature, say hello to those boys. There were no women allowed in Censorship. Some members of the Committee were secretly hoping there'd be No Women Allowed in Ireland, which would be fine, except for the vexed issue of ironing.)

So, if you like, do your own sex scene. You know you want to, as Tommy Marr said to Aoife O'Keefe the time of the Apostolic Social in Ryan's. That was his come-on. That, half a can of Lynx deodorant, low-slung trousers that showed his Saint Bernard underpants in case of that saint she was a devotee and a big slow wink that was more or less the image of Haulie Roche the time he got the stroke. *You know you want to.*

Either way, please yourself. Doctor Mahon is here and we have to take our Intermission.

*

70

Fortunately, at that time, Ireland wasn't in the world. So we weren't in the World War. Old Roundrims came up with that. Brilliant, really. World War II was *toirmiscthe*, he said, which people had to look up but basically turned out to be verboten in Irish. Twitter went crazy, saying it was shameful and backward, but back then twitter was only spoken by birds. The thing is, Irish people don't like to refer to a thing *directly* as Jimmy the Yank found out the time he came home, went into Burns Chemist in Kilrush and asked full volume for something for the blood coming out of his backside. There's nothing direct about us. It's not coincidence we have no straight roads, not for nothing we use the back door. People coming to our house sometimes parked in the yard and waited for my father to appear, so they weren't really calling at all. So no, we weren't in The War. We were in something else called The Emergency. No one else in the world was in it, just us. The Munich Bother as Paddy Kavanagh calls it (Book 973, *Collected Poems*, Martin, Brien and O'Keefe) didn't bother us.

Grandfather wasn't exactly courting material. For one thing he was *old*. He'd been born in 1895 and was now past forty. And for another he had been Off-the-Circuit since before Oriel College and had pretty much forgotten the existence of females of the human variety. (Curly ear hair, mad wiry eyebrows like tangled fishing line over rheumy eyes, and his version of the Reverend's stippled jaw-mask offered in evidence.)

But it must have been something to do with the Big Catch, the last salmon, or his own private Emergency, because when Grandmother saw him, caught a sniff of Eau de Salmon and her heart went butterflies, he didn't run out of there.

At that time Grandmother was going by the name Margaret Kittering. She was what in those days they called a handsome woman, in that gaunt angular long-necked Anglo-Irish way. I think it means you could see *breeding*. Like horses, you could see by the teeth, the jaw. Let's take a look, her dentist must have said, and then just stood back and applauded. Anyway, whatever the breeding, the Kittering jaw met the Swain. (Later of course the MacCarroll made a cat's melodeon of it. But that's for a different volume, *Teeth of the Swain*, ed. D.F. Mahony.) Margaret's other features of note were light-curled auburn hair, delicate ears and the small perfect Kittering nose that later swam downriver and landed on my brother Aeney.

Teeth, ears *and* nose, what more could a man want?

For her part Grandmother had that no-nonsense Headmistress thing that made her think this man could be Knocked Back into shape, he could be Straightened Out, and with her fine boneage and those awesome elbows Grandmother was a born Knocker and Straightener.

The extent of her task was made clear when Grandfather brought her back to Ashcroft House. When they came in the avenue and she saw it, the jungle of briars he hadn't noticed, the broken windowpanes, the rooks making attempt number 576 to get back up the chimney, she didn't allow herself any expression of dismay. In *The Salmon in Ireland* it says that once she finds a spawning ground the hen salmon is fiercely focused. She will assume a vertical position and fan her tail furiously to dislodge pebbles big as balls until she has made a suitable pit.

Only a small *Oh* escaped Grandmother when the wolfhounds bounded up to join them on the bed.

Another when she caught the salty whiff of Grandfather.

Another when she got a first peek at his Catullus.

Sorry, fecund.

Still, Kitterings do not shirk, no, they have that good German-English blood in them, and the First Round of Knocking and

72

Straightening (which lasted until Germany said *Mein Gott* and surrendered) produced a daughter, Esther.

Rounds Two and Three produced Penelope and Daphne.

By that time, Grandfather's — what Brendan Falvey called *lions* — must have been nearly exhausted. He'd started late. But he still lacked a son. And seeing his three daughters already on their way to becoming little Kitterings he must have felt he was seeing Swains disappear from the world. By then he was already locked in the first silent skirmishes with Margaret, moving a chair back where he wanted it, leaving open a newspaper he knew she wanted folded away, opening windows she closed, already engaging in the ding-dong, attack-and-retreat that was their marriage as he realised with a peppery gall that he was the one who had been hooked.

But in those days once you were wedded you were in Holy Deadlock, and in Ireland the priests had decided that once a man entered a woman there was No Way Out. The vagina was this deadly mysterious wrestler that could get you in a headlock, well, metaphorically-speaking, and then, boys, you were rightly *stuck*.

That Will Teach You, was Number One sermon at the time.

Number Two was Offer It Up.

And so, with no way out, following the floods of September that year (Books 359–389, *Old Moore's Almanacs*. Volumes 36–66) and the catch of a Salmon weighing 32lbs, he gave it, as Jimmy McInerney says, one last shake.

My father was landed in May. He swam out after fourteen hours of labour, was not yet dried of the birthwaters when Grandfather Abraham appeared in the nursery like strange weather, jutted the Swain jaw to study his only male progeny, and asked: *what weight?*

And in that moment, like a pinch of salt, he passed on the Impossible Standard.

He calls his son Virgil.

Honest to God.

Virgil.

Abraham eschews saints and when he's asked for a middle name for Virgil he considers only a moment before replying: Feste. (See Book 888, *Twelfth Night*, W. Shakespeare, Oxford Classics.)

Could have been worse.

Could have been Worm.

'Fester?' In the front pew Clement Kittering dispatches an eyebrow. (The Kitterings consider the Irish in general to be Decidedly Odd, but often Quite Charming, and this curious Abraham is gone native, is turned Irish.)

'No dear. Feste.'

The moment the christening is complete Abraham startles Grandmother by taking the child from her. With quick leather shoeslap he bears my father down the aisle like a trophy. The boy is brought out and on the gravel apron before the front archway he's raised towards the glowering sky of the County Meath.

It's as if Abraham believes the old Reverend won't have been able to stay away. He'll have stridden across the stippled coals of Purgatory to see the new Swain, and to see if maybe this baby will be The Next Big Thing in holy world. Abraham holds his son and behind him like a murmuring river the congregation flows out and around the front porch, and the baby's not crying, God love him, he's not, he's gazing up out of the intricate lacework of what looks like a mini-priest's robe that Margaret had made for him, he's sort of fluttering his eyelids with the breezes that are trapped there. And then to the Reverend, and for all and sundry to hear, Abraham declaims, 'This boy will never step inside a church again.'

9

Uncle Noelie, who was not an uncle but a cousin, dressed for his death every night. One time he woke in the morning with a holy fright. (It was probably the fooking forestry that had surrounded him, unbeknownst, Sean Hayes says. You'll hear words like that here, little bits of leftover Shakespeare. Unbeknownst. *Unbeknownst* to itself the Department had destroyed the countryside with pine trees. Unbeknownst, they're going to do the same with windmills.) Anyway, Uncle Noelie woke up in a mortifying panic in his holey mouse-coloured underpants and vest, went to Patrick Bourke's in the Square in Kilrush and asked for a funeral suit Best Quality and right enough they sold him the suit, shirt, tie, socks and shoes and asked who it was that had passed on.

Which, I'm sorry, is just weird. *Passing on.* It's not even grammatical. It just hangs there, vague and inconclusive. It's like saying *he went up to.*

Passed on to *where,* exactly?

Anyway, the outfit was for his own funeral. Uncle Noelie came home, laid the suit shirt and etceteras on the bed, the shoes beneath. All day he worked his few fields in his farming trousers boots woolly jumper and what-have-you, but when he went to bed at night in that small farmhouse he put on the suit shirt and tie, left the shoes, laces undone, below, then he lay out, hands-joined, posed, so if he died in the night he'd be dressed for Departure.

Joe Brogan passed his house most days on his way to the buildings back in the time when there was buildings happening and between them down in The Crossroads one evening they'd worked out that Uncle Noelie was to open his curtains when he woke and that way there was no need for Joe to come in to check on him. He could just drive by, because, both bachelors, they weren't intimate on that level, there'd be no calling in, no need for tea and goldgrains, they were both clear on that, none of that, no, there'd just be this business of the curtains because Uncle Noelie had related his two mortal fears. The first was Not Being Found, of Mouldering Away, Sean Hayes says (and you'd moulder faster in among all those trees). How long you would be mouldering would depend on whether you went to Mass or not. Not because of mystical preservation but because if you were a Regular you'd be missed after two Sundays. There'd be that gap in the back of the Men's Aisle where you stood with the Head-downers. That was the unsaid secret advantage to church-going. But if you were an Irregular like Uncle Noelie then who knows, you could be Not Found until the trees fell through the roof and some of the Hourigans came in to rob the place.

The second fear was Being Found. If you were taken unawares, if you were found in what Nan calls your All Together, then the shame of that, the thought of the whole slew coming poking around your kitchen nosing into the front bedroom and seeing you with your what Mona Moynihan calls *croissant* just sort of sitting here, would be enough to ruin the first several weeks of your time in Heaven.

So Uncle Noelie came up with his plan. Each night he pulled the curtains, combed the little bit of hair crossways on the front of his head, put on the suit and lay out on the bed ready for take-off.

76

And it worked too.

It worked two ways. It worked first that when he woke up in the morning in the suit and he realised he wasn't at his own funeral he smiled. He smiled that lovely small round nut face of his and thought how well he looked and what a surprise it was no woman had ever found him. He rose and undressed with the sort of secret knowledge of his Happy End ahead. And it worked too because when one morning Joe Brogan drove by and the curtains were closed Uncle Noelie was only Gone a short while, and later that evening Mrs Quinty told my mother he made A Beautiful Corpse.

I was thinking about Uncle Noelie today when I was in the Regional. I was thinking about being Gone and wondering where Gone was and what it would be like and what the weather there would be. It's a thing you just never hear, the weather in the next life.

On the one hand it can't be raining there all the time.

But then if you were an African maybe that's what you'd be hoping for.

On the other hand if it was blazing hot like it was that one summer when Nan went salmon-coloured and couldn't stand up for falling down, Mick Mulvey started sporting the sombrero and olive-oiling himself and Father Tipp had to ask Martin Malone to stop wearing the micro-shorts to Mass, well that would be no fun at all. Irish people would be a freckled show in a sunny Heaven.

Just before Doctor Naradjan came in to do my Check-Up I was starting to wonder if you can only get to Heaven if you believe in it. Is it like Santa, where once you stop believing he stops coming? I know, *thinking too precisely on th'event*, but when you're lying in bed with your body going nowhere your mind sort of heads off. Anyway, just for a minute then I had maybe a glimpse of Ruth's Version because I was seeing Uncle Noelie in the Good Suit walking across his own fields and none of the forestry was there and across the river the hill fields weren't thumping with windmills and it was just the right kind of All-Ireland weather in September. Noelie's hair was still combed crossways and he had his teeth so he was smiling natural and he was back in a better version of his own familiar place. He was carrying a small Clare flag for the hurlers like he knew this year with Davy the lads were going to do it, and he was coming closer and I knew he had something he wanted to tell me and I tried to say his name out loud but I couldn't because I was in a ward in the Regional and I lost belief or vision or whatever and the whole scene sort of passed into nothing, the ground unreal and the story failed.

10

A salmon egg dropped from waist-height will rebound, quite in the manner of a tennis ball.

I thought you'd want to know that.

My father wasn't immediately aware of any burden on him.

Perhaps on Sunday mornings when Grandmother led the girls to church in Trim, that formidable line of what Nan calls the Polished Shoe Brigade, Head Girl material each one, marching up to that front pew in pleated wool coats with natural imperiousness and sitting so astonishingly upright because Nan says something in the breeding meant they had no backsides, perhaps then he wondered. He was left to himself in the house, and played Orphan.

He read. He read everything he could find. He loved books about explorers. Marco Polo, Christopher Columbus, Ferdinand Magellan, Vasco da Gama, Francis Drake, Hernán Cortés. The names alone took him away. I see him looking up from a page, it's the strange deadened quiet I know on country Sunday mornings when the Christians are at Mass and you feel so *other* that you have to occupy your time or you fear the Old Testament God himself will come up the stairs and say YOU! The rain is streaking down the long rattling windows of Ashcroft. The unfired chimneys are singing. He reads of those ships sailing into the New World and after a time he looks up and to no one but his own imagination says, 'Hernán Cortés,' which is maybe the only time anyone has said that name aloud in the County Meath but works as a kind of super-economy SwainAir flight to take him into the Aztecs. He can feel the sun scorch his brow. Those ancient oak floorboards of Ashcroft are a softly swaying deck, arriving under an azure sky, creaking in the surprise of the sudden furnace, discovering salt in all its wounds. And he says 'Vasco Núñez de Balboa' and in that damp room in the dead Sunday morning my father becomes the first European to see the Pacific Ocean.

One Sunday in the attic Virgil found his father's rubbery black gasmask. When he put it on he became an alien, sucking breath through the heavy nozzle filter and crawling along the floorboards like he was a creature out of his element or newly landed on the planet. He loved that. He loved the strange *privacy* of being different. He loved the secret life inside him and could stay there in that inner country all day. What he thought of not going to church he never said. He never went. That was that. And when Aeney and I were old enough to realise this was a little odd, and that no one in Faha had a father who played Mozart at full volume to the river while the rest of us went to Mass, it was just another small piece of the puzzle we already knew: our father was a genius.

Eventually, Virgil was sent to Highfield School to Mr Figgs. Figgs was a bald low-sized little sneeze who came from Brighton and was soon dismayed to find Irish weather the perfect seedbed for head-colds. His face was never free of his handkerchief. It dabbed, wiped, rubbed and *received* the sniffled sneezed and blown expressions of the Figgs nostrils. Still, Figgs knew his figures, knew language too, and quickly saw that Virgil Swain had Serious Potential. To save him from contamination from the Dolts he put my father in the front row next to the Sniffleodeon that was his own desk. While the Michaels and Martins, the Tommys and Timothys of Highfield got about the business of educating each other through Advanced

Ink-drinking, Higher Thumping, Desk-kicking, Flicking snot and/ or spitballs into the miry curls of the boy up front, Mr Figgs taught my father in a conspiratorial whisper. His handkerchief he lay on the desk at the ready. Across a pale nimbus of free-associating germs he craned his damp pink face and spoke Algebra.

My father took the bait. He liked being singled out. You'll already know he liked feeling that he was *rising*. He didn't mind the hook in his mouth. Beneath the curls the head hummed. The class he left in his wake. At breaktimes he stayed in, avoided games of War in the yard, and Figgs opened a little further the doors of his mind.

And what a mind it was. It devoured everything. Figgs could not believe his luck. He took my father's first name as a hint and tossed him a piece of the *Aeneid*. My father leapt and took it. A little Horace (Book 237, *Horace's Odes*, Humphrey & Lyle, London), a book whose cover is neither paper nor card but a kind of amazing amber *fabric* that makes the softest whisper when you flick it, a snippet of Cicero (Book 238, *Cicero's Speeches*, Volume I, Humphrey & Lyle, London), burgundy card-covers, stiff and formal, and smelling of asparagus, some Caesar's *Gallic Wars* (Book 239, De Bello Gallico, Volume I, Humphrey & Lyle, London) which Father Tipp thought was Garlic Wars, and I didn't correct him, it made no difference. My father devoured them all. He read at the same rate and with the same enthusiasm as the other boys excoriated their nostrils.

Nor was Latin his only excellence. On language and literature his brain fired. Figgs fed him poetry. Gave him Milton's 'L'Allegro' and, while working his own nose behind the fumigate flag of his handkerchief, watched as *Hence loathed Melancholy, of Cerberus and blackest midnight born* worked its way into my father's imagination.

Each day my father carried home the neatest copies ever written, each page scored with so many half-winged ticks of Mr Figgs's

Merit Marks it appeared a coded language of flight. And it was too. It said: *This boy is ascending.*

What it might also have said was: *This boy has no friends.*

But back in those days nobody read those parts. Child psychology hadn't reached Ireland yet. Not that it has exactly left the starting blocks now either. Seamus Moran, whose wiry black hair all migrated to his knuckles after he ate out-of-date tinned sardines, told my mother once that his son Peter was Special Needs. 'You know, Authentic.'

'Mr Figgs says Virgil is an excellent student,' Grandmother tells Grandfather one wet evening in March.

See two studded-leather wingback armchairs, battle lines, either side of the fire, two table lamps, twin amber glows. A large room with high ceiling, long sash windows, a floor rug of brown and orange, once thick and vibrant but now flat and lifeless with a going-threadbare patch where the hounds lie their drool-heads sideways before the hissing fire, logs are burning but not satisfactorily. Rain somehow spits down the full length of the chimney. The room smells of damp and smoke, that particular combination Grandmother believes is Ireland and against which she combats day and night with several purple squeeze-ball perfume bottles, shooting little sprays at the enemy with only momentary success, but impregnating her with a permanent cheap air-freshener scent as the ultimate triumph of Ireland over Kitterings.

Grandfather sits one side of the fire, Grandmother the other. Without television, they do a lot of that. Watching-the-fire is Number One on the TAM ratings back then. Grandfather smokes his cigarettes to the butt and looks in the fire at Morrow, Eacrett, Cheatley & Paul in the Next Life. He's pure Swain like that, the distant, the invisible, the depths, all big draws for the Swain mind. And he's arrived at that place where he wishes the Germans had been a bit more efficient and aimed two inches to the right and found his heart.

'What did you say?'

'At Highfield. Mr Figgs says Virgil is excellent.'

History repeats. That's all there is to it. Patterns keep coming back, which either shows that people aren't that complex or that God's imagination just kept bringing Him back to these same obsessions. Maybe we are a way for Him to work things out with His Father.

Now that's Deep.

Anyway, it's not the Narrator's weakness at characterisation. It's that Grandfather is turning into Great-Grandfather.

He shifts his long legs back from the fire. Unbeknownst to him, the soles of his boots have been cooking nicely, and as he withdraws the long pole-vaulting legs and places the feet there's a little singe-surprise, a little *dammit* sting, but he won't betray it and give his wife that little I-told-you victory. Though Sarsfield, the more loyal of the hounds, raises an eyebrow in concern, Grandfather won't let on. He just hears the word *excellent* and, as they said in those days, his hackles are raised. 'Excellent? How is he excellent?'

He hates to hear it said out loud. That Swains never, ever, *ever*, praise each other openly, nor are they comfortable hearing other people praise them, is a dictum. They want their children to be excellent, to be beyond excellent, and invisible.

But, at the same time, the last thing Grandfather can tolerate is that any excellence of Virgil's is claimed to be Kittering. It's enough that Grandmother has scored three for her side already.

'Generally. Excellent generally,' she says. And then, out of that haughtiness she has, what in Flaubert is called *froideur*, and what in the Brouders is just Class-A Bitchiness, she adds, 'He takes after my father.'

Phrase isn't out of her mouth when Grandfather is walking his hot bootsoles to the door.

'Virgil? Virgil, come down.'

Ashcroft House has two floors. (A Developer lives there now, but as Margaret Crowe says he bankruptured himself.) The upstairs rooms are too large for children and my father's has a bed and table at opposite ends.

'Virgil!'

He raises his head from Tennyson (a gorgeous red-covered gilt-edged edition, Book 444, *The Works of Alfred Tennyson*, Kegan Paul, Trench & Co., 1 Paternoster Square, London, inside which there is a bookmark, Any Amount of Books, 56 Charing Cross Road). He's in 'Idylls of the King'. *There likewise I beheld Excalibur, before him at his crowning borne, the sword that rose from out the bosom of the lake.* But on his father's calling of his name his heart leaps. He has that small boy adorableness and rushes down the big stairs. He opens and closes the door to the Drawing room swiftly and as a result sucks a great purgatorial pall of smoke out over his parents.

Margaret shoots off a spray.

'Tell me. School, Virgil? How is it?' Abraham asks.

My father has no idea he's a cannonball. He has no idea he's being readied, rolled in, prepared to be fired at his mother.

'Good.'

'Good?'

My father nods. 'I like it.' He smiles the big-eyed-boy adorable smile I will see in Aeney.

'I see.'

'It seems he's very good at Latin. So Mr Figgs says,' offers Grandmother. She has a way of speaking about you that makes you seem elsewhere. She allows a pause, before throwing to the window an under-her-breath: 'Just like my father.'

'I see.' Abraham is backside-to-the-fire, hands behind back, chin at up-jut. 'You find it hard, Virgil?'

'No.'

'I told you, Abraham. He's excellent.'

Grandmother wasn't great at smiling. She never got the hang of it as an expression of contentment. She approached the smile from the wrong end and started with the lips. The lips pulled back and up a little at the ends, but the eyes were saying something different.

The smile does it for Grandfather. There's a moment he's looking at Virgil and suddenly his blood stops. A chill comes up his back. It's the same chill he had that night in Oriel College. It's the chill that in three seconds is followed by a flush of heat and the flash of illumination. He's helpless to stop or resist it. He's looking at his son and in him he's seeing Meaning, he's seeing here's the reason he fell wounded in the hole, here's the reason *Tommy's okay*, because although he's fought against it ever since the Reverend died, although he's tried to believe that in this life there's nothing to believe in, in the end Swains can't escape their nature.

'Virgil,' he says, 'you will not be returning to Highfield School.'

Spray-spray. Spray-spray-*spray*. 'What are you talking about, Abraham?'

'That school has nothing more to teach him.'

'Don't be silly. How will he learn?' She does the smile again. This time she adds an eyebrow in the manner of the Colonel.

Grandfather won't have it. He won't have eyebrows like that aimed at him. 'That's the end of it,' he says and fires the full chin back at the raised eyebrow.

She gives him both eyebrows; he gives her the nostrils.

He's taking Virgil over for himself, and that's that. Let Grandmother have the girls – she already has – he will take Virgil. He will have one proper Swain. My father will be the reason the bullets missed Abraham's heart. He will become The One.

For a more profound insight into the problem from a salmon's perspective, see Mr Willis Bund's *Salmon Problems* and *The Life of the Salmon* (Books 477 & 478, Sampson Low & Co., London). For my perspective, read on.

While his sisters went to school, a parade of tutors came to Ashcroft House for my father.

Some days when I am Poor, when I haven't the energy to lift myself on the pillow, when the rain washes down the skylight and I want to sleep for ever, they visit.

Mr O. W. Thornton.

Mr J. G. Gerard, Mathematician.

Mr Ivor Naughton, Latin, Greek & Classics.

The young Mr Olde.

The old Mr Ebbing.

Mr Jeremiah Lewis.

They are walk-on parts. Each of them was hired and eventually fired once they made the fatal flaw of declaring Virgil brilliant.

Only one, Mr Phadraig MacGhiolla, makes a lasting impression. He's the one who brings the folktales. He's the one in the too-tight black suit with the up-forked red hair and fiery eyes of a nationalist who speaks Irish mythology. Teachers don't always know when they've lit the torch paper. But MacGhiolla knew. He knew he'd entered Virgil Swain's imagination and held up a flame when he told him of a boy who fell in love with a girl called Emer who said he could not have her unless he completed Impossible Tasks. The boy was sent to study warcraft in Scotland under the tutelage of the female warrior Scathach-the-Shadow. Scathach-the-Shadow was about twenty centuries ahead of Marvel Comics. Gaming was in the early development stages back then. One in every two gamers died. Being Scottish and a warrior meant that Scathach was ferociousness itself. She didn't have a Console, she had a hawk with talons. The boy was sent to her to learn how to achieve the impossible, and when he did, when Scathach had brought him up through all the Levels, showed him all the Cheats, and listed him on the Roll of Honour as All-Time Number-One Player, he came back and entered the fortress where Emer was guarded.

He entered it by going upriver against the current.

The method he used was salmon-leaps.

Not kidding.

Virgil tried it out for himself. One day he sneaked out the back door into the rough tufted grass that looked like a green sea behind Ashcroft. He put his hands down by his sides, straightened himself to salmon-slimness, sucked in as much breath as he could and then, with face turned to blue sky, he blew hard, arching his back into bow-shape, and tried to leap upward.

Maybe it did work. Maybe he'd inherited something from the pole-vaulting legs. He felt sure there'd been some take-off. Definitely more than if he just jumped. Yes, there was definitely some *ascent*.

That was the beginning. And MacGhiolla, Son of the Fox, knew. What he didn't know was that his own position was guaranteed the day he told Grandfather that Virgil was hopeless in Irish History, Culture & Language.

In the meantime, between husband and wife battle proper was commenced. Knocking and Straightening long over, Grandmother now took to a new field; she would not be outdone by Grandfather and so marshalled the girls into various endeavours of high achievement.

Piano was a particular favourite. Esther, Penelope and Daphne were each instructed by a Mrs Moira Hackett whose sense of humour was no longer intact and who personally had no music in her but employed the Irish Academy ruler-on-knuckles method to

87

significant effect. The three girls were soon able to perform like upright porcelain pianists, backs a perfect plumb-line, shoulders squared, and only the curved claw-shapes of their fingers moving, producing a kind of flawless mechanical music only a little worse than the cheapest wind-up musical boxes. One evening when Abraham returned from fishing he was called in to the drawing room to hear three sequential versions of Chopin's *Fantasie Impromptu*.

My father began the piano the next day.

His three sisters were all started on the violin.

II

We pause here because The Narrator has to go to Dublin.

In general, I no longer go outside. It's hard to explain. Unless you've felt it yourself, once you hear that you think *Oh-oh*, you look away but you think *She's bonkers*, a little case of the *Do-Lallies* here, because who doesn't go outside? Well, excuse me, I don't. Get over it. Once I returned from university I had this dread pressing in on my chest. If I got to the front door my legs stopped working. That was it. I couldn't breathe. I'd turn back in and sit on the arm of Nan's chair. But the feeling didn't pass. Glasses of water, air, deep breaths, blowing in a brown paper bag that had been emptied of onions, arm-pinches, Vicks inhaler, hot water with Vicks, more air (fanned *Clare Champion*), more water (sparkling), vinegar, a squirt of lemon, and a mouthful of whiskey, made no difference, neither did the little parade of the parish's amateur psychiatrists who came and sat on the bed and played a game of Questions-with-no-Answers. *What is it you are afraid of, dear?*

Please.

But now I have to go to Dublin. For Timmy and Packy this is a Big Day. Uniforms are ironed, boots cleaned, and Hair has met Comb. It's like we're going up for the All-Ireland, only instead of a team of lads in those too-short shorts and shin-high socks they wear in GAA, I'm going to be facing The Consultant.

In a secret room somewhere long ago, Jimmy Mac says, the leaders of the Medical Profession decided the best way to turn consultants into millionaires was to only have about four for the whole country. Once they had the four the doors were locked. So it takes about ten years to get to see one. Consultants are mystical as Magi, but in inverse, you have to travel to them. You have to be in Serious Condition to be sent, and if you are it's pretty much the end of the yellow brick road. Mary Houlihan in Knock was three years buried when she got called. Her husband Matty said he'd a right to dig her up and bring her corpse, only Dignam the ticket inspector in Ennis probably wouldn't allow her the free pass.

I come down the stairs in the stretcher. I'm trying to breathe all the time but it feels like I'm underwater.

'It's okay, love,' Mam says. 'It's okay.' Her hand takes mine at the bottom of the stairs, and with Timmy holding up the top and Packy the bottom we sail out the front door.

The sky is huge and jellyfish-grey and there's no light in it at all. There's just this watery expanse leaking drops as we go down the garden to the ambulance.

Timmy and Packy have the inside of it shining. Mam sits beside me. You can see the bravery in her. You can see how she will *not be defeated*, how the world has thrown sadness after sadness at her and knocked her down and she's still getting up, she's older than she was and there's these few silver hairs coming at her temples and her eyes have that extra deepness of knowledge that makes her more beautiful in a kind of lasting way. It's like she's this eternal Mother, my mam, this wall around me, holding back the sea that keeps coming for me. I can see it in her eyes. I can see the way she's hoping so hard that this might be the time, this might be Help Coming.

She's hoping and trying not to hope at the same time.

And that's the saddest thing.

Hope may or may not be a Thing with Feathers. But it's definitely a Thing with Claws.

We drive out of Faha for Dublin when the fields are just waking to today's rain. Today it's a soft silveriness that Packy says suits Intermittent 4 on the wipers but Timmy thinks should be 5. They talk the whole way. If we were driving to Moscow they'd talk the whole way there too.

I'm okay inside the ambulance, because somehow it's not the world.

Conversation follows the road. While we're still in the parish the talk is all Faha. It's Martin & Maureen Ring whose daughter Noelle has gone off with one of the Muslims of Mayo, the Ballyhaunis Meat Men. It's the bachelor Brothers Hayes, who are in their sixties, who each buy a copy of the *Champion* even though they live together in the same three-room bungalow. The brothers have a teabag mountain outside the front door, a giant steaming mound that's supposed to be composting in the front bed but is resisting because of the rain Timmy says, lends the air at their front door a bit of a tang of India in monsoon season. If we have a flood there'll be a tea-Ganges heading down to McCarthy's.

The talk is of the Apostolic Works whose workers are all women in their eighties now and who still meet in Faha N.S. seven o'clock on the evening of the First Tuesday, carrying their glowing Ever-Readies along the road like genuine Illuminates and making the decision now to team up with the troop of the Legion of Mary whose Legionnaires are down to two. It's the news that when Sean & Sheila Maguire came down to Faha graveyard Wednesday to dig up her grandfather that got buried in the wrong grave they found an actual snake slyly slithering between Ciaran Carr's plot and that of the woman he was meant to marry, Una Lyons.

We pass Dan Byrne in his black suit and string vest out by the Cross. A big believer in the visuals, Dan lost his shirt on bank investments sometime after the Banks passed their first Stress Test.

The dogs in the street knew the country was cooked, Packy says. Because of me he won't say fooked.

The Nationwide got narrow, Timmy says.

We get out on to the Ennis road and down to Icarus at the Roundabout. He's in the conversation for twenty miles. Icarus used to be inside at the Market but flew over to Greece for a bit and came back not the better for it, Packy says. He needed a bit of hammering. He's not gold enamelling or anything, he's not the full Byzantium, but he's Clare's best Greek and people are kind of fond of him, even if a naked man with arms out and legs akimbo was a bit much for the youth. People didn't take kindly to his wings getting dinted. He's erected now in the centre of the Rocky Road roundabout with the CCTV because Packy says The Lads would have him for melting if he was out there without the Eye on him.

'They would,' says Timmy. 'He's better there anyhow.'

'He is.'

'When he was in The Market the scholars from Flannan's were always putting the traffic cone on his head.'

'They were.'

'One time he had a bra and panties.'

'I didn't see that.'

'One time they strapped a traffic cone over his . . .'

'I remember that all right.'

'Flannan's lads.'

'Good hurlers though.'

'They might do it this year.'

'They won't.'

'You have no belief. That's your problem.'

The National Conversation takes the new motorway all the way from Ennis to Dublin and between those shallow naps you have in seatbelts I hear: Why the country is destroyed; why the last crowd were the worst crowd to ever run this country; why bankers should be locked up and criminals let out; why we'll never see the like again.

The best thing we could do, Packy says, is cut ourselves free.

'How do you mean?'

'Just what I said. The best thing we could do as a country. Just cut the rope. Cut the rope and sail away.'

The Consultant doesn't have an office. He has Rooms. He has some really nice furniture. All his magazines are this month's. And they have no creases in the covers. When you're waiting for the Consultant you don't really want to read about the Ten Best Places to Eat by Moonlight.

I sit with Mam and we wait. I get so tired I can't even

＊

The piano-playing Aunts come to visit us after Aunt Esther dies. I am eleven years old. Their visit is announced well in advance, the Aunts are very Old School like that. I think they imagine it's proper to send word ahead so that the maids and servants can start fluffing floors and polishing pillows. They imagine there must be buffing to be done. I think it's well-intentioned but Nan won't credit it. She believes my father's sisters are powdered witches sent from the east with the sole aim of denigrating the people of the west.

Unlike everyone else who uses the back door, the Aunts come in the front. They make the latch of the kitchen door seem a contrivance of intentional backwardness.

Here they are:

'Hellooo? Hellooo?'

They peer in and at the same moment both angle back their heads, as if they have taken a position a little too close to a pano-ramic screen. They are tall and big-boned and look like men playing women's parts in a play by Oscar Wilde.

'Nan, Verge's sisters are here,' my mother says loudly.

But Nan already knows, and furiously pokers the fire to try and smoke them back out. Nan here is The Aged P only with more mischievousness than Mr Wemmick's in *Great Expectations*, the only book of which my father kept two copies (Books 180 and 400, Penguin Classic & Everyman Classics editions, London), both of which I have read twice, deciding each time that *Great Expectations* is the Greatest. If you don't agree, stop here, go back and read it again. I'll wait. Or be dead.

Grandmother Bridget, the Aunts call her.

'Grandmother Bridget, hello!' they call out.

Nan doesn't reply but flaps the *Champion* at the fire and sends out a great curling cloud of smoke.

In reprisal, by way of commentary on Nan's deficit and I suppose in testament to the superiority of their side of the family genetic, and the east of the country in general, the Aunts smile their full fierce perfect teeth.

'O and here's Ruth. Little darling Ruth. Come here, my dear, let us look at you. There is such intelligence in that face, isn't there, Daphne? And what an interesting dress, dear.'

Another great pall of turfsmoke.

'Now, Ruth, come and tell us everything. Let us look at you.'

What is it they see? I am thin but not of the sylph kind, more the gawky lanky kind which may be what constitutes the Swain Beautiful but feels Rangy Ruth to me. My knees are actually *sharp*. At that age I am officially Waiting for My Chest. The Chest Fairy is on the way from Boozoomia or somewhere and all the girls in my class are going to sleep at night in their own state of Great Expectation, waking up and checking: is that it? – throwing their shoulders far back and breasting the world, as if the task of womanhood is to balance the weight that lands on your chest and could easily topple you over.

Which in a way I suppose is true.

Anyway, The Chest Fairy passes me by. I'm still Waiting. So when the Aunts look at me there can't be much that impresses.

I've learned that you can never see yourself as another person does. You can never really know who you are for them, at least not until much later. That's what I think now. I stand and look at my aunts. They have amazing coats and dresses. Their dresses are of a woven cloth on which patterned flowers in subdued colour have been embroidered the way I've only seen on wallpaper. Their coats have huge black buttons and when they hand their coats over they are heavy as blankets and smell like cupboards.

'I'm sure you're best in your class, Ruth, aren't you? Good girl, good girl. You're such a bright girl you will just grow up and dazzle. Won't she, Daphne? She'll dazzle.'

'Dazzle dazzle dazzle.'

'Mother says you like to read. Do you?'

I do.

'Of course you do, because you're so bright, you little angel. If your grandmother was alive she'd – No. No, Penelope, I'm not. I'm not no.'

'Handkerchief?'

'Thank you, Penelope.'

'We've brought you a present, dear.'

'Really?'

'It's just for you.'

It's a hardcover of Jane Austen's *Sense and Sensibility* and on the inside front page there's this little oval black and white picture of her with a baby's bonnet on her head and a kind of ironic smile like She Knows. Jane knows what stupid insensitive people there are in the world and that's what is behind every word she writes. Look at her portrait, She Knows. I think Dear Jane had a bit of the Impossible Standard herself although maybe it wasn't even that impossible, maybe it was just some kind of decency and awareness she was expecting.

'It's Jane Austen, dear,' Aunt P says.

'What?' Nan asks from the fire.

'JANE AUSTEN,' Aunt roars.

'EXHAUSTING?' Nan bellows back. 'YES,' and starts the Aged P nod.

Neither of my aunts, I am convinced, ever drank tea from a mug. The china cups are out for them.

They are a pair in the world, the two of them, and trade in exchange one to the other an entire currency of startled, dismayed and disapproving looks. The world fails the Impossible Standard constantly. Sometimes I imagine a whole gallery of their failed suitors, scrubbed jowly farmers of Meath, tweeded-up and cow-licked down, sent up to evenings in Ashcroft. The Meath men have surnames like Castlebridge, Farns, Ainsley. The sisters kill them off afterwards with cutting remarks. One sentence will do for each one.

'Those hands he has.' Castlebridge.

'Did he seem to mumble terribly, dear? Could you, I couldn't understand him. But perhaps you're fond of him?' Farns.

'Actually I've never seen a fork used quite like that.' Ainsley.

Pursed mouths, raised chins, arched eyebrows: each sister destroys the other's suitors like she's scissoring paper dolls. They find none up to standard. Their souls select their own society as the best and they become the pair they are.

'Is that a?'

'Tart,' Mam says.

'Tart. Pie, yes. I see. Apple?'

'Rhubarb.'

'Rhubarb. Well, well. Rhubarb, Daphne.'

'Yes. Rhubarb.'

From care, or meanness as Nan says, the aunts are thin women. When they lift the cups of tea they do so with thumb and forefinger only, the other three fingers an extended fan for balance and grace. They lean ever so slightly forward and, eyebrows raised and lips tightened to the smallest puckered nub, sip the startling dark brew my mother has made.

'Rhubarb? Well well, Daphne.'

Dad arrives late. He comes into the kitchen in his wellingtons and there is sudden excitement. His sisters fly up like ravens.

'O Virgil.'

They flutter about him a few moments — 'Virgil, are you getting thin? What is this you are wearing?' — and show their love in questions.

My dad is easily embarrassed.

That man is an ocean of emotion, Jimmy Mac said.

Knowing the aunts were coming, Mam has everything just as tidy as can be. She's put a load of things away inside the dresser, she's hidden the tea-towels we usually use and taken out these cream ones I've never seen; for the duration of The Visit the Normal Life of our house has been tidied away. I like it in a way. There's a sense of occasion. So here's my dad standing in his wellies and he can see how tidy the place is even as his sisters circle. He can see all the effort Mam and I have made and his eyes have that kind of shining they get when the feelings are these waves rising in his heart.

'O Virgil, are you getting thin?'

My father was always thin and his hair was always silver. His eyes were the bluest blue, the way the water looks when in the sky over it you think you can see Heaven. In my mind the thinness and the silveriness and the blueness were all connected.

'He is getting thin, isn't he, Daphne?'

Aunt D twitches her beak. She wants to be nicer than her sister; she wants to speak to her brother in his world, and so all the way across Ireland she has considered what she will say. Now she makes this high, brow-pencilled smile and asks: 'How are your cows doing, dear?'

97

Men are private. This I have learned. They are whole continents of privacy; you can only go to the borders; you can look in but you cannot enter. This is something I have learned. All this time Aeney is sitting in the narrow stairs that go up over the dresser to our bedrooms. He broke his leg falling from the sycamore and is perched up there, his cast out in front of him, and he's watching and listening. He has a smile people describe as winning, a winning smile, a smile that wins you to him no matter what, you just love him.

'Oh now, Aon-us,' Aunt P says. She can never get the hang of his name and wants to say Aeneas and Aengus together and she's a little surprised he's been there all the time but she's not cross because you can't be cross with Aeney, you can't be cross with that smile. You see that golden hair and that smile and some part of you is sort of quietened, like you know he's different somehow. I don't mean that in the way some people do, like it's a bad thing, I mean just the opposite, like you feel a little awe, a little O my God. You look at him and you think *golden boy*.

'Oh now, there you are. Come down here and tell your aunts all about you.'

*

We drove for four hours to see The Consultant. We saw him for thirty-three minutes.

Something in your blood is wrong, he said.

Then we drove back across the country in the ambulance, Mam holding my hand, and Timmy and Packy not talking at all. The daylight was all gone and the road was this long winding river of yellow headlights going home towards the west. When we passed Tipperary we were back in the rain.

12

Your blood is a river.

13

The drizzling dawn of my father's fourteenth birthday, Abraham appeared in the big draughty bedroom and shook his son awake.

'Come on.'

Virgil dressed at top speed, was down the stairs and in the kitchen in no time, buttoning his last buttons as his father finished packing their lunch, a hodgepodge of bread, spread, pickles, cheese and apples.

They stamped into wellingtons, Abraham shook the tin box of flies, gave a kind of up-flick of his head and went out the front door, Grandfather banging it to so the bang fired into his daughters' dreams upstairs and startled a flush of blackbirds off the front lawn.

It was one of those perfectly still mist-laid mornings, the fields wearing that silver drapery in imitation of Heaven, the air smelling green, sticky new leaves unfurling, and father and son with rods skyward heading for the river. I leave them on that road a while, soft clump-thud of their boots, metal-clasps jinglejangling on Grandfather's shoulder-bag. They're a good way gone when Grandfather says: '*Arma virumque cano.*'

He doesn't slow down, doesn't break stride or look sidelong at his son.

My father is not sure he's heard. Grandfather's pole-vaulting legs carry him in two strides what takes Virgil three. He's always a little in the old man's wake. He looks at Abraham who is not looking back but marching on. And without question or comment Virgil replies: '*Troiae qui primus ab oris italiam.*'

And away they go, playing a little game of Aeneid and cutting across the fields of the County Meath.

When he's had his fill of the Latin, Grandfather says, '"O that this too sullen flesh . . ."'

And Virgil gives him back '". . . should melt, thaw, and resolve itself into a dew . . ."' He knows the five soliloquys spoken by Hamlet. He can go from the sullen flesh to the rogue and peasant slave to how all occasions. He's learning the four in *Macbeth*.

Not once does Grandfather stop. He doesn't look sideways at his son nor show any outward marvel at him but somewhere inside, somewhere in the Swain Unreachable, out in the unknown deeps where that part of him that was once a gleaming youth in Oriel College, somewhere there I know his spirit leaps.

Fat Meath cattle, tongue-tearing the first right succulent grass of spring, look up and watch Hamlet & His Father passing.

My father is in a new version of Heaven. He hasn't time to consider it yet, whether he is happy because he is hastening along the road with his father as day breaks, or just because he was asked to come and that now this is actually happening, or because he has been asked for a speech from Shakespeare and the phrases are coming like a long golden thread out of his mouth even before he has time to think of them. The words are there, and flow, as he works hard to, and now matches the long pole-vault strides of his father.

In some ways my father's whole life is in this moment. In this are all the years ahead, all the poems, all the rapture and the yearning and the grief too.

Abraham makes no comment, but my dad knows. He knows he is being heard. He knows this is a kind of perfection, and everything – the morning light, rods over shoulder, glistening fields, the thick and intense gaiety of the birdsong – enters him and leaves this permanent shine far down in his spirit. He knows it. And I think that for just these moments, the two of them hurrying to the river for the first casts, leaving the world behind, crossing the fat fields of the Fitzherberts to the dark rush of the waters, for just these moments Virgil Swain meets the Impossible Standard.

When Grandfather comes back to Ashcroft that evening he draws a sheaf of pages from the top drawer of his desk, dips his pen, and writes the first sentence of *The Salmon in Ireland*: 'Ireland is a paradise for the salmon fisher.'

14

When my father told it, they caught a salmon that day.

I think it is an imagined one, but I didn't say so.

From the look on my face he could tell. 'O Ruthie, you don't believe anything,' he said and crumpled his face to a small boy's dismay.

I do, Dad. I do. I believe everything.

'Ruth,' Mrs Quinty says. 'I'm so sorry.'

Her face is smaller, her eyes larger than ever. She keeps them wide open to hold all her tears. In them is the news of my blood gone wrong.

'It's all right, Mrs Quinty.'

'Life is so unfair.'

There's nothing I can say to that. Life is unfair is in History of Swain, Volumes 1 through 20. It's not only unfair it's outrageous. It's harder than anything you could imagine and on top of that It Makes No Sense. God calls you and then changes His mind. Germans shoot at you then save you. You try and die quietly and someone gives you a fortune.

'I've brought you this,' she says.

It's a cassette of *The Shawshank Redemption*.

(Have I told you I have TV up here? Jimmy Mac ran the wire up through the floorboards so I could watch *Home and Away*. And even though I'm The Smart Girl and was studying Thomas

Wyatt — *they flee from me that sometime did me seek* — and Philip Sydney and the whole Gartered Stocking Brigade of Poets I still like going Down Under to those beaches in Sydney. It's the only time I see the sun.)

'Thank you, Mrs Quinty.'

'I haven't seen it myself, but Mrs Quinlavin says it's good. She showed it to the Transitions and it kept even them quiet.'

'Because it's about an impossible escape.'

'Well,' she says, 'maybe it won't be any good.'

'Mrs Quinty?'

'Yes, Ruth?'

'Did you ever hear of a story where a character separated from his shadow? He separates from it and spends the rest of the story trying to catch back up to it. Something like that?'

About a month after the Aunts visited a package arrived in the post, brown paper, neatly tied string, and inside it the mixed company of Charlotte Brontë, Mrs Elizabeth Gaskell and a rather bulky, I might say contented, Thomas Hardy lying between them. I read them all, read them one by one with a kind of constant hunger as if they were apples that fed and made you hungry at the same time. I don't mind saying I loved nothing as much as having those books upstairs in my room. Maybe it was because I knew they were Swain, maybe because it was true that deep down I was Snoot Ruth and didn't want to be MacCarroll or because there was something kind of appealing about the Philosophy of Impossible Standard so that when you were told these books were beyond you it meant those were the very ones you wanted to read, and did read. What Sister Margaret-Mary in Kilkee did for Mass-going, I did for reading, World Champion Standard. When I was eight and Mum took me to Ennis to get my first pair of glasses the very first question they asked was *Does she read a lot?* like it was A Sign, like it said Smart Girl right there on your face, and when I got them and wore them to school you'd swear I was Little Miss Porcelain-face – Jane Brouder who had elected herself Mother Hen of our class, and who at age eight had an encyclopedic knowledge of Things That Could Go Wrong With You, sort of cordoned me off and screamed at anyone who came within ten feet of me: 'Mind! She's got glasses!' I was just that bit more delicate than the others, or less vain or more posh or something, because there were others who couldn't see well, others you saw squinting or looking into the copy next to them when there was something to be taken down from the board, but either they wouldn't allow their beauty compromised by the thick brown-rimmed glasses the Mid-Western Health Board had decided was the best anti-boy device they could think of, or their parents didn't think seeing was so important for girls.

In Faha it was easy to be different. One time the aunts sent me yellow satin slippers and when I wore them to Mass you could feel the whole church noticing and Mary Maloney thinking *Protestant Shoes* and *Swain Notions* and making her whole self shudder a little in her good coat as she coughed on this great hairball of resentment until between the Offertory and the Consecration she found solace in the idea that the slippers would be filthy in a day. I saw her. I knew. I am the kind of girl who notices. But that wouldn't have stopped me wearing them. I'm that much a Swain anyway. I'm that much like my dad with whatever stubbornness foolishness or willpower he had to have to arrive here with a name like Virgil Swain, Latin-speaker, when the first question anybody back then asked would have been just – *Swain?* That would be enough. In that would be the whole story. It wouldn't be like now with the Kwietcowskis and the Secas and the Pawlavs; back then the worst thing would have been to say: *Not Related*. When you're different you've got two choices. You can stand out or you step back.

I was already different because I was a twin. Funny how you can say that: I am a twin.

Not I am one of twins, but I actually am A Twin.

Like there's two of me all the time, this other one right here beside me whether you can see him or not.

Or as if you're saying, I'm a Half.

Twins are not rightly understood as a concept in the parish anyway; before us there were the identical twins Concepta and Assumpta Talty who somehow merged in the parish mind into the one, Consumpta; whichever one was met was called that and if both were together people said Hello Consumpta and the girls said hello right back. The parish can be odd like that. Mary Hegarty pushed a pram through the village for nine years after her son Seanie had died as a baby and not one person ever said, 'Mary, your pram is empty,' they just let it be and she went on wheeling her grief through the village and out the back roads by the river where all grief flows.

Down in Faha N.S. Mrs Conheedy was the principal. She had come over from some mountainy place in Kerry and all I'll say is when I first met her I thought she was Mr Conheedy. I know it's not polite but when you're in my position with *something in the blood* you have Special Privileges, and number one is you can tell the truth. Mrs Conheedy had a face lumpy as a turnip and shoulders you could imagine her carrying a sheep on. There were no dentists where she came from. She was the last disciple of Crimplene, a sensible cloth that couldn't wrinkle or fade, that defied both time and humanity and always looked the same. Her dresses had this big zip on the back of her neck. She always left it sticking up, a little square hole in it, like she had a secret hope that one day a hook would come down from the sky and get her. I certainly hoped it would. Jimmy Mac said she had Gone-into-Teaching because it was the only place where she could rule without reprisal; where she could give free rein to the awesome dimension of her need to crush things. Mr Conheedy it seemed had enjoyed this for the first three months of their marriage, but then had run off, Nan said, to try and find a female Mrs Conheedy next time round.

'Ruth and Aengus Swain come here.'

'Yes Miss.'

Aeney gave her the Winning Smile at Full Power. He tilted his head slightly so the quiff of his wondrous fair hair added to the effect of general adorableness. He went to Full Luminous. But it didn't work.

'Ruth, you will be in Miss Barry's class; Aengus, you will be in Mr Crossan's.'

We didn't even look at each other. We didn't say a word. We just stood there feeling the knife along our sides.

You can't know. Maybe you can imagine in your head, but you can't know. You can't know what it feels like in your blood.

'Miss?'

'Go now, Miss Barry's. Mr Crossan's.'

'Can't I stay with my brother?'

'No you cannot.'

'Please Miss.'

'There is no Please Miss. Miss Barry's, Mr Crossan's. Now. It will be for the better for both of you.'

I'll never forget walking down that corridor after we came out of her office. I'll never forget the clammy air and the blurred voices coming from the teachers inside the classrooms. It was like we had slipped from the world, like there was all this activity going on, half past ten on an ordinary Monday morning and everyone in their proper places behind doors except us. The corridor had these square dome skylights spaced along it and the sun fell down in actual beams that showed the dust and the particles of the otherwise invisible so you felt you were crossing someplace, but for just that while you were neither in one world nor the other. Sunbeam shade sunbeam. Shade. And maybe I was aware everything was changing and that I was losing my brother, that from that moment he would begin slipping away. Maybe in that walk down the corridor I could feel the days of summer falling away from us, the playing together in the fields behind our house, games of hay-hide, of Aeney and me climbing in the sycamore tree, of being in the Big Meadow, of me telling him Ruth's Version of the books I was reading, of calling across the upper air at the top of our house, my sky-bed to his: *Are you asleep yet?*

Are you?

I reached over and took Aeney's hand. I tried my trick of Making Everything Stop so it would stay just us, floating in a sunbeam, out of reach of change.

It seems to you such a small thing. Maybe you're even in the Conheedy camp and believe it would be For the Better. It says so in many books, Separate the Twins.

But not in any books written by twins.

Mrs Conheedy came out of her office. 'Ruth Swain, stop dallying. Into class now.'

I let go of Aeney's hand. He looked at me. He smiled one of those brave smiles small boys smile. But he was afraid.

I remember feeling the cold handle of the classroom door. I remember Aeney walking past me down to Mr Crossan's and his not turning back and my watching him go and thinking *I love my brother* and feeling this hopeless loss that I had no words for but later found in the fairy-tale word *banishment*.

Miss Barry was an angel. In total I had fourteen teachers in all my time in school. Only one was an angel.

I didn't hear about Mr Crossan from Aeney that day. When he came out into the yard he stayed on the edge of a group of boys. They were pushing each other and being loud and he was trying to attach himself to them, just sort of walking along a little behind them, trying to find a glue he was just discovering he didn't have. I didn't have it either. Go down to any schoolyard at breaktime and look in and you'll see. You'll see the ones who have no Human Glue, who run out the first day with this perfect unrumpled optimism and trust, who still think of every boy and girl as their undiscovered friend and believe What Fun We'll Have. And then, in the schoolyard, day one, there's someone sprung from evil genes like Michael Mooney or Hen genes like Jane Brouder and they feel something off you, feel that field of difference you don't even know you're giving off, and boom you're out, you can't stick on. The group runs down the yard and you run too but it's like the signal was given on a wavelength you didn't receive in time so you're a few steps back. Look at the pictures of Aeney's class. You'll see. It's like he's been photoshopped in and there's this clean line around him, no Human Glue.

I watched him that day even as I was becoming The-Girl-with-Glasses. I was thinking *Okay, if I am to be on my own island I'll have Aeney come over and join me.*

Swain Island would be fine with me. But when I went across the yard from Girls' side to Boys' to speak to him he turned away. He wouldn't look at me. He wouldn't be saved.

'Separates from their shadow?' Mrs Quinty says.

'Yes.'

'No. No, Ruth. I don't think I know that one.'

15

If your blood is a river, where is the sea?

A central principle underlying Mrs Quinty's Rules for Writing is that you have to have a Beginning Middle and End. If you don't have these your Reader is lost.

But what if Lost is exactly where the writer is? I asked her.

Ruth, the writer can't be lost, she said, and then knew she'd said it too quickly and bit her lip knowing I was going to say something about Dad. She pressed her knees together and diverted into a fit of dry coughing.

This, Dear Reader, is a river narrative. My chosen style is The Meander. I know that in *The Brothers Karamazov* (Book 1,777, Penguin Classics, London) Ippolit Kirillovich chose the historical form of narration because Dostoevsky says it checked his own exuberant rhetoric. Beginnings middles and ends force you into that place where you have to Stick to the Story as Maeve Mulvey said the night the Junior Certs were supposed to be going to the cinema in Ennis but were buying cans in Dunnes and drinking them in the Parnell Street carpark and Mrs Pender saw Grainne Hayes hanging off the salt-and-vinegar lips of some pimpled bean-pole at The Height, wearing enough eyeliner and mascara to make her look like a badger in Disney and that micro-mini that wasn't more than two inches of black-plastic silage wrap, all of which required they chose the historical form of narration and Stick To

Their Story since she'd left the Hayes's house earlier that evening in jeans and hoodie. But there's a different kind of stickiness here, there's the kind that gets inside your skin when you've been in the river and you come out and shower and dry off but it's still there, and you know you've been in a river. Here's the day Mam took Aeney and I to the circus. Duffy's Circus had been coming to Faha since Duffy first bought a camel. They came annually in summer and set up in the GAA field, bringing with them a giant yellowy tent that smelled of magic when magic was elephant dung and hay and tobacco and that when erected was home to an exotic collection of flies moths and mosquitos, some of which I imagined orbiting the head of Melquíades when years later I read my father's yellow-paged copy of *One Hundred Years of Solitude* (Book 2,000, Gabriel García Márquez, Picador, London), the one that has *A mi amigo V, que me ha ensenado un nuevo modo de entender la vida, Paco* written inside it, but I never found out who Paco was or what new way of life V had shown him. Duffy's came until their animals were dust, they came the year after that too when their camel was dust with two humps and whose performance consisted of a coarse hair skin you were allowed to rub and which felt exactly like the hairy couch the Mulveys bought from Broderick's in Killenena. (Once Duffy's was gone the Great American Circus came with stars and stripes painted on everything and accents of Pure Mullingar, but by then sadly I was Beyond Circuses.) Aeney and I sit in the front row. The trapeze is high above us. We lean back to look up at this glittering girl. She is maybe fourteen years old. We are seven. Cymbals are crashed together by the moustached barrel-shaped man we presume is Duffy, his face, like Mr Micawber's after he had drunk punch, appears *varnished*. He cranes back to gaze above and then the girl walks across the upper air. We can't see the line. She just walks across nothing, her arms extended for balance, her chin slightly raised, as though the Nuns were right and only perfect posture will get you into Heaven. She walks above us, pays no attention to the world below. Aeney turns to me and his eyes are wide with amazement. He doesn't say anything. He doesn't say *wow* or *god* or *d'you see her?* He knows that with me he doesn't need to. He just looks and smiles and I smile, and without for a second thinking of it he squeezes my hand one quick squeeze of just joy and then he lets go and we both look up at that impossible girl.

And then the moment twists, slides away from me, and is gone downriver. Down this narrative all manner of things will float. But not Mr Crossan. I'm sinking him here. And if God asks for cause I'll give Him cause. I'll give Him that two yards of bones topped with a sprig of ginger, that narrow-jawed rat-faced misery with the pinched whine for a voice, the head to one side growing wiry nostril hair as he looks down at who he'll pick on for humiliation today; I'll give Him the Pride and Prejudice of Mr Crossan, that skinny shiny-suited blister with the complexion of uncooked sausage who went into teaching so that he could belittle others, so that he could say: 'Aonghus Swain, is that handwriting? Tell me. I can't read it. Is it? IS IT?'

I've had stupid teachers, lazy teachers, boring teachers, teachers who were teachers because their parents were and they hadn't the imagination to think of anything else, teachers who were teachers because of cowardice, because of fear, because of the holidays, because of the pensions, because they were never called to account, never had to actually be any good, ones who could not survive in any other profession, who were not aware they had trod on butterflies. But none of those compared to Mr Maurice Crossan. He was the one who first stamped on my brother's soul. He was dark, as they say here. For those who want more of him visit the dark character of Orlick Dolge in *Great Expectations* and cross that with a ginger-headed weasel.

He's not getting in here. He's not in The Ark.

When the bell rang I waited by the gate for Aeney. When he came he didn't want me to be me. He walked past and I knew not to say anything but to just step silently into his wake. When we came in Mam had the table set and one of those thin smiles mothers have when they're hoping so hard for their children all day and the hope is kind of butting up against the fear and the foreboding and really they are this massive mess inside with this smile plastered on top.

'Well? How was it?'

'Fine,' Aeney said.

That's the thing about boys. Maybe just Irish boys. Boys have No Go Areas, they have an entire geography of places you can't go because if you do they'll crack open, they'll fall apart and you won't be able to put them back together, not ever. Girls know this. We know. Even love can't reach some places.

Fine, Aeney said, when there was no way in the world he was fine. When fine was as far as you could be from a true description of what he was feeling. But that was it. That's all he said, and Mam sort of bit her lip and poured us MiWadi and said she had his favourite, Petit Filous, for after. He ate his dinner. He didn't want any Petit Filous. He went up to his room and shut the door. When I came up I asked him through the door if he wanted to learn our spellings together, he said no. I sat in my sky-room, he sat in his. Then I heard him crying. I heard it at first like it was choked breathing. Like when you've sunk in deep water and had the life terrified out of you and you come up into the air eyes wide and mouth gasping not sure if this is your last and you're about to be dragged back down again. He sucked in spasms, then he moaned and made this sound that wasn't like anything except the sound a spirit makes when it's sundering.

'Aeney, let me in. Aeney?'

But he didn't answer. He just cried on, this hopeless hard retching as if the tears were shards and each one cut as it came out. He was sitting on the floor up against the door so I couldn't get in and Mam was gone to take Nan to Murphy's so I just sank down on the floor on the other side of the door and because of the force of his crying the door and the whole partition wall kind of gave a little, these jagged ebbs and flows, as if the whole upstairs was in a storm, and my brother was in another boat sailing away, and no matter how much I wanted to, no matter what I did or said I would never be able to get to him.

*

Mr MacGhiolla *was* a teacher. He was the one who taught my father about the King-Under-the-Wave. He had this old book of tales (Book 390, *Hero-Tales of Ireland*, Jeremiah Curtin, Little, Brown, Boston), a kind already out of fashion then, but which he employed to keep my father's imagination greenly lit. He didn't want my father doing just Shakespeare and Homer. I'm not sure if he explained to Virgil that Shakespeare was Irish (see Book 1,904, *Ulysses*, James Joyce, Bodley Head, London) and that in fact all great writers can be traced back here if you go far enough, but he instilled in him the belief that this was a country of unrivalled imagination and culture. He threw out mythological names his pupil had never heard of, each of them exotic bait he knew the boy would rise to. In the long room upstairs in Ashcroft where no one could hear, he spoke to my father *in Irish*.

Ireland had gone wrong at some stage, according to MacGhiolla. Some kind of spell had been thrown and the country began forgetting itself. It began turning into Lesser Britain was the gist of Mr MacGhiolla's argument. Our history, our folklore and culture were being washed into the sea and must be defended. MacGhiolla was too passionate to worry about mixed metaphors. He was too passionate to worry about generalisations or broad strokes or let the rational get in the way of his argument. Neither was he bothered by the fact that his pale complexion was deeply unsuited to passion and blotched in disparate patches as he rose to his theme. He spoke standing, hands clasped when not released to fork his red hair with exasperation, eyes locked on the upper left air when not locked on Virgil and burning his point home. He spoke on rising toes, on rolling ankles, he spoke with forward tilt, with lifted shoulders, with forefinger pointing and fist punching. He did verbal pirouettes, he did elongated sentences, he let clauses gather at the river and foam until they found spittle release. He spoke hushed, he spoke his big points in whispers, then drove them in with urgent balletic waves of arm and extended eyebrow as he said the same thing again only louder. He was not then a guns and bombs nationalist. He was the more dangerous kind. He was a poems and stories one.

As proof of his impact, my father kept all the books Mr MacGhiolla gave him: Book 391, *The Crock of Gold*, James Stephens, Pan, London; Book 392, *Irish Fairy Tales*, James Stephens, Macmillan, London; Book 393, *The Three Sorrows of Storytelling*, Douglas Hyde, T. Fisher Unwin, London; Book 394, *Death Tales of the Ulster Heroes*, Kuno Meyer, Hodges, Figgis & Co., Dublin; Book 395, *Silva Gadelica* Volume II, Standish Hayes O'Grady, Williams and Norgate, London; and the tea-ringed Book 396, *Cuchulainn: The Irish Achilles*, Alfred Nutt, D. Nutt, London. From Mr MacGhiolla my father heard about the King who lived under the waves, about the Glas Gainach, the cow whose milk was almost butter. He heard about the Queen called Mor who lived in Dunquin and the herder who came from Under the Sea. Cathal the Son of Conor, the Black Thief, the Tuatha Dé Danann, the Children of Lir, the Voyage of Bran.

For my father it was as if the world split open and out came this parade of The Remarkables.

If this was America they'd be Blockbuster material, there'd be CUCHULAINN VII in 3D by now with Liam Neeson in his long *Star Wars* hair, the Gáe Bolga instead of a Light Sabre, there'd be a side franchise for Oisín in Tír na nÓg and Diarmuid and Grainne would get a revamp as Greatest Love Story Ever and run for seven seasons as a daytime soap.

That material was *deep*.

And in all of it, in all of those tales, the hero faces impossible tasks. And he triumphs.

With a brilliant student Mr MacGhiolla shone. It was simple: we are the storytellers. Imagination in Ireland was beyond the beyond. It was out there. It was Far Out before far out was invented in California, because sitting around in a few centuries of rain breeds these outlands of imagination. As evidence, think of Abraham Stoker, confined to bed until he was eight years old, lying there breathing damp Dublin air with no TV or radio but the heaving wheeze of his chest acting as pretty constant reminder that soon he was heading Elsewhere. Even after he was married to Florence Balcombe of Marino Crescent (she who had an unrivalled talent for choosing the wrong man, who had already given up Oscar Wilde as a lost cause in the Love Department when she met this Bram Stoker and thought: *he seems sweet*), even after Bram moved to London he couldn't escape his big dark imaginings in Dublin and one day further down the river he spawned *Dracula* (Book 123, Norton, New York). Jonathan Swift was only settling into a Chesterfield couch in Dublin when his brain began sailing to Lilliput and Blefuscu (Book 778, *Gulliver's Travels*, Jonathan Swift, Penguin, London). Another couple of deluges and he went further, he went to Brobdingnag, Laputa, Bainbarbi, Glubbdubdrib, Luggnagg and . . . *Japan*, before he went furthest of all, to Houyhnhnms. Read *Gulliver's*

Travels when you're sick in bed and you'll be *away*. I'm telling you. You'll be transported, and even as you're being carried along in the current you'll think no writer ever went this Far. Something like this could only be dreamt up in Ireland.

Charles Dickens recognised that. He comes to Dublin August 25th 1858 for an imagination Top-Up. Stays in Morrison's Hotel on Nassau Street (I know, scary that I know that, but I do. Roast Pork with apple sauce, Bread and butter pudding). He heads down to Cork four days later, checks in to the Imperial Hotel, where, according to the porter Jeremiah Purcell, the clock in the front foyer has been stopped at twenty to nine for about a year waiting on one of the Stokeses of Mac Curtain Street to come fix it. (Charles Dickens is a punctual man. He values punctuality above church-going. He stands looking at the clock. Jeremiah comes over and explains. *She's stopped.* Charles looks at him. 'She's stopped?' *She is, Sir. Stopped. Wound, but won't go beyond twenty to.*) Next day Charles takes an early-morning carriage to Blarney Castle, which is dark stone and dreary on the day on account of the rain, and that place sets him thinking. He skips up the steps, gets a small bit drowned, but carries on, lays down and does the whole backwards lean-over-the-edge, osteopathy no-no, to kiss the Blarney Stone.

Reader, he does, even the World's Most Bountiful Imagination, the Inimitable, needed a little of the Irish. And it works too; Charles Dickens isn't back in London two days, size 8 walking brogues not yet dry by the fire, overcoat still smelling of turf smoke and Clonakilty blood pudding, when he begins ruminating on a dark stone house. He sits in his study, says to himself: twenty minutes to nine. Stop the clocks. Twenty minutes to nine. That's all it takes. That detail is all he needs. Good man, Jeremiah. Thank you, Stokeses of Mac Curtain Street. Because now, Boz O Boz, Charles sucks a segment of orange in attempt number 37 to clear his palate of the Cork fry, spits a

117

good-sized pip, *ping*, into the metal bin beside his desk, picks up his quill and creates Philip Pirrip.

'Is that true, Ruth?' Mrs Quinty asked, eyes enormous and brows lifted, missing altogether the point of stories.

For three years Mr MacGhiolla came to Ashcroft. The mark he left on our narrative was in my father's mind. He made my father believe this was a country apart. He made him think it could be Paradise. And Mr MacGhiolla was the one who first inspired Virgil to think of writing.

Everything that followed flowed down the river from that.

Did you ever see how fast a river runs?

Maybe you did. Maybe you stood once on the banks in late springtime when the rains are running off the hills and the whole country is sort of flowing away faster than anything you can imagine. Maybe when you were small like Aeney and me you pulled the branches off ash trees and threw them on to the Shannon just to watch the whish and pull of the riverwaters, the way the branch landed on the moving world and went faster than your eye told you it could, faster and swirlier, bobbing and twisting before easefully floating just for a bit and going under and coming up again black and slick and smaller now flowing away off into the for ever after.

Grandfather Abraham went to meet the Reverend one afternoon in June when the salmon were running. He had finished writing *The Salmon in Ireland* the previous evening and sent it, wrapped in brown paper and tied with fishing line, to Messrs Kegan Paul, Trench, Trübner, Broadway House, 68–74 Carter Lane, London, E.C. He walked out with the inner lightness of an author who has delivered. He wore a green tweed with flap pockets, cast into the river at Rosnaree, began his heart attack, and entered the Afterlife just after his fly was taken.

16

I have a suitor. His name is Vincent Cunningham.

Because I have Something, because I am Plain Ruth Swain and Snoot Ruth and bedbound and read too much, because I don't go outside, because I am the pale untannable oddment of a freckled river child and there could be no right reason for a suitor as sweet as Vincent Cunningham to choose me, you might already have supposed there is something wrong with him. There is. He's got that thing Mr Quayle has in *Bleak House*, a power of indiscriminate admiration. To him everything is a little bit luminary. Everything is fantastic and I it seems am beautiful.

That's just mad.

As Margaret Crowe says, That boy is Un-real.

He first proposed to me when I was eight. Having little time during Small Break, and the yard of Faha N.S. not being listed on Most Romantic Spots for Lovers in Ireland, he chose the direct approach.

'Ruthie, will you marry me?'

'No.'

Like with Estella, and cream crackers, I thought it best to just snap his heart across. Otherwise there are all these messy fragments. To underline my position I added a deep frown, a shocked shake of my head, a sharp turn on my patent-leather shoes and the quickest possible walk across the yard.

But Vincent Cunningham being Vincent Cunningham he took encouragement in that, and set out off on a course of Distant

Loving, which I think is in Ovid, and in the Primary School Edition must include putting Lovehearts in your pencilcase, tangled daisies in the pocket of your duffelcoat and writing the Adored One's initials on the inside of your wrist where the lads won't see it during Football.

He proposed again when he was ten, only slightly less directly. This time we were walking home from school. At least I was walking in the direction of home, he was walking in the exact opposite direction of his, a fact of which I took no notice at the time.

'Ruthie,' he said, 'when we're older, do you think you'll like me?'

'No.'

He nodded his Vincent Cunningham nod, like he'd expected that answer, like Ovid had already covered that and counselled the next approach should be: 'Okay.'

Just that, and Walk Alongside Her in Perfect Quiet, which to give him credit he did beautifully right until we got to our gate and then he blew it by going pink-faced and frowny and boy-combustible, toeing a little urgent hole into the gravel, studying the excavation and not looking up as he said, 'Well, I'll love you.'

'Vincent Cunningham.'

'Yes?' His eyes didn't come up. They too are brown as hazelnuts. But he kept them down, reviewing the hole he'd made.

'Don't be silly.'

I didn't mean it to sound like that. Some things happen before you've thought them through, the way Seamus Mac slashes the flowers off the fuchsia with a length of hydro-air pipe when he's going for the cows. The smashed red blossoms are strewn all along the road making you think that's why they call them Tears of God.

'Okay,' he said, like he was saying Fair Enough, and it hadn't mattered at all, and he had to hurry home anyway because there was an Under-12s match in the park that evening, which there was and at it I heard later he played Out of his Skin, throwing himself into tackles, Most Valuable Player and whatever other medals they give out, until one of the over-age Quilty lads came over and broke his leg.

After that his suiting went underground. In the Tech when it was discovered I was in fact useless, *Nul Points*, in Maths, he came to the house and gave me classes. His knees tried to do some suiting then. So did his Pythagoras. Because Vincent Cunningham helped Dad on weekends and in the summer holidays and because he could drive a tractor at fourteen he was in and out of our house and yard and only sometimes would he let loose his Ruth-I-Want-To-Marry-You look, the way smouldering boys can, just to let me know it was still there. It was a little W.B. Yeats Syndrome who, until he was fifty, proposed to Maud Gonne every couple of weeks even though she said no way no how, was addicted to unsuitables, and her name was Maud.

So now here we are, Vincent Cunningham grown streaky tall with mad long eyelashes over the hazelnuts, a nature sweet as anything, and two years of Engineering among the micro-skirts in Galway failing to budge him from his eight-year-old certainty.

The thing is, the more he pursues his line of admiration and wonder and general sweetness the more I find myself being sour. It's part Swain-contrariness, part Estella Syndrome. I can't help myself.

'I look like . . . I don't know what I look like. What do I look like?'

'You look beautiful.'

'There are no beautiful women writers.'

'Yes there are.'

No there aren't. Well, except for Edna O'Brien, who is actually a kind of genius and gained my undying admiration when she said plots are for precocious schoolboys (Book 2,738, *Writers at Work, The Paris Review Interviews*, 7th Series, Secker & Warburg, London).

'Here, look at Emily Dickinson,' I said, and showed him the passport-sized photo on the back cover of the *Collected Poems*. 'Her face, two prunes in porridge.'

'I don't know, I think she looks nice,' he said.

'*Nice?*'

'She does. She looks interesting.'

Reader, pick any Brontë. Any one, doesn't matter. What do you see? You see intelligence, you see an observer, you see distance, you don't see beauty. Look at Maria Edgeworth, Mrs Gaskell. Look at Edith Wharton, she's Henry James in a dress. Henry called Edith the Angel of Devastation, which is not exactly Top Score in the Feminine Charms department. Agatha Christie is a perfect match for Alastair Sim when he was playing Miss Fritton in the Tesco box-set of the old *St Trinian's*. You can't be beautiful and a writer, because to be a writer you have to be the one doing the looking; if you're beautiful people will be looking at *you*.

'I don't care. You are beautiful,' Vincent Cunningham says, and with those three words firmly keeping his place in the Least Likely Irishman. Even I think I must have invented him.

'You're a hopeless idiot.'

'I know.' He smiles. He sits here beside the bed and his whole big face just beams. It's ridiculous how happy he can be. It runs in the Cunninghams. His father is a Stop-Go man for the Council. Johnny Cunningham appears around the county wherever they're doing roadworks, sets up with his big red and green lollipop and when he makes the traffic flow he gives a thumbs-up and shines the same smile. For some people the world is just heaven.

Vincent was in the same class as Aeney once. He sat behind him in Mr Crossan's, and for a while became his only friend. He's thin and made up of angles. If you had to draw him using only straight lines you could. Even his hair is straight. It's a little brown hedge rising evenly off the top of his intelligence. According to him I brought him to Literature. He says it like it's this far-distant place and there was no way he would find out how to get there if it wasn't for me talking about some book I'd read and him going off to find it. Of course once I knew that I started intentionally mentioning some of the Obscures. That's part MacCarroll and part Impossible Standard. I'd say I read a great story by Montague Rhodes James, 'A School Story' (Book 555, *The Collected Ghost Stories of M.R. James*, Oxford), which told of a man found dead in his bed with the mark of a horseshoe on his forehead, and Vincent would head off, driving Eleanor Pender potty in the Mobile Library until she tracked it down and he'd read it and come hurrying back up the stairs here to say you were right Ruth, that was a good one.

'Which one was that?'

'"A School Story". You remember. The horseshoe on the forehead.'

'That one? I've forgotten all about that one. I'm reading *Riceyman Steps* by Arnold Bennett now.'

Goodness provokes bitchiness. It's mathematical. It's somewhere in the human genes. Any number of lovely people are married to horrible ones. Read *Middlemarch* (Book 989, George Eliot, Penguin Classics, London) if you don't believe me. There's something in me that can't just let it be. Goodness is a tidy bow you just can't help wanting to pull loose.

Besides, there's the added complication: I'm not well. If I wasn't, if I wasn't the Number One Patient in the parish from the family that has already been visited by Doom, would he still be coming calling? Am I Vincent Cunningham's path to Sainthood? You see, you just can't trust goodness.

Sometimes after he's gone I've wondered what it would be like to slip into a different story and actually end up being Mrs Vincent Cunningham. You know, Chapter XXXVIII, 'Reader, I married him. A quiet wedding we had, he and I, the parson and clerk were alone present.' (Book 789, *Jane Eyre*, Penguin Classics, London.)

Cunningham is a bad surname, but it's not dreadful. Not as bad say as Bigg-Wither. Mr Bigg-Wither (not kidding) was Jane Austen's suitor. He fell in love with the sharp bonnet-pinched look, was very partial to one flattened front hair curl, and tiny black eyes. He pulled in his person and fluffed out his whiskers to propose to her.

Now that took courage. You have to grant him that. Proposing to Jane Austen was no walk in the park, was in the same league as Jerry Twomey proposing to Niamh ni Eochadha who had the face and manners of a blackthorn. Still, Bigg-Wither went through with it. He got out his proposal.

And Jane Austen accepted. Honestly, she did. She was fiancé-ed. She did her best impression of a Jane Austen smile then retired straight away to bed. Up in the bed she lay in her big nightie and couldn't sleep, not, surprisingly enough, because of the bonnet, but because of the suffocating way the name Bigg-Wither sat on her. That, and the thought of giving birth to little Bigg-Withers.

The following morning when she came down to him negotiating his toast and marmalade in past the whiskers, she said, 'I cannot be a Bigg-Wither,' or words to that effect, the engagement was off, and all the world's Readers sighed with relief. Because a happy Jane Austen would have been useless in the World Literature stakes.

One day, to advance his suitoring, Vincent leaned forward to the bed, raindrops sitting on the hedge of his hair, and told me that Robert Louis Stevenson's beloved nurse was a Cunningham.

He knows I have a soft spot for RLS and not just because he was sick or because we have the same initials but because there's something impossibly romantic about him and because before he started writing *Treasure Island* he first drew a map of an unknown island and because he believed in invisible places and was one of the last writers to know what the word *adventure* means. I could give you a hundred reasons why RLS is The Man. Look in his *The Art of Writing* (Book 683, Chatto & Windus, London) where he says that no living people have had the influence on him as strong for good as Hamlet or Rosalind. Or when he says his greatest friend is D'Artagnan from *The Three Musketeers* (Book 5, Regent Classics, London). RLS said: 'When I suffer in mind, stories are my refuge, I take them like opium.' And when you read *Treasure Island* you feel you are casting off. That's the thing. You are casting off and leaving behind the ordinary dullness of the world.

For Vincent, bringing me the news of the Cunningham connection was the same as bringing me chocolates. He sat there by the bed looking as happy as, well, a Cunningham. He'd been reading up on RLS (as an engineer Vincent used the Internet; it's slow and dial-up here, the minister is still Rolling Out broadband, but he must be Rolling It Out around his own house, Paddy Carroll says) and it had taken Vincent hours but he'd gathered up a fair bit of RLS knowledge and even learned off a bit of *The Land of Counterpane* in which RLS is sick in bed and plays with toy soldiers in an imaginary world on his blankets.

'Aeney had soldiers,' he said. 'I remember them. He kept them in a biscuit tin. And he had a farm in there. Do you remember? Little plastic cattle and horses and pigs and things.'

I didn't say anything.

'He had fences too, didn't he, and . . .'

I didn't say anything.

'I'm an idiot,' he said after a little while.

Give me credit. I know this is when I'm supposed to say, 'No, Vincent, you're not, not at all,' and take his hand nineteenth-century-style and let the moment be a little bridge between us, but of course I didn't. You can't go encouraging the Vincent Cunninghams of the world because the truth is boys can fall deeper in love than girls, they're a lot bigger and heavier and they can fall much further and harder and when they hit the ground of reality there's just this terrible splosh that some other woman is going to have to come along and try to put back into the bottle.

'RLS,' he said, getting back to safer ground after another while. 'The chest wasn't great with him.'

Clare people don't like to be too blunt.

'He had tuberculosis, Vincent,' I said (Book 684, *The Life of Robert Louis Stevenson*, two volumes, Thomas Graham Balfour, Methuen, London). My father only had a falling-apart second-hand Volume Two, a book that has been to sea, has water-buckled pages, two Chapter Fours, and smells of Scotland.

'Still, he bought four hundred acres in Upolu, Samoa,' Vincent said. The Cunninghams are addicted to looking on the bright side.

'He fell in love with a Fanny,' I told him.

He allowed that a moment.

'When he went to live there he took the name Tusitala. It means Teller of Tales,' he said, smiling like this was a deeper layer of chocolates.

'So did Keats.'

'Took the same name? Wow.'

'Loved a Fanny.'

'Oh.'

The rain tattooed the skylight while his brain went back a few Windows on the search, then he remembered: 'He was supposed to design lighthouses.'

'His father did.'

'So he was a sort of engineer really,' he said triumphantly, having completed his own feat of mental engineering, connecting Vincent Cunningham to RLS and so to me. This kind of thing doesn't feature in Ovid, but it will in *Vincent's Way* if I ever get to write it.

He was just too happy-looking then so I said, 'He hated engineering.'

There was no coming back from that. He sat quiet for a bit and I lay back against the awful pillows and thought *Ruth Swain you're horrible*. And the rain fell some more and Vincent studied his hands in his lap, until at last I said: 'When he died on the island on Samoa they cleared a path through the jungle all the way up to Mount Vaea so that he could be buried on the summit and see the sea. So I suppose there was some engineering in that.'

And Vincent said, 'Ruth Swain,' just that, just *Ruth Swain*, and he shook his long head like I was a wonder of some class and his face broke into this big smile he has like something was mended or Hope Renewed or I'd actually kissed him.

Un-real.

17

My father loved Aeney more than anything in the world. I'm allowed to say that. I'm not saying it out of hurt or disappointment or to undo some twist in my heart. I'm not saying it in a Bitch-of-the-Brouders God-Forgive-Me way, back of the hand covering the mouth, eyes wide and a hot whisper spreading some vicious-ness sideways into the world. I'm saying it because it's true and because you'll need to understand that. Aeney was a magical boy. I knew. We all knew. Some people make you feel better about living. Some people you meet and you feel this little lift in your heart, this *Ah*, because there's something in them that's brighter or lighter, something beautiful or better than you, and here's the magic: instead of feeling worse, instead of feeling *why am I so ordinary?*, you feel just the opposite, you feel glad. In a weird way you feel better, because before this you hadn't realised or you'd forgotten human beings could shine so.

Aeney's shining started Day One. He swam down the River Mam ahead of me and when he was landed he landed in the amazed wet eyes of my father. He was lifted gleaming in the gentling giant arms of Theresa Dowling, District Nurse, and she said *There now* and smiled the big dimple smile she has even though Aeney had started crying. He cried as if crying was a language he alone knew and in it there was something urgent he needed to say. Not the bumping rocking in the plump boat-hams of the District Nurse, not the view he was carried to of the swirling Shannon, not the first super-delicate cradling of Dad nor the warm damp breast of Mam stopped him. In the family legend, Aeney cried until I swam downriver after him, until Theresa Dowling said *Oh* and out I came, Australian front-crawling, red and gasping and apparently particularly hairy. Then he stopped.

Because, just like his father, our father was not young when we were born, there was an extra-ness to the joy. It's not that we were unexpected, it's that until his children were in his arms he hadn't actually gotten further than the imagining of us. He was a poet, and the least practical man in the world. And a baby is a practical thing.

Two babies, well.

Right away Aeney was better at things than me. He knew the first skill of babies, Put On Weight, and thrived into early handsomeness before he was one year old. He was the kind of baby people peered in at. He was Number One Baby at Mass. Our first Christmas Maureen Pender wanted him to play Jesus on the altar, and he only lost out because Josephine Carr on the committee disqualified him saying Jesus was not a twin and put forward her tiny three-year-old Peter who God Bless Him she must have been feeding birdfood because he ended up not growing at all, playing the Faha Jesus until he was five, and is a trainee jockey above in Coolmore now.

Aeney had the golden hair nearly right away. His eyes blued. We both have the same eyes, but his grew blue as our father's, as if he'd swam up through some underworld Mediterranean and some of it glinted still in the pools of his eyes.

How do you capture a brother as elusive as Aeney? How do you capture someone who was always slipping away?

His favourite foods, apples, Cheddar cheese, purple Cadbury's Roses, Petit Filous.

His favourite colour, red.

His favourite sound, the singing of the cuckoo when it came, and which he always wanted to be first to hear, and for which he would go hunting by Ryan's and McInerney's, but would always be beaten by Francie Fahy who held the title: First in Faha to Hear the Cuckoo. But as Jimmy Mac says, Francie had family connections there.

Aeney's favourite clothes, a pair of muddy blue no-brand runners whose laces were so stained you couldn't tell they were once white except for the places beneath the eye-hole flap, a pair of khaki trousers whose knees Nan patched so many times they looked padded, a red jumper that was two sizes too big for him and which he wore holding the cuffs that came halfway down his palms. The cuffs frayed from being held and every so often Mam trimmed back the strands. He wore the jumper again and they frayed again and she trimmed them again but she never threw it out. He liked holding on to something. When he was small he held the label inside his pillowcase when he slept. Only I know that. I was not a sleeper. His hand in sleep searched to find it. He would take the label between thumb and forefinger and just move it slightly against itself, over and back, as if the smallest friction was sufficient, as if with that he knew he was still in the world.

His favourite thing to do, run. He's a flier, Mr Mac said the year he formed the new Community Games Committee and decided Faha was going to be Put on the Map. Aeney was going in the Under-Eights on Honan's field.

At that stage it was generally presumed that I was not someone who was going to Put Faha on the Map and so once the races started I was to share with Dympna Looney the important job of Holding the Ribbon at the finish line, which I didn't think very important but my father said was Homeric, and though I didn't know what that meant it made me feel a little flush of importance.

'Breasting the ribbon, Ruthie,' he said, 'you're the line between one world and another.'

He could say things like that. He could say things no other dad could say, and because parents are mysterious anyhow, because they belong in another world, you don't ask, you just nod and feel you've entered a little bit into the mystery yourself.

The field was lined with these triangular flags Margaret Crowe had cut out of a pale-blue bolt of Virgin Mary cloth she'd got from Bowsey Casey's and Rory Crowley had hand-painted a big lop-sided oval on the cow-plopped field. There, various of our able-bodied were desporting themselves as Homer says, which in this case meant doing Serious Stretches and running back and forth in little show-offy dashes they'd seen on RTE Olympic coverage with Patrick Clohessy alongside doing demented Jimmy McGee commentary into an empty Coke bottle. The whole clan of the McInerneys were there, tearing around like brown-nosed bluebottles, no hope that a single one of them would ever run in a straight line.

In order to put Faha on the map the entire parish showed up. Jesus Mary and Joseph Carty, Father Tipp, Monica Mac, Tommy Fitz, Jimmy Mac, the Major, the Saint Murphys, Vincent Cunningham and his father Johnny, John Paul Eustace in his navy suit, even Saddam. Everyone gathered in good-humoured admiration of their own seed and breed as Marty Mungovan says. Honan's cows were exiled to a rushy wasteground where a loose string of electric fence kept them, looking on with mournful moo-faces or maybe they were cow-smiling that the plenitude of their dungs in the running track had supplied the setting with bountiful midges and flies. In Faha Community Games you ran with your mouth closed.

Dad was always awkward in scenes like this. He was a Swain and Swains are not for joining in. They're not part of the General Population somehow. There's this little remove, this stepped-back quality that means Dad is going to be the one over at the edge of the field. While Mam is in there helping out, getting Mona Halvey's wheelchair across the tufted ground, selling Draw tickets, filling little plastic cups with MiWadi and trying to keep the McInerneys from drinking them all before the games begin, Dad is over on his own, he's in red corduroy trousers that are seriously baggy and bunch at his waist where the belt tries to make them fit, he wears two shirts instead of a jacket. His silvery hair is grown long and occasionally wild strands fly in the wind. But he doesn't care at all. He has a book with him. It's going to appear to those who don't know him that he doesn't want to be part of this, that he holds himself apart on purpose and that it comes from the fact that he's not one of them.

The truth is, he's not one of anything or anyone. It's not pride, it's not even a choice. There's a skill he doesn't have, and as he stands on the edge of the field his heart must fall a little when he looks up from a page and realises his children don't have it either.

Aeney is having his paper number pinned on. Mr Mac is down on one knee telling him tactics for seven year olds. I'm getting ready to unroll the ribbon when Jane Bitch of the Brouders, God-forgive-me, says tell your brother not to win. Noelie Hegarty is to win because his baby brother Sean died. She has her little entourage with her, a white ankle-sock brigade of holy head-tossers. Their aim is to out-nun Mother Teresa.

'I'll tell him no such thing.'

'Then I will,' she says, and flounces across the field to him.

I'm holding the ribbon taut when Aeney comes running. I can see the wild delight in his eyes. He's ahead of the rest of the field, legs flashing so superfast you think he'll have to fall down, running so quickly that everyone watching him smiles. You can't help yourself. He's going so fast his number flies off. There's actual July sunlight glancing off his hair. The whole parish roars him on. He's coming up the not-so-straight straight, chest out and his little arms flashing, and he can see me just ahead holding the ribbon. Ribbon-holders are not supposed to cheer, but inside the roar I do a little *go on Aeney go on Aeney* and the ribbon wavers a little until Dympna gives me her future-headmistress look and tugs it taut.

And then Aeney's going in slow motion.

Slow and slower still.

And Noelie Hegarty is coming up alongside him.

And Noelie Hegarty is going past him.

Come on Aeney.

But he doesn't. Noelie Hegarty breasts the ribbon.

Afterwards, Jane Brouder goes and says something to Aeney, she talks to him like they're New Best Friends, and then she walks past me, pout-and-button nose raised to ten o' clock and ass eloquent.

Dad said well done to Aeney. He said it quietly, firmly, and the way he looked at him he seemed to be seeing deeper, as if the two of them shared some secret and it was a Swain thing.

The following year Aeney didn't run. He only liked running on his own after that, after that he only ran by the river. Dad never said Aeney, you should take part in races, or You have to, he never said a thing, never showed any disappointment, but, years later, folded carefully in Book VI of Virgil's *Aeneid*, I found the creased rectangle of Aeney's paper number that had fallen off that day.

Aeney preferred outdoors to indoors. He didn't freckle, he tanned, which if you ask me is a clear sign of being Chosen. It's up there with perfect hair and teeth that actually fit inside your mouth.

Aeney climbed every tree he could find. I think it was Jim Hawkins Syndrome, wanting to be Up Top in the crow's nest in the *Hispaniola*. I'd stand below on the ground and watch him work his way up into the big chestnut at the gate into the Long Meadow. If the tree didn't end, if there wasn't a highest branch, I think he'd be climbing upwards still. That's my brother. I'd lose him in the leaf canopy and then be sitting below reading a book, every so often craning my neck to look up the way you look when a bird disappears into a tree but sings still. He wasn't a bird though; often out of the treetop I'd hear this sudden clatter and quick-snapping and a cry, all instantaneous, and I'd drop the book and shout out his name and look up and not see him but see the tree come alive somewhere above, a flutter of leaves descending, a white-snapped branch sailing down, and Aeney unseen coming crash spin grab-falling through the upper greenery, a kind of antic acrobatics bred in certain boys in which danger is neither seen nor felt. He falls fifteen feet inside the tree, but clings on somewhere, I see only the blue runners dangling for a moment, pedalling the air until they find the branch.

'Aeney? Aeney, are you okay?'

I hear him laughing. Up in the tree he's laughing. Then he calls down, 'Yeah.' And he climbs upwards again. He climbs like he's in his own inner Duffy's Circus and somewhere up here is the glittering girl. He climbs until he must be out in the sky and see the river from above.

God, Pauline Dempsey said, has His hand on certain people's shoulders.

He'd be better covering knees, Nan said.

Despite Nan's knee-patching, by the time Aeney was seven both of his knees bore raised wrinkly scars in crescent shapes. He showed me but he didn't care. Blood-crusted, pebble-embedded,

134

skin-flapped, and often an iodined purplish blue, on his knees were written his adventures. I thought of that one day years later in Mrs Quinty's class when we read Elizabeth Bishop's poem about the tremendous fish. The fish had escaped many hooks but bore their marks. He was caught at last. (Book 2,993, *Collected Poems*, Elizabeth Bishop, Farrar, Straus & Giroux, New York.) But that fish was old.

The first time Dad took Aeney fishing Dad didn't know what was going to happen. I was asked if I wanted to go, but by then I was already working on my Twin Theory, that if one twin loves the outdoors the other loves the indoors, one likes books the other music, one red the other black. The back pages of my copies had whole lists. So when Aeney said yes to fishing I said no. I didn't know then the history of salmon in the Swains, I hadn't seen Grandfather's Salmon Journals, read *The Salmon in Ireland*, or thought my ability to remember everything, to amass knowledge, was in any way connected to fish.

My father by that stage was already Elsewhere. He was already writing the poems that were coming into his head now like weird butterflies in March, already farming the fourteen acres of the worst land in Ireland, growing rushes and puddles and rearing the thinnest Friesian ladies to ever make an appearance at Clare Marts. I should have known something when he took out the fishing rod. I should have seen in the way he assembled it, the way he stood in the front garden practising a cast, throwing a line through the midge-veils trying to hook the invisible, that salmon fishing was serious business.

So too was starvation. You have no money but you have a river full of fish passing your front door. You figure it out.

Dad loved Aeney more than anything, but he couldn't show it. He just couldn't. There's a Code for fathers in Ireland. Maybe it's everywhere, I don't know, I haven't cracked it. My father followed the Code. He was careful about his children, he didn't want to ruin us though somehow felt sure he would. He thought Aeney and I were marvels but he didn't want to make a mistake. Maybe he thought Abraham was watching. So he'd probably thought about it for a long time before he came in from the casting and decided he should go fishing with Aeney. Dad could be sudden like that. He couldn't help it. It's the nature of Poets. You don't believe me, look up William Blake, say hello to those impulses, go meet Mr John Donne in a dark church some time, spend a summer's day with young William Butler, Ace Butterfly-catcher.

Dad shook Aeney awake early in the morning, said, 'Come on.'

I lay in my boat-bed listening to them whispering downstairs at breakfast, the soft rubbery stamping as they put on their wellies, the small rattle of the tin container that held the flies, the hard fallback *clack* of the latch when they went out the door.

I should have gone.

At that moment I knew I should have gone. But I was addicted to my own cleverness and wouldn't go round twin theory.

In families it's hard to trace the story. If you're in it the Plot Points aren't clearly marked. You don't know when things turn until much later. You think each day is pretty much as dull as any other, and if there is something happening it's not happening in your family and it's definitely not happening in Faha. You think your own oddness is normal. You think Nan harvesting a lifetime of *Clare Champions* is normal. You think having a grandfather who published a book but didn't want his name on it is normal, having a father who wants to be a poet but has to be a farmer, who has no clue about farming, and won't publish any poems, all Normal.

My father and Aeney didn't catch a salmon that day. They caught some other fish. The thing that happened was not about

136

the catch. It wasn't about a father and son standing on the Shannon riverbank, it wasn't *Now listen here, Son,* it wasn't directed by Robert Redford or lit gorgeously like *A River Runs Through It,* it wasn't that my father opened his heart and said I think my life has been a colossal mistake, that every poem I write fails, that we have no money, or that Aeney told him he had a secret crush on Jane Brouder. What happened was at first neither discernible nor understood.

It was just this: that day my brother Aeney fell in love with the river.

18

When Grandfather Abraham was gone Grandmother had a brief moment of Victory, as if by outliving him she could lay down her cards and declare that she'd finally won the Game of Marriage. It wasn't until the long evenings of the following winter, hounds gnawing on the stringy twines of the Indian rug and developing the first stages of what my father said was curry-scented incontinence, sash windows rattling like denture laughter, and the fire blowing down these great black puffs, that she realised he might be the one laughing now.

The aunts were away in the kind of school where books are balanced on your head. Esther, the eldest, would graduate in a year and go directly into The Bank. It was how it was done in those days. If you were smart and proper like Esther and could wear a skirt and blouse and had been trained by a crack squadron of nuns to sit perfectly upright and keep your knees together and your hair in a really really really tight bun you could be Mr Enright's Secretary. You could live in a flat in Rathmines and own a Raleigh Ladies' Bicycle, spend your evenings with Persil washing powder and a Philips steam iron and head into Dublin in the mornings fresh as Palmolive. The Sixties were starting then, but not in Ireland. Maybe the Ministers were thinking of Rolling Out the new era but they had to run it by the Censorship Board, and anyway Aunt Esther was always a few decades behind. Poor thing, she was of a nervous disposition and couldn't bear the thought of things not being just so. Mr Enright never had a pencil out of place. Banks in those days were pretty much like churches; you put on your best clothes to go into them, and a Banker was a Very Good Catch. Aunt Esther had her hopes I suppose, but Mr Enright realised he'd ruin a perfectly excellent secretary by marrying her. Instead he chose the deeply unsuitable daughter of the bank's president and took up golf. Aunt Esther attended the wedding. When I think of her I think of her as the tall girl in the back of the wedding photos, the big-boned one with the abashed air who has tirelessly shopped for just the right dress for the occasion but who says Yes of course when the photographer suggests maybe a better position for her would be in the third row. Aunt Esther attended a lot of weddings, I think, and only gradually did the corroding disappointment of the world work its way into her soul. Hope, you see, takes a long time to die. When we visited her in St Jude's, the nursing home that would later change its name to Windermere and eventually welcome Aunt Daphne, Aunt Esther had to hold on to her hands tightly they shook so much. She wore a pale-blue cardigan and white blouse with the cuffs just showing and a white linen handkerchief pressed in next to her left wrist. She couldn't keep her head still, it sort of juddered like these bolts of electricity were hitting it but she kept fighting them, she kept trying to keep herself still and proper and Receive her brother's children because that was the right thing to do and I just stood there with Aeney beside our father seeing Dad's eyes glass up and thinking it was pretty much the definition of Impossible for a woman suffering this badly to have such grace.

Daphne and Penelope had each other. They were never a problem to Grandmother. They were their own mini-company and, as I said, from early on they Selected their own Society and shut the door.

But what was Grandmother to do with Virgil? Without his father she feared her son would, well, I'm not sure what she feared exactly, but considering Abraham and considering The Reverend, maybe it was safe to suppose something Swain-odd. By that stage Ashcroft was in the first stages of dilapidation. It's another truth universally acknowledged that a woman without a husband suddenly notices the frailties of her accommodation. She knew it hadn't happened overnight but she woke one morning and noticed that dry, wet and medium damp rot had settled throughout the house, that paint was leaving the upper walls of the drawing room in alarmingly large bubbled flakes, the floorboards in the foyer were being eaten at their ends, the piano lid had a subtle but certain buckle and the guest-room chimney was lying out in the middle of the Front Circle. So while she figured out what to do with Virgil she told him to attend to these.

That was Grandmother's style. *Attend to these please, Virgil.* And off out the door with her, doing the Kittering version of Queen Victoria, and keeping her nose tilted up just enough to keep breathing in sweet denial.

Clearly she had never met my father.

Two things were certain. One, that he would set about the tasks with that fierce boy-concentration I remember seeing in Aeney, and two, that he would fail hopelessly. Still, he banged and sawed, he painted over the dark stains coming on the walls and he stuffed the gaps between the window sashes with newspaper.

Ashcroft was in a time warp. I'm not sure it was even in this country. Whenever my father told of it the story was always in bits and pieces, fragments he'd drop into some telling, but the moment I heard them I was already creating the imagined version. The version where the boy is expected to become the man in the big house that's falling down and where these beefy Meath-men

140

Gaffney and Boucher come up the drive with ladders tied to the top of their van and scratch their heads that there are still people living like this in Ireland. The men are served tea and biscuits in the back kitchen, but they're served it in Aynsley china cups with hairline cracks in them. My father does the serving. He's Little Lord Swain I suppose. His clothes come from Switzers in Dublin which is Top Notch but they're threadbare and wrong-sized, and to Messrs Gaffney and Boucher eccentric. He wears slippers inside the house and out and his red-stockinged toes peek through. He has three layers of shirt, some with collars some without, none tucked in. He has that English kind of hair that is too unruly for a comb and is now speckled with paint but he seems not to mind in the slightest. While he brews the tea on the Aga the men talk of things in Meath and my father stands reading a book. He has no idea what they're talking about, they may as well have been telling the news from Brobdingnag. I've looked for this scene in Elizabeth Bowen (Book 1,365, *The Last September*; Book 1,366, *The Death of the Heart*, Anchor, New York) and in William Trevor (Book 1,976, *The Collected Stories*, Penguin, London) and Molly Keane (Book 1,876, *Good Behaviour*, Virago, London) and in *Birchwood* (Book 1,973, John Banville, W.W. Norton, New York) but I've never quite found it, and so have to believe my father didn't invent it, it must be true; he stands reading Hemingway's *The Sun Also Rises*, holding the book in his left hand while with his right he pours the tea, his eyes not leaving the page. This act stops the men's talk. Oddball they expect him to be, he's a Swain in Ashcroft, but tea-pouring and Hemingway has a certain skill to it they recognise. That's what Lost-in-a-Book looks like they're realising, and they have a kind of natural countrymen's appreciation. When Boucher asks my father why he's not at school Virgil doesn't stop reading, he's feeling the pain of Jake Barnes and the fascination of Lady

Brett Ashley. He's standing in the damp basement kitchen of Ashcroft on an overcast summer's day but he's on his way to the boiling-hot bullfights in Pamplona, and so without taking his eyes from the page says, because I'm going to be a writer.

Teenage boys can be insufferable with certainty. It's true. It's their horror moans, Margaret Crowe says.

But Virgil was right in one way. There was no point in his going to school. He'd have to pretend he didn't know as much as he did. School in Ireland back then was pretty much a priest and civil-servant factory depending on your proclivities. Rejects were sent into trade, because money and making money were generally frowned upon. If you failed at the Higher Subjects and didn't show any skill at Maths and Latin you were sent into Commerce, which was basically a dirty word back then. I guess it took half a century to reverse this, to get to the place where the Maths and Latin boys were the lower division and a newsagent like Seanie O could buy four hotels in Bulgaria and like a Lesser Dictator drive through Faha in a black-windowed Land Rover. Either way my father was not going to school.

But he was next to useless around the house. For a time Grandmother didn't notice, or she pretended not to. To keep him busy she gave him chores.

'The banister, Virgil, will you see to it?'

'Virgil, the door to the guest room on the upper landing,' she said in passing, handing him the porcelain knob that had come off in her hand.

Things like that. They were strangers to each other and were living in the big vacuum that came after Abraham. It happens in the Bible too, a big character leaves and there's a natural hole while God figures out who He's going to send on next. In the Bible Abraham dies when he's 175 years old. He was a good character and God didn't want to let him go. After a while He sent on Esau. He was a doozie. When he first came forth, it says, he was red all over *like a hairy garment.*

I'm just saying.

Dad was able to fix nothing but between chapters he tried. There was just him and his mother rambling around in the big house then.

'Virgil, be a dear and bury Sarsfield.'

History had turned violent again and Mr MacGhiolla with a special gleam in his eyes had departed for the North. He left my father books with trapped strands of red hair and a faint sulphuric whiff of nationalism trapped within the pages.

My father and his mother lived on in dust and dilapidation, ate little nothing meals of Branston Pickle on toast, tinned kippers, the unfortunately named Bird's Custard, and had BBC radio crackling on in the background. Grandmother didn't believe things should have Eat Before dates. She didn't believe things went off until well after you had cut off the blue parts and the parts that were furred, and even then there was always a portion that was perfectly fine, Virgil. *Perfectly fine.* Eat Before dates were all nonsense as far as she was concerned, a conspiracy of shopkeepers to fool the less discerning into purchases. Here was some Marmite that was supposed to be gone off a year ago. But it was Perfectly Fine. *Marmite cannot go off, Virgil.* Her shopping was virtually non-existent, and without speaking of it there developed inside Ashcroft a strategy of improvisation; you looked in the cupboard and you chose a tin of something, you opened it and sniffed. If you were still standing you went ahead. There was still a large wine cellar, and Grandmother began on the oldest bottles, reasoning, like your narrator, that she could be dead before she reached the present. In Abraham's study my father found a vast supply of cigarettes, and in the autumn evenings when he read Hemingway at the top of the stairs under the one bulb that was replaced he took up smoking, and almost at once arrived by his father's side in the battlefields of France.

One summer's day a banker called Mr Houlihan, for whom I always see Mr Gusher in *Bleak House*, a flabby gentleman *with a moist surface*, rang the non-ringing doorbell. He attended a while, turned to consider the fallen chimney in the Front Circle, turned back, dabbed his forehead to no effectiveness, chewed the blubbery excess of his lower lip, rang the non-ringer again, looked up at the ruined majesty of Ashcroft, looked down at the polish of his shoes, knocked on the knocker peremptorily, three firm raps as befitted his station, attended once more, dabbed once more, and was in the process of his third attempt when Virgil came round the side and told him that door didn't open any more.

Virgil was wearing his pyjamas under a too-big blue blazer of Abraham's. He brought Mr Houlihan down the steps and in through the basement, passing through the kitchen where Purvis the cat licked the Branston lid and four empty bottles of milk of various period soured the general air, then up the back steps, Mr Houlihan's shoes squeaking, taking care to put no weight on the fourth from top, arriving into the gloom of the windowless corridor where a lightless lightbulb hung, Virgil leading with the confidence of the blind in a world gone blind, Mr Houlihan feeling his way with a moist horror.

Circuitously then, they arrived in the front hall just inside the same front door and Virgil said, 'I'll get Mother.'

Mr Houlihan attended and dabbed and considered the aspect. He had not been inside Ashcroft before. As a boy he had once climbed the orchard wall. He'd once viewed the exotic kingdom it was from the wild grass of the Long Meadow, and once, walking home from the Brothers, Abraham had driven past him in the dusty old Humber that was such a dark brown it looked *plum*. But now here he was, in Ashcroft, on the bank's business. He gave a firm down-tug to the bottom of his jacket. Dampness foreshortened it. He chewed at his lips and blinked. In the front hall were two tall mahogany chairs against the wall either side of the front door. They were chairs that no one ever sat on. They were the sort of excess furniture people had in houses like that. These were wedding gifts, one-for-Him, one-for-Her sort of thing, His and Her Majesty kind of chairs with stiff backs and faded embroidered seats that some seamstress had done in the early Louis times. They were the sort of thing French people love, because they're beautiful and completely impractical and because only French derrières could ever really fit in them. When I saw the Hers one day in Aunt Daphne's I couldn't imagine an Irish backside ever sitting on it.

But Mr Houlihan's did. Perhaps overcome by the anxiety of the occasion, perhaps to escape the squeak of his shoes which seemed to undermine his authority, Mr Houlihan sat up onto the chair.

No sooner had he landed then he realised the proportions of the chair were more decorative than human because his feet did not touch the ground.

'Mr Houlihan,' Grandmother boomed.

Grandmother's English heritage meant that she had that Empire voice, that come-out-of-your-grass-huts-and-give-us-your-treasures-for-our-museums kind of voice. The woman could boom. It was seriously terrifying. Even years later when my father imitated her and she seemed part Margaret Thatcher and part horse Aeney and I were still frightened.

She boomed out his name and walked ahead of him into the drawing room. She didn't say *How do you do* and she didn't ask his business, she just led on. There's a certain kind of presumption that comes with Kitterings. They can't help it. They expect people to follow in their wake. Mr Houlihan scrambled to get down out of the chair and followed in his squeaking shoes.

Grandmother took the best seat at the top of the dining table, the window behind her so she was statuesque and mostly bust.

Like Mr Gusher, Mr Houlihan found his moistness getting excessive. He shone. Shining was in itself not problematic and could be interpreted as passionate. But then shining produced a general appearance of actual *wetness*.

'Are you hot, Mr Houlihan?'

'Not at all, no thank you, Mrs Swain.'

'Kittering-Swain.'

'Excuse me. Mrs Kittering-Swain. Well, perhaps yes, just a bit. Warm, actually. Hot. Yes. Is it hot in here?'

'I don't believe it is.'

The drawing room in summer produced flies. Though the long windows were never opened and my father had stuffed the gap between the sashes with newspaper, the flies found their way. Perhaps they came down the chimney. They lived in the middle air between floor and ceiling and though many died and remained on the floor until dust there always seemed what my father called a general population. Within five minutes they had found the moist peeled onion that was Mr Houlihan. No sooner had he opened his case and taken out a slim file and said, 'The actual finances, Mrs Kittering-Swain,' than he had to start batting away at the first of them.

Flies did not dare approach Grandmother.

'The finances?'

'Yes, well, Mr Swain didn't actually . . .' Houlihan ducked below a bluebottle. He paused, gnawed some more on the rubbery consistency of his lower lip. 'The mortgage that he took on the house . . .' The bluebottle came back at him.

146

And so it went on. Years later my father made a pantomime of it. He lay on the bed and Aeney and I played the flies. We buzzed our fingers through the air and sought out the florid face of Mr Houlihan as he tried to tell Grandmother that Grandfather had borrowed against the house and not repaid a penny. We flew into Mr Houlihan's mouth as he asked her to agree to a repayment schedule he had drawn up. We screamed with laughter when Mr Houlihan swallowed a fly and coughed and spat and flapped his fat hands and made big wide bulbs of his eyes. We tickled Mr Houlihan in the place below his ribs where he was helpless to stop and couldn't finish his sentences except to cry out *But the money, Mrs Kittering-Swain, the money!* and then he fell off the bed crash! on to the floor and was silent and Aeney and I giggled a bit and then got worried and looked over the edge and down to where Dad lay, his face soaking wet with laughter or tears we couldn't say.

19

Where are you, Aeney?

You slip away from me as you always did. Where are you?

20

'Mrs Quinty, can you see the earth from Heaven?'

'O now, Ruth.' Mrs Quinty pulled herself up a bit tighter and clutched the balls of her knees.

'Can they see us? Right now? Through the roof or through the skylight? What do you think?'

Mrs Quinty doesn't really like to say.

'I don't really like to say, Ruth.'

'But what's your opinion?'

'I really don't think it's right to talk about it. And I'll tell you why.'

'You believe in Heaven?'

Mrs Quinty took a little sharp inbreath, like the air was bitter but medicinal and had to be taken.

'Well, can you or can't you see what's happening here when you're there?'

Mrs Quinty made dimples of dismay. She gave herself a little tightening tug and glanced towards the door where she could see into Aeney's room where Mam had all the washing hanging on chairs and stools because there's no drying outside now and because despite the rain up here in the sky-rooms is the driest place in Faha and though it looks like a kind of ghost laundry, like that description I read in Seamus Heaney of spirits leaving their clothes on hedges as they went off into the spirit world, like Aeney's room is this secret Take-off Launching Pad, it's practical. Mrs Quinty kept looking in there while working her way up to an answer. Maybe she was thinking of an official response. Maybe she was doing her own inner mind-Google and really for the first time looking up *Heaven*. She didn't have to go Pindar, Hesiod, Homer, Ovid, Pythagoras, Plato, Augustine, Aquinas. She didn't have to open some of those books of my father's, the ones that came from a monastery sale and smell like frankincense or blue cheese, *De laudibus divinae sapientiae* of Alexander Neckham, the *Weltchronik* of Rudolf of Ems, the translated *Le Miroir du Monde* of Gauntier of Metz, composed 1247, who located Paradise precisely 'at the point where Asia begins'. All those writers who got themselves in a geography-bind trying to explain how it was that Paradise didn't get washed away during Noah's Flood. Or those who had to explain that when Heaven was generally considered to be *above* us that was when they thought the world was flat. Because for the Departed say in, I don't know, Australia, if they went *Up* to Heaven they'd likely come up in Leitrim, which might be Paradise to wet-faced welly-men from Drumshambo but would be a holy fright, as Tommy Fitz says, to sun-loving sandal-wearers from Oz. No, Mrs Quinty didn't have to go from Saint Brendan to Dante, all she did was turn the shining eyes to the rainlight and she was back in Low Babies in Muckross Park College, Dublin, one rainy afternoon looking at a picture of holy people standing on clouds and a white nun saying: 'Now, girls, this is Heaven.'

Heaven's specific physics and geography were Unknown, and that was the way it was meant to be.

Until you arrived.

Then, even if you were dim as bat-faced Dennis Delany who couldn't learn the calendar and spelled his own name Dis, you suddenly understood. The entire workings of the mind of God suddenly became clear to you and you went *Ah*. Until then, it's a Mystery.

'I don't believe in it,' I said.

Mrs Quinty returned from Low Babies. 'O Ruth.'

'I don't. Some days I just don't. I think there's no point in any of it. It's just rubbish. It's just a story. People die and they're gone. They don't see you and you never see them again. It's just a story to lessen the pain.'

Mrs Quinty looked at me. She looked the way you look at a dog who fell in the river and only just made it back to the bank. 'Maybe it is a story,' she said at last. 'But it's our story, Ruth.'

By the end of that summer in Ashcroft my father had nearly run out of stories. He'd almost read his father's full library and arrived at last at *Moby Dick*. The edition I have is a Penguin paperback (Book 2,333, Herman Melville, Penguin, London). It's been well-thumbed, at least triple-read, there's that smell the fat orange-spine Penguins get when their pages have yellowed and the book bulges, basically the smell of complex humanity, sort of sweat and salt and endeavour. Like all the fat orange Penguins, it gets fatter with reading, which it should, because in a way the more you read it the bigger your own experience of the world gets, the fatter your soul. Try it, you'll see.

My father revisited *Moby* a lot.

Maybe it's because there's no other novel in the whole world that better captures the Impossible Standard.

The end of that summer in Ashcroft he was reading *Moby*, and then, one evening maybe because he was bored, maybe because he was in one of those mad chapters that detail the physiognomy of whales, he went and took down one of Abraham's unused Salmon Journals, and shortly after, amidst the Havishammy dust and cobwebs of Ashcroft's non-dining Dining Room, he began a novel. It was set on a ship in the sea.

151

Now it takes a certain twist of mind to be able to write anything. And another twist to be able to write every day in a house that's falling down around you with a mother who's working her way through the wine cellar and a moist Bank Manager who's expecting *At the very least, Mrs Kittering-Swain, a gesture.*

My father had both twists. As Matty Nolan said about Father Foley, Poor Man, when he came back with the brown feet after thirty years in Africa, he was Far Gone. Virgil had that power of concentration that he passed on to me. He filled one Salmon Journal and started on the next. He went a bit Marcus Aurelius who (Book 746, *Meditations*, Penguin Classics, London) said men were born with various mania. Young Marcus's was, he said, to make a plaything of imaginary events. Virgil Swain meet Marcus. Imaginary events, imaginary people, imaginary places, whatever you're having yourself. Gold-medal Mania.

I suppose it was just pole-vaulting really, only with a smaller pole.

Point is, he was very Far Gone.

And that's where he was when they came to take the furniture. Mr Houlihan didn't come in person. He stayed out at the gates in his car, dabbing and moistening and peering in, blinking the rapid blinks of the obscurely guilty and finding he had chewed his lips into looking like burst sausages in an over-hot pan. Gaffney & Boucher it was that were sent. They parked the lorry in the Front Circle beside the fallen chimney and came in like long-necked birds calling various polite but unanswered hellooos through the house, both of them with the low-slung shoulders and downcast eyes of the deeply apologetic. Grandmother did not appear. They arrived in the foyer and began taking the gold mirrors off the wall. One screw wouldn't loosen. It would only turn and turn, and Gaffney gave it elbow grease and Meath meatiness and broke a piece of the nineteenth-century artisan moulding getting it free. Boucher shouldered the front door and Ashcroft opened to the daylight for the first time in years. They took the long sideboard (leaving the twin China dogs on guard on the floor), the standing Newgate clock, the embroidered Louis chairs, the studded Chesterfield, four armchairs of stuffing various, huffing and puffing as they moved the long oak dining table that bashed against the door jamb and wouldn't fit – sideways or backways or anyways, Phil; You're right there, Michael – and at last had to be left just inside the dining-room door.

At teatime Virgil landed back in this world. He didn't realise anything had changed until he came downstairs and crossed the front foyer and felt something under his foot. He bent down to pick up the piece of gold moulding. That's when he saw the mirrors were gone. That's when he saw the front doors were wide open. He called his mother. She failed to answer. He called her again, this time climbing the stairs, thinking *we've been robbed* and that this had happened when he was whaling just off the coast of Nantucket.

He knocked on Grandmother's door. He called to her. When he opened the door he saw her slanted across the bed, one arm hanging over the side as if she'd been caught and pulled askew and then had either shaken free or been thrown back. Her face was lopsided, her lip pulled low on one side where the fish-hook had been.

A stroke is not the word for it, the philosopher Donie Downes says. It's more a Wallop. It's a flaming wallop somewhere in the inside back of your head. Bang! like that. And you're switched off same as the Mains is down and you lie there in the Big Quiet silently cursing the closure of Emergency in Ennis General Hospital and hoping Dear God Timmy and Packy are coming. In Dan's case everything returned to normal, TG, he says (Thank God), except for the compulsion to tell every passing soul in Ryan's or Nolan's, Hanway's, the post office, going in or out of Mass, about the exact nature and dimension of his Wallop.

Grandmother did not recover. Maybe she wouldn't have wanted to anyway. Maybe once she was transported out the front doors of Ashcroft and was loaded bumpily up across the fumy exhaust of the ambulance, *rolled* into the grim metal interior and strapped in place, her one imperious eye still good for glaring, maybe she realised she wouldn't be getting any further in the wine cellar. She had the second stroke. In Faha the word that's fatally attached to *stroke* is *massive*. This one was Massive. To her eternal mortification it was not in some private room with stacked goosedown pillows, elegant bedclothes, and attendants with proper accents. It was in the ambulance, stopped on a narrow bend somewhere near Navan, waiting for skittish young cattle to cross. Her son was sitting alongside her.

Three weeks after Grandmother died, Virgil too left Ashcroft. There was no natural place left for him to fit into the world.

He took *Moby Dick* and went by bus to Dublin. Two days later he stepped on to a Merchant Navy ship docked on the River Liffey.

Then he went to sea.

TWO

Mythologies

I

Back in the time when we were all seaweed, Tommy Devlin says, and adjusts himself on his seat for the long story.

Tommy Devlin is Nan's cousin. He's a strictly brown-trouser man. He's an *Irish Independent* man. He's a fist socked-into-his-hand man in Cusack Park when the boys from Broadford are putting points on the board. *Now for you.* Tommy's History of the World is not written down but firmly fixed in his mind in the same way that Chocolate Goldgrains are the only biscuit, Flahavan's the only porridge, and Fianna Fáil the One True Rulers (like all mythological heroes presently enduring a temporary period of exile).

Back in the time when we were all seaweed, he says, there was some seaweed already had the MacCarroll microbes or genomes or whatever and after that it was only a matter of time and creation.

Back then Ireland was down at the South Pole. So I'm thinking it would have been frozen seaweed of the sort Paddy Connolly started selling above in Quilty thinking in the Boom it would catch on like frozen yoghurt but hadn't calculated on the power of the salt making your lips swell up like slugs in a wet June while you stood there sucking Quilty seaweed. But then the Bust came and the Japanese had the earthquake and the mini-meltdown and couldn't eat their own and started sending delegations worldwide in search of good seaweed. A Mr Oonishi arrived in the County Clare, had a taste of frozen carrageen and went *odorokuhodo yoi*, which was *boys o boys* in Japanese, and the Connollys were back in business.

Sorry, drifting. It's a river narrative. Once, we were all frozen seaweed.

Then, Tommy says, America split off of Africa, said *See you boys later*, and did the American thing, it went West.

Ireland of course did its own thing and went north. All of us were seaborne. Whatever microbes were paddling Ireland they were fierce stubborn and didn't bother stopping at any of the sunnier climes, didn't say *Lads, what about the Canaries for a location? Didn't say Madeira looks nice*. No, they kept on, getting away from everyone, and would have kept going, Tommy says, except that Iceland had broken off above and was already in situ. The microbes were like the McInerneys who head off to Donegal each year, any number of children sardined into the back of the old Peugeot, three per seatbelt, and somewhere north of Claregalway dement their mother and father with *Are we there yet*. Enniscrone, County Sligo, is as far as they've ever made it. Tommy's basic point: the microbes were getting restless by then. The sun had livened them up. Then the rain got them in a right stew. Suddenly we were bestirring ourselves.

Ireland came to a stop. And the seaweed-people started moving about on the land.

And some of them were MacCarrolls.

Because we were once seaweed we all long to get back there. That's the premise. The sea is the Mother Ship. That's the explanation for Kilkee Lahinch Fanore Ballyvaughan and all the bungalows built up and down the Atlantic coast. That's the reason the planners couldn't say it'll look a bit mad and make the whole country look like we're some kind of perverted sea-voyeurs.

So the seaweed people started moving around in the rain. Some of them, who resented their mothers, and figured out right away that the west was the rainiest part, went into the Midlands to vent their feelings and invent hurling. The MacCarrolls stayed where they were. They'd just about dried out when The Flood came, Tommy says.

'And they all drowned?' I asked.

'Some of them survived,' he said, 'by becoming birds.'

'That was clever.'

'Others were swimmers.'

After The Flood withdrew things were grand for a time. Then the Partholonians came. They were already bored with sunscreen and deckchairs down in the eastern Mediterranean and arrived into Donegal on a salty gale, had a bit of Killybegs Catch, and headed south, where they met the Fomorians. The Fomorians were the misshapen one-eyed one-legged offal-eating hoppers who were peopling Offaly at the time.

Having only the one leg, they weren't that great at fighting. The Partholonians made mincemeat and pale spongy bodhráns out of them.

By the year 520 Tommy says there were 9,046 Partholonians in Ireland. Then in one week in May a horde of midges came, brought a plague and wiped them all out.

Except for one.

Tuan MacCarrill survived by becoming a salmon.

Fact. It's in the History of Ireland.

It's not all that strange when you consider that story is written in the Book of the Dun Cow, which is Book Number 1 in Irish Literature and was written on the hide of Saint Ciaran's favourite cow in Clonmacnois.

Not kidding.

Tuan survived by becoming a salmon.

Now, before you go saying *those Irish*, or *Come off it*, I will point out that though Tuan was maybe the first to use this method he was not the last. In the fat yellow paperback of David Grossman's *See Under: Love* (Book 2,001, Picador, London), one of the few books in which my father inscribed his name (blue biro), Bruno Schulz escapes the Nazis by becoming a salmon. Check it out.

Anyway, years later (according to the hide of Saint Ciaran's favourite cow), the salmon that was once Uncle Tuan was caught by a woman who ate him. It's true. She caught him, ate him, and then, in the kind of plot twist you get when you're writing on the hide of a Dun Cow, she gave birth to him again. He was a fine lad with distinctive red hair and salmon-coloured freckles, who had inside him the history of Ireland.

Not kidding.

The MacCarrolls were always into the stories. But first the stories were inside them.

Tuan MacCarrill had seen the Nemedians, the Partholonians, the Fir Bolgs and the Tuatha de Danann. The Tuatha de Danann were the followers of the Goddess Danu. They'd come to Ireland in long wooden boats and, tough men, burned them the moment they landed so there would be no turning back. Some of the locals looked up, saw this great boat-shaped cloud from the boat-burning and believed these fellows had sailed down from the sky.

'The stories of them lads would fill all the libraries of the known world,' Tommy said. But Tuan knew them all. He was the only one who could tell of the great battle against Balor of the Evil Eye, which was the first All-Ireland, but took place on the Plain of Moytura. The referee was a crow called the Morrigu. She whistled for the Throw-in and watched from a tree. When the last of the Fomorians were dead, the plain slippery with black blood and the ground underfoot spongy as figrolls in tea, the Morrigu blew up for fulltime.

Tuan MacCarrill had seen it first-hand. He was the first Embedded, the original Eyewitness Reports, a one-man Salmon

News Corporation, he'd been there and seen that, getting fish-eyed Exclusives of everything from the Fomorians to the Fianna.

And so, because he'd been here since seaweed, he told the early history of Ireland to Saint Finnian of Moville, who, being a monk, had a quill handy.

It's the way Tommy tells it.

If Ireland's first historian had been a girl instead of a salmon-boy it would have been a different story. If the man writing it down hadn't been a saint there'd have been other parts for women besides Goddesses, witches and swans.

So, there were seaweed people and sky people.

In time the seaweed people and the sky people found attraction in each other, and intermarried and became the Irish. That's the short version. That's why some of us are always longing for sky and some are of us are longing for the sea, and some, like my father, were both.

We're a race of elsewhere people. That's what makes us the best saints and the best poets and the best musicians and the world's worst bankers. That's why wherever you go you'll see some of us – and it makes no difference if the place is soft and warm and lovely and there's not a thing anyone could find wrong with it, there'll always be what Jimmy the Yank calls A Hankering. It's in the eyes. The idea of the better home. Some of us have it worse than others. My father had it running in the rivers of him.

The MacCarrolls stayed near the river. Beside the river there are two things you never forget, that the moment you look at a river that moment has already passed, and that everything is on its way somewhere else. The MacCarrolls weren't poets. They were too stubborn for metre and rhyme schemes. They were knuckle- and knee-scrapers and collarbone breakers, they were long-hair growers. They were fisher and boatmen. They had a wild streak in them about the same width and depth as the Shannon and they

161

had no loyalty to anyone but themselves, which was as it should be Tommy says, because Ireland then was in a complete dingdong between kings and clans and Vikings and Normans and whatnot and a lot of it was to do with O'Neills from Up North, which in Tommy's narrative means *Enough Said*.

In any case, the MacCarrolls stayed out of all that. Because of the salmon-time that was in their bloodstream they had a fair bit of knowledge and they hadn't forgotten the important thing the river had taught them: things pass. The place under their feet changed name a dozen times, but they stayed put.

A share of them got in boats and headed for the horizon. Stands to reason, Tommy says. Wouldn't there be a restlessness in any man who was once salmon and floating seaweed?

There's no arguing with that.

I wouldn't argue with Tommy anyway. Mrs Quinty says three months ago when they brought Tommy to the Regional the surgeon opened him up, and then just closed him up right away again, as if Tommy Devlin had become The Book of Tommy and on every page was written *Cancer*. Afterwards, Tommy took his book home again to Faha and carried on regardless. He has a kind of Lazarus glow now. There isn't a person in the parish would deny him anything.

'My point,' he says, 'restlessness a natural by-product of salmon-ness.'

That's why there's MacCarroll cousins in Queens and White Plains and Lake View Chicago and Michigan and San Francisco and why there's a Randy MacCarroll who's a horse-breeder in Kentucky, a Paddy MacCarroll a sheep-breeder in Christchurch New Zealand, and Caroll MacCarroll who breeds the turtles in Bali.

But a share of them stayed in what became Clare too.

'The family has a certain contrariness in it,' Tommy says. 'D'you see? From time to time the family would burst up in rows, one gang taking a position, the other gang taking the contrary, even if only for the virtue of being contrary, which is a peculiar twist in the Irish mind that dates back to sky and sea people. Some of the MacCarrolls would take a huff and splinter off over the mountains into Kerry or even, God Help us, Cork.'

What you had in the chronicle of the country then was a few centuries of a game of Rebellion-Betrayal, Rebellion-Betrayal, Uprising Put-Down, and Hope Dashed.

The History of Ireland in two words: *Ah well*.

The Invasion by the Vikings: *Ah well*.

The Invasion by the Normans. The Flight of the Earls, Mr Oliver Cromwell. Daniel O'Connell, Robert Emmett, The Famine, Charles Stewart Parnell, Easter Rising, Michael Collins, Éamon De Valera, Éamon De Valera again (*Dear Germany, so sorry to learn of the death of your Mr Hitler*), Éamon De Valera again, the Troubles, the Tribunals, the Fianna Fáil Party, The Church, the Banks, the eight hundred years of rain: *Ah well*.

In the *Aeneid* Virgil tells it as *Sunt lacrimae rerum*, which in Robert Fitzgerald's translation means 'They weep for how the world goes', which is more eloquent than *Ah well* but means the same thing.

There were MacCarrolls on both sides each time. They were Pro and Anti in equal measure. The only thing you could be certain of with a MacCarroll, Tommy says, was that opinions were Strongly Held. It was a seaweed–salmon thing. Salmon aren't reasonable. They're the boys for going against the current.

'Which holds a certain attraction for the Opposite Sex,' Tommy says, using Capitals.

'It does?'

'Oh it does,' he says.

That's when he goes Old Testament and starts listing the Begetting. Cearbhall MacCarrill married Fionnuala Ni Something who begat Finn who married Fidelma Ni Something Else and begat Finan who married a Fiona and begat Fintan, and so on. When they emerge out of the seaweed-smelling mists of time they are still marrying and begetting, some of them have dropped the A, others the Mac and some have gotten above themselves and taken up the O, so there are MacCarrolls, McCarrolls, Carrolls and O'Carrolls, all of them with a seawide streak of stubbornness and a character composed of what Nan simply calls salt. Some of them have twelve in the family, one of the Ni's wins Ovaries of the Year and gives the world eighteen MacCarrolls before sending the ovaries to the Clare Museum in Ennis and lying down on a bed of hay with a bucket of milk.

Tommy is hardcore into the folklore, he's far gone in *ceol agus rince* as Michael Tubridy says, has printed his Boarding Pass and been literally Away with the Fairies several times, believing we Irish are Number One folk for lore and in fact in our most humble and affable selves most if not all of the history of the world can be explained. He does the whole MacCarroll seed and breed, draws short of *And it Came to Pass*, the way Joshua does it in the Book of Joshua but he gives it the same ring. Like some of the women I may have dozed off during routine rounds of begetting but I come back in time for my Grandfather Fiachra who, thanks to Tesco's box-set, is played by young Spencer Tracy in *Captains Courageous* when Spencer is a Portuguese-American fisherman called Manuel Fidello, and later by old Spencer Tracy when he plays Old Man in *The Old Man and the Sea* and gets an Oscar nomination, but the Oscar goes to the thin moustache of David Niven and that salty deepwater Irish melancholy settles for ever into Spencer's eyes.

Grandfather Fiachra has the Spencer Tracy eyes and the Spencer Tracy hair that is this uncombable wavy stuff that makes it look like he has just surfaced into This World and has a last bit of silver sea still flowing crossways on his head. I never met him. Grandfather MacCarroll is in two black-and-white photographs in Nan's room. In one of them he's at his own wedding. He's in the front porch of Faha church in a black suit with pointy gangster lapels. He's big and barrel-chested and looks like there's nothing in the world he won't meet head on. Back then everyone looks serious. You get a shock when you find out he's twenty-eight, because the suit and the look and the pose make him older than anyone that age now. There's a smile around the corners of his mouth and something dancing in his eyes. He's waiting for his Bride.

She's a Talty.

Do I need to say more?

(Dear Reader, time is short, we can't even open The Book of Talty, because if we did we'd get sucked out in that tide. We'd be Gone for Some Time and away into the stories of Jeremiah Talty who was a doctor only without a degree, Tobias Talty who kept a horse in his house, lived on apples and grew the longest beard in the County Clare, his sister Josephine who conversed with fairies, & brother Cornelius who went to the American Civil War and fought on both sides. We might never get back.)

Bridget Talty is coming to the church by horse and cart. She's coming from fifteen miles away in Kilbaha by the broken road that's in love with the sea. She's sitting in that boneshaker beside her father in a wedding dress she's fighting because she didn't want to wear one, and has already thrown the veil into a ditch this side of Kilrush. They're rattling along in sea-spray and salt-gale and suddenly the regular rain turns to downpour. It comes bucketing and her father says rain is good luck for weddings but she doesn't answer him. She's foostering with the buttons at the collar of the dress because they're pinching out her breath and ping! one of them flies off, and ping! another. And she tugs back the collar and

165

holds her head high, so soon face, neck and the upper curve of her breasts are all gleaming with rain and her hair is wild streels tumbling. When she arrives outside Faha church in the cart she's this drowned heap, proud, beautiful and feckless as she gets off the cart, lands down into a fair-sized puddle, strides through it, muddied shoes and splattered stockings adding the final Bride-à-la-Talty touches as she comes through the church gates.

And standing there waiting, not at the altar but at the front door because that's the way he's doing it, Grandfather releases the Spencer Tracy smile around the corners of his mouth, sees the whole of his married life ahead, and thinks: *Well now. This is going to be interesting.*

The second photo is years later. It was taken by Martin Liverpool the time he was home for the Fleadh, Tommy says. Martin had been working on Merseyside ten years and came home with a touch of the John Hinde's, the freckled folkloric, seeing Ireland in panoramic Technicolor and Kodak-ing every turf barrow, ass and child, so that when he went back to the sites he had the country kind of captured in snaps that he kept in small cardboard shoe-boxes, taking solace from stopping time, and not admitting emigration had lacerated his heart. Martin Liverpool came past our house the day Grandfather was up thatching.

In the photo Spencer Tracy is still recognisable as Spencer Tracy, but his hair is white now. It tufts out from under the flat tweed cap. You can see his hair still has the waves but they're softer. The big wild tides of his youth are gone. Already passed are the years of *ruile buile*, the shouting and roaring, the storming in and the storming out, the flying dishes, the sudden wordless reconciliations he always instigated because despite his toughness and salmon-streak Spencer was hopelessly sentimental the way only men can be. The birth of Mam, the years in this house when it had to accommodate two big hearts and minds bashing against each other and making fly the sparks in which the love happened, I can't really imagine them. You can't imagine your nan like that. She's too Nan to accommodate younger versions. All I know is that before Bridget Talty became Nan, before she became guardian of *Clare Champions* and Watcher of the Fire, before she took to pretending deafness and day and night wearing Spencer Tracy's cap, she was a young married woman who found herself to be fulltime baker of bread, washer of shirts, getter of turf, raiser of hens ducks and geese and that she did not mind any of it as long as she could have a pack of ten Carrolls Number One cigarettes and go set dancing in the evenings. That's her legend in the parish. To Comerford's, Tubridy's, Downes's, to Ryan's, Daly's and McNamara's she went, as well as skipping across the fields to house dances, bringing her big bashful Spencer Tracy with her, crossing under kissing starlight, the two of them coming flushed in the back door on to flagged kitchens, doing the Caledonian, the South Galway and the Clare Sets, five Figures, with glistening faces and battering steps, Tops and Tails, shouting 'House' and dancing the world simple.

In the photo Grandfather has a white shirt with sleeves rolled, big coarse tweedy trousers the thatch won't penetrate. The roof has two homemade-looking ladders hanging on it. They are hooked over the apex so it looks like Grandfather is heading up into the big bluer-than-blue sky. Martin Liverpool has given him a shout so he's turned halfway up the ladder and now he's in the perfect position, blue sky behind him and straight ahead the same sweeping Shannon river view that I have from the skylight. He doesn't know his heart attack is on the way. He doesn't know he has only time to get the thatch finished, the turf home, and two horses shod.

Jaykers God, Tommy says. But he was a fine figure of a man.

Ah well.

That's where Tommy's history ends.

But that's not the end.

The next bit is the fairy tale.

There's a day in April when it's raining. The river is running fast. The girl whose father had died, whose mother raised her in the crooked house by the river, who grew up with that broken part inside where your father has died and which if you're a girl and your father was Spencer Tracy you can't fix or unhurt, that girl who yet found in herself some kind of forbearance and strength and was not bitter, whose name was Mary MacCarroll and who was beautiful without truly knowing it and had her mother and father's dancing and pride in her, that girl walked the riverbank in the April rain.

And standing at that place in Shaughnessy's called Fisher's Step, where the ground sort of raises a little and sticks out over the Shannon, right there, the place which in *The Salmon in Ireland* Abraham Swain says salmon pass daily and though it's treacherous he calls *a blessed little spot*, right there, looking like a man who had been away a long time and had come back with what in *Absalom, Absalom!* (Book 1,666, Penguin Classics, London) William Faulkner calls diffident and tentative amazement, as if he'd been through some solitary furnace experience, and come out the other side, standing right there, suntanned face, pale-blue eyes that look like they are peering through smoke, lips pressed together, aged twenty-nine but looking older, back in Ireland less than two weeks, the ocean-motion still in his legs but strangely the river now lending him a river repose, standing right there, was Virgil Swain.

That's us, from Seaweed to Swain.

I used the long run-up. You have to; otherwise the pole won't carry you over.

It's the way Charles Dickens does it in *Martin Chuzzlewit* (Book 180, Penguin Classics) where in Chapter One he traces the Chuzzlewits back to Adam and Eve. The MacCarrolls go back further. They go back beyond, Martin Feeney says.

The Swain are the written, the MacCarroll the oral. Ours is a history of tongue marrying paper, the improbable marrying the impossible. The children are incredible.

When I call my father Virgil Swain I think he's a story. I think I invented him. I think maybe I never had a father and in the gap where he should be I have put a story. I see this figure on the river-bank and I try to match him to the boy I have imagined, but find instead a gristle of truth, that human beings are not seamless smooth creations, they have insoluble parts, and the closer you look the more mysterious they become.

Nobody in our parish ever called my father by his name. They called him Verge. And one time I wrote that down along a page of my Aisling copybook, *Verge*, and thesaurus-ed to find Edge, Border, Margin, before I came to Threshold, and then I thought of it as a verb and got a shiver when I wrote Approach.

My father never really told us where he had been. Deep, deep, and still deep and deeper must we go if we would find out the heart of a man, old Herman Melville says in my father's copy of *Pierre; or, The Ambiguities* (Book 1,997, E.P. Dutton, New York), a book that has the smell of basement and on page 167 a tea-stain in the shape of Greenland.

The years between my father's leaving Ashcroft and his standing on Fisher's Step are lost. When you're a child who has grown up on Adventure stories, who had Spencer Tracy for a Talty grandfather and a rushing river outside the door, there was a certain prestige in being able to announce in Faha N.S. that before he lived here my father was *Gone to Sea*. In a parish where the river opens into the sea the happy children dream of voyaging out, the sad of being sucked out, but either way the sea is magic central. Gone to Sea inspires a certain status. But the prestige was short-lived because I couldn't expand beyond that phrase, because I got flushed when asked and because that little bug-eyed Seamus Mulvey kept following me around the yard singing 'Where did he go? Where did he go?' in that high strangulated whine all the Mulveys got from burning plastic bottles in their fire after the Council starting charging for recycling. 'Did he go to Africa? Did he go to Australia?' the round head of him bobbing side-to-side, the bug-eyes shining like sucked Black Jacks, singing scorn and teaching me the universal truth the human mind abhors vagueness, even a tiny mind like Seamus Mulvey's.

Our father went to sea with Ahab and Ishmael. That's a fact. But he didn't find the whale. He came back with the same restless seeking inside him, and added to that a sense of things being infirm.

'Where did you sail to?' Aeney asked.

Dad lay between us on Aeney's bed-boat. We were eight and in school had started doing Geography. At night-time Aeney took the Atlas to bed and before Mam called up Lights Out I joined him under the blue duvet with the white floating clouds on it and we looked at maps and took a kind of comfort from the way no matter how big a place was, if it was big as all of South America say, it still fitted inside a page. Aeney was a boy who dreamed. And so when he was looking at the maps you could sort of feel his brain whirring and you knew that afterwards in his sleep he'd still be travelling in those places.

'Where did you sail to?'

Dad lies between us on top of the floating clouds, his long thin body a ridge of mountains that I can walk two fingers on. That April day when Mam first found him on Fisher's Step he had D.H. Lawrence's ragged reddish-brown beard, the one from the madly wrinkled cover of the *Selected Poems* (Book 2,994, Penguin, London), but we weren't born until long after that, so by now his beard is silver and I can walk my fingers right up along his shoulders and over his collar into it and I get a good way into the softness of his beard before he makes a pretend snap and a shark sound and I scream and save my fingers for another while.

'Where did you sail when you were a sailor?'

'Well,' he says, 'I'll tell you, but you mustn't tell anyone.'

'We won't. Sure we won't, Aeney?' I lie, looking across at Aeney to make sure he won't mention Seamus Mulvey.

Aeney shakes his head the way small boys do, with a kind of complete and perfect seriousness. His eyes are Os of wonder and gravity.

'Tell us.'

'Well,' Dad says. 'Do you know where the Caribbean is?'

Aeney flicks the pages of the Atlas. 'Here.' He holds it across the mountain ridge so I can see.

Dad smiles that smile he has that's near to crying. 'That's right.'

'Did you sail there?'

'I did.'

'What was it like? Tell us.'

'It was hot.'

'How hot?'

'Very very hot.'

'And why were you there? What were you sailing there for?' Aeney wants to understand how you can get into a map that's on page 28 of an Atlas.

'Why was I there?' Dad says.

'Yes.'

My father's eyes are looking straight up at the slope of the ceiling and the cutaway angle where the skylight is a box of navy blue with no stars. The question is too big for him. I will see this often in the years to come, the way he could suddenly pause on a phrase or even just a word, as if in it were a doorway and his mind would enter and leave us momentarily. Back then we thought it was what all fathers did. We thought that fatherhood was this immense weight like a great overcoat and there were all manner of things your father had to be thinking of all the time just to keep the over-coat from crushing him. 'Well,' he says at last, 'that's a long story.'

'All right.' Aeney props himself up on his elbow. One look at his face and you know you can't disappoint him. You just can't. Before they are broken small boys are perfect creations.

'Well,' Dad says. 'I'll tell you the short version.'

I move in closer. My head is against my father's side. It's warm in a way only your father's body is warm and his shirt smells the way only your own father's can. It's a thing impossible to explain or recapture, because it's more than a smell, it's more than the sum of Castile soap and farm sweat and dreams and endeavour, it's more than Old Spice aftershave or Lux shampoo, more than any combination of anything you can find in the press in his bathroom. It's in the heat and living of him. It goes out of his clothes after three days. That's a thing I learned.

But then I am not thinking of any of that. I press myself into the warmth of my father and his arm lifts and comes around me. His other arm comes around Aeney.

'Well, it was a big-enough ship,' my father begins. 'It belonged to a Mr Trelawney.'

Aeney needs details. 'What kind of man was he?'

'A good man. But he couldn't keep a secret.'

'Why not?'

'It was just his failing. But he had a cool head, so that was good. Anyway, he owned the ship and he came with us. And brought with him his friend, a Doctor Livesey.'

'Was he good?'

'He was. He treated everybody the same.'

'That was good.'

'Yes.'

'What was the Captain's name?'

'Smollett. He was a good Captain.'

'You need a good Captain. Who else?'

'There were plenty. There was a Mr Allardyce, Mr Anderson, and Mr Arrow.'

'They are all As.'

'Quiet, Ruth. What was Mr Arrow like?'

'Mr Arrow drank. Even though it was not allowed.'

'Did he fall overboard?'

'Yes. He fell overboard during the night when we got to the Caribbean. His body was never seen again.'

Dad allows a pause for Mr Arrow's body to sink without trace.

'There was also Abraham Gray.'

'What was he like?'

'He was a carpenter. At first I didn't like him, and when you're on a ship with somebody you don't like that's no fun. But then he did some good things and I saw a different side of him. And in the end he saved my life.'

'Did he?'

'He certainly did.'

'How?'

'That comes later. First, who else? There was John Hunter, there was Richard Joyce. And Dick Johnson. He always had a Bible with him. Everywhere he went. He thought it would protect him in the seas.'

'And did it?'

'He didn't drown. But he got malaria.'

'Was that bad?'

'Yes, Ruthie.'

'He died?'

'He did.'

We pay our respects to Mr Johnson as he follows Mr Arrow into the dark.

'George Merry, Tom Morgan, O'Brien. We never knew O'Brien's first name. He was just O'Brien.'

'Good?' Aeney's O eyes.

Dad makes tremor an invisible whiskey bottle at his lips. Poor O'Brien.

'The Caribbean, you know, is not a place. It is many places. Islands. Some of them are so small they're not even on that map. But all of them are beautiful. The water is this marvellous blue. It's so blue that once you see it you realise you've never seen blue before. That other thing you were calling blue is some other colour, it's not *blue*. This, this is blue. It's a blue that comes down from the sky into the water so that when you look in the sea you think sky and when you look at the sky you think sea.'

Aeney and I lie there and realise we've never seen blue, and how amazing it must be, and for a while I try the difficult trick of seeing what I've never seen except through my father's telling. I set him sailing in the very best blue I can imagine, but know that is not blue enough.

'Close your eyes to see it,' he says.

We both close our eyes. Just when I think I am seeing it he lifts his arms from around us and our heads slide back deeper into the pillow on Aeney's bed. The bed rises as the mountain ridge goes away and my father eases himself off. I'm in the warm space that still smells like him and I'm thinking of sailing towards an island in the marvellous blue.

Aeney doesn't want to imagine. He wants the real thing. He wants to be there. 'Tell us more.'

'I will,' Dad says. 'But just get to the island now. Just arrive. Tomorrow I'll tell you about Mr Silver.'

'Mr Silver?'

'Shsh. Lie back.'

'But who is he?'

'His name was John. We called him Long, even though he wasn't.'

My eyes are closed, but I can feel Dad pull the covers up around Aeney. His voice is quiet because he thinks Ruthie is already asleep. Very gently he pats Aeney's head and at his ear whispers, '*He had a wooden leg.*'

3

We tell stories. We tell stories to pass the time, to leave the world for a while, or go more deeply into it. We tell stories to heal the pain of living.

When Mary MacCarroll sees Virgil Swain on Fisher's Step she doesn't fall in Love right away. She falls in Curiosity, which is less deep but more common. She sees a man with a sunburned face and ragged beard and presumes he's a fisher. She has come out of the house to clear her head and walked in the April rain without purpose or destination. Often she walked the riverbank. The Shannon is a masculine river. It's burly and brown and swollen with rain. It shoulders its way out between Kerry and Clare with an indifferent force but when you walk alongside it down where the fields fall away and the line of the land is this frayed green edge you can get a kind of river peace. I used to love walking there. Running water is best for daydreams, Charles Dickens said, and he was right.

Mary sees the man and knows he's a stranger. He is standing looking at the river the way only fishermen do. But she sees no rod or tackle, and as she approaches she has enough sense of her own beauty to expect him to turn to look at her.

He doesn't.

She walks three feet behind him, and he doesn't turn. She goes on down the bank, discovers a seed of curiosity is cracking in her, and opening now, unfurling a first feathered edge as she thinks *he's looking now* and makes as though tossing her hair but is checking to see if his head has turned.

It hasn't.

She is only eighteen but has already taken enough possession of the world to know her own impact in it. It isn't vanity like Anna Prender in Kilmurry who'd be happy if you carried a full-length mirror alongside her or Rosemary Carr inside in Kilrush who Nan says is in love with her own backside, it's a natural thing. It's what happens in small places. It's what happens when your father was Spencer Tracy and you come to Mass walking with your head MacCarroll high and have a kind of ease and grace that people notice. It's what happens when the timbers of the Men's Aisle groan under the forward strain as you come up to Communion, or the biggest male attendance in Faha church occurs the evening of the Feast of Saint Blaise when Father Tipp is going to bless your arched bare throat. Something like it is in a poem of Austin Clarke's in *Soundings* which Mrs Quinty used to teach us in TY. The 'Sunday in every week' one.

She's used to it, that's all.

And he doesn't turn.

Well that's fine. She doesn't really care. She walks on down the river to the end of Ryan's and she crosses out over the place where the wire ends. She goes along by O'Brien's and up to Enright's, all the time the rain falling softly and all the time the seed feathering some more.

Who is he?

She stops to talk with one of the Macs who are out counting cattle and says there is a stranger back along the way, but she only gets a *that right?* in reply and that doesn't satisfy the thing the Curiosity craves. It wants to talk about him. It doesn't matter what is said as long as something is, as long as somehow the mystery of

177

him gets out of the place inside where the feathering is madding now.

She goes back along the bank, back past O'Brien's and Enright's and over the wire into Shaughnessy.

There he is, in the very same place. He hasn't moved.

This time she can look at him as she approaches. She can allow the Curiosity what it needs, it needs detail; the way in profile his hair looks roughly barbered, the way the beard runs down into his shirt collar, the way the sun and sea have early-aged him. Details: boots without laces, she has never seen boots like them, trousers foreshortened by long wear and knee-gathers, the shirt that had once been white, the jacket he wears, tan leather, square-cut, thousand-creased, both dark-polished and dulled by weather, the jacket which later she will learn he got in Quito in Ecuador and from which he cannot be separated. There's a paperback book that's too tall for the jacket pocket. (It's the Collier Books edition of W.B. Yeats's *Mythologies*, Book 1,002, published in New York, priced $4.95, and on the cover the poet is young and melancholic, forelock falling on to his left eyebrow. It's the book that brought Virgil back to Ireland, the one that begins with 'A Teller of Tales' where WB says the stories in it were told to him by Paddy Flynn in a leaky one-roomed cabin in the village of Ballisodare. It's the one where he says *In Ireland this world and the world we go to after death are not far apart.* The tops of pages are river-and-rain-warped, the whole book buckled a bit from travel, age and pockets, but it's a book that feels *companionable* somehow, if you know what I mean. In it there are many pages with lines underscored, or in some cases with just ascending wing-like Nike tick-marks next to a paragraph. Sometimes the marks have been made in different inks and therefore different times, so that in 'Drumcliff and Rosses' after Yeats tells of Ben Bulben and Saint Columba there's a wavy black line under how he *climbed one day to get near Heaven with his prayers*, but in 'Earth, Fire and Water' there are two red strokes slashed down in the margin next to *I am certain that the water, the water of the seas and of lakes and of mist and rain, has all but made the Irish after its image.* Between pages 64 and 65, 'Miraculous Creatures', there's one of those old grey cinema tickets on which is printed Admit One.)

Mary hasn't seen a man so still, she hasn't seen a man with a jacket like that, with a book in his pocket.

She walks back towards him. He'll say hello this time, she thinks. He'll know it's me. Somehow he'll have seen me the first time without my knowing and this time he'll turn and say hello.

Maybe he'll just turn and nod, she thinks. But at least then she will see his face.

She goes along the track by the river, it's muck-tacky with rain, heels of her boots sucking. She is ten yards from him, then five; then she is passing behind him. He hasn't turned.

What is the matter with him?

If she reaches she could put her hand on his back. If she reaches she could shove him into the river, and for a flash moment she is the girl who will do it, who will suddenly stop and push her two hands into the small of his back and send him spinning into the Shannon.

What is the matter with him? Is he deaf or blind or just rude?

She goes ten yards past when she decides to turn and tell him that this is Matty Shaughnessy's field and it's private. Fifteen when she thinks no she won't. Twenty when she thinks she will fall over, go the full Jane Austen, hurt her ankle and cry out, twenty-five when she's too mad and won't give him the satisfaction and thirty when she comes through the stile out of the field and looks back to see him still standing there.

'There's a stranger down at the river,' she tells her mother. And that is a first relief. It's relief just to say *stranger* because then he is already somebody, and she is already connected to him.

That's how I see it anyway. That's how I see it when I ask Mam 'How did you first meet Dad?' and each time she tells me the story of Not Meeting, of Passing by, and how it seems to me God was giving them every chance not to meet, and the singular nature of their characters will mean their stories will run parallel and never do a Flannery O'Connor. Never converge.

'Is there?' Nan says. She's flour-elbows in this scene. It's a bit Walter Macken meets John B. Keane because she's breadmaking the loaves she sells in Nolan's shop to keep them alive. Her dancing days are over and Spencer Tracy is on black-and-white reruns in her head now, but she knows this day is coming. You can't have a daughter that beautiful and not know.

'A stranger?' she says. Nan is sharp as a tack and cute as buttons. She won't look up from the dough but she'll let her daughter get it out.

'I don't know who he is,' Mary says.

'No?'

'No.'

Mary throws her coat on the door hook, sits to toe the heel of a boot.

Nan gives the dough thumbs. She gives it Almighty Thumbs. Her thumb knuckles stick out like shiny knobs from years of breadmaking. 'What's he like?'

'I don't know. I hardly saw him.'

'Didn't you?'

Mary goes to tend the fire, roughly rakes down the grate and assembles the embers in a little heap.

'Tall, I suppose?' Nan asks.

'I think. I don't know. I told you, I hardly saw him.'

Nan kneads the story some more. 'What was he doing? In Shaughnessy's, I wonder?'

Mary doesn't answer. She's not going to speak about him any more. 'Nothing,' she says, after a while.

'Nothing?'

'Nothing. Just looking at the river.'

That night he's with her in her bed.

Not in that way.

She's lying in her bed with the curtains drawn and the window open because the April night is softer than tissue and because she can't get enough air. She's lying on her side facing the window and the room is loud with that song the river has when the rain is spring heavy and the Shannon flowing fast. She can't sleep. He won't let her. What was he doing there? Why did he not turn? She's angry with him, which marks a deepening and keeps him there, as if already their relationship is a living thing and he is already someone with whom she can get angry. She moves on to her other side and puts the pillow over her ear. But it's useless. Somehow the river is louder when you cover your ears. It's like the sea in shells. You hear it in your blood. I used try to escape it with headphones when I told Mam I couldn't bear to hear the river running any more and for weeks she tried everything, taping the vent in the skylight, hanging chimes made of shells, bringing up Dad's music and playing it loud, but even J.S. Bach had to pause sometime and between his Movements the river sang and in the end I stood in my nightie and opened the skylight and screamed at it, which is neither great for your reputation or stopping river noise.

Mary's angry at him. Then she's angry at herself for even think-ing about him. And so in the bed they are joined. It's not an ideal relationship, but it's a start. I have the same thing with Vincent Cunningham, so I know. She tells herself to forget about him, but if there's one sure way not to forget something it's to say Forget That.

Why is her pillow so lumpy?

Why is the sheet so twisted around her legs?

Why, why, why is there no air in April?

They have a hell of a night together.

In the morning the birds are singing with that extra-demented loudness they have in spring in Clare, they're all ADHD and they've got this urgent message they're trying to deliver but because God's a comedian they can only speak it in chirrup. Mary comes into the kitchen. Nan is there already. Since her husband died she can't bear being in the bed and sleeps in the chair so she's up before the birds, the bread loaves that were out upside down overnight are now being tapped on their backs before Marty Mungovan who was sweet on Nan from her dancing days comes to collect them.

'Morning,' Nan says to her daughter.

But Mary goes straight out the back door and across the haggard to the hen run. She lifts and pulls open the mesh-wire gate and the hens raise an excited clucking. The older ones see that she's bringing no margarine tub of Layers Mash and turn away and the younger ones in terror run into the wire and poke their heads through it, for a moment scrabbling at the ground for propulsion going nowhere but squawking mad because they know something unusual is happening. Which is true, something has happened. She crosses the Run and stoops in to the House and from the wooden crate that has Satsumas inked into it and a bed of patted-down hay she takes six eggs.

She comes into the kitchen and starts cracking them straight away into a bowl.

Nan knows enough of the human heart not to pass comment.

The eggs get beaten. They get beaten big-time. They get salted and peppered. Then they get beaten some more.

Then they get abandoned. She just stops beating them mid-whisk and leaves them and goes out the back door again, this time not going into the haggard but out the pencil-gravel way where the grass grows up through it in wet April and makes a kind of slug-road into the garden. She goes out the gate and walks with her arms folded across her and her green cardigan pulled over but not buttoned. She never buttons it. There's something in her can't stand confinement. It's a MacCarroll thing. She walks down the road and Marty Mungovan passes her in his van coming to collect the breads and gives her the nod and she just inclines her head slightly in briefest greeting. She hasn't brushed her hair, she hasn't done one thing of all the things she might have done in getting ready to go and meet her future husband.

Because right then she's just curious, she wants to know, that's all. And she marches down the road that runs parallel to the river and takes its curves from it until she gets to Murphy's gate and for an instant she hesitates, just one moment, just one moment in which she might say to herself *what the hell are you doing?* and turn back, just one moment which flies away into the mad chirruping of the birds, then she climbs the gate.

She sees him right away. He's there, in the same place, in the same pose, watching the river in the same way.

Just the fact of it, just the strangeness and the stillness and the *solidity* of him of whom she'd been thinking all night, takes her breath. She's aware her heart jumps into the side of her throat. She's aware the ground has a spongy spring to it and the sky is huge. He's there again, standing, looking westward. He's there. It's like the French Lieutenant's woman in the *The French Lieutenant's*

Woman only in reverse, and with the river instead of the sea, but there's the same inevitability, the same sense of things just about to go bang.

What's he doing there?

Mary hasn't worked out the next step. She didn't really expect him to be there and came half in the hope that his having vanished again would free her of thinking about him. But now she has to figure out what happens next. She's crossing the field to the mucky track again and she's got her arms tighter around her and her head lowered a bit now, but she's thinking *Has he been here all night?* And in that there's madness and attraction both. Right then she doesn't have the words to explain it. It's like Colette Mulvihill over in Kilbaha who left The Church and took up Leonard Cohen and when Father Tipp asked her why she just said Mystery, Father, which was a blow to him because the Church had spent fifty years taking the mystery out of it so that now uncaught criminals like Kieran Coyne and Maurice Crossan could become Eucharistic Ministers and the Hosts arrive in a blue van from Portlaoise that says Maguire Bros, Clergy Apparel & Supplies, All Religions, right on the side and *Wash Me Please* in finger-writing underneath.

Mystery, Father, was about right.

Mary walks along the track. She's not looking at him. She won't. But she's fallen so far in Curiosity there's no way she's going to be able to go home again until she's found out something. Her mind is pulling at the mystery, and it's flying past River-stalker, Inspector of Riverbanks, Surveyor of Soils & Erosion, Fisher-scout, Salmon-spy, Pathfinder, Priest, but it never gets to Man at the End of Living, it never gets to Man Who has Come to Drown, because she's not yet acquainted with anything Swain. She doesn't know about Grandfather Absalom waiting in the candles for The Calling or the pole-vaulting or the Philosophy of Impossible Standard. She doesn't know poets can have ash in the soul, or that after so much burning there comes a time when there's nothing left but blowing away or phoenix-rising. She hasn't read Eileen Simpson's *Poets in their Youth* (Book 3,333, Picador, London) or John Berryman's *The Freedom of the Poet* (Book 3,334, Farrar, Straus & Giroux) or Peter Ackroyd's *Blake* (Book 3,340, Vintage, London), Paul Ferris's *Dylan Thomas* (Book 3,341, Dial Press, New York), Paddy Kitchen's *Gerard Manley Hopkins* (Book 3,342, Carcanet Press, London) or any of the others my father gathered together in a mad company under the slope of the skylight where once the fire smoked and the hose soaked them all. She doesn't know that he has seen much of the world, but she feels it. She doesn't know he has come back to Ireland carrying a caustic disappointment in himself, that he feels *is this all there is?*, that his life has amounted to nothing, that nothing has happened but Time, and that now he has walked across Ireland Swain-style, fishing the rivers his father described, and is that most dangerous of things, a man looking for a sign. No sign had been seen, until yesterday, when he came to that spot in the river and for no reason that can be explained fell into the conviction that he was *meant* to be there.

He has no more idea of why than she does.

But he has that Swain ability to believe in the outlandish. The family has history in it.

'What are you doing here?' she asks him. The thing is too big in her to get out delicately.

He doesn't move. He's been standing too still and too long and maybe he thinks it is his own mind asking. But then there's the difference in the air. There's something he can't see but feels and he turns and looks at her.

The French Lieutenant's woman's face is unforgettable and tragic. Its sorrow wells out as naturally as water, Fowles says.

And I think that's what Mary sees too. He turns and she sees the sadness and right away she's sorry for her bluntness and being so MacCarroll and she wishes she could wind the moment backwards.

'I'm sorry,' he says. 'I didn't realise I shouldn't be here.'

'No,' she says, a little too quickly. 'It's all right.' Her arms are still about her and she rubs her hands a little back and forth on them as if she's cold but she's not cold.

'I'll go.'

But he doesn't go. He uses the future not the present tense, and between those two is our life and history.

She feels him looking at her. She feels for a moment arrested by it, and in that arrest there's danger and warning and dizziness, but mostly there's the irresistible pull of when a pair of eyes are matched, because although she doesn't know it yet here's Love and Death in the same breath, here's one of those moments upon which a story turns, and right now, just by the way she lifts her face and smiles, my mother is about to save my father.

'It's okay,' she says. 'You can stay.'

('Mam, how did you meet Dad?'

'I just met him.'

'But how?'

'He was just there. That's all.'

'There?'

'Yes. He was just *there*.')

I've decided it's the Elsewhere in him that draws her. Like now, Faha back then was a parish of two minds. In one, there was nothing that happened anywhere in the world that was nearly as interesting or noteworthy as what happened in your own parish. To them travel was a waste of time and money. *What would you be wanting to go there for?* was delivered with such vinegar disregard that the legs were cut from under the very idea and to even consider travelling beyond the Faha signpost was evidence of some genetic weakness. To the others, there was nothing of any significance that ever happened inside the bounds of the parish. As proven by the RTE evening news, in which Faha had never appeared, the world happened somewhere else. Thus far the whole of human history had bypassed the parish and the sooner you could get on the N68 and out of it the sooner you could encounter actual life. It wasn't until the Bust when those with Mindset One had no choice and all the tilers and painters and chippies and plasterers had vanished and the Under-21 team stopped existing altogether that Mindsets One and Two, Home and Away, started getting mixed up. Then girls like Mona Fitz and Marian Callinan set up Faha-in-Queens, Faha-in-Melbourne and started e-publishing versions of the parish newsletter with times of Mass in Faha, this week's Epistle Readers, the WeightWatchers meeting, the Old Folks Cake Sale and the Under-14 fixtures, just so people could pretend they weren't Elsewhere.

It's the Elsewhere in Virgil Swain that draws her. He is a stranger. It's the oldest plot. But it's a good one. She tells him he can stay, as if it is in her power, as if she is somehow already in charge, and she's decided the best way to hide her attraction to him is to deny it exists.

It's in the Book of Women's Stratagems.

She says he can stay and then she walks away.

But really they are already in a relationship. Already she's think- ing of the places he's been and already she wants him to tell her, and that telling will be the first bridge between my mother and father. His stories will bring her across to him.

He stays in the village in the unofficial B&B that Phyllis Thomas opened when her husband left her for a Gourmet Tart in Galway. After three days he is no longer just a stranger but The Stranger, like a DC Comics version that's drawn in purple or grey, because that was when the only strangers in the parish were there for funerals or weddings and there was no such thing as tourists in Faha and it was still twenty-five years before Nolan's would start selling the Polish beer and the kind of bread that tastes like wood. He stays in the village and he walks the roads of the parish in a way that's already noted as peculiar. Farmers don't walk if they can take tractors. Men only walk if their cars are broken. Nobody back then walks just for walking. The only time there are Walkers on the road is when Mass is on. So Virgil is already building a mythology. He's tall and quiet and the Readers of Character who occupy the tall stools in Carmody's or prop on Mina Prendergast's post-office windowsill before and after Mass are already tonguing their thumbs and flicking the pages of Who He Might Be.

Mary doesn't know what to do with him. She knows she wants him in her day. She likes that he's there, that if she goes out on her bicycle with eggs or bread she'll see him somewhere. She'll see his tall figure over a stonewall, see the looping stride, the long back, the uplift of his chin as he goes, that Swain angle, as if he's always half-looking above.

And then he's so quiet. And there is something irresistible in that.

They become what Dilsey Hughes from Dublin calls An Item.

It's a walking item, mostly.

They walk. That's what Mam says. They walk everywhere. Sometimes he doesn't talk and she sticks these little barbed comments in him to get him to respond. She says something to get his seriousness to collapse and when it does she laughs and then he smiles and she feels this flood of warmth coming over her and she knows now this is more than curiosity, but she won't say the word Love. He'll have to say it first.

188

But now she's afraid he might go. She's afraid that one day she might wake up and he will be gone in the same way that he came.

So she sees if she can drive him off. The MacCarrolls have that little perverse streak in them. She'd rather break her own heart than have it broken. There's an Irish logic to it. But maybe you have to be here a hundred years in the rain before you understand it. She tries Not Showing Up. That's another stratagem. She's mad to be out walking and bumping against him but she won't let herself. She stays in the house and beats eggs. She keeps an eye to the window to see if he'll come in the gate. But he doesn't. He has the Swain thing where disappointment and hurt are first nature and he stands out by the river and feels the nails being driven into his heart.

Between the Swain thing and the MacCarroll thing it's not looking great.

When I tell it to myself at this stage I'm worried for me and Aeney.

Because both of them are so good at suffering. Dad has come back to Ireland and believes that in Mary MacCarroll he's found meaning. And I mean Meaning. Which in ordinary language is significant enough, but in Swain-song is pretty much the tops. He believes everything up to now has been pointless. *What have I been doing?* The voyaging, the high-walled seas, the lightless-night horizons, the fevers, sicknesses, the frizzled scorched skin of his brow and the tops of his ears, the sailings in and the sailings out, the whole kit and caboodle, the whole Boy's Own, Melville and Conrad, conceit of it, all of it has been a running away, an avoidance of what has been flowing in his blood all the time, the sense that *there is something I must do*. And what must be done is in fact here, in this parish, by this river, with this woman.

I'm not an expert, but when a man finds Meaning in a woman it seems to me you know two things. One, you know you're going

189

Deep, and Two, you know this is the most high-risk kind of love there is.

For Mam the risk is already clear. She knows there will be no other Virgil Swain coming through Faha. She knows she has to stay there and take care of Nan because Mam has that good big heart of Spencer Tracy in her and she will never let you down. She'll sacrifice whatever she has to. Some people are just that good, they have this soldier-saint part of them intact and it takes your breath because you keep forgetting human beings can sometimes be paragons. So she's caught because she knows this is it. *This is it.* And despite every caution that the Central Council of the Faha Branch of the Irish Countrywomen Association might have offered, that a man not born in the parish, a man not born in the county, or even in The West, a man with no soil on his hands or cattle in his blood, would find it impossible to be happy here, Mam wants to believe he will love her enough to stay, and that once he does everything will be all right.

But she won't ask him. She won't go any further in the Book of Stratagems. There's no summer dresses or lipstick or hairdos or perfume, no invitation to tea, no *here's a cake I baked* or *there's a dance in Tubridy's* or *I saw you fishing yesterday.*

Nothing.

She waits and she suffers and he waits and he suffers, both of them like characters in a cliffhanger at the end of a chapter.

4

I'm an incurable romantic, according to Vincent Cunningham.

Incurable anyway, I said.

Then I told him that the Latin word for waiting is pretty much the same as suffering, and he went Wow, like I was the keeper of Cool Things and if he could he would have kissed my Knowledge.

My father started fishing. Right down by Shaughnessy's he started. Mary saw him in the morning when she went to collect the eggs. She stalled in the pen, heard the softest *whish* wrinkling the air and turned to see his line floating its question mark over the river. 'He's fishing,' she told the hens, who were not indifferent to the news because she spared a few eggs that day.

You and I know that Virgil Swain was not going anywhere. We know he had that same Swain certainty his father had in the candles in Oxford. *This is what I am meant to do.* And that was unshakeable iron in him.

Faith is the most peculiar thing. It's Number One in human mysteries. Because how do you do it? Where do you learn it? For the Believers it doesn't matter how outlandish or unlikely the thing you believe in, if you believe it, there's no arguing. Pythagoras's early life was spent as a cucumber. And after that he lived as a sardine. That's in Heraclitus. That's what he believed. Beside the east bank of the River Cong in Mayo was a Monks' Fishing House and the monks laid a trap in the river so that when a salmon entered it a line was pulled and rang a little bell in the monks' kitchen, and although there were strict laws forbidding any traps nobody ever stopped the monks because they knew the monks believed the salmon were Heaven-sent and even unbelievers don't want to tax Heaven. Just in case. That's in *The Salmon in Ireland*. Bridie Clohessy believes her weight is all water, Sean Conway believes the Germans are to blame for most things, Packy Nolan that it was the red M&Ms gave him the cancer. With faith there's no arguing.

Virgil Swain believed this was the place he was meant to be. This was the place of which, when I imagine him lying fevered and delirious below decks in the West Indies, or landed in Cape Town and gone ashore with whoever were the real-life versions of Abraham Gray and John Hunter and Richard Joyce, he was dreaming.

It was not so much that it was Faha itself. It was this bend in the river.

River bends have their own potency. Ever since some hand wrote *a river flows out of Eden* rivers and Paradise are pretty much inseparable. If you're reading this in Persian think *Apirindaeza*, in Hebrew *Pardes*. As far as I can make out there are rivers in every Paradise. Though not always fishermen. Bishop Epiphanius in 403 AD had an epiphany and decided Paradise had in fact two rivers, the Tigris and the Euphrates, but whether these flowed into or out of Paradise was not clear and Augustine made this even more confusing by saying a river flowed *out* of Paradise and watered Eden, which led to serious problems because according to all maps of Paradise that meant the water had to flow *upwards*. A conundrum until John Milton solved it by explaining that paradisiacal water defies gravity. We are all looking forward to that.

So, for my father it was this bend in the river.

It was probably only the land from here to McInerney's and Fisher's Step, the water thick and wide and the feeling of imminence that the river is about to meet the sea.

So the truth is he didn't fall in love either, he fell into Faith, which was onetime maybe the Champions League of Love until the sponsors pulled out and now it doesn't get coverage any more. It's still in poetry though. That's where you find faith. I'll get to that later.

Virgil Swain stayed and fished. He out-waited the length of time it took for Mary MacCarroll to defeat her doubts and start thinking that maybe he was The One. Maybe he wouldn't be going away.

The first time Dad stepped inside this house he had a salmon with him.

It wasn't as odd as it sounds. Mam had seen him catch it. She'd seen the non-catching first, the days he spent casting the line and catching a large amount of nothing so that in the village the story was Your Man had nothing on the end of his line, no bait (or hook according to Old Brouder), that he was escaped from somewhere, or was Simple, and was hoping the salmon would catch him.

Mam had seen him and knew he *was* fishing. She'd seen the way he went about it, the rhythmic rituals he had, the musclework of back and forearm, the interplay of rod and line, pulling and unreeling, that little freeing of shoulder he did before casting into what was above him. She'd seen the fishing going on for days, the actual vigil it was as he stood there, remarkable both for persistence and patience, and the sort of trancelike state it seemed you could get into when you were a man hooked into a river.

But she didn't know Virgil was trying to catch his father.

She didn't know that once he stood on the mucky bank at Shaughnessy's and the hook went into the water he had to plant his feet to stop the tide of regret pulling him in. He knew he was on the threshold of real life, that real life was just behind him up in our house and that here was an Impossible something he was going to

193

do. And now he was stricken by the urging of some kind of basic human need: he wanted to tell his father. He wanted to say *Dad* because he wasn't sure he'd ever actually said that to Abraham when he was alive. *Dad, I've found what I'm going to do. I'm going to do what you couldn't do. I'm going to make happiness. And I'm going to make it here.*

Abraham didn't reply. But maybe he looked down and saw the candles burning in his son's eyes because right then and there Virgil caught a salmon.

To you, Dear Reader, this may not seem a Major Plot Point. But to those of us versed in Swaindom, we know it was a blessing.

If you're like Mona Boyce, who has the narrowest nose in the parish and is permanently engaged in the science of hairsplitting, you'll say it was a sea trout. But I know it was a salmon.

Nan looked at him in the doorway. He was a jumble of angles. If he wasn't cradling the salmon his arms would be too long. His hair and face were wet and his eyes glossed with a dangerous amount of feeling. 'Mary!' she called over her shoulder, not taking her eyes from him. 'Mary!'

Mam had come in only moments before him. She'd seen him lift the fish in the sky and had come home running. She'd come in and gone to the blurry grey-speckled mirror in the bathroom and had a fight with her hair. She tousled it loose and it laughed at her, then she tied it up too tight and it felt like a hand had grabbed her from above and was pulling the top of her head off, then she released it again and patted it like it needed reassurance and if it got enough it would *sit just right, for just this once, please.*

'Mary!!'

When she came out Dad was still standing in the doorway with the salmon and Nan was still looking at him, like there was a language barrier, like between Swains and MacCarrolls there was this ocean, which of course was true because Swains were basically English and MacCarrolls Irish and I am the child of two languages and two religions, and the most male female and the oldest young person to boot.

'Hello,' she said. In my version she said it the Jane Austen way, like he was Captain Wentworth and they were in Lyme Regis and a covering of coolness was needed in case she just went over and grabbed him by the wet jacket and started kissing him, for although they'd Gone Walking, which was the first step on the road to intimacy, this was another step altogether, this was coming inside the house and meeting Nan.

'I caught one.'

'At last,' she said.

He looked at her, but he didn't move.

The thing that was moving was Nan's mind. She was flicking the pages fast, like when you read every third paragraph to try and get ahead of the story. Nan stood looking at the two of them looking at each other. 'I'll cook it, so,' she announced.

Sometimes when I'm lying here and the day outside is that warm mugginess we get in wet summertime, when you know the sun is shining somewhere high above the drizzle but all we have is this jungle-warm dampness thronged with midges, my mind goes a little García Márquez-meets-Finn MacCool and when Nan cooks the fish by the fire the whole house becomes imbued with salmonness and foreknowledge. The whole history of us fills the air.

Virgil is to sit at the table.

'Sit at that table,' Mary says. She's all business. She has that no-nonsense practicality of a countrywoman and in a flash she's back and across the kitchen with mugs, plates, cutlery. She's filling the milk jug from the larger jug, sawing into a loaf, plating slices, feeding turf to the fire, and at no time looking at Virgil Swain.

He sits. In Spencer Tracy's chair.

'That was my husband's chair,' Nan says, taking the head off the fish.

'I'm sorry.' He shoots up like he's been stung, stands in the perplex of the moment until Mary says, 'It's all right, go on, sit.'

'Are you sure?'

'Sit.'

'Will I take this . . . ?'

'Sit.'

He sits back down but on the very edge of the chair. His trouser legs are dark flags to his thighs, boots leaking the river, and down the slope of the floor run two little streams of his arrival in their lives.

'Not a bad fish,' Nan says, head-down and doing serious industry with the knife.

It is in fact an incredible fish. It's an Elizabeth Bishop fish and can be found in her *Collected Poems* (see Book 2,993), but Nan believes that praise is a forerunner of doom. The head and tail go in a pan with butter and salt. They spatter out the possibility of conversation. Then Mary carries them on a plate, calls 'Sibby Sibby Sibby' at the front door, and although I've never met a cat in Clare not called Sibby this one knows it's her and comes from where all day she sits on the roof of the henhouse watching the Hens Channel. Virgil can see Mary through the window. He watches the way her hair falls as she bends to the Sibby, her dress holding the line of her knee, her fingers playing on the cat's head and confusing it into choosing between two pleasures, wanting the caress and the salmon at the same time.

Mary comes back in. She doesn't look at Virgil as she passes. She has the air of having so much to do. The air of Feeding the Guest. It's a country thing. Maybe it's an Irish thing. The Welcome is more important than anything else. You can be dying, you can have no money in the bank, your heart can be breaking from any number of aches, but still you have to lay the Welcome. Feed the Guest. Tomatoes have to be sliced, lettuce run under the tap and dabbed dry, three leaves on a plate. A scallion. Are there boiled eggs? There are. Bread, butter, salt. Whatever is happening in your life is of no consequence when you have to do the Welcome.

'You sit,' Nan says to Mary. She isn't used to being Cupid. This is her first and only go and she's that bit rough.

'I'll get napkins.'

Nan gives her the look that says *Napkins?* which is in subtitles only MacCarrolls can read.

Do they have napkins?

They do. They are paper Christmas ones. Mary puts one on each plate. Then she turns and presses her hands together and looks at the kitchen like there must be something more she could bring to the table. 'You want something to drink,' she says. It's not a question. 'We have Smithwick's.' She looks to Nan. 'Don't we?'

'There's a bottle of Guinness.'

'Smithwick's or Guinness?'

Her face turned to him makes his answer choke at the base of his throat. 'Actually . . . just water would be fine.'

That's when Nan turns. That's when she knows this is a story she hasn't read before.

'Just . . . water. If . . .' The words are trapped somewhere.

Both of the women look at him. What is he going to say? *If you have any?*

'I don't drink.' He lends it the tone of apology. 'When I was at sea there were many . . .' That's all he says. That's the whole story. He lets the rest of it tell itself. There's a moment of stillness while that story passes. Fighting the salmon-head Sibby makes the plate rattle on the flagstone outside. 'Just water would be lovely.'

197

'Water,' Nan says to her daughter and turns back to tinfoiling the salmon.

Mary fills the big white jug with the blue bands on it. She fills it too full and lands it with a topspill on the table in front of him.

'Lovely,' he says. 'Thank you.' He doesn't just mean the water. There is this thing about him then, this quality that I imagined when I sat in lectures on Edmund Spenser or Thomas Wyatt, an old-world gentlemanly chivalry and courtesy about Virgil Swain, as if everything that comes to him in those moments is so unexpected and marvellous that what he feels is grace.

'You sit now,' Nan says, still not quite managing the Cupid.

And because once the table is set and there's absolutely nothing left in the press that can possibly be put out – cold-slaw, Colman's mustard, pepper, ketchup – the next bit of The Welcome is to sit and ask *How do you like it here?*; Mary pushes her palms twice down her dress, jabs her fingers into her hair, gives up, crosses the kitchen, sharply pulls back the chair opposite him, and asks, 'So, how do you like it here?'

'Very much.'

'Good.'

That exhausts the dialogue. She realises she hasn't folded the napkins and takes hers and begins to press it in halves. Virgil does the same. Both of them are useless at it. Maybe evenness is a thing intolerable to love. Maybe there's some law, I don't know. She lines up the halves of hers, runs her forefinger down the crease. When she picks it up the thing is crooked. So is his. She undoes the fold and goes at it again, but the napkin wants to fall into that same line again and does so to spite her, and does so to spite him, or to occupy both with conundrums, or to say in the whimsical language of love that the way ahead will not be a straight line.

She doesn't give up, and he doesn't give up. And in that is the whole story, for those who read Napkin.

Mary and Virgil are sitting by the set table at the river window, Nan's folded *Clare Champion* is on the sill, and at the fold there's this ad saying *The Inis Cathaigh Hotel for Weddings*, so maybe Nan has more of sly Cupid in her than she is given credit for. They sit and look out at the all-knowing river rushing past and the Sacred Heart light is burning red overhead and the smell of the salmon rises and takes the place of conversation.

It's not a fish smell like Lacey's where since Tommy lost the job they only eat mackerel and out-of-date Lidl bread, or the Creegans, who since the buildings stopped live off river eels, and like the Zulus Dickens saw in Hyde Park and said were fair odoriferous; it's this warm pink insinuation into the air. It's lovely and gentle and penetrating and smells of the supernatural. To my mind that cooking salmon is pretty much the Swain version of the Thurible, and Nan has become the Thurifier, pokering the turf into life, turning the fish, peeling back the foil to check the progress, reveal-ing the pink flesh and releasing a great waft of the impossible.

And I think right then Virgil looks at her. He looks across the table and when she feels him looking she flushes pink and warm and keeps her eyes on the river outside. She's looking at the river and he's looking at her looking at the river and there's no way back for him now. This is his life right here, the salmon is telling him. This is it, the salmon says, and because the salmon is knowledge and knows everything Virgil knows it's true. The air itself is changed, and what seemed impossible, that he might stop travel-ling and stop seeking a better world somewhere else, is suddenly not only possible but inevitable and here, in this woman's face, it begins.

'That's done now,' Nan says, licking the burn on her finger, and ferrying the fish to the table.

5

You can't really imagine your parents kissing. I can't anyway.

You can't imagine your own origin, the way you can't imagine the beginning of the world. Not everything can be explained, is a standard Swainism. You just can't imagine the consequences that led to you, or imagine those consequences not happening. You can't imagine the world without you because once you do everything else takes on this kind of temporary sheen like breath blown on a window. I know I shouldn't even be thinking of this, but maybe it's because like Oliver in Chapter the First of *Oliver Twist* I am unequally poised between this world and the next. That's my excuse anyway. You can't imagine your own origin. It's like this mysterious source or spring somewhere. You know it happened; that's all.

Mam and Dad married in St Peter's Church, Faha, and had a dinner after in the Inis Cathaigh Hotel, Kilrush. The Aunts were the only guests of the groom, and all of Faha came for the MacCarrolls, filling the Bride's Side pews to bursting and giving the church the perspective of tilting to starboard. Though Mam didn't know it yet, their wedding day was my father's first time in a church since his own christening. He had never been confirmed, but Father Mooney, not a big believer in paperwork, a lover of roast beef, and in his last year before retiring into the saintly surrounds of Killaloe, supposed the certificate was on its way in the post and went full steam ahead.

It was a noted wedding in the parish memory. I think it was because Dad was still that DC Comics figure, The Stranger, and because none of the men in the parish could believe that Mam hadn't chosen one of them. Long before the Consecration, before the head-bowing part when the Bride and Groom are up there kneeling together and there's this sense of Something Big happening, men's hearts were already breaking. Bits of longing and dreams were cracking off and sliding away the way Feeney's field did into the sea. Father Mooney must have felt it, this giant ache that filled his church. In the Men's Aisle there were some with prayerhands clasped knuckle-white, cheeks streaked with high-colouring, thin nets of violet, and their Atlantic blue eyes boring down into the red-and-black tiles hoping for an Intercession. When it didn't come they did what men here do and by midnight had emptied the bar at the Inis Cathaigh and the emergency crates and barrels that were brought up from Crotty's.

Mam didn't care. She was only thinking *here is my life*, here it was beginning, and although she had only heard the vaguest bits of the Swain story, only knew a few paragraphs of different chapters, she didn't mind. When she was a girl, Mam had some wildness in her. She had a bit of the Anna Karenina thing, not in the Other Man sense but in the way Anna longed for life with a capital L. I've read *Anna Karenina* (Book 1,970, Penguin, London) cover to cover twice, and both times couldn't help thinking that in that largeness of heart, that capacity for feeling and desire and passion, there's some kind of holiness. I'm with Anna. She's the greatest woman character ever created and the one I most wish would come up the stairs and sit by the bed and tell me what to do with Vincent Cunningham.

Mam took a leap. That's the thing. She took a leap with a man who had no employment or apparent friends, whose sisters were strange gazelles in long wool coats with fierce buttons, a man whose mystery was encapsulated in the phrase *Away at Sea*, who had come back for no reason other than to find her. She couldn't possibly *know* she would be happy with Virgil Swain, not really. But she was the daughter of Spencer Tracy, and there was something in him she trusted. She couldn't have explained it. It was a mystery. But she believed in it. It's that MacCarroll thing, Tommy says, belief in mystery. It's well known. He married his Maureen because they ran out of crisps in Cusack Park and she had a bag.

The honeymoon was one night in Galway.

When they came back Nan had prepared The Room. Dad moved in with the baffled deepsea shyness of a character just arriving in a story already underway. He had the awkwardness of an alien. It was his first home, but it wasn't his. Like Mr Lowther in *The Prime of Miss Jean Brodie* (Book 1,980, Penguin Classics, London) he'd never be quite at home in his own home. There were MacCarrolls in the stones, MacCarrolls in the rafters, MacCarrolls up the chimney. And then there was Nan.

In those first weeks he had to sail around her. The kitchen was hers. She was already in it when he woke. She was still in it when they went down to bed in the evening. The first sounds of morning were the leaden thump of the bread dough.

'Morning, Bridget.'

He sounded like an American to her. She took a puff on her cigarette. 'Morning.' She couldn't get around his name yet.

He had to stoop to look out the deep-sill window. 'Not raining,' he said.

'Yet.'

'Would you like tea?'

'I've had tea.'

'I'm going to make some for Mary.'

Thump. She flipped the dough on its back, knuckled its swollen belly, picked up the cigarette and gave it another puff. Because she hated the sight of butts, because she associated them with the men with Italian accents who always got shot first in the black-and-white movies, Nan had already developed the ability to smoke cigarettes entire without losing a fragment of ash. After the first few goes she smoked *upwards*, turning her head sideways and in under the cigarette chimney-style so the little tower of ash balanced off her hand and never fell.

Virgil moved the kettle from the side of the range on to the hot plate, and stood, heating his hands that didn't need heating, his eyes travelling the shelves, the walls, the dresser, taking in everything, the small silver trophy one of Grandfather's greyhounds won an age ago in Galway, the little stack of Memoriam Cards standing face out with the memory of the latest Late, the plastic Infant of Prague, the twist of brown paper holding unused carrot seeds from Chambers's in Kilrush, the Sacred Mission Fathers calendar with the one picture of black African children, the Saint Martin de Porres one that was never used with a picture of Peruvians and permanent January, the ESB bill standing upwards in a mug so as not to be forgotten, the three white porcelain eggcups with miniature hunting scenes that were a gift from Peggy Nottingham and were never used for eggs but hoarded thumbtacks and sometimes hairclips and two spare red Christmas lightbulbs, a whole history of things that made Our House.

Everything was already in place; that was the thing. If he opened a drawer in the dresser he'd find it crammed with what appeared to be rubbish – dried-out Crayola markers, worn-down stubby pencils, tangles of string, rubber bands, playing cards with the Seven of Diamonds and the Three of Spades missing, a single red battery, a round flat box of hard sweets long stuck together, a golfball, a tiny screwdriver that came in a Christmas Cracker, matchbooks, a yoyo, a mouth organ – things unremarkable except in the aftermath of death when they take on themselves a portion of haunting.

Where would he fit in this house?

The kettle began to boil. 'Are you sure you won't have tea?'

'That's not boiled. Leave it boil a while.' She didn't look up. The dough was surrendering. 'What are you intending to do?'

'To do?'

'Here. For a living.' With full forearm force, bang!, she flung the dough down on to the floury table.

'Well, there's the land,' Virgil said.

'The land is bad. You're not a farmer.'

'I could learn.'

The kettle was at full steam now, an urgent plume racing to ten o'clock, but he didn't lift it.

'Do you know anything else?' She didn't look up. She gave the kneading the thumbs.

What did he know?

He knew Ahab, he knew Mr Tulkinghorn, he knew Quentin Compson and Sebastian Flyte and Elizabeth Bennet and Emma Bovary and Alyosha Karamazov, he knew Latin Declensions and French Verbs, Hernán Cortés, Euclid, Knots, the Capitals of the World, how to parse a sentence, how to live on tinned food and powdered milk, he knew what the sun looked like in the evening-time in December off Punta Arenas, how the wind off Cape Town carried the scent of sage in spring, he knew tides and tempests, he knew there was an island in Cuba called La Isla de la Juventud that bore exact resemblance to the geography of RLS's Treasure Island, but Virgil Swain did not know anything he could do in the County Clare.

Nan worked the dough into a rough circle, and then with the base of her hand chopped a cross into the top. 'The land it will have to be then,' she said. She rubbed her hands together, balling crumbs she slapped off her palms. 'I'll have tea, so.' She drew on the last of the cigarette, turned on the tap and doused the ash, looked out the window at the haggard and the haybarn with the three panels hanging loose. 'If you're making it.'

Irish people hate to lose face. That's Number One dictum. That's why the Bust was what Kevin Connors called an unholy show, and why the whole nation was *mortified* at the carry-on of the bankers and developers. Not so much because it happened, but because everyone in the world now *knew* that it had happened and we were once again Those Irish. We'll bear anything in the privacy of our own homes, as long as the world doesn't have to know.

How Public, like a frog, is dear Emily's version (Book 2,500, Emily Dickinson, *Complete Poems*, Faber & Faber, London).

So, right then and there, Nan decided that if Virgil Swain was going to be a farmer he wasn't going to be one that people would laugh at.

She opened the kitchen door, shouted, 'Mary, come get your tea!' and told Virgil, 'Come with me.'

They went out on the acres, Nan in cuff-down wellies and hooded green army coat, Virgil in a too-long woollen jumper under the leather jacket and the low fishing boots that were already drinking mud before they crossed the Fort Field. They went in sinking Suck Mode, each step announcing itself, a kind of spluck-splosh procession that scattered the blackbirds back up into the rain and down into the next field, Nan travelling faster because she knew how to do the swaying-hip swing, dip and recover that people here know is how you walk these wet river fields, which means you don't step down you sort of roll across them, which is great for waterland walking but maybe the reason the parish is Number One in Clare for hip replacements. She spoke curtly as she went. 'The drain on the western corner needs clearing every month.' It looked like it hadn't been cleared in years. 'A wet spring and you can't travel this field till August.' It had several silver ponds in it. 'This is The Big Meadow.' 'This is the Small Meadow. My husband cut it by hand.' She took him across every inch of the land in which we grew muck puddles, rushes and occasional grass. He didn't say anything. They climbed the wall into Lower Meadow, because the gate was no longer attached to the pier, was tied with twine and looped with crazy brambles. He offered her his hand but she didn't take it, stepped in front of him and crossed with goat nimbleness, turned to look back when she heard the clatter of falling stones as he came after. In the Bog Meadow she showed him the four cows. She called 'Hup!' to them on the top of the stile, maybe to alert them that here was the new farmer, to have them do that whole-body-shiver thing horses do and present their best profiles. But whether from the mesmerism of the rain, the dullness of having several stomachs full of twisted mulch or the fact they were wearing brown-stockings of mud to their hocks, the cows were in cow stupor and didn't move. 'That's our stock,' Nan said.

Virgil looked at them. He had no clue what to say. The rain that was not called rain was falling on both of them. The river was running the way it is always running to get away and there was a little edgy breeze coming across from McInerney's to remind you the back of your neck was wet. 'Beautiful,' he said.

Now that was not what Nan expected. She had no answer for that. She looked at him.

But Virgil was already away in the Philosophy of Impossible Standard. In a way, it helped that the land was as bad as it was. It meant that here he would not only have to Out-Wiltshire Wiltshire he would also have to Out-Ashcroft Ashcroft. So the effect was not to discourage him, it was the contrary. I may be the only one who thinks that here in Muck-and-Drizzle land is the least-like-paradise place there is in the whole country, but even so you'd have to say it was going to take dreaming.

'That's all of it,' Nan said, with the kind of low voice people use at the end of a long confession when everything terrible has been told. 'We'll go back so. Mary will be up.'

'I'll stay here. I'll be back in a while.'

'There's no need.'

'I know. But I'd like to.'

His eyes were dangerous. That's what Nan must have thought. They had that look that told you they were seeing more than you were.

'If you're sure.' She didn't look at his eyes.

'I'm sure.'

'Right so.'

She hip-swung her way back across the fields. When she came in to the questions in her daughter's expression in the kitchen, she said, 'He wants to stay out.' And in a single moment the two of them shared a look that said those things in silent mother-daughter language that would take a hundred books and more years to tell.

After the hens and the ware and the ashes and the peeling, Mary went out to find him. She was afraid his heart was cracked. She was afraid the reality of the place would have overwhelmed him, that she'd find him under a dripping hedgerow in a distant corner ready to announce they couldn't make a life there. Then she saw him. He was on the far edge of the Bog Meadow inside a silver nimbus.

It was a trick of the light. Wanting to make his first impression on that landscape he had come upon a length of barbed wire buried in the grass. He'd started to pull it up and found that time and nature had firm holds. But he'd persisted in the way only my father could. The hopeless was his domain. He just kept at it. Barbs bloodied his fingers. One tore a long meandering scar on the back of his hand that years later Aeney and I said was like a river and my father said which river and we said the River Virgil. At last the grass made a resentful ripping and surrendered the wire. He'd worked his way along it then, finding the forgotten bounds, lifting the rotted sticks that were once the fence posts. But as he did, the wire freed from tension began to coil and tangle behind him. It was the way God played with my father. Even a small success was mercilessly pursued by failure. He'd gone back to try and straighten out the wire and by the time my mother saw him he was standing *inside* it, the coil shimmering glints in the rainlight and my father this soaked figure laughing in the trap of the practical.

I think she knew then he wasn't giving up.

'You look drowned,' she said.

That evening Virgil went out after dinner to check on the cows. That, he knew, was an important part of farming. Just before darkness, Check on the Cows. If you're getting some idea of my father you'll already know he had no idea what to check for except their actual presence. If they were standing he pretty much thought they were okay. If they were lying down he'd Hup! a few times to get them to stand and then walk away, leaving the same ladies wondering why they were gotten up and wearing the cow expression of People are Puzzling. That first evening, while Mam and Nan did the dishes, he went across the fields. Darkness was falling. He was used to sea-dark which is darker than any. What he wasn't used to was the sense of things flying invisibly above him. He had the impression the air was full of nightblack cloths, shreds, rags, falling out of the heavens. But not landing. With impossible swiftness one swooped, arced, vanished, and another came. He ducked, raised his hand over his head, and then realised the air was thronged with bats.

I know them. I've seen their grandchildren. They go home into this tiny hole in the angle of the eaves at McInerney's. More come out than go in, which has always been true of McInerney's house. I've grown up in the country, bats don't frighten me. But Virgil's blood was chilled, as if bats were a portent, as if he was being reminded right then paradise isn't going to be easy, there's darkness in the world, and instead of coming back across the field he clambered out over the crooked gate on to McInerney's road.

The gravel underfoot was helpful. The bats didn't overfly the road. He walked between the high shoulders of the wild fuchsia.

Then he saw the torches.

In the wide deep dark we have in Faha a single torch can be seen a long way. These were dozens. They were a lighted river, winding out from the village, thinning in places, thickening in others, but all coming towards our house.

Virgil's first thought was guilt. Father Tipp says the two signs of saints are guilt for no reason and being caught in a constant tide of undeserving. I think my father thought he deserved what was coming. I think he knew he had taken the most beautiful girl in the parish and so his first thought was *They are coming for me.*

He'd been away, remember. He'd been on the sea with his imagination a long time, and in that imagination this was the kind of thing that happened in William Faulkner, they came with torches. They let their disapproval out in fire. They were going to come and burn down our house.

But this was not a few men.

This was everyone. The whole parish was on its way.

He stood in the road. That's the thing that gets me in this story. That's the thing that surprises me when I force Tommy Devlin to tell it. Virgil just stood in the road. He didn't come running to tell Mam and Nan, didn't rush in, bolt the door, push the table up against it cowboy-style and say *Injuns*. He stood in the road and waited and that river of lights kept coming.

When the river turned the corner near Murphy's he saw it was not made of men. They were figures out of phantasm, Tommy says. He enjoys that word. *Phantasm*. Some had cone heads and misshapen bodies. Some had masks and were huge tall women with dresses that couldn't button over bosoms. Some were white and mountain-shaped, a sheet thrown over them, others in sacks and straw, their faces blackened. There was not a single recognisable human being.

When the river turned the corner near Murphy's it saw Virgil Swain.

And it stopped.

To stop a river that long is not easy, and so all the way back along it there was jostling and pushing and a great murmuring that rose and went along the length. The murmur didn't materialise into language proper. But there was a chorus of *shshshshshshshshshsh* and then Virgil was standing a hundred yards from our house face to face with a figure whose head was a wicker cone that rose to eight feet.

'Turn back,' my father said. He said it just the way Spencer Tracy would have, because, although outnumbered by three hundred and twenty-seven to one, he wasn't going to let them come burn down the house.

Coney shook his head. The river wouldn't turn back but wouldn't say why either. Cone Head didn't want to give himself away. That was the bit that made it difficult. He shook the cone more eloquently. The whole front row of cone-heads shook theirs. There was a whole lot of shaking going on.

'Turn back!' my father shouted out over the entire river, which was swelling and thickening now at the headwaters. Masked figures were pressing forward to see what was happening.

'Turn back. Go home!'

There was more head-shaking, gestures of confusion and refusal. But still none would speak.

And I suppose it might have remained a stand-off but for Mam calling 'Virgil!' in this hard whisper behind him. 'Virgil!' He turned to look back at her and she was waving frantically for him to come to her. 'They're our *bacochs*,' she said. 'Straw Boys. They're here to celebrate our wedding.'

Virgil looked at the river that was made of the men and women of the entire parish in what varied ingenious and bizarre disguises they could manage, and he saw that some were carrying not weapons but fiddles and bodhráns and he took a step backwards, and then another, and Mary put her hands over her mouth to hold the laughter but it was giggling up in her eyes and she took his hand and they ran the last of the way back along the road and in the gate and were in the house just moments before the river poured in after them.

6

Are you there?

Days like this when I wake and feel more tired than I did when I went to sleep I can't quite believe in you.

Dear Reader, are you a figment?

It's hard to live on hope. Living on hope you get thin and tired. Hope pares you away from the inside. You're all the time living in the future. In the future things will be better, you hope, and you'll feel better and you won't wake up feeling like someone has been taking the life out of you drip by drip while you slept. The whole country is living in the future now. We're in this Terrible Time but in the future we'll be all right again. We just have to keep hoping. But Moira Colpoys got first-class honours in her Social Science degree and Mrs Quinty says she sent out a hundred CVs in Dublin, every and any kind of job, got only one reply and when she went to the interview there were three hundred people and two hundred of them had been working for ten years and so yesterday Mr and Mrs Colpoys took her to Shannon and by now she's arriving in Perth and tomorrow she'll start looking to find the Davorens who she doesn't really know but they're from the parish and went out there last year and got a start in a tyre factory. The Colpoys are both in their sixties and she's their only. Mrs Quinty says when Mr and Mrs Colpoys stopped into Maguire's for petrol and milk on the way back they looked ten years older. They're just going to hope things improve, Mrs Quinty says. They have that big damp old house they rattle around in, the one that looks like a tall grey shell and was my first model for Miss Havisham's Satis House and has already been robbed twice since the Bust, and in there they'll be, wearing three pairs of socks and sitting close to the fire, and hoping.

To have hope you have to have faith. That's the crazy bit. You have to believe things *could* get better. You have no idea how exactly, but somehow. It's a blindness thing, faith. But I seem to see too much. I lie here in the boat-bed when I wake up. I'm supposed to call Mam right away so she'll come and pull open the curtains and use her best cheery voice to banish any gloom, but some days I don't. I wake and feel the exhaustion of morning. I wonder where I go from here, and how any going could possibly happen, and look across the room at all the books and I wonder if maybe I am doing what I set out to do, if maybe I am finding my father.

I look *grey*. I actually do. Mirrors should be banned, the same way Uncle Noelie banned the News. Both are enemies of hope. Uncle Noelie said he couldn't take listening to the wall-to-wall Doom experts who were the Boom experts before, most of them like a dark neighbour secretly delighted to be part of an important funeral, and so, because the time called for extreme tactics and because your heart has to be sustained by something, he switched over to Lyric FM for Marty in the Morning and shook hands with Mozart. But you can't switch off the mirror, it's right there over the bathroom sink, it's hard to avoid, and in it I'm *grey*.

'Do I look grey?' I asked Vincent Cunningham.

'What?' He did that thing people do when they hope a question will go away. He did his Robert De Niro, which is to smack three invisible bits of lint off the knee of his trousers, and then examine his fingers closely and frown at what only he could see there. If, like Mr Pecksniff, he had a hat he would have looked inside it for an answer.

'Which word do you not understand? Grey? My face, does it look grey?'

'No. No. Of course not.'

'What colour would you say I look?'

'Normal colour.'

'That's ridiculous. Obviously I'm not, never have been, and never will be *normal*.'

'No but you know what I mean.'

'Under my eyes. Circles. What colour?'

'Normal.'

'Vincent.'

'Blue-ish.'

'Blue-ish grey?'

'Blue-ish pale.'

'Which is what people call grey.'

'If you don't feel well maybe you should go to hospital.'

There were so many reasons why that was ridiculous I didn't even begin. In the county hospital the Winter Vomiting Bug had arrived, the Autumn Vomiting Bug having presumably departed for Africa, greyness was not a condition with swift remedy, as my eating any amount of beef, lentils, beans, spinach, and double doses of Hi-Dose Iron tablets could already testify, and the fact that my insides at this point were a magical swings-and-slides play-ground for Pfizer, Roche, GlaxoSmithKline, and the Star Trek-sounding folks at AstraZeneca, meant that I gave this sugges-tion only My Look.

'Just admit it. I look grey.'

'You do.'

'Thank you.'

'You're welcome.'

I got less satisfaction than I had hoped. 'My hair is like old straw.'

'Ah, Ruth, no it's . . . Yes, yes it is.'

'Thank you.'

If you're feeling hopeless you want someone else to feel hopeless too. That's one of the better contradictions in human nature. But Vincent Cunningham has one of those cork hearts that keep bobbing up when you try and push it under.

'I'll wash it,' he said.

'What?'

'Come on. I'll wash your hair.'

'Fly around the room first why don't you?'

'Come on, it'll make you feel better.'

'I'm not letting you wash my hair.'

He was already heading to the bathroom. 'I'll get the water ready.'

'Vincent! Vincent?' I could hear the taps running. It takes a while to get the hot water up here. My father put in the bathroom using a second-hand *Reader's Digest Guide for Homeowners* (Book 1,981, Reader's Digest, New York) he got from Spellissey's in Ennis. The bathroom proved an arduous task, the book's spine is broken on the water-warped pages showing Basic Home Plumbing and it appears that either my father or the original owner near-drowned the book in the attempt. You turn on the tap and nothing happens. When I was younger I used to imagine the water had to come from the river, and didn't mind waiting because of the engineering miracle my father had worked. At first nothing happens; you turn the tap full on, and it's as if you are being tested in a prime belief, that water will in fact come, and once you believe that you can actually hear this tiny suspiration escaping the spout which affirms your belief that soon the air will become water if you can just put up with standing in the cold a bit longer. The water runs cold for ages. It runs cold until you get to the place where you're thinking *there is no hot* and then begins a knocking out of *Macbeth*. It's somewhere in the house, but no one's sure where. The knocking becomes a clacking behind the wainscoting and the pipes sound the way arthritis must feel, an achy resistance to fluidity, but at last you know your belief has paid off and the hot comes with a series of airy belches and a sudden splashy gulp of triumph.

Vincent came in carrying the bath towel. 'Right,' he said.

'Right what?'

'You'll feel better.'

'Gone insane, is that it?'

'Yep,' he said, hedge-hair high and mad eyelashes batting as he began to pull back the duvet. 'Come on.'

'Listen, Vidal, it's not that I don't appreciate . . .'

He'd already got his arm around my back and under me. He was already finding out that I was lighter than he had imagined, that I had such little *substance* that for a moment he must have thought his arm had passed through me, that he had dreamt me, except if he had he probably wouldn't have dreamt the grey skin or the straw hair or quite possibly the attitude. He held me up. I held on to him. 'You're mad,' I think I said. I was too surprised for long sentences.

He had the wooden chair backwards against the sink, a towel double-folded as a neck support. The water was steaming.

'Here.'

'You'll scald me.'

He seated me gently then lifted his arm away, pausing just a moment to see that I was still sitting there. Shoving up his sleeves, he turned to the sink.

216

'Vincent.' I had my back to him.

'I know.' He dipped his elbow.

'No but . . .'

'Now.' He took my hair. 'Lay back.'

'Have you ever . . . ?'

'Ruth, lay back.'

I put my head on the support. And now my hair was in the water. His hands were drawing the water to it, treating it the way they might treat the golden hair in a fairy tale. Then he was cupping and letting the water flow on to my head and dipping his hands and cupping again and letting flow again, in what was somehow now the most ancient and natural rhythm in the world, the flowing of water over a head. And I was leaning back and my eyes were looking up at him, but he was looking only at my hair and the job he was doing, and he had that look you see in boys and men when they are engaged in a task grave and intricate and vital. His fingers moved the shampoo through my hair. My head was a comforting hardness, I knew, a bone at last of substance, and he worked a foam against it, and then smoothed the length of my hair, sometimes letting the hair move between both his palms, sometimes one hand laying the soap and the second pooling water over it. It came over my brow and he apologised and I said it was all right but with a kind of supreme gentleness he dabbed my eyes with the towel end and then returned to the washing with the same intensely focused tenderness. By now there was nothing I could say. I lay there in the towel while he changed the water. Then he began the rinsing. Water did not feel like water. It felt like a dream of water flowing over me and I closed my eyes and felt Vincent's hands and the water and the flowing and a kind of impossible sensation of freeing and pouring and cleansing, as if this was a baptism, simple and pure and fluent in grace, as if there were grounds for hope yet.

217

7

My father did not know how to drive. He had gone from the hothouse island of Ashcroft away to sea and bypassed the years when he should have learned. Mam knew how. She had learned in the big back meadow in her father's cabless Zetor when she was eleven, sitting on Spencer's lap, thrilling to the loud and bouncing propulsion across the open ground and the fact that you could go here, or there, or over there, just because you wanted. Mam drove the same way she walked, freestyle, also known as bumpily. She didn't really go in for right- and left-hand lanes, which was fine this side of Faha where the road is cart-wide and Mohawked with a raised rib of grass and when two cars meet there is no hope of passing, someone has to throw back a left arm and reverse to the nearest gap or gate, which Faha folks do brilliantly, flooring the accelerator and racing in soft zigzag to where they have just been, defeating time and space both and making a nonsense of past and present, here and there. As any student of Irish history ancient and recent will know, we are a nation of magnificent reversers.

In the lower cabin which was once the Original House of the MacCarrolls and then became the Cowhouse and then the Carhouse there was a pale blue Ford Cortina. In the early evenings after the farming and before the light died Mam took the key and drove them west along the rim of Clare. Both of them favoured edges. They liked to follow the Shannon seaward, see the end of land on their left, and where current and tide met in choppy brown confluence. Their destination was, like Ken Kesey's bus, Further. They went like escapees, Mam employing that driving style that was basically blind faith, speed and innocence, hurtling the car around bends, ignoring cracked wing mirrors, whipping of fuschia and sally, birds that shot up clamouring in their wake, hitting the brakes hard when they came around a corner into cows walking home.

I like to picture them, the blue Cortina coming along the green edge on Ordnance Survey Map 17, Shannon Estuary, one of many dog-eared and crinkled maps that for reasons obscure are all pressed between Dostoevsky's *The Idiot* (Book 1,958, Penguin Classics, London), David Henry Thoreau's *Walden* (Book 746, Oxford World Classics, Oxford) and Samuel Beckett's *Molloy* (Book 1,304, Grove Press, New York). On the map there are four different tones of blue for the river, High Water Mark, Low Water Mark, and 5 and 10 Fathoms. I've looked at it a long time, the way the green of the land seems to reach out, even off the edge of the page, so that the most western point, Loop Head, doesn't fit, and is in its own little box on the top. They go everywhere along the southern shore, different evenings to Labasheeda, Knock, Killimer, Cappa, into Kilrush and out again, to Moyasta and down left around Poulnasherry Bay, to Querrin and Doonaha, taking roads that end at a gate on the river, reversing, into Liscrona and Carrigaholt, down to Kilcreadaun Point where Virgil wants to go but the road won't let him, on again, summer evenings all the way down to Kilcloher for the view there, back up again, into Kilbaha, and finally, racing the sunset to get to the white light-house at the Head itself where the river is become the foaming sea. There is no further.

On those drives Virgil felt light, felt illumined. He'd look at Mary and his heart would float. That was the kind of love it was, the kind that radiates, that begins in the eyes of another but soon has got into everything, the kind that makes the world seem better, everything become just that bit more marvellous. Maybe it was because he'd been at sea so long; maybe it was because he was realising how lost he had been and that now here real life was beginning; maybe it was because he was feeling rescued.

Virgil sat in the passenger seat, his eyes on the fields, the ascent and arc of birds, the glassy glints of the river, the broadening sky.

And he *looked* at things.

I know that sounds ridiculous, but there's no other way to say it. My father could fall into a quiet, arms folded across himself, head turned, eyes so intently focused that you'd know, that's all. We would anyway. Strangers might see him and think *he's away in himself*, he's lost in some contemplation, so still and deep would he get, but in fact he was not away at all. He was *here* in a more profound way than I have the skill to capture. My father looked at things the way I sometimes imagine Adam must have. Like they were just created, an endless stream of astonishments, like he'd never seen just this quality of light falling on just this kind of landscape, never noticed just how the wind got caught in the brushes of the spruce, the pulse of the river. Raptures could be little or large, could come one after the other in a torrent, or singly and separated by long dullness. For him life was a constant drama of seeing and blindness, but, when seeing, the world would suddenly seem to him laden. *Charged* is the word I found in Mrs Quinty's class when we did Hopkins, and that's a better way to say that in those moments I think the world to him was probably a kind of heaven.

He'd see in quiet, and then would come the release.

'Here, stop. Here.'

Mary looks across at him.

'We have to go down here.'

She bumps the car on to the ditch. Parking is not in her skillset. Virgil is already out the door. 'Come on.'

She hurries after him. He reaches back and catches her hand. They cross a field, cattle coming slowly towards them as if drawn by a force.

'Look, there.'

The sinking sun has fringed the clouds. Rays fall, visible, stair-rods of light extending, as if from an upside-down protractor pressed against the sky. The river is momentarily golden.

It lasts seconds. No more.

'It's beautiful,' she says.

'We shouldn't miss these.'

'No. We shouldn't,' she says, looking at him and trying to decide for the hundredth time if his eyes are blue like the sky or blue like the sea.

I'm guessing Mam knew right away this wasn't a farmer. I'm guessing that if she wanted a farmer she could have chosen from a martful. But maybe she didn't know he was a poet.

He didn't know himself yet. He wasn't thinking of poetry yet.

Having devoted himself to seeing as much of the world as he could, my father now employed the same devotion here. He did exactly what his father would have done. He threw himself into the work on the land. Straight off he demonstrated that he had a genius for making nails go crooked; also an expertise in bending one prong of the fork, blunting hayknives and breaking the handles of spades. Things just went wrong for him. He went out to clean a drain in the back meadow, hacked at the grass till he could see and then clambered down into the rushy sludge.

I, you will already have deducted, am inexpert in farming matters, but I do know that in our farm stones were gifted at finding their way into the very places where no stones should be, weeds were inspired in their choice of Mam's flowerbeds, and black slugs the size of your fingers came from the river at night on the supposed invitation of our cabbages. Basically, at every moment our farm is trying to return to some former state where muck and rushes thrive. If you look away for one moment in summer your garden will be a jungle, one moment in winter it will be a lake. It's from my mother that I have the stories of my father's first attempts at farming. When I was younger and she told how hard it was I wondered if stones, weeds and slugs didn't fall from the sky, if there wasn't a sign on our door, or if the Reverend wasn't somewhere up there pacing Up-jut across the heavens, spying us below, saying *here, I'll send this. This will try him.*

Virgil stayed in the drain all day. He worked the spade blindly in the brown water, brought up slippery planes of muck he slathered on the bank so the stained grass along the meadow showed his progress. He thought nothing of spending an hour freeing a rock, two digging out the silted bottom. Why drains clog at all I am not sure. Why when the whole thing has been dug out and the water is flowing it just doesn't stay that way I can't say. I don't know if it happens everywhere, if something there is that doesn't love a drain — *thank you, Robert Frost* — or if Faha is a Special Case, if in fact it's a Chosen Place where God is doing a sludge experiment he couldn't do in Israel.

When the handle of the spade snapped he worked using just the head, rolling his sleeves but dipping beyond that depth, the rain coming in after a long time at sea and letting itself down on the back of the man stooped below the ground. The cows gathered and watched. In the late afternoon Mam came out in one of the oversized ESB all-weather coats everyone in Faha procured when they started building the power station and she told him he'd done enough for today. Down in the ditch he straightened into a dozen aches, his hair aboriginal with mud, face inexpertly painted with ditch-splash, eyes mascara'd. By rain and drain his clothes were soaked through.

'Virgil, come in home.'

He smiled. That's what he did, he smiled.

It was a rapture thing. But also, Swains are extremists.

Just like saints. And mad people.

'There's a bit more,' he said.

'You're drowned.'

'I'm fine.'

It was straight-down rain. It was washing his face. It was hopping off the shoulders of the ESB all-weather.

'Virgil.'

'I'll get this cleared. Then that'll be one job done.'

She looked down at him, her new husband, and looked back along the three-quarters of the drain that had been cleared but was not yet running. Dark patches of dug-out muck lay along the bank like a code, symbols in an obscure proving in mathematics that had progressed so far but was still short of conclusion, still short of anything being proven.

'Are you going to be impossible?' she asked. She knew the answer before he gave it.

Rain and ardour were glossing his eyes. 'I think so.'

She had to bite her lip to stop herself from smiling. She had that falling-off-the-world feeling she often got around him, a feeling that came swift and light and was so unlike the weight of the responsible that had come into the house after her father had died that it felt like wings inside her.

'All right so,' she said. And then she turned and walked back across the puddle-meadow, three luminous bands on the back of her coat catching the last light and making it look as if in her tiers of candles were lit.

There was no boiler or central heating in our house then. There was the range and the fire and large pots for hot water. When Virgil came in evening had fallen. Nan was gone to the Apostolics. He stooped in under the rain-song on the corrugated roof of the back kitchen smelling prehistoric. 'I freed it,' he said.

'Take off your clothes,' Mary said. To escape the compulsion to embrace him, she turned to the four pots she had steaming.

He saw the stand-in tub on the floor.

'Take off everything.'

When I read the white lily-scented paperback editions of D.H. Lawrence's *Sons and Lovers* and *The Rainbow* (Books 1,666 & 1,667, Penguin Classics, London) that's where I find them.

Mary dips and squeezes the sponge. Steam rises.

Virgil steps naked on to the flags of the floor.

8

Today when they carried me out into the ambulance Mam held my hand tight. I had my eyes closed. Timmy and Packy have got the hang of the stairs and the narrowness of the doors and there was no banging on jambs or jerkiness on the steps and when the rain touched my face I didn't panic, and I didn't open my eyes until I was strapped into that small space and we were moving. Then Mam dabbed my face two gentle dabs and took my hand in hers again, and I was glad of it, even though I'm not ten years old or even twelve. It's because people are so perishable. That's the thing. Because for everyone you meet there is a last moment, there will be a last moment when your hand slips from theirs, and everything ripples outwards from that, the last firmness of a hand in yours that every moment after becomes a little less firm until you look down at your own hand and try to imagine just what it felt like before their hand slipped away. And you cannot. You cannot feel them. And then you cannot quite see them, there's blurry bits, like you're looking through this watery haze, and you're fighting to see, you're fighting to hold on, but they are perishing right before your eyes, and right before your eyes they are becoming that bit more ghost.

We were in Tipperary before Mam took her hand from mine.

Because this was going to Dublin again, because this was The Consultant, Timmy and Packy went Extra Reverential, and because Timmy could see I was paler and thinner than last time and because he knew I was Book Girl he tried to leaven literature into the conversation.

'Ruth, tell me this. Wouldn't Ireland win the World Cup of Writing?'

'There is no World Cup of Writing,' Packy told him, and then, discovering a hair of doubt across his mind, turned back to me and asked, 'Is there?'

'I know there isn't,' Timmy said. 'But *if* there was, I'm saying. Do you know what the word IF is for?'

'You're some pigeon.'

'If is for when a thing is not *but if it was*. That's why you use If. If you didn't use if then the thing would be. That's the distinction.'

Packy's response was to put the wipers up to Intermittent Four.

'Most of life depends on If,' Timmy said, going deeper.

Maybe a mile of road went by and he resurfaced with: 'We'd have eleven World Class, wouldn't we, Ruth?'

'Living or dead?' Packy asked, and when Timmy threw a glare across at him Packy shrugged and said, 'What? I'm only saying. You need to know the rules.'

'With writers it makes no difference.'

'All right so,' he said and started trying to think of the poems he'd done in school.

Timmy reached across and put us back on Intermittent Three.

'Yeats is one anyway,' Packy said.

'Centre midfield,' Timmy said.

'That other one was a goalkeeper.'

'Who was that?'

'Your man, we did him for the Leaving.'

'Who?'

'The goalkeeper.' Packy looked ahead into the rain for him. 'Paddy Kavanagh.'

'Was he?'

'He was. I heard that once. Goalkeeper. Blind as a bat too. Who's centre forward?'

'Who do you think, Ruth?' Timmy's eyes were on mine in the mirror.

'Both sexes?' Packy asked.

'What?'

'Well if living or dead, then men or women, right?'

Timmy looked at him like a man who had just taken up golf, a wrinkle of perplexity across his brow.

'What about your one who won the prize? Who's she again?' Packy went fishing for the name.

The rain was coming fast, sitting a long time on the windscreen between wipes so we sped sightless then saw then were sightless inside the rain again.

'We'd have a good team all right,' Timmy said. His eyes were back on mine. I looked away. I hadn't the energy for conversation. I was feeling that kind of weakness you feel where you imagine there must be a valve open somewhere inside you. Somewhere you're leaking away. It's slow and silent but all the time something is flowing out of you, there's a lessening and a lightening and sometimes you get so tired you don't want to fight it, you just want to close your eyes and say *all right then, go on, flow away.*

'Enright!' Packy said. 'That's her.'

Timmy half-turned back to us, spoke through the sliding window. 'Did you read that one, Ruth?'

Mrs Quinty had given me *The Gathering*, partly because it had won a prize and partly because it was a Serious Book by a Woman, and she wanted to encourage me, she wanted to say See, Serious Girls Can Win, but she would be afraid to say anything so direct so the book had to do the saying as books often do. I loved it, but the publishers had put this staring boy in black-and-white on the front of the paperback with only his eyes in colour and they were a piercing blue that I just couldn't look at so I had to bend back the cover. Then when I got to page 71 where she writes about a man with an indelible watermark of failure I had to stop because of sinking.

'How's your own book coming, Ruth?' Timmy asked. 'Ruth wants to be a writer,' he told Packy.

I didn't want to be a writer, I wanted to be a reader, which is more rare. But one thing led to another.

I'm not writing a book, I'm writing a river, I wanted to say. It's flowing away.

'I think I need to sleep,' I said.

Mam stroked my brow. Three soft strokes. 'You go ahead,' she said. 'Close your eyes.'

'We'd beat the Brits anyway,' Packy said. Then, after a time, he added, 'Of course they'd have Shakespeare.'

And after another while: 'And Charles Dickens.'

And after another while: 'And Harry Potter.'

The Consultant says we need to take a more aggressive approach. He says the Stage of Monitoring is over. I will need to stay for an extended period. He prefers Dublin to Galway but the choice is ours. There will be two stages of treatment, remission induction therapy and post-remission therapy. I will need a venous access device, he says. Interferon-Alpha has to be injected daily. The side effects may be fevers, chills, muscle aches, bone pains, headaches, concentration lapses, fatigue, nausea and vomiting.

But he is very positive. Very.

We need to go home and prepare ourselves. He'll see me in a couple of weeks' time.

Then we'll start to turn back the tide on this thing, he says.

9

Astonishingly, after sex my mother did *not* become pregnant. She may have been the only woman in Ireland not to. At that time women got pregnant by wearing short skirts and high heels. High heels were notorious for it. Kilrush was virtually all high-heel shoe shops.

That first year the whole parish was waiting for Aeney and me to show up. The women in the Women's Aisle, convinced that the real reason Mary had married The Stranger was that she was already Expecting, were chancing sidelong glances during the Consent-creation as Margaret Crowe calls it to see if there was a curve like a river bend coming in my mother's wool coat. The men in the Men's Aisle were intentionally looking away, because men's dreams die with slow stubborn reluctance and denial is a strong suit in these parts; *She-isn't-married, she-isn't-married* running like a bass line in low hum into the candle vapours.

Aeney and I were still out at sea.

In the meantime my father's farming went poorly. Our cattle were unique in being able to eat grass and get thinner. They added to this a propensity for drowning. One drowned is bad luck, two is the devil himself, three is God.

But God (or in Freudian, Abraham) wasn't going to beat Virgil. My father took every setback as a trial, doubled the lines of wire, re-staked the fence, then made a double perimeter along the river when he came out one morning to see a whole portion of it, posts and wire both, had been pressed forward into the water. The

229

following night he camped out in the field. He sat hunkered in a greatcoat in the rain, peering through the dark for the ghost-shapes of the cattle, listening inside the running of the river for the approach of hooves. He would not be defeated. Not another beast would drown even if it meant he had to camp there every night. When at last he saw the bruise of dark upon dark that was a cow coming to the fence he stood and waved his arms wildly and hallooed. The cow jolted out of its cow-dream and looked at him like he was the one was mad.

'Back! Go on! Back! Hup! Hup!'

The old cow didn't move, so determined was she in drowning.

Virgil had not thought to bring a stick.

'Hup! Go on! Hup!'

Still she stood there, her eyes wilding a bit looking past him at the river and puzzling on why he was not letting her pass. She swung a half-step around to see if that would placate him.

It didn't. Virgil smacked his hand on her backside, 'Hup!', and in surprise she kicked out both hind legs, a not undainty lift and back-flick that caught him on the shin and buckled him. He was lying on the ground beside the wire before his brain had time to tell him she had broken his tibia.

The cow still had her backside to him. Now others of the herd approached through the dark.

Were they all come to drown? He grasped on to his shin with both hands, pressing, as if he could squeeze the parts together, but the pressure only shot the pain deeper. He roared out. And maybe because the cattle knew the sound of pain or because they had been distracted on their way into the river, or because cows can't keep two thoughts in their head at the same time, they stopped. They stood and watched him. After a while one of them got the idea there was maybe sweeter grass over in the far corner where she had been an hour earlier and where there certainly was not but she went anyway and the others in cow fashion followed and that night none drowned.

My father crawled back across the field. He banged on the back door because he could not stand to get the latch.

The following afternoon, when Virgil's leg was set and he was seated in two chairs inside the window, Jimmy Mac called in to see him. He listened to the full account of our cattle that were bent on drowning. Then he nodded slowly, scratched at the starter beard he always wore except on Sundays. 'It wouldn't be,' he said, 'because they're looking for water to drink, would it?'

My father told that story. Like all the stories he told it was against himself. He was never the hero, and from this I suppose we were to learn a kind of grace, if grace is the condition of bearing outrageous defeat.

One year he decided to put the Big Meadow in potatoes. I think that's how you say it, to put it in potatoes. The principle was simple. You bought the seed potatoes, you opened the drills, popped in the seeds, closed them again. For each seed you had bought there would be a minimum tenfold yield. Maybe twenty-fold if the year came good. Tommy Murphy had a Cork cousin with a harrow. The cousin had moved to Clare and was only just making the adjustment. He came and stood on the wall and looked over into the field. 'There'll be a few stones,' he said. 'They'll need picking.'

Turns out he had the Cork mastery of understatement. Who knew one field could harbour so many stones? If they were laid out end-on-end there would be no field. If you were of an Old Testament bent like Matthew Bailey you'd suppose the stones rained each night from the sky. Maybe they did. Or maybe every farmer in the parish had already dug out their stones years ago and dumped them in our fields when the MacCarrolls were wistfully watching the Atlantic and sucking seaweed. It turns out we had a world-class collection. There were top stones, mid-stones, deep stones. Then there were rocks.

Virgil gave his back to them. The skin of the tops of his fingers too, the joints of both thumbs, the exterior knuckles of both hands, the balls of his knees. He'd be out before the birds in the March morning, stamping heat into his wellingtons, letting himself out the back door, breath hawing, ear-tips freezing as he crossed up over the opened field to the top corner where he sank to his knees, having decided kneeling was a better method than bending. He scrabbled at the ground, picked out stones, tossed them towards the barrow, dawn rising to the hard mournful *clack clack* that startled the magpies until it became habitual and they came and took the worms that had risen without realising what the birds knew, that men opened ground in Spring and potatoes went in around St Patrick's Day.

What does a man think of when he's all day on his knees in a field beside the river? I have no idea. I suppose it would have occurred to some that maybe the field was unsuitable. But like me, in matters farming my father was an innocent, and so I'm guessing he just supposed this was what it meant to work the land. If you're a Latin reader, take a break here, have a read of Virgil's *Georgics*, written about 30 BC, and you'll see that Virgil had his troubles with farming too. But he didn't have our stones. On our farm there were always too many stones.

My father filled a barrow to the brim and shortly discovered he had invented a new ache, straightening. He went to hoist the barrow handles, and had a blinding insight out of Archimedes: stones were heavy, ground was soft. He couldn't push it. The wheel sank.

'Only the birds witnessed your father's ignominy,' he told us. 'Taking stones back out of the barrow again.'

Instead of the barrowing he decided to make mounds, conical clamps of stones at the edge of furrows. They are still there. The grass has overgrown them and so they make our back meadow look like an artist installation or a green sea with frozen wave caps rising. They are a monument to the Potato Years, I suppose. Mac's cattle use them as backside-scratchers.

Virgil devolved a Swain Method. Day after day he went along on his knees taking out the stones. Then he went along on his knees putting in the seed potatoes. His hands were like old maps. Every wrinkle and line had some of our field in it. When he had the seeds in, Murphy's cousin came back and covered them. The cousin stood on the wall after, my father a curved C-shape beside him. 'This place is nicely cursed with stones,' the cousin said in Corkish. He gave this insight air and time, then he threw a curt nod towards the now invisible potatoes and added the Pagan-Christian Superstition-Blessing combo we use here to cover all bases, 'Well, may they be lucky for ye. God bless 'em.'

God, it turns out, is not a big fan of potatoes in Ireland. It may be unfinished business between Him and Walter Raleigh. Maybe, like tobacco, the potatoes were never supposed to have been brought to this part of the world. Maybe God hadn't put them here in the first place because He knew what He was doing and they were supposed to stay in South America. They definitely weren't meant to come to this country. That much is clear. If you recall He'd already sent a pretty major message to that effect. Stop Living on Potatoes, Irish People, was the gist of it. Catch Fish was the follow-up, but it didn't take.

Still, two weeks before Easter my father's first potatoes had sprouted. Mary came to the back gate and looked out at her husband inspecting the ridges, and in the green shoots I'm guessing she saw a vindication. He was not mad, he was just a dreamer. Men are much bigger dreamers than women anyway. That's a given. Read *Nostromo* (Book 2,819, Joseph Conrad, Penguin Classics, London), read *Jude the Obscure* (Book 1,999, Thomas Hardy, Macmillan, London), read as far as my father and then I got to, page 286, Volume One, in Marcel Proust's *Remembrance of Things Past* (Book 2,016, Doubleday, New York), read the 1975 *Reader's Digest Condensed History of the World* (Book 1,955, Reader's Digest, New York), and tell me men aren't dreamers. But this was a good dream. Maybe it was the best dream, the original one, that a man and woman could live together on a piece of land beside the river, the dream that you could just be. Although every window-sill-sitter outside the post office had said MacCarroll's field wasn't suitable to grow five acres of potatoes, there the potatoes were. Mary entered the kitchen like a dancer. Her mother was knuckling dough. 'They're growing,' Mary said.

Nan knuckled the dough some more.

'They're growing,' she said again. 'The potatoes.'

'My bones are telling me I don't like the weather that's coming,' her mother answered, and slipped her mouth in under the ash tube.

It wasn't rain exactly. It was weather that descended like a cloud. It was there in Holy Week, a fog that was more than a fog and a mist that was more than a mist because it was dense like a fog and wet like a mist but was neither and was neither drizzle nor rain proper. It came between the land and the sky like a blindness. It just hung there, this mild wet grey veil through which the river ran and escaped. But the potato stalks relished it. Maybe because it was a kind of South American jungle weather, maybe because it was mythic like them, the potatoes flourished, rising quickly towards the promise of May. My father was out with his spade, mounding earth against the sides of them, thinking nothing of the weather that was sticking to him or the fact that for forty days the field hadn't seen the sun.

It was a triumph. Despite the weather the blossoms came. My father had a shining shook-foil dazzlement in him, that extra-ness of light or energy or just life which Aeney and I would come to know so well. Literally a kind of brilliance, I suppose. You saw it on him and in him. He had to find ways to let it out and he hadn't found the poetry yet.

It was another week before Virgil saw the blight.

The neighbours knew it before him. Maybe the whole country did. But nobody wanted to say. As Marty Keogh says, we can be fierce backward about coming forward. No one likes to be the bearer of bad news. Maybe they think that if no one picks it up and bears it then the bad news will rot away where it is, which Marty thinks not a bad thing and might have saved us from the Bust only for the fact that we were paying the lads on the radio to tell us we're doomed. In any case, the potato stalks started withering. Virgil went out one May morning, the drizzle cloying, the birds I suppose with diminished eloquence, and at last saw what was blatant. He didn't at first think it was blight. Although it was raining and had been raining and would continue to rain, he thought it looked more like drought. The green of the leaves was dulled as if from an absence of water. He took a leaf in his hand. It was in the softness of dying and curled instantly to a crêpe consistency. He stayed out in the field. He tramped up and down the ridges. He had not sprayed against blight because it simply had not occurred to him. Because he was in that innocent or ignorant state depending, where you believe God is good and hard work alone will bring reward.

The stalks blackened overnight. It turns out there was a given wisdom that potatoes beside rivers are doomed, and that wisdom

235

was aired generally now, only not in my father's company. He dug up a plant. Beneath it were potatoes smaller than stones. They were savagely acned. When he held one in his hand he could press his thumb through the pulpy heart.

He did not call the Murphy's cousin. He did not tell anyone but my mother, and that afternoon went out with the barrow and began singlehandedly to dig up the five acres of that failed crop. It took days. The cattle in the next field over watched as he mounded the stalks. The mounds smelled like disease. They had to be burned. But they would not. Twisted tubes of the *Clare Champion* flared and went out. He walked into the village and bought kerosene from Siney Nolan who sold it to him with grave lowered eyebrows and knew but did not say *What do you need that for?*

The following year he tried the potatoes again.

This time he sprayed.

This time there was no blight.

This time it was river worms that destroyed them.

Those potatoes were all right, Mam said, when she told it. Aeney and I were maybe ten. All of us were at the table. A large bowl of floury potatoes had summoned the story.

'The way I remember it, those potatoes were all right,' she said. She looked closely at one she held upright on her fork, 'If you cut around the worms.'

I screamed and Aeney ughed and Mam laughed and Dad smiled looking at her and letting the story heal.

'Mammy!'

'What?'

'Don't say that word,' I said.

'What word?'

'Worms worms worms,' Aeney said, scratching the table with the wriggling fingers of both hands, quoting but not exactly performing Hamlet.

'There's nothing wrong with . . .'

'Don't!'

'As long as you cut around them,' Mam said.

I screamed again and Aeney came at me with the worm fingers and slimed them gleefully along my neck. I scrunched my chin down which is, I know, pathetic Girl's Defence, Baby Edition, but all I could think of given that my brain was all *worms*. And he kept doing it, which in my experience is Typical Boy. Anyway, next thing, Dad had come with his two hands palm-to-palm like snappers and *whop!* He'd golloped up Aeney's worms. He kept them imprisoned in his snappers and Aeney yelled and Dad laughed and I was saved and in turn now laughed at Aeney captured in Dad's hands. Somehow the worm-ruined potatoes had become this happiness, somehow the years-ago hurt had transformed, and I think maybe I had a first sense then of the power of story, and realised that time had done what Time sometimes does to hardship, turn it into fairy tale.

10

And still we were not born.

Your narrator, you may already have grasped, is not gifted in matters chronological. Chronos, the God with the three heads who split the egg of the world into three even parts, and started the whole measuring-out business, never appealed to me.

Neither did the DC Comics version Vincent Cunningham says is right cool.

Aeney and I were not yet on the horizon of this world. Sometimes I like to think we were in another one, having just a wonderful time. I like to think not of The World to Come but of The World That Came Before, for which so far in Literature I have found no descriptions. There is something in Edward Joseph Martyn's peppermint and mothball-smelling *Morgante the Lesser* (Book 2,767, BiblioBazaar, South Carolina) but it's more a World Elsewhere really. When Mr Martyn wasn't helping W.B. Yeats found the Abbey Theatre he squeezed in a little time to do the bit of writing, and in this he describes the perfect world of Agathopolis. In Agathopolis Mass is attended every morning after everyone has a good thorough full-body wash. After Mass you sit around on grandstands and watch military reviews.

Unreal.

Here's a better one. Think of any of your favourite characters, and then picture them in the time before they entered the story. They existed somewhere, in a World Before. Hamlet as a small boy. (*Hamlet Begins* in the Warner Brothers version.)

Macbeth as a teenager. (Out of his pimples The Dark Prince Rises. Sorry, fecund.)

Anna Karenina in school. She probably had someone like Miss Jean Brodie in her prime for a teacher not Mrs Pratt who we had and who, like Miss Barbary in *Bleak House*, never smiled and because I was Plain Ruth Swain told me I shouldn't rule out the nuns, she herself who had a gawky face on her that Tommy Fitz proved by Google was identical to a Patagonian Toothfish.

In the World Before This One, Aeney and I were waiting. We knew there was longing for us. We wanted to come. But once we did we knew that time was going to start and that meant time was going to end too, so we hung out in distant seas a while longer. We didn't mean any harm. And anyway the story wasn't ready for us yet. There are precedents. It's ten chapters before Sam Weller appears in *The Pickwick Papers* (Book 124, Penguin Classics, London), nineteen before Sarah Gamp arrives in *Martin Chuzzlewit* (Book 800, Penguin Classics, London). But Mary and Virgil were losing hope of ever having children. My father was certain it was his fault. Thanks to the Reverend and thanks to Abraham he had the Swain genius for finding fault in himself. He came up short of the Standard in everything. What it was like to live with that inside you, what it meant to be subject to the constant duress of failing the Impossible, to aspire and fall, aspire and fall, to flick between the cathodes and anodes of rapture and despair, I can only imagine. I don't aspire. My hope has a small h. I hope to get to the end.

Because, first-off, Mary was a woman, and secondly because she was a MacCarroll, Mam took the news of being unpregnant stoically. She didn't go do-lally. She didn't drama-queen. Maybe she knew about the Late Arrivals thing, or maybe Mam just has more faith.

In the evenings after work Virgil would go out in a long buff-coloured coat he had brought back from somewhere in Chile, the one that was split deep up the back so you could ride vaquero-style, that had two tails that flew out and in a crosswind came up like wings. He walked miles along the riverbank. It was chance. It was a fluke of biology. That was all. Don't be stupid. There was no message, no meaning in it. It was not a Judgment.

But it felt like one.

To save my father from himself my mother took him dancing; Nan's set-dance addiction had gone down the bloodstream and transmogrified into Jive in Mam at which Virgil was hopeless but did anyway because it made her smile and he was addicted to that. His long frame sole-shuffling was not exactly dancing. Elbows crooked, arms out, he seemed to be doing The Coat-hanger. By living in Ashcroft with Mother Kittering he had missed out on that whole stage of development where bad clothes, peer pressure and pimples combine to teach you how to mimic the cool people. My dad literally had no clue. But Mam didn't mind. Everything about him was evidence of something special, when special was still a good word.

They went to plays in halls. They went to the Singing Club. They went to the Kilrush Operatic Society's production of *The Bohemian Girl* at the Mars Theatre, with Guest Artists (all of whom have sung at Covent Garden, the flyer says. It lies folded inside the yellowed dog-eared and generally dirt-smelling copy of John Seymour's *Complete Book of Self-Sufficiency*, Book 2,601, Corgi, London). One night they went to see Christy Moore who sang with shut eyes the Christie Hennessy song that became Virgil's favourite because in it was the line 'We'd love to go to Heaven, but we're always digging holes' which my father said summed up we Irish and was more profound than Plato.

Back then same as now the sea-salty village of Doonbeg had the best amateur-drama group, that parish was all theatre, and they went there to see John B. Keane's *Sive*, and afterwards my mother came out moved and upset. They went across the street into the graveyard and stood a time in the starless dark waiting for the sorrow to pass. She held her arms across herself and he wrapped his around her. They didn't speak about the play. They didn't talk out the upset the way they would if we moved the scene to America. My guess is that something in the play had caused her to think about having a daughter and that had led to thinking maybe it was true that they were not going to have children. When Mam gets upset she goes quiet. A whole battle goes on inside her, but unless you know her eyes you can't tell.

Dad knew. It was his fault. That's the default Swain position. The indelible watermark of failure. He wanted to apologise. But he wouldn't know where to begin. He held on to her. They stayed in the quiet of the graveyard as the hall emptied and the audience went to Tubridy's and Igoe's, they stayed long enough so the seagulls that slept inland there on the grave of the two Dunne boys that drowned in the Blue Pool had become accustomed to them.

Then Dad said, 'Come on.' He led Mam back to the car. Even though he didn't drive he was Keeper of the Keys, and this time he got in the driver's seat.

Reader, you'll think she said, 'But you can't drive.'

And he said, 'I've been practising,' or, 'It doesn't look too hard.' Or any better dialogue you'd care to add here.

But I don't think she said anything at all.

Then they were driving out of Doonbeg, Dad using that jerky pedal-down pedal-up technique he always had so the Cortina went down Church Street in spasms of hesitation, indicator flashing first left then right as he tried to find the windscreen wipers and at least see what they were going to crash into.

Maybe everybody got out of the way. I don't know. I can't drive. I can't imagine how you do it. How you go around bends without knowing if there is going to be somebody standing there, if there mightn't be someone who has fainted in the road like Mrs Phelan say, or that idiot boy of the Breegans who likes to stand in traffic. I can't imagine how I'd progress at all, how I'd ever have the confidence to just trust that it would be all right, that the unexpected wouldn't happen, because in fact that's all that does happen.

Virgil had no such problem. He drove leaning forward, hands at ten and two hooked over the steering wheel, mouth tight, eyes fixed on the illumined way. He went faster than he realised. He was not like the Nolan brothers who took corners at a hundred, did the Olympic Rings in doughnuts on the Ennis Road and whose driving skills were mostly testament to a childhood devoted to Pac-Man, and who, Thank the Bust, Kathleen Ryan says, are sharing their talents with the people of Australia now. But he was a wild driver. It was as if he was determined to race her away from the place where the sadness was, as if the Cortina were chariot and horses both and something grave was in pursuit. He drove the way the blind might drive, by faith, ignoring white lines, hurtling away from the Atlantic and heading south by zigzag, sweeping aside veil after veil of mist until they came out on the familiar, the dark slick waters of the estuary. Virgil drove the car up on to the ditch. For a moment he must have thought that would do to stop it. He didn't actually apply the brakes and the car bumped along aslant, two wheels up on the grass and Mam shouting 'Virgil!' And a louder 'VIRGIL!' (which certainly startled Publius Vergilius Maro in the Afterlife where I picture him in the sheet-toga Seamus Nolan wore when age eight he gave a sort of boxing interpretation

242

to who he called Punches Pilot in Faha N.S. production of The Nativity. Publius though had probably managed to gather some young lads around him and was telling them about the Trojan War, *again*, and stalled mid-dactylic a little proud because somebody from Faha down in Earthworld was calling his name). They went jouncing along the bank, the car whipping bits of hedge, dipping in hollows, rising on crests before Dad thumped what he discovered were the brakes and Mam screamed, was jolted forward, and Pop! smacked her head off the windscreen the way the doll figures do in the Road Safety ads.

Only her head didn't come off.

It was only a small *pop* probably. Because she just rubbed her forehead and blinked her eyes and Dad said, 'Jesus, I'm sorry.'

There were ten blank seconds maybe.

You only need to wait five.

'Mary?'

Mam looked across at him. She stared, wide-eyed. 'Have we stopped?' she asked.

She let him think he'd hurt her another ten seconds then she punched his arm. 'You're mad, you know that? Mad.'

'Starting and stopping are the hard bits,' Virgil said. And he smiled.

When my father smiled it was like he had unlocked the world. It was that huge. It made you want to smile too. It made you want to laugh and then it made you want to cry. It was in his eyes. I can't explain it really. There was this sense of something rising deep in him, and of *shine*.

Mam put her hands to her mouth and into them she laughed.

'Come on,' he said. He was already getting out of the car. In the movie version Mam'll say, 'Where are you going?' but the dialogue is edited out here. Here there is only his figure become white as he

243

takes off his jacket and leaves it on the driver's seat. He's out in the mizzling night rain. His shirt gleams. Across the field the river is black and slick. 'Come on.'

I know what the river is like at night. I know how it tongues the dark and swallows the rain and how it never ever sleeps. I know how it sings in its chains, how steadily it backstrokes into eternity, how if you stand beside it in the deeps of its throat it seems to be saying, saying, saying, only what you cannot tell.

'Come on.' He takes her hand.

And now they are running.

I know that field. Years ago I went there. It's rough and wildly sloping, hoof-pocked and rushy-bearded both. Running down it is bump and splash, is ankle-twist treachery. You get going and you can't stop. You're heading for the river. And you can't help but scream.

Mam screams. Virgil yells out. And they charge down the dark to the river. The bank is plashy from long river-licking. The muck is silvered and without footprints. It sucks on their shoes. Virgil stops and pulls off his. Then he's taking off his shirt.

'Virgil?'

Then he's taking off his trousers.

'You're not?'

The rain is already beaded on his hair. He looks up into the sky. Then he smiles at Mam, turns, goes three steps and dives into the Shannon.

She yells out.

He's gone. He's disappeared into the river. She looks at the place where he went in but it's moving, and quickly she loses the spot, tries to refind it but she can't. She imagines where he must be gone, the line the dive would have taken him, and she traces that as far as she can but it's lost in the seamless dark. 'Virgil?'

Nothing.

A rush of questions, like swimmers entered a sea-race at the same moment, splash-stroke in her mind. How long can you hold your breath underwater? How far can you go? Does a current take you? Is the Shannon deep? Are there river weeds? Malignant river-creatures? *Can he swim?*

She looks out into the nothing. Then for no reason she can explain she turns and looks at his shoes on the bank. Empty shoes are the strangest thing. Look at a pair of anyone's worn shoes. Look at the wear on them. Look at the scuffs and scratches. Look at the darkened heel-shine inside, where the weight of the world rubbed, the dent of the big toe, where the foot lifted. Tony Lynch who's the son of Lynch's Undertakers and who grew up a pall-bearer says putting the shoes on the corpse is the hardest part. The empty shoes of someone who's gone, there's a metaphysical poem in there. You don't believe me, look in Pablo Neruda's poem 'Tango del viudo' in the thin white *Selected Poems* (Book 1,111, Jonathan Cape, London) with the bookmark *Alberto Casares, libros antigos & modernos, suipacha 521, Buenos Aires* inside. '*Los mejores libros para los majors clientes*'.

Empty shoes. Weird, I know. But true.

Mam looks down at Dad's shoes on the bank, and that's when suddenly it hits her: *he's gone.*

Her heart flips over. *He's gone.*

My father is gone from this world and in the next moments my mother experiences the kind of dread foreknowledge widows in Latin American novels do, where black birds are sitting in the tops of trees and the wind rustles like black crêpe and smells like charcoal. He's gone. His story is over.

That's it.

The immense loneliness of the world after love falls upon my mother. She stands there. She can't speak, she can't shout out. She's just taking this ice-cold knowledge inside her.

Then, forty yards downriver, Virgil comes up through the surface. He yells.

It's not a yell of panic or fear but of joy, and at that moment my mother discovers that my father is a wonderful swimmer. He's learned in deep waters and distant places and not only has he no fear he makes fear seem illogical, as if water and current and tide are all graces and a man's movement within them natural as it is on earth. His stroke is unhurried. There is a kind of elemental delight in crossing the pull of the river, in feeling it, allowing it, resisting. He swims like he could swim for ever. I think he could. I think he can.

He comes back to her and holds his place in the water at her feet. 'Come in,' he says.

'I could kill you.'

It's not the reply he was hoping for. When I get around to writing it, it will not feature in *Chat-Up Lines for Girls who Don't Get Out Much*.

She's serious, and not serious. Her heart has not yet flipped back and she's in the deep waters of realising that if he was gone her life would be over, which in my book is basically substance essence and quintessence of Love.

'I'm sorry.'

She looks at him. He is naked. His upper body has the strange luminosity of flesh when most vulnerable. It's that pale tone the holy painters use, the one that makes you think what the sound of the word *flesh* does, that it's this thin-thin covering, *flesh*, and so easily it can be pierced.

'I can't swim,' Mam says.

'I'll teach you.'

'You will not.'

'It's not hard. Mary, take off your clothes.' He is floating below her, his arms doing a kind of backward circling I've seen him do so he's moving but not going anywhere.

'You're mad.'

'I'm not.'

'It's freezing. I'm freezing right here.'

'You get used to it. It's lovely. Come on.'

'I'm not going in.'

'Then I'll have to come get you.'

'Don't you dare.'

He puts his feet down, finds the mud floor of the Shannon, which is like a dark paste, tacky and cold, and he wades in to the bank.

'Virgil!' She's watching him, she's warning him, but she's not running away.

He puts his hands up, leans forward, and like a strange white river-thing coming ashore flips himself up on to the bank.

'Virgil! Don't.'

He stands, the river runs off him, leaves a river shine.

'Come on. I'll show you.'

'Virgil!'

'You'll love it.'

'Don't you touch me!'

He takes a step towards her. And because she doesn't want to run away and she doesn't want to go in the river, and because the whole scene is unscripted and mad, she bends down and takes his shoes and fires them out across the dark and into the water. The surprise in his face makes her laugh. Then she grabs up the rest of his clothes.

'Mary!'

She throws them, shirt and trousers making briefly an Invisible Man, briefly winged, until he lands on the face of the river.

247

Clothes-man floats seaward. They watch. It seems he'll swim to the Atlantic. Then a twist in the current takes them; soundlessly my father's clothes slide under and are gone.

Virgil looks at my mother.

She looks at him.

Then she laughs, and he laughs, and then he comes after her and she runs but not so fast that he cannot catch her. And when he does, her hands feel the chill slippery skin of him and she smells the river that is on him and in him and his kiss is a shock of cold becoming warm, river becoming man.

Nine months later, Aeney and I swam downriver and were born.

II

When I wake some parts of me are dead. My arms get under me during sleep. As if all night I have been doing backstroke, slow mill of arm over arm towards unseen destination until exhaustion arrives and I give up. I always wake with a feeling of things unfinished. I wake and feel these lumps under me and sort of wriggle to get them alive. Then the room and the house and the parish gradually assemble around me again and Mam looks in and says 'Morning Ruth' and lets up the blind on the skylight and opens it a crack so we can see and feel today's rain.

Here, in what Shakespeare calls The Place Beneath, the rain that falls from heaven is not so gentle. If once, it's definitely not twice blessed. Safe to say Dear William & his gartered stockings were never abroad in the County Clare.

'How are you, pet?' Mam sits on the edge of the bed. She pats and straightens and fixes the duvet and the pillows while she talks. She can't help herself. My mam never ever stops. She's just this amazing machine that somehow manages Nan and me and the house and keeps us all afloat. She's on all decks, crewman, boilerman, purser, Captain. My mam is a miracle.

'How are you feeling?'

I can't say. That's the thing. I can't say how I am feeling because once I start to think *what's an honest answer to that?* I lose my footing. There's this huge dark tide and I feel *O God* and I can't. I just can't. I used to think that no one who hasn't been inside your life can

249

understand it. But then I read all of Emily Dickinson, the nearly eighteen hundred poems, and afterwards thought *I had been inside her life* in a way that I couldn't if I had lived next door and known her. I'm pretty sure you could have sold tickets to see the look Emily gave if you asked, 'How are you feeling today, Miss Dickinson?'

But I don't want to be cold, or hurt Mam, and I don't want to get into a discussion either, so I say, 'I'm okay.' And Mam smiles the smile that isn't one, but has that patience and understanding and sadness in it, and from the pocket of her cardigan she takes the yellow and blue and white tablets and gives them to me. The water in the glass is room temperature, and on a single swallow the tablets vanish into me and taste like nothing, which, to anyone with even weak-grade imagination, is disconcerting. You want them to taste like something. You want them to be more substantial, and significant, in a way, though I cannot explain that.

'Now,' Mam says, 'I'll bring you up something in a little while.'

'Okay.'

'Okay.'

She doesn't get up for a moment. For a moment there's something silent sitting between us and I know it's the untold story of our family and it's like this sea-mist has come up the Shannon and into the room and hangs nebulous and opaque and tastes of salt. Then Mam pats my legs under the duvet two gentle pats and she rises and goes.

From the moment we arrived, Aeney and I were noteworthy personages in the drama of the parish. First of all, we nearly weren't landed alive. Mother being Mother, she took the perfectly practical no-nonsense approach to pregnancy and paid no heed to the powdered ladies in Mina Prendergast's who began their stories by saying *I don't like to say but* or to those who cast their what Margaret

Crowe calls Asparagus at the fact that Mam was older than the Faha norm for having a first baby, and in boyfriend terms Dad was An Ancient. The fact that Mam seemed so happy, which in Irish Catholic translates into Doom Imminent, was another portent. The whole parish was waiting for The Delivery. It was not that anyone wished us harm; it was just that people like to be right. They like Next Week's Episode to turn out exactly as they expected *and* to surprise them. Nurse Dowling came and measured Mam and leaned over to listen to us and said hello. We said hello back. We were perfectly polite. Only we spoke at the same time so she didn't hear that there were two of us. Everything is Grand, just Grand, and after that we stopped listening to the World to Come and swam the warm swimming that takes you back to being seaweed.

The plan was that we were to be born in hospital. Ennis though had been Downgraded. One morning a vicious sausage heartburn twisted the Minister sideways at his mahogany desk and he had a pregnancy epiphany, decided no one was to be born on the outer edges of the country. Any more, the excellent Irish people would be born in Centres of Excellence. There would be none of these in the County Clare. There would be one in Limerick though, which at that time was a Centre of Fairly Alright, but if you lived in Kilbaha or out on the Loop Head peninsula you'd have a hundred-mile drive on roads the Council had given up to the mercy of the Atlantic which rightly owned them and was in the process of taking them back. Still, the hospital in Limerick was the intended setting for our long-delayed arrival in the narrative, and in the blue Cortina Virgil practised delivery-driving. He didn't want to fail this. He had a sense of enormity, as if for every inch swelling in Mam's belly there was growing around his heart a feeling of immensity, as if his life had reached a verge and this great leap was about to happen, and he would be ready. He made the car spotless, or as near as, given that some spots were actual holes. He went on his knees and took every weed out of the garden. He got new gravel for the gravel way and raked it smooth, then raked it smoother. One day he cleaned the kitchen windows and the bedroom windows and then The Room ones, then the kitchen ones again, going round the house the way Tommy Devlin says a cow circles before calving. He whitewashed the house, limey spatters flecking the clean windows, flecking his hands, face and hair which he had no time to clean because Mam's cry came and when he ran in the door she had already slid down on to the floor before the fire and Nan had stood her still-smoking cigarette on end, pushed the kettle across to boil and taken down two blankets and three towels so the flagstones would be softer landing and to New Arrivals this world wouldn't seem penitential.

In minutes the parish was on its way. Moira Mac, who had several PhDs in what, with unfortunate phrasing, her husband Jimmy called Dropping Babies, was there before Mam cried a second time. By the time Nurse Dowling came there was a full gathering of women in the kitchen, their men sitting outside on the windowsill, painting the mark of whitewash across their bottoms, smoking, watching the river running and wondering could that be fresh rain starting.

The labour lasted an age. The journey to Limerick was considered and dismissed. Still we didn't make an entrance. Gulls came up the river. Clouds came after them. The word *Complications* leaked outside in a whisper. The men took turns to go round the corner and pee against the gable. Dad came out, strode right down the garden and out the gate, stood alone in the river view in commune with Abraham or the Reverend or the General Invisible, turned on his heel and without a word strode back in.

Young Father Tipp came, parked his Starlet the way priests park, on the outer edge, carried his missal low down and a little behind him the way Clint Eastwood carried his gun, like he'd only use it if he had to. He took the nods, said what names he knew – 'Jimmy, John, Martin, Michael, Mick, Sean, Paddy' – to the ground-mumble chorus of 'Father' and then stayed outside amongst them.

'Is there any . . . ?'

'No, Father.'

'Nothing yet, Father.'

'No. Right.'

'Could be a while yet, Father.'

'I see.'

Eventually, to relieve Father Tipp of feeling *spare*, as Aidan Knowles says, Jimmy Mac asked, 'Would you maybe say a few prayers, Father?'

And so they started up. A kind of human engine.

From where Aeney and I were it sounded like murmuring waves. Wave after wave. Which fooled us into thinking it was maybe the sea.

Mam screamed. Nan fecked the fecking Minister. The room heated under the scrutiny of the female neighbours, none of whom would chance but sidelong glances at Mam, all of them sitting Sufi Clare-Style, hands folded in their laps and eyes fixed faraway on the emerging plot. In the chimney the wind sang, the rain proper started, and finally, between prayers and curses, Aeney Swain swam, landing with some surprise not in the salty Atlantic but in the giant Johnson's baby-oiled arms of Nurse Dowling.

We were notable personages in Faha, first, because of our birth, our natures being immediately established as precarious and untimely, and second, even as the blankets and towels were tidied,

Mam was laid on the couch and the men called in for tea, we were notable for being unexpected twins. Briefly we enjoyed the celebrity reserved for the two-headed.

'*Two?*'

We were not alike, but likeness is a thing expected of twins and expectations lean to their own fulfilment.

She's very like him, isn't she?

Spitting image sure.

Which, Dear Reader, is revolting. When I asked her Mrs Quinty gave the more polite interpretation saying that she thought it was not spitting but *splitting* image and that it came from splitting a piece of wood and matching the pieces perfectly, the join of the back of a violin say. But Vincent Cunningham says it's *spit and image*, a person being literally both the fluid and picture of the other, which to an Engineer brain apparently makes perfect sense and is not disgusting at all.

Either way, we began as marvels. Faces peered in at us.

Can you tell them apart?

It is something to be innocent of your own marvellousness, to just have it, the way the beautiful do, and to bathe in the knowledge of being blessed. For me of course it did not last, but there was a time, and on good days I like to think some radiance of that entered me and no matter what happened after, no matter the pale thin face I see in the mirror, no matter these eyes, no matter the exhaustion and the sadness, somewhere inside it remains and there could yet be a time when what I feel is marvellous.

When Dad held us he could not speak. His eyes shone. I know I've said that. Reader, be kind. I have no better phrasing. It was like there was excess of shining in him. He kept *filling up*. Brimming. He lifted us in his arms and had to tilt his head skyward to stop the tears falling out.

When you are born into a great tide of love, you know it. Though you are only minutes old you know. And when you are days and weeks old and can only receive you know that what you are receiving is love. Aeney and me, we knew. We knew when we were being pushed in the big-wheel pram down the Faha road, when Mam and Dad's faces, sun and moon, came and went over us, when we lay on the blanket in the kitchen and found a huge finger fitted into our tiny hands, and how by just holding tight you made a smile, we knew when we were in handknit jumpers laying on a blanket in the bog while Mam and Dad footed the turf, picked bog-cotton ticklers for our noses, when the cuckoo sang and Mam sang back to it, when she played butterflies under our chins, we knew and learned the strange and beautiful truth that being adored makes you adorable.

Vincent Cunningham comes up the stairs with Vincent Cunningham bounce. He's off for Reading Week, which is the only thing not done that week.

'What's new?' he says.

'Well. I'm still here. Still in bed. Still exactly the same. So, that would be nothing.'

Turns out engineers don't get irony.

'Hair is good,' he says. He puts his hands down between his legs and rubs the palms together in a kind of boys o boys way. 'Your mam says you've had no breakfast.'

'I have to wait an hour or I vomit.'

He tries to let that pass. He has to negotiate a route around the fact that I will be going to Dublin for a while, and he has to do so without mentioning illness. I watch the skylight. The clouds are closed doors in a hospital sky.

'I couldn't wait an hour,' he says. 'No way.'

'Why? You'd die?'

I don't really mean to be so, aspic. It just comes. And I have the face for it.

'Still raining?' I say at last to help him, like I can't see it on his shoulders and on his hedge-cut hair and how always it makes the skin of his face so amazingly fresh-looking.

'Still raining,' he says, and then turns on me his great big Little Boy Smile and adds, 'Wettest year since Noah.'

12

It was the brimming that brought my father to poetry. We were to blame. By the time we were born Virgil was already a familiar in the second-hand bookshops of the county, knew the floorboard groans under the twenty thousand volumes in Sean Spellissey's in Ennis; the busted book boxes in the Friary that on them said Donal O' Keefe, Victualler, but were filled topsy-turvy with donated paperbacks, Corgis and Pans mostly but also occasional mottled hardcovers with peeling-off *From the library of* nameplates; the backdoor bookshelves of Honan's Antiques, where the volumes smelled of candles and Brasso; the haphazard find-it-yourself emporium that was Nestor's where brandy-smelling books were thrown in for free if you made a purchase, explaining why on separate occasions Virgil bought the quarter-ounce, the half-ounce and the ounce weights that sit on the second shelf of the dresser; Mulvihill's where deceased priests' libraries were sold, all hardcovers; Neylon's bar in Cranny which as draught-excluders had bookstacks in the windows and from which *Our Mutual Friend* was rescued, *M. Keane* written in blue biro on the flyleaf; Madigan's in Kilrush into which the Vandeleur library dispersed and where Maurice Madigan guarded over it, wearing the moustache he got from his father, who got it from his back in the day when shoe-shine brushes were a facial style of command.

Before we were born, Virgil knew them all. Perhaps because he did not go to university, perhaps because he felt a lacking which proved impossible to ignore, my father wanted to read everything. Because he could not afford new books, and because he disliked the temporariness of library loans, wanted to keep a book that mattered to him, he haunted the second-hand shops. If, as was rare, he read a book that he thought valueless he would bring it back to Spellissey's or Honan's and return it, in the kindest way letting them know the book was worthless, and suggesting he choose something else. I know because I have stood beside him at these mortifications, turning my shoe and pulling down from the hand holding mine while with his most reasonable voice he negotiated the unreasonable. These encounters were sweetened by the fact that after, in my father's quiet triumph, we would go (literally) to Food Heaven, on the Market, for Chocolate Biscuit Cake, or take possession of one of the soft deep couches of The Old Ground Hotel, and there, while the fire heated the twin ovals in Virgil's soles, and Mr Flynn flew up and down the hall addressing crises, we shared Tea for One and read with the leisurely disregard Jimmy Mac says is the hallmark of proper gentry.

The library that grew in our house contained all my father's idiosyncrasies, contained the man he was at thirty-five, and at forty, at forty-five. He did not edit himself. He did not look back at the books of ten years ago and pluck out the ones whose taste was no longer his. So absorbed was he in the book he was reading that the library grew without his noticing. Though he needed new clothes, though his fashion sense evolved into Too Short Trousers, Mismatched Socks, The Patched and the Missing Button Look, Mam became his conspirator and on birthdays and at Christmas gave him not clothes but books. It was in her way of loving. She was selling brownbreads and tarts then, and would come from town with flour and bran, apples, raisins and rhubarb, and a paperback she'd leave by his plate for when he came in from the land.

Perhaps because my father had discovered that, despite the weather, there was some profound affinity between the Deep South, Latin America, and the County Clare, on his shelves in various editions are almost all of what Professor Martin called the dangerously hypnotic novels of William Faulkner and Gabriel García Márquez. Dickens is the only other whose work is so present. Prompted perhaps by his own name, Virgil liked the epic quality, the messiness of generations, the multitude of figures drifting in and out and the certainty that time was not a straight line. Ever since Ashcroft he liked to be lost in a book. It was firstly the Elsewhere thing. It was the pull of other worlds that, though he would jab Up-Jut at me for saying so, went all the way back to The Reverend. Old Absalom, Old Shave-Shadow, was the forerunner because there was something in a Swain that was drawn out of this world, something that made them Look Up or Out or Over and which at its best was somewhere between pole-vaulting salmon-sense and Robert Louis Stevenson Syndrome and at its worst resulted in the Reverend's ignoring wife and child to go graveyard-walking under starlight and becoming addicted to beeswax candles.

But it was also *nourishment*, a thing I only came to understand later.

So yes, Virgil liked to be lost in a book, and he read with the smallest rocking of his upper body, a kind of sea-sway that if you listened hard because you were laying in his lap and were supposed to be asleep was accompanied by the thinnest murmuring. I was already The Twin Who Doesn't Sleep (which, Dear Reader, is an out-and-out lie. I did sleep, in fact, slept sweetly and soundly, beautifully actually, but only when held, which is *not* weird but perfectly sensible and if you don't believe me you haven't read your *Hamlet* and should sit in a corner and do some deeper thinking about the Undiscovered Country then you too will want to be held while sleeping. So, *please*) so I was on his lap and could hear the steady sound of his reading. It's not that he mouthed the words. It's that they sort of *hummed* in him. It's like there was a current or a pulse in the page and when his eyes connected to it he just made this low low thrum. John Banville would know the word for it, I don't. I only know the feeling, and that was comforting. I lay in his lap and he read and we sailed off elsewhere. Dad and I went up the Mississippi, to Yoknapatawpha County, through the thick yellow fog that hung over the Thames or in through those dense steamy banana plantations all the way to Macondo. We went in the large lumpy blanket-covered Sugan boat-chair that was placed in by the Stanley range where our cribs were put to keep us warm and where Aeney slept like the Pope Nan said but I cried and was lifted, swaddled in West Clare Tropic, sucked my tiny thumb and was ready for departure.

I fell asleep in strange places. Dear Emily said there is no frigate like a book to take us away, and as I told Vincent Cunningham even though Emily couldn't put a straight parting in her own hair and had a face that Never Saw the Sun she was World's Number One Explorer of the Great Indoors, and in that too she was right. Dad and I went some places, and because some things, most things in my experience, are more vivid when you haven't seen them, I know Mississippi better than Moyasta.

What none of us realised and what at first of course Virgil didn't realise either was that the library he was building would in fact become a working tool, a consultancy, and that it was leading somewhere.

He had no intention of writing.

He loved reading, that was all. And he read books that he thought so far beyond anything that he himself could dream of achieving that any thought of writing instantly evaporated into the certainty of failure.

260

How could you even start? Read Dickens, read Dostoevsky. Read Thomas Hardy. Read any page in any story by Chekhov, and any reasonable person would go *ah lads*, put down their pencil and walk away.

But Swains and Reasonableness, you already know, are not best acquainted. And anyway the certainty of failure was never a Swain deterrent. (See: Pole-vaulting.) Besides, I think there was already something in my father that wanted to *aspire*. It was pre-set in the plot, and only waiting for the day when the brimming would reach the point of spilling.

Aeney and I were that day.

First he went outside. He went out through the nods and mumbles, the drizzle-heads, the Well-Dones and the Good-Mans, marched down to the river which was sort of his version of church and tramped along at Reverend-pace, wordless and grave and impossibly full, rain veils billowing the way old Richard Kirwin tried to convince me once was how angels appear in Ireland, between sky and earth this vaporous traffic.

Virgil couldn't believe it. He couldn't believe that we were born, that he was a father. It's not that he was ignorant of biology, or that for months my mother hadn't carried us with MacCarroll aplomb. She had. The whole parish knew that at least one of us was coming, and though our sex was polled variously, Mam carry-ing-to-the-front, to-the-side, to-the-other-side, depending on personal bias, political affiliation and glasses prescription, there was never a doubt that Virgil was about to be a father. But still our arrival was a shock. The moment we appeared in the kitchen, Aeney pink, shining and wondrous, I hairy, Virgil's life was changed. And he knew it. It was risen up. That's the part you have to understand. I suppose it may be so in all fathers, I don't know. It was a sort of epiphany, Ecstasy even, which as far as I can tell has more or less disappeared out of life now ever since the Church went wonky and sport took over the terrain of Glory. But if you cross your Swain & Salmon lore, add in a little of the lonely depths of Virgil when he was a boy, you'll come to it.

At the plashy bend just past Ryan's wet meadow, there where they have the bockety homemade sort-of-jetty where for reasons private the Ryans keep loops of baler twine, rope and buckets, he stopped, turned his face to the sky. He had to breathe. Joy was a huge balloon inflating in his chest. Or a white flame scorching it. Or a dove rising. I wish I was a poet.

Point was, he couldn't contain it.

He was a father. And in the same instant, by the curious calculus of the heart, he missed his own father. It was not Abraham himself but a better, kinder interpretation, an Abraham that had not existed except as possibility, but who now took over the role as in my father was proven the truths the New Testament is more humane than the Old and the world looks joyous to the joyful.

He wanted to shout out. He wanted to wave his hands in the air, to halleluiah, do a few steps, go Big Gesture, the way Burt Lancaster does in the video of *The Rainmaker* which Mrs Quinty gave me and which I can't give back because the machine ate the tape when Burt went spittle-spraying and just a tinsy-winsy little bit Over the Top.

None of which, thank the Lord, Brothers and Sisters, Virgil actually did. What he did was stand beside the river.

That's where he found the rhythm.

There were no words at first. At first there was a kind of beat and hum that was in his blood or in the river and he discovered now somewhere in his inner ear, a pulsing of its own, a kind of pre-language that at first he wasn't even aware he was sounding. It was release. It was where the brimming spilled, in sound. To say he hummed is not right. Because you'll suppose a tune or tunefulness and there was none, just a dull droning inside him. He went up and down the riverbank. He went the way Michael Moran the Diviner goes when he's going round and round a source, head bent and almost holy, shoulders stiff, serious neck-crane like Simon the Cross-carrier, wispy hairs on the back of his neck upright and all of him attentive to an invisible elsewhere.

Virgil walked the rhythm the river gave him. Over and back. Back and over. Lips pressed shut now, brow like a white slab, eyes watery and in a way unseeing. And now he was tapping. Three fingers of his right hand against his thigh, *da-dumda dumda dum dum-da*. The ground softened and mucked under the weight of the not-yet-poem, was printed and overprinted, boot-marks rising little ridges, small dark river waves, as he tramped and hummed and heard the hum turn into a first phrase.

He had something.

Was it wonderful? Was it like the moment the fishing line tautens in the stream and what was slack becomes a clean and perfect angle of intercourse? Was there that same electric flash of feeling, a *zap!* eye-startle, muscle-tension, torsion of body to river? Did the urgency and unsettledness and rapture crash-combine, did his whole spirit cry out? Did he think *yes, here, I have one!*

And was it wonderful?

Well, at the time I was one hour and twenty minutes on the planet and mostly concerned with figuring out how there was two of me. But in the coverless edition of *The Compleat Angler* (Book 900, Chatto & Windus, London) that smells not so much of fish but certainly of yearning, Izaak Walton says angling *is* just like poetry, and so that's how I picture it. He had one.

I've read dozens of interviews and accounts that basically come down to How Poets Do It and the truth is they're all do-lally and they're all different. There's Gerard Manley Hopkins in his black

263

Jesuit clothes lying face down on the ground to look at an individual bluebell, Robert Frost who never used a desk, was once caught short by a poem coming and wrote it on the sole of his shoe, T.S. Eliot in his I'm-not-a-Poet suit with his solid sensible available-for-poetry three hours a day, Ted Hughes folded into his tiny cubicle at the top of the stairs where there is no window, no sight or smell of earth or animal but the rain clatter on the roof bows him to the page, Pablo Neruda who grandly declared poetry should only ever be handwritten, and then added his own little bit of bonkers by saying: in green ink. Poets are their own nation. Most of them know. Philip Larkin, writing from Belfast to his *Dearest of Burrow-dwellers*, My Dear Bunny, told how he bought a shilling's-worth of mistletoe and was walking home with it to his flat, feeling jolly and like the reformed Scrooge, then noticed that the dark-coated, to-the-chin-buttoned, people of Belfast were all staring at him, the Blossom Carrier, as if they expected at any moment he might erotically explode.

They are a parish of peculiars, poets. But they all generally agree, a poem is a precarious thing. It is almost never landed clean and whole in one go. Virgil had a bite, one phrase, that's all. But he wouldn't let it go, and because poetry is basically where seeing meets sound, he said the phrase aloud now. He said it aloud and tramped it along the riverbank, said it again the moment he finished saying it and found in repetition was solace of a kind. In the dull consistency of the beat was that universal comfort babies know and people forget. He teased the line, waiting for the next movement. When it didn't come he said the first line over. He didn't give up. The sensation was so new and in it the certainty that *this was something* that he kept at it, and was still crossing over and back on the mucked strip beside the river when Father Tipp came looking for him in order to arrange the date for the baptisms.

*

264

Father Tipp was glad to see my father was praying. He heard the murmuring on the breeze, saw the head-bent pacing, and was consoled that though Virgil Swain was not a frequenter of his church fatherhood had now returned him to God. This would make easier the task that had troubled him in our kitchen, namely how to save Aeney and my souls before his annual holiday home to Tipperary.

Not knowing the fields Father Tipp missed the track, crossed Ryan's not Mac's, and so laboured through muck and plop, waving an arm at my father that he might see him and shorten the journey. But Virgil saw nothing, so absorbed was he in his prayers, and Father Tipp had to carry on, neat black Clarks size sevens having a little brown baptism of their own and the heat of his effort bringing the midges.

'Hello? Hello there?'

He did another big drowning-man wave, smacked too late the first triple bites on his forehead.

'Virgil? Hello?'

Still my father didn't see or hear him. By the time Father Tipp crossed the loose rusting wire on random sticks the Ryans favoured as fencing, catching his inner trouser leg a twang, he could hear the praying and thought what he was seeing was Pentecostal.

Father Tipp was still young then, Shock and Awe still belonged to the vocabulary of the cloth and the Church was not yet in the toilet as Sean Mathews said. He was still inclined towards the miraculous, and came along the bank believing he was seeing what in fact he believed. Or believed that he believed. It's a vicious circle.

'Virgil?'

My father didn't stop. He kept on, pacing and repeating, pacing and repeating, until, with a purple flush of authority, Father T stepped at last into the way of the poem. 'A word?' he said, hands behind his back, eyebrows up and face pinched, more or less exactly the way Timothy Moynihan did in Faha Hall when he was playing the Vicar in that English farce and Susan Brady opened the door with her knickers in her hand.

Father Tipp realised in an instant the awfulness of his intrusion, knew when he saw my father's eyes flash, Virgil stopping sharp, falling silent. There was a moment of acute diffidence, as though they were high-standing bishops of different flocks. Because by then he knew that what he had heard was not after all a prayer.

'Father.'

Briefly the priest considered his shoes, and the moment he did the toes of them lifted slightly from the suck muck and his heart fell. West Clare was just not Tipperary. 'I was wondering if I might have a word?'

'Yes, Father?' My father looked dazed.

Father Tipp compensated for self-consciousness by bubbling. 'Well, isn't it marvellous? It is. Marvellous now. Twins. You had no idea, I'm told? No. No but marvellous now.' A penance of midges came to his brow. He went after them with a white linen handkerchief. 'Warm, isn't it? Close. Terribly close.'

The two men stood and considered the closeness. 'Not good this time of year the farmers tell me,' Father Tipp said, and ran a finger round the inside of his collar.

Silently my father was repeating the phrases of the poem just departing.

'Not that I understand why exactly,' the priest said. He kept the hanky handy. Father Tipp was and still is a man skilled in the art of avoidance, black-belt level at the cryptic, but the heat of what he had to propose was making a glistening *Here Midges* landing strip of his forehead. 'They're not like this in Tipperary,' he said and dabbed, letting the sorrow of his exile air before chancing a first proper glance at my father. 'Momentous day for you. Of course it is. Of course it is.' He watched the river run. 'Yes.' The midges took a moment to regroup. This time they came to his moisture moustache. He flicked the hanky at the air as if giving a kind of general dispensation.

'Well,' he said at last, 'I'll be off. Just wanted to say my congratulations.' He didn't risk a handshake, but turned, took three steps and shot one hand upwards so his departing benediction was backwards. 'God bless.'

He got five yards down the bank when he stopped, shook his head in this performance of contrariness, and turned back. 'I nearly forgot,' he said. 'The baptisms?'

'What?'

'I'm actually away week after this. How will we? I wonder. No. Could we maybe? No. No no. I suppose not. Only . . .' A black diary had appeared in his hand. 'We couldn't . . . ?'

'We'll do it now,' my father said.

'What? No. That's not . . .'

But before he could finish his sentence my father had taken one of Ryan's buckets and, *slurp*, dipped it in the river to clean it out, *slurp*, dipped it again, and was now carrying it slapping and brim-spilling back across the field towards the house.

Or so the mythology goes.

'Virgil, no. I didn't mean. There's no need for . . .'

'We'll do it now,' my father said again. He was already past the priest, going the easier track home, and Father Tipp was already hurrying after, already wondering what the hell had happened, in the confusing cloud of his midges trying to figure out where in his strategy the error had occurred. 'Stop! Wait a minute,' he called, knowing that my father would not stop or wait a minute.

'I won't do it,' the priest said.

'Then I will.'

And he would. That was one thing Father Tipp said he knew. Everyone in the parish knew Virgil Swain enough by then to know that when he made a decision, no matter how ill-advised, mulish, in fact ass-backward as Seanie the Yank says, he stuck to it. So as Father Tipp came scampering after him he had to change tack, hurry through the broad headings of the Act and its Consequences: on the one hand the fact that this would mean the baptisms were done, on the other it would not be in the church; on the one hand he would be enlisting two more into the Faith, on the other this man had a bucket of river water. On the one hand so more or less did John. On the other-other, if word ever got to the Bishop.

'I think I have holy water in the car.'

Whether my father was afraid that we would not survive until the priest returned from his holidays, whether he was saving us from an afterlife of wandering among the unblessed, had over-Dante-ed on the short fat green-backed edition of *The Divine Comedy* (Book 999, Modern Library, New York) that has *M.P. Gallagher, Rome* written on an unposted envelope inside, whether it was in compliance with Abraham's thinking or in defiance of the Reverend's, whether it came abruptly out of the fracture and loss of the poem, whether the poem itself was to be about river-birth and renewal and the priest's question had been trigger for the outlandish fact of it, I can never decide.

When Father Tipp went to his car the plastic bottle of Holy Water was empty. He'd been over-liberal at Prendergast's the day before. When he came in the front door to tell them he'd send to the Parochial House for more he came face to face with the chastening truth that there is a tide in things, for Ryan's bucket was in the centre of the flagstone floor, my father was kneeling, cradling Aeney in his arms, and the waves of praying were just waiting for his blessing to dip us into the brimming water.

Nearly twenty years later, still in exile and sitting up here in the attic room beside the bed, that's how Father Tipp told it. Lest I fear our baptism sub-standard in religious terms, he added that no sooner had he started proceedings than there was a general shuffling among the gathered witnesses pressed tight and pretty much steaming inside our kitchen. Everyone closed in around us, everyone wanted to see. It was as if our story was already being told and was moving the hearts of Faha, making people think *These two will need help*, for right then there was an opening of shirt buttons, a rummaging in handbags, in wallets and coat pockets, a general flurry of rooting about, and then, as the river water was being scooped from the bucket, into our swaddling on the kitchen floor came assorted Miraculous Medals, rosary beads, Memorial cards, brown and blue and green scapulars of various antiquity (and body odour), two Padre Pios, two Pope John Pauls, one Little Flower, Saint Thérèse of Lisieux, Patron-of-the-Missions card, several (because we had been Lost & Found) Saint Anthonys, one Saint Teresa of Ávila, Patron of Headache Sufferers, and from the handbag of Margaret Crowe a sort of crouched-down Lionel Messi-looking Saint Francis of Assisi, all of them well-worn and *used* and in our first moments in this world falling around Aeney and I now like holy human rain.

13

My father used Aisling copybooks. He wrote in pencil. Like Robert Lowell (and Margaret Hennessy, who looked like she had been returned to Faha after abduction by aliens), he often put his head to one side, as if one ear was leaning towards a sound that was not yet in this world. He hummed. He also tapped. I was afraid of sleep. I lay in his lap, small as a sonnet, and just as difficult.

He sat and hummed. Then suddenly he leaned across and I was lost in the deep coarse smell of the river-fields in his jumper and heard, somewhere invisibly above, the soft rubbing sound of pencil on paper.

He leaned back, hummed what he had written. We rocked on.

Aeney had no jealousy in him. I think at first he didn't know he was a twin. It is different for boys. Boys are born as masters of the universe, until a bigger master knocks them down. I cried; Aeney slept. I was picked up and carried out from where our cots were in Mam and Dad's, taken up the steep stair that RLS would be delighted to know was called a Captain's Ladder, on to the little landing and into the chill space that Before Conversion was then the attic and later Aeney's and mine. Up here, spilled pool of light and stack of books, was my father's pine table and chair. Up here by the bar-heater he wrote the first poems with me on his lap. When I woke in the mornings I was back in my cot, and felt, well, *composed*. My brother did not care. Even when later he discovered

I could not sleep unless held, when he sometimes woke and looked across and his sister was vanished, he appeared unperturbed. Maybe he wasn't that attached to me. Maybe he had a finely developed and fearless sense of the world to come, or had the unshakeable confidence of the first-born, that first landing in the plump arms of Nurse Dowling, which had informed him that *things would be all right*. The only fracture in this, the only inkling of otherwise was what only I knew, the way Aeney's hand in sleep went to his sleeve or the label of his pillow so that he was always holding on to something and never adrift.

Each family functions in their own way, by rules reinvented daily. The strangeness of each of us is somehow accommodated so that there can be such a thing as family and we can all live for some time at least in the same house. Normal is what you know. In our family it was unremarkable that my father had no income, that he hummed above the ceiling, only went into a church when there was no Mass on, fished religiously, had a book permanently sticking out of his pocket so his pockets were always torn at the edges, or to himself sang undervoice and off-key what I didn't know then was the Psalms. It was not curious that he liked jam with sausages, was no more odd than Nan sitting on *Clare Champions* and smoking up the chimney or Aeney's craving for salt on everything, cornflakes, hot chocolate and cake. Nothing in your own family is unusual.

I think nothing of it on the morning the Tooth Fairy has come to be brought by my mother out in the not-quite-rain to find my father, and to find him waiting for a cow to calve while reading aloud. It's the dirty white paperback of William Blake's *Songs of Innocence and Experience* (Book 1,112, Avon Books, New York) but back then I think it's a story for the cows.

'There she is!' The book goes into his pocket. He kneels down to me. Always in happiness my father seemed on the point of tears.

I thought it normal. I thought every adult must have these huge tides of emotion rising. Every adult must feel this wave of undeserving when they kneel down and see the marvel of their children.

'Did she come?'

I smile my crooked smile, hold out the shining coin.

'Let me see. Well well well. Isn't that something? Will you give me a loan?'

I will. I offer it, but he presses my hand closed inside his.

'You hold on to it for now, Ruthie,' he says. 'But I'll know where to come if I need it.'

The colour of his eyes deepens with feeling and he has these twin clefts either side of his lips where feeling is checked. 'You must have been very very good to get that much. Did you see her?'

I didn't.

'Do you know I think I did hear something,' my father says. 'It was very late. I was awake and working and I heard this gentle *whh whh whh.*' He blows three times to make the wings of the Tooth Fairy as she circles and then descends upon our house. *Whh whh whh.* 'She must have folded her wings then because I didn't hear her inside the kitchen, and the wings would have knocked against things, wouldn't they?'

They would.

'But the latch. That's why I heard the latch. I was wondering about that. It made just the softest clack, must have been when she was going down to your room. You didn't see her at all? But you felt her maybe?'

I did. I do now.

I nod my solemn five-year-old nod and fly up into the air in my father's arms. He turns me around in the sky above him, which is where I want to be always, but cannot, and must take succour in

272

the knowledge that though human beings can't fly soon I will lose more teeth.

When Mam takes me back across the meadow, rain-starred, gummy, dizzy, my father is back reading Blake to the cows.

One day we get a dog, a golden retriever my father christens Huckleberry. He's not golden but white, which is the best kind I tell God-forgive-me the Bitch of the Brouders when she says your dog is a fake. Aeney and I take Huckleberry down to show him the river and to tell him not to drown. He's puppy-manic and piddle-happy, scampering on the end of our blue baler-twine leash like his dream-legs are longer than his real ones. Aeney runs with him, and I run after, realising instantly that Huck is to be Aeney's dog, that in a way inexplicable unless you've known it, they *recognise* each other.

Huck will not swim. He may be able to, we don't know. We throw sticks into the water thinking to fool him into having his retrieving instinct override his desire not to get wet, but he just sits and in the deeps of his brown eyes the sticks float away down the river.

My father says we should skip our homework, we should take him to the beach, and we all load into the Cortina and drive to Kilkee. Huck loves the car. He loves to be moving. He sits up and looks out and Aeney winds down the window that later won't wind up but has to be fingertip-pulled and then pressed the last inch. I think Huckleberry knows we're going to the sea. I'm thinking he smells it and is already working out his strategy, How To Avoid The Sea.

That's the kind of mind I have.

It's still the time when dogs are allowed to run free on beaches. The Minister for Poo hasn't been elected yet. So when we come down on to the big horseshoe beach Aeney lets Huck go and

273

Huck goes running like he's never run before, like sand and shore and sea-wind are marvels particular for dogs. He runs and you feel joy. You can't explain that. He runs head out and ears back, like he can't get to where he is going fast enough, like his blood remembers beaches from a world before and what beaches mean is freedom. Aeney tears after him. He yells *Huck! Huck!* and is not dismayed when Huck doesn't slow, but runs on regardless, arms flying, carefree in the way we all want to be but suppose only exists in fairy tales, the pair of their prints briefly present in the sea-washed glare of the gone-out tide.

'Swim, Ruthie?' Dad asks, though he knows I won't. Then he is in his brown trunks walking towards the ocean and Mam and I are standing, the way girls always are, watching, holding the clothes, peering into the distance, first for Aeney, and then into the far-out sea for Dad.

One sunny birthday we get a horse, a grey mare, who because Dad's wrestling Homer at the time he calls Hippocampus, which in mythology was part-dolphin part-horse and part-bird, could go speedily on land sea and air, none of which dear Hippy actually managed in her lifetime. A man called Deegan brings her from Kilrush in a horsebox behind his dusty old Mercedes. Hippocampus is going by the name of Nancy and keeping her mythological powers under deep cover.

Mr Deegan gets out of his car says great day great day thank God and smacks his hands together. He wears a small felt hat. He wishes Aeney and I happy birthday and asks aren't we the lucky ones. This is a lovely quiet horse for you, he says. Oh Jeez she is. He releases the catches either side of the horsebox and makes a shout of Hup! as he lets down the back. Mam is standing beside the cabin with her arms folded and this held-in smile she reserves just for Dad, for when he has done something she thought impossible. Nan is at the kitchen window scowling her opinion of horse-dealers. Mr Deegan goes inside the box and unties Hippy and maybe because of the drowse of the drive or the torment of flies she has had to ignore, she does not move.

'Hup now, hup. Come on. Come on, young lady.' Hippy backs down the ramp with stiff-legged reluctance, comes down into our yard and turns out. Her eyes spook a little until Aeney tells Huck to be quiet.

'There now, take a look at your horse,' Mr Deegan says. 'She's a classy lady, this one.' He pats her neck, harder than I would have, but Hippy doesn't seem to mind.

'What do you think of her, Ruthie?' Dad asks.

'She's lovely.'

'Will you pet her?'

'She likes to be petted,' Mr Deegan says. 'Oh Jeez she does.'

'And she's quiet?' Mam asks him.

'Very quiet, Mam.' Mr Deegan has a broken china smile. Because by horse-dealer's instinct he knows Mam is harder to impress than Dad he clicks his fingers on an idea. 'I'll show you how quiet,' he says, and then he crouches down and gets in under the horse, so that he is actually in there, squatting sitting-room-style between her four legs. 'It rains you can always shelter under here,' he says. 'She won't mind.' He holds a hand out towards me. 'Want to have a cup of tea in here? I'll ring for service.' He tugs twice on her tail. Hippy doesn't mind. She doesn't move.

I, who by age eight am already fearful of all cattle and beasts general, who have already decided the natural world is a misnomer, think this is the best horse there ever was. This is Hippy the Wonder Horse. I take Mr Deegan's hand and go in under her. So then does Aeney.

'Will she have babies?' Aeney asks.

'Foals they're called,' I tell him.

'Will she have foals?'

'Please God,' Mr Deegan says. 'Please God.'

And I think I know then this will be a day I will be remembering. I know it even before Aeney and I get the giggles under there and cannot stop ourselves, and Hippy doesn't mind or move and the giggles get worse, and they spread to Mam who passes them to Dad in the form of the smile she releases now, because Virgil is wonderful, because somehow, she doesn't know how, he has got us a horse for our birthday.

It doesn't matter that Hippy was never actually ridden, that she just stood in the field, and grazed and wanted to be petted, that when we came home from school I petted her because I had read *Black Beauty* and wanted a good part if Hippy wrote her own autobiography, that Aeney lost interest in her when she wouldn't go and instead he went river-hunting with Huck for whatever it is that boys hunt. It didn't matter that months later when Tommy the vet came and examined her he explained that Hippy was approximately a hundred years old, stone deaf, and was employing all of her energy just to stay standing, that my father's softheartedness had been trod on, that he had paid twenty times what she was worth out of money he didn't have, somehow none of that matters now, for in these pages now here we are on that hot birthday, my brother and I, giggling mad beneath the mythological horse and making the mark in my heart that says *I was happy here*.

14

There is a scene I love where a brother and sister meet after many years and little communication. They meet in an arranged café in mid-afternoon. The light is dying and the city outside rumbles softly in the complacent time before rush hour. The café is unexceptional and quiet. She comes first, sits at the far end, a table facing the door, nervous in her buttoned raincoat. The waiter is an older man. He leaves her be. The brother enters late with the look but not the words of apology. He kisses her cheek. They sit and the old man brings them teas they do not want, two pots, strong for him weak for her. It is long ago since they said each other's names aloud, and saying them now has the extraordinary shyness of encounter I imagine on the Last Day. At first there is the full array of human awkwardness. But here is the thing: almost in an instant their old selves are immediately present. The years and the changes are nothing. They need few words. They recognise each other in each other, and even in silence the familiarity is powerfully consoling, because despite time and difference there remains that deep-river current, that kind of maybe communion that only exists within people joined in the word *family*. So now what washes up between them, foam-white and fortifying and quite unexpectedly, is love.

I cannot remember what book it is in. But it's in this one now.

15

Writing of course is a kind of sickness. Well people don't do it. Art is basically impossible. Edna O'Brien said she was surprised Van Gogh only cut off *one* ear. Robert Lowell said what he felt was *a blazing out*, flashes, nerve jabs in the moments the poem was coming. I myself have had no blazing out, and don't suppose it's all that good for your constitution. To stop himself from taking off into the air Ted Hughes had to keep repeating over and over *Beneath my feet is the earth, some part of the surface of the earth*. The thing is, writing is a sickness only cured by writing. That's the impossible part.

Once he had started proper, my father never stopped. He was *always* writing. That's what I understand now. There was no rest, no pause. It was not that he only wrote when the dishes were cleaned and cleared away in the evening, when he went off alone to the table in the pool of lamplight. It was not that he only wrote when he had the pencil in his hand. It was that whatever part of his brain brought the rhythms and the sounds, whatever part of his mind saw things in the everyday not-really-beauty that was here around our land and the river, that part had clicked On and gotten stuck. There are two things, Tommy Devlin says, that are the mark of genius: one is non-stop buzzing in the brain, the other seeing the next move when there is no next move. He was speaking about Jamesie O'Connor hurling for Clare back in the day but the non-stopped-ness is right. There's seeing in it, and there's transformation. Things are seen differently to what they are. Not that they are always better or brighter necessarily. It's not like Bridie Clohessy whose vision was blurry coming from WeightWatchers and mistook Declan Donahue for the Archangel Michael, or Sheila Shanley who took a notion after her husband died, woke one morning and decided to paint everything Buttermilk, walls, windows, stairs, threw out everything she owned that was not a creamy off-white, and became a one-woman effulgence show. Sometimes things are darker, worse, and with inexplicable torment you hear the gulls, whose complaints are complex and constant when they come in over Cappa with cries crazy it seems from banishment.

I didn't understand that my father's brain could not rest, or that when he was out in the fields, driving us to town, or sitting to tea, all the time there were words, rhythms, running like one of those programs that don't shut off somewhere in the back of the computer. All the time there was gathering this sense of mission.

Once people got to hear about it in the mystical way that people of Faha can hear a person taking off their underpants and are the *ne plus ultra* in the Intelligence & Surveillance league, once word was out that Virgil Swain was writing poetry, there were two immediate first reactions; the men's: that it was his own fault for marrying Mary MacCarroll; the women's: her own fault for marrying The Stranger. But after that initial wave had passed a third reaction came and endured, a quiet awe and respect reserved for someone who had chosen such a serene and perfectly impractical career as that of Poet. We're like that as a people. We can't help but admire a bit of madness. Even Tommy McGinley was quietly admired despite the kind of hit-on-the-head mouth-open expression he got from eating cork, after hearing on RTE it was the main ingredient in Viagra, and not what they actually said, that the main ingredient was made in Cork. No, in Faha a bit of madness is all right. So, people started giving us books, books they had read and ones they knew they would never read, books that were left to them, books that were bought because they were the cheapest things at church sales, books that came free with newspapers, books that were found in trunks and attics whose titles and binding and print combined to say *this is a serious book* and to which the finders in our parish invariably responded by thinking: Virgil Swain.

'This is a book for an intelligent man,' JJ said, handing over Yeats's *Essays and Introductions* (Book 2,222, Macmillan, London) before sitting a while in our kitchen, big hands on his knees, genial eyes smiling and that kind of lovely old-fashioned gentle courtesy you can find in the older people in Faha. After a time he nodded to the fire and added, 'I don't think we've ever had a poet.'

Of course my father hadn't exactly *chosen* poetry. But it was always rising in him; that's what you get if you read your Abraham Swain and know your *The Salmon in Ireland*.

At first I didn't even know that it was poetry. Dad was working, that's all. I knew it was writing, and I knew it was humming. When you're young you're protected by a cloud of vagueness. How our whole household actually worked, how the farming progressed, how many bread loaves were baked and sold, eggs trayed and delivered, how in fact we survived at all – I had no idea. I never wondered, never asked. I may have heard a cow had died, a pine marten had raided our hens, that the car was resting this week, but because Mam was basically Genius Level Ten at guarding her children I never computed these facts, never added them up with Nan mending our mended clothes, Aeney's trouser legs being let down and let down until they couldn't be let down any more, fish for dinner again, or the large earthenware jar of coins my mother kept in the window.

Then one day the cloud lifted. In Miss Brady's class I answered that my father was a writer.

'Really? That's wonderful, Ruth.'

I had said it out loud for the first time, *a writer*, and felt a little ascension myself.

'Where are his books so?' God-forgive-me, the Bitch of the Brouders asked, because her father, Saddam, was our leading celebrity and she wasn't going to be dethroned from Best Father.

I had no answer, *Ascension Ends with Crash Landing* running in a Breaking News banner across my forehead. Then Miss Brady said, 'You can be working on a book and be a writer.'

But later when I was standing alone in the yard and trying hard To Look Normal Jane Brouder crossed over with that hideous Anne Jane Monaghan who had only added her middle Jane out of some Cool Girls thing, who believed herself the model for Miss Perfect in the Mr Men series but who I voted Girl Most Likely to Be Lady Macbeth, who later, after her mother had paid a dozen tutors to more or less crow-bar off the top of her head and stuff everything they knew in there, got six As in her Leaving and is now in teacher-training polishing her dictator skills.

'Is it *poems* he's writing?' she asked, with flawed grammar. She used a tone which implied poetry was something like impetigo, which had devastated the school when the Resettled came from Dublin and for three weeks turned our class into good casting for a leper colony. 'Is it *poetry*?'

The two of them looked at me with the exact same look.

'It's a story,' I said.

Still the look.

'It's a story, like *Black Beauty*.'

That's what I wanted it to be. I wanted it to be a book I brought to school one day. I wanted it to be unsurpassably jaw-droppingly eye-poppingly amazing, a book Loved By Everyone, and somehow through that I would conquer my own oddity and might even be asked to add a middle Jane, which I had briefly decided I would consider but for the misfortune of the rhyme, Ruth Jane Swain, which suggested hooped dresses, wisteria on the veranda, and a haughtiness I personally could never aspire to.

The Janes stood and scrutinised me.

'It's a lie,' Anne Jane said, triumphantly.

'No it's not.'

'Yes it is. I can tell. It's a lie.'

'I'm going to ask your brother,' God-forgive-me said.

'He doesn't know.'

'Why not?'

'He just doesn't.'

'Come on, Anne Jane. Let's ask him.'

'Yes, let's.'

'Wait.'

'What?'

'What?'

'It's not finished yet. The book is not finished yet.'

'Your father's not actually a writer, is he?'

'Is he?'

'Is he?'

That afternoon I walked home pulling overripe blackberries and throwing them into the ground, finding in the purple staining small consolation but adequate image. Aeney had run ahead. Aeney always ran ahead, was always happiest in speed and in any case would be no help in this. In me, exhausted from the defence of having a special father, had bloomed the first dark cloud of betrayal, a small but persistent whispering: *I wish my father was not a writer.* Why could it not have passed over? Why couldn't somebody else's father be a writer and mine a teacher or doctor or councillor?

I brought my frown into the kitchen.

'Mam?'

'Yes, Ruth?'

'Nothing.'

'Are you sure?'

'Yes.'

'All right then.'

'Only.'

'Yes?'

'What's Dad writing? Is it poetry?'

'Yes.'

'Have you read his poems?'

'No.'

'Why not?'

'Because they're not ready yet.'

'You can still be a writer when you're working on a book,' I said.

'Of course you can,' Mam was working dusting flour. Her arms are basically flour and dough. If she's not making bread in Heaven when she gets there it'll be because Bread of Life doesn't need flour and aprons are only for this world.

'When will the book be done?'

'I don't know, Ruth. Some day.'

'But soon?'

She paused, as if it was a thing she hadn't considered, or hadn't considered until that moment that I might want the book to appear, that in fact my whole status and future happiness and the happiness of all the world, Hello, actually depended on it.

'Yes, I'm sure. Soon,' she said. 'Okay, pet?'

'Okay.'

*

That eventually the poems would coalesce or coagulate, or what-ever it is that poems do, was not in doubt. The pressures of brain, paper, pencil and time made it inevitable. Because the secret to writing, the entire syllabus, booklist, coursework, of Ruth Swain's Master's programme in Creative Writing is four words: *Sit in the Chair.*

Or, in mine and RLS's case, *Lie in the Bed.*

There's a book inside you. There's a library inside me.

Sit down.

The words will come, the pages will gather. That's it. Course over.

So it was just a matter of stabbing a pen into his heart, and putting in the time. And more and more that's what he was doing. In the morning, my father's eyes would be gone Japanese, extrava-gant puffed bags of sleeplessness making them narrow, his silver hair forked on the right-hand side where he had held his leaning head.

'Was the writing good, Dad?' was basically my version of *Are we there yet?*

'You know you are the most wonderful girl in the world? Have I ever told you that?'

I nodded, full glob of Flahavan's with honey swimming in my mouth.

'No. I don't think I ever have.'

'You did!'

'How can I have forgotten?'

'You did already!'

'No, no. I never did. But I will now. Do you know what you are? The most . . . ?'

I had to finish his sentence. Otherwise he would keep at it. And although even then I feared those critics creeping behind the wainscoting or under the linoleum who would consider me a Sentimental & Exaggerated Character, I will admit I did say: '. . . wonderful girl in the world.'

Go on, shoot me.

Once, when I got chickenpox, and had to be separated from Aeney, who never caught anything anyway, a bed was made for me beside Dad's table and I was back for three nights in his night-composing. At first before writing he read. It was a warm-up. It was sort of like taking the pole down the cinderway, feeling the wind, trotting down to the vault and looking up at it. He read aloud from those writers that he knew were beyond him. When I got to Trinity I would understand they were his canon: Shakespeare, · Marlowe, Blake, Wordsworth, Keats, Coleridge, Hopkins, and of course Yeats. They were the bar. They were the ones laid out across the sky overhead if you were a sky person, the salmon if you were a sea one. Basically, The Impossibles.

My chickenpox nights, Virgil read Hopkins. (It was years later, when in the stale yeast-and-socks air of the Arts library I went in pursuit of Hopkins, that I came across GMH's letter to Richard Watson Dixon, where he says: 'My vocation puts before me a standard so high that a higher can be found nowhere else.') Back then chickenpox Ruth was not sure her father was speaking English. *Dappled things, couple-colour. Rose-moles all in stipple upon trout that swim.* He spoke the lines aloud, plugged in to what Seamus Heaney called the powerpoint of Hopkins, and soon his head fizzed, fried, sizzled.

Transcendence is the business of poets. That's what they're for. They're not like you and me. They have that extra bit that's always ready for take-off. Poets understand why God didn't give us wings: he wanted entertainment. He wanted us to aspire, to ascend. He wanted poetry.

My father could read a poem five or six times, more, over and over, reading quietly but intently, the lines like a ladder or a prayer rising until the time when he put the book aside and then was utterly quiet. He sat, leaned forward, stared at the page. I did not move. The room contracted. The rain and the rain-wind rattled the slates, whipped the loose wire from the TV aerial, *whp whp*, against the roof. It didn't stop, *whp whp whp*, and in time became a charioteer who rode down the sky, *whp whp*, came in over the dark river that had swallowed the stars, and settled just above our house.

Slowly then, the slightest angling back and forth of his body that pressured the back legs of the wooden chair into a thin creak, my father rocked and began to hum. He picked up the pencil. He moved his whole body towards the page. I lay in my unsleep as the under-voiced hum turned to phrase. And though I had not words for it I knew that we were in Lift-Off, I knew that I was hearing the poem *happen*, that there was air under us and we were away, in some other place where marvels were and dazzlement common. I knew that nothing in the ordinary world was quite like this and I lay there, hoping the spots on my skin would not vanish for a time, for a time happy in the confluence of sickness and poetry.

16

When the book didn't come, and didn't come, I perfected my skill of Standing Alone in the yard. Silently I worked on my narrative voice. *My dear Jane-sows. You are dunghills. Pissed-on nettles. Spews of vomit. Period pains. You are stuck-up vindictive ignorant pony-tailed piglets. I wish you misery and pimples, hair that will never come right, husbands with hairy backs and breaths of cauliflower.*

(Later, in Editorial, fearing Mrs Quinty might think my narrator a bit Swain Extreme, and that use of Black Arts might be held against me in the next life, I amended that to the blessing Tommy Devlin says Mona McCarthy used after the exhausting three-day – two-geese, four-duck, five tart – visit of her American third cousins. She waved them a serene goodbye from the front door, said, 'May God preserve them, at a distance.')

Distance is something Swains do well.

Because I never made friends, because if you think about it *making* friends sounds fairly contrived and deliberate and sort of selfish, *making your friends*, and until the world taught me otherwise I'll admit I always believed friends would somehow find me, would detect Ruth Swain-ness in the stratosphere and head out on their camels, I am used to being on my own. But now that I am imminently departing rounds of callers come to our house for A Last Look, or to Get Ahead of the Funeral, a local science.

The first was Baby Jesus.

He arrived unannounced at the front door. He did not ring the bell but lay just in out of the rain which by then was torrents. Mam found him when she was letting out Huck. Jesus was exactly the same as he'd been when he was kidnapped. There wasn't a mark on him. He hadn't aged a day. Mam let out a cry.

Well you would.

And she looked out the yard for who had brought Him. There was no one. Huck looked at Jesus and looked at Mam with dog puzzlement and then Mam said 'Business Huck' and he remembered what he had come out for and trotted diagonally to that bush Margaret Crowe calls the Anonymous to do the only Business being done in these parts now. Mam picked up the Baby Jesus. Then she saw how the river had risen. The lower edge of Ryan's meadow was gone. The next five yards were a dull silver pocked with rain and pierced with rushes. All along our side the river had come up. She stood holding Jesus and looking at the rain.

Here in Faha, of rain we have known All Kinds, the rain that pretends it's not rain, the rain that crosses the Atlantic and comes for its holidays, rain that laughs at the word *summer*, sniggers at the dry day in Ennis twenty kilometres away, hoots at what pours, streams, teems, lashes, pelts and buckets down. But this was different.

It had intent. That's what Mam thought. And the intention was Flood.

Huck came back and looked at Mam and she said 'Good Boy' and let him back in to his place before the fire where he would lay his general ancientness and act as slipper-warmer to Nan. Mam brought Baby Jesus in.

'Somebody's left this,' she said to Nan.

'Give him to me.' Nan took Jesus and dried his face, with biblical accuracy, only using a page of the *Clare Champion*.

'There's going to be a flood,' Mam told her. But Nan was already saying her prayers. I could hear the murmurs rising as Mam came up to tell me.

When Jesus comes to your house there's only one message: you're doomed.

I hadn't realised I was done for until that moment. That whoever had taken the Baby Jesus and kept Him ten years in what had to be pretty secret captivity for whatever Special Needs the kidnapper had, that they had decided that now I was the one who most needed His Presence was enough to give you the heebie-jeebies.

'Hellooooo?' came up the stairs.

'Jesus!'

'Ruth!'

'Sorry.'

'Just me,' said Mrs Prendergast, who had not in my lifetime visited our house, but now entered my bedroom wearing the flushed look of Mrs Peniston in *The House of Mirth* (Book 1,905, Edith Wharton, Everyman Library, London) who cherished a vague fear of meeting a bull.

Mrs Prendergast came in the door and stopped, relieved and holding her hands together so that we might get a better look at her and get her portrait right. 'What dreadful rain,' she said. 'Mary,' she gave my mother a hand then turned to me a little pained smile. 'And how are you, dear?'

I'm not sure she expected an answer. She patted my bed, then held her hands together in more or less the exact replica of how I realised I had written Mrs Cissley when her Oliver had died and she had come to visit Abraham.

'Sit down, Mina,' Mam told her.

'I won't stay,' she said. 'I just wanted to see poor Ruth, and offer my best wishes.'

'Sit. Please.' Mam turned the chair around.

'I won't.'

'Please.'

'Perhaps just for a minute then.' Mrs Prendergast drew the tails of her long tweed coat forward and like Mrs Peniston sat on, not in, the chair. (*Thank you, Edith.*) The coat buttons were immense and green. Her hat was round and rimless, made of threaded rows of tiny beads and had a concertina effect, as if it had once been sat upon, which it seems is The Look in Limerick, if not Paris. To allow herself be taken in, and give gravity full play, she looked down, considered her tiny feet.

'I'll make tea.'

'Oh no, not at all. Not at all, Mary. No no no.'

'It's no trouble.'

'I wouldn't hear of it. I just called to see poor Ruth.'

'Hellooo?' came up the stairs.

'Come on up,' Mam said.

'Mary. Ruth. Mrs Prendergast,' the Major Ryan said, entering and showering a fair bit of rain off his person. A big square man with a barrel-chest, he was a little bit Mr Hubble the wheelwright in *Great Expectations*, the one who had a sawdusty fragrance and always stood with his legs very wide apart, which in those trousers was disconcerting. Major Ryan had a boom voice he had to keep under restraint except during Lent when the plays were on. Now he went to whisper-power to ask, 'How's the little lady doing? All right?'

I was right there looking at him.

I was not and never have been The Little Lady.

'Sorry now. I was just passing. Sorry,' Mr Eustace said, coming in the door, stooping and craning, easing in past the Major. 'Sorry now.'

290

'Mr Eustace.'

His surname was an offence to him. 'John Paul, *please*.'

I had only seen him in our house once before. You saw him that time you were first driving through the parish and he was standing in a doorway selling Life Assurance but noticed your car was not a Clare Reg. That time you probably didn't realise his face was so *white* or that he was just perfect casting for Mr Sowerberry.

'Sorry now. Sorry,' he said, 'just. Well.' He looked at me like I'd already died. It was a Fondly Missed look, like I was The Departed and he was the Deeply Regretted By, setting his long black eyelashes to Down & Flutter and paying his respects with a letter-box mouth and palming his hands off each other. 'Sorry.'

'Can I come up?' Monica Mac said. Monica has a quiet personality but compensates with loud lipstick.

My Last Day it rained visitors. It's in the secret tactics of how to keep the patient from thinking of what lies ahead. But here it proves a country truth: it takes a parish to rear a storyteller.

And God bless them, they came. In No Particular Order, as they say on *X Factor*, Tommy and Breda, the Saints Murphy, who smelled of candles and left after Breda kissed my forehead and sneaked a set of opalescent rosary beads under my pillow, Finbar Griffin who I had never actually spoken to, who always wore the pained look of a man who had spent the day castrating bullocks, or was just the look of a man married to Mrs Griffin, Kathleen Quinn who had developed a gift for seeing personal insult everywhere and secretly thought she should have been offered the chair, Margaret Crowe who told Kathleen the weight suited her, big Jack Mannion who just came to the top of the stairs, gave me two thumbs-up, and went down again, because some things couldn't be said in words, Seamus O'Shea who had been Customer Services in the bank before the economy took a haircut and who'd since opened a barber shop in his sitting room, Louis Marr who wore thin-legged bright-red trousers and Faha's only flower-print shirt, was not gay, but just a bit fabulous, Charlotte, one of the Troy sisters, who brought impossibly beautiful flowers, Noeleen Fry, God Love Her, with the permanent scowl of a woman who couldn't locate the bad smell in her kitchen, Eamon Dunne who had the original Bluetooth device, a Blue Tooth, which when he smiled communicated only one thing, awesome disregard for the opinion of others, the two thin Duffys who hadn't a penny to their name now and survived mostly by watching afternoon cooking shows, the button-eyed Maurice Kerins who was innocent of everything except murder by accordion, Nora Cooney whose husband Jim, like Mr Skimpole in *Bleak House*, considered thoughts to be deeds, and that by thinking of paying a bill supposed it needed no further action, had in fact thought himself into enormous riches, pin-striped ownership of property in Bulgaria, Romania and Hungary, none of which made material impact on Nora's plain green coat and worn-out muddy ankle boots.

They kept coming.

There may have been a schedule nailed up on our front door.

The black-and-white Frank Morgan who played Professor Marvel then The Gatekeeper, The Carriage Driver, The Guard and finally the Wizard of Oz looked in the open window and said: 'I just dropped by because I heard the little girl got caught in the big –'

Sorry. Fecund.

After a first general enquiry about my health, conversations ran over and back above me, unbounded. A universal truth is that in the company of an ill person people speak of illness. Hereabouts Illness-tennis is played by masters. No sooner did someone serve a burst gall bladder – A Tony Lyons in Upper Feeard, cousin to Eileen who was a McDermott and had the Hospital Bug – than they got a backhand pancreatic cancer, with topspin – Sean O'Grady of the O'Gradys beyond in Bealaha, not the one who was married to the one of the Kerry Spillanes who had the red hair and went off with the Latvian, the other one, who had the arm after the accident, was going out for it must have been on to ten years with that wonderful Marie of the O'Learys, had already survived a family so numerous that two of them were named Michael, and the father who went into Crotty's pub in Kilrush and woke up in Paddington, him.

'Is that right?'

'That's right.'

The true masters were all women. From what I could tell, *Bless-us-and-save-us, poor man* generally signalled the end of a set.

The men, because of their higher nature Vincent Cunningham says, were generally more squeamish, spoke of matters National, Meteorological and Agricultural, from which I learned that on Clare FM Saddam said Green Shoots of Recovery had been seen, to which Jimmy Mac added, coming out of his own backside, that the rain was biblical and had just officially Gone Beyond a Joke, that Father Tipp was going to say a Mass for Dry Weather, and that Nolan's bull had sore back feet and so, much as he wanted to, he couldn't *incline* himself to Do the Business.

But before they left, all of them, one way or another, told me that I would be grand just grand, *you wait and see*; some undercut their own statements of confidence, or supplied the grounds for it, by adding they would be lighting candles and praying for me.

They came and went the way Irish people do, like ones doing rounds on what they hope is Holy Island under the unknown chastisements of the rain.

When they went downstairs I expect they saw Nan holding Baby Jesus and had this inner *O shit* feeling but which in Mrs Prendergast came out as *O my goodness.*

By then Mam was too worried to have dialogue. The river was coming across the field.

Jimmy Mac stood in the kitchen; 'Jesus,' he said. But he was looking out the window. And when he turned back he told Mam, 'We'll get sandbags,' and was gone out the back and wellying across the tongue of water coming in the drive before she could say thank you.

He came back in his tractor in fifteen minutes, a transport box of sand and cab full of empty 10-10-20 bags and any number of McInerneys, most of who were not believers in coats. By rain-telegraph Mickey Culligan and Finbar Griffin came too, my Gentleman Callers, sputter-roaring their tractors out into the river-field and using whatever you use to reopen the drain that never drained and to make these brown scars across the field to delay the progress of the flood, each of their tractors going bogging good-o, little Mickey Mac said with ten-year-old glee, eyes polished and nose dripping free and clear and unheeded when he came in to say they were going to sandbag our front door now. The first of the bags thumped down a minute later, then the next, as men and boys passed the windows, swinging over and laying in the bags, working tenacious and resolute, with a kind of uncomplaining Clare defiance and goodness, putting a pause on the river, and whether saving me or Jesus at that point immaterial.

17

I cannot sleep.

Tonight it seems impossible that anyone sleeps. How can they? My blood aches.

The rain won't stop. It just won't, it's like the sky is irreparably holed. I think *it can't keep up like this*, I think *nowhere does it rain like this, soon, soon it will ease*, and when it doesn't, when it just keeps on hammering, I think of Paul Dombey hearing the tide and thinking it is coming to take him and saying 'I want to know what it says, the sea. What is it that it keeps on saying?' and I sit up in bed and hold on to my knees and close my eyes and rock slowly back and forth and back and forth and back and forth until it comes to me clear and sure so that somewhere inside my rocking and my darkness I know that what the rain is saying is *Sorry*.

That day it was not raining. We got a half-day for the holidays and ran out into summer when summer was still a word plump and generous and there was actual sunshine and time was impossibly deliciously luxuriously long and the idea of summer stretched out ahead so that now as you entered it you could not imagine it ever ending. The whole school ran out the school gates, schoolbags bouncing on backs, and last watercolour paintings buckling a little in the hands holding them. There was pushing and yelling getting through the gate. Parents were standing by their cars. Noel

McCarthy was in his mini-bus, the window down and the radio letting Martin Hayes's fiddling float-dance over us.

Aeney ran; I didn't. He always ran. I'd like to say it was because he knew he was finished with Mr Crossan, I'd like to give a reason, but the truth is he ran just for the sake of running and I suppose for freedom. His fair hair went round the corner.

I let the school go. When I saw Vincent Cunningham had stayed waiting outside the gate I said, 'Go home. I'm not walking with you,' and he said 'Okay' like I hadn't hurt him and ran on. I walked around the yard pretending to look for something and when every-one was gone except the teachers who were having holiday coffees and doing whatever teachers do in empty schools I walked out the gate. I walked with what I hoped was the reserve and maturity befitting Our Last Day, the end of Primary. Aeney and I were done. We would not be back there.

The cars were already gone, the road returned to that quiet it kept all day except for at nine and three o'clock. I walked the bend for home. The air was warm, the fuchsias so full of buzz you imagined if you stopped and looked, as I did, that you would see nothing else but bees. But you didn't see them. Hum and drone were just there, like an engine of summer, tirelessly invisibly turning. I took my time because time was suddenly mine. I had been waiting for this day all year. I had been waiting for it ever since I realised that Aeney and I did not belong in the school, that Aeney maybe belonged in no school, and that without intention I had read myself away from girls my age and was in the true sense of the word, Alien, other. That Secondary school would be better, that there I would encounter like-minded girls, *Serious Girls*, as Mrs Quinty said she hoped to find, was then not in doubt, in the same way that at the end of Secondary I would cherish a brief confidence that in Third

Level things at last would be different and intelligence and oddness found to be normal.

I dawdled. I plucked a buttercup and rubbed out its yellowy heart on the tartan pinafore which I had always, always hated, flushing a little with the thrill of staining with impunity and the anticipation of seeing my uniform thrown in a corner. It was my slowest walk home ever. When I came in the back door Mam said, 'Well,' and came and hugged me. 'You did it,' she said. 'That's the end of that.'

She held on to me longer than my new status would allow in the future, but right then I did not resist, my head in against her, and coming around me warm and deep and smelling of bread the many things that are contained in the word *mother*. I think I knew it was a hug I would remember always.

'So proud of you,' she said. She knew my battles and knew too that she could not fight them. Her eyes were so green. 'Holidays!'

'I know. I don't believe it.'

'A whole summer.'

'Yes! Yes! Yes!'

'Do you want to get changed or will you eat first?'

'Changed. Definitely.'

Nan was sleeping in her chair. I went upstairs and took off my uniform. Then I pulled open the skylight and because Aeney and I had promised it was what we would do on our last day I fired jumper blouse and pinafore out the window. Just like that they were gone, and with sudden lightness I jumped on the bed, and bounced, rising with implausible impossible happiness and bringing my hands to my face to catch my giggles.

I put on grey jeans and a yellow T-shirt that said 'Always'. There was so much summer ahead of me I didn't know what to do first. All the things I had thought of through March April May and June now jostled at the starting gate. How could I begin? How could one minute be Hell and the next Holidays? I lay on the bed and opened a book. I had all the time in the world to read now. And because I knew I had I didn't. I went downstairs.

'Will you have something now or wait for dinner?'

'I'll wait for dinner.'

Peggy Mooney came in the back door. 'Mary,' she said. 'Ruth. Holidays today.' She was a nervous woman at the best of times and she held her arms across herself, as if she was afraid some part of her would fly away. 'Only that tomorrow is Sheila's,' she said, 'and I was wondering, Mary, if I could get a few flowers for the altar.'

'The wedding,' Mam said. 'Of course you can, Peggy.' She wiped her hands down her apron.

'O thanks. Thanks very much now, Mary.'

'Don't be silly. You didn't need to ask. Come on.'

The clock of one day is not the same as another. We invented time to make it seem so, but we know it's not. Things speed up and slow down all the time. The kitchen window was open. There were three flies in the ceiling. The new *Clare Champion* was on the table, still fresh and folded beside a white plastic bag of sliced ham Dad had brought from the village. Aeney's cup and empty Petit Filou and spoon were in the sink. The oven was doing that ticking it does when the power has been turned off and the hot metal is contracting. The five-day pendulum clock tocked. The cold tap dropped a drip. *Drp!* like that, and then another, *drp!*, the way it always did because Dad was always going to fix it so that generally we took no notice, but right then I did. I was standing by the window and I turned the tap extra hard and looked at it until I was sure it wouldn't drip. Then *drp!*, it did. Mam went through the garden with Peggy Mooney, cutting more flowers than were needed, a generosity of flowers bundled into Peggy Mooney's arms that would make such display that ever after people would come to Mam for flowers, but right then I thought *why is she giving away all our flowers?*

Standing at the window I ate a piece of brown bread. I heard a tractor coming from Ryan's and heard it going past and heard it until it must have turned out by McInerney's. Then Peggy Mooney's old car drove away with a passenger seat full of flowers and Mam came in.

'You don't know what to do with yourself, do you?' she said, smiling.

'Why did you give away all our flowers?'

'Poor Peggy,' Mam said. 'They have nothing, and we have flowers.' She ran the tap over her hands. 'Dad will be home soon. He had to get a nozzle for the sprayer,' she said, and turned off the tap, tea-towelled her hands, and the tap started dripping again.

'Go find your brother,' Mam said.

'All right.'

There were more birds. That's what I thought when I came outside. There were definitely more birds or the ones there were sang more. I went out around the haybarn and the haggard and all of it was sort of busy with birds. I went up to the gate and the stonewall stile and I called 'Aeney?' and the birdsong stopped or went elsewhere, and I went into the field that smelled rich and sweet because of the sunshine. The light had that kind of white dazzle you're not yet used to if you've spent all of June in a class-room. The dazzle gave me these stray things moving in my vision, these little fissures or threads that some people call floaters and some fishhooks. They're sort of what invisible would look like if it was visible and they just move down your seeing and if you follow one down to the end you think that's the end of it but then there's another one starting. Light causes it, or tiredness, or just

contrariness of blood brain and sunshine. They start when they
start and they stop the same.

I went down the field to the river. I knew where Aeney would
be. I knew he would be running the beaten track with Huck,
throwing sticks, or sitting down on the far side of Fisher's Step
with the fishing rod, believing that once they passed our bank the
fish were catchable there. To prove in myself that these were the
holidays I took my time. I told myself *You have all the time in the
world*. I plucked random grasses and let them go. Ryan's was in
meadowing. If you stepped off the track the hay was high to your
waist and in that sunlight even I thought it was beautiful. There
were bees and flies and midges sort of flecking or flawing the air
and that hum which was overtaken by the song of the river as you
came to it.

I could see fifty yards along the bank now, to the point where
McInerney's bushes came down and blocked the view. The other
way I could see to Fisher's Step, and in neither way could I see
Aeney.

It was just like him, to have gone somewhere new.

That's how he was. He'd have tired of here and gone
elsewhere.

Go and find your brother.

Why should I? He'd come home when he was hungry, and
Aeney was always always hungry.

I stopped looking for him.

I walked along the bank and looked across at Kerry. 'I have all
the time in the world now,' I said across the river, and then I
watched the floaters and fishhooks descend.

In the distance there was the noise of a tractor, and that was lost
inside the noise of another, and you knew there was coming and
going happening somewhere and that everything ordinary and

everyday was continuing the way the world continues around you and for just these moments you're the still point at the centre.

Then I saw Huck.

He was a white gleam, sitting on the very edge of the bank up at the far end of Fisher's Step.

'Huck! Here boy! Huck!'

He didn't move. It wasn't surprising. He was Aeney's dog. He just stayed there, sitting erect and facing the river, but something in his sitting passed into me. For whole seconds I didn't move. I didn't run. I just stood there and felt this *departure*, this separation. The air was buckled. The moment wouldn't turn right. My heart was in my throat. Something had reached in and seized it and was now taking it out of my mouth. I think I cried out. But the sound was swallowed by the river. Then I was running and time was moving, lurching, too fast, so that soon it would be wrecked and pieces would break up and never come right so that here I am squatting down beside Huck and saying *Where is he? Where's Aeney? Find Aeney, good boy* and Huck barks at the river and the suck hole and the water in it is twisting clockwise faster than clocks, and here I am running back through the meadow for no reason not taking the track except the reason that nothing makes sense and I am running in risen clouds of hay dust gold and choking and shouting *help help* though I know there is no help and here I am breathless in the kitchen where Dad is just home and the tap is dripping *drp!* and I'm saying *He went in the river I know he went in the river* and here is Dad diving in the river, and here the whole parish coming, and the Guards and the ambulance and Father Tipp and the summer evening hopelessly horribly beautiful and a hundred men carrying sticks *to poke into the rushes* and walking out along the length of the bank in the coming dark and being back there the next day at sunrise where Dad years ago had first stood and felt

301

the sign and where now he had spent the night calling *Aeney?*
Aeney? with hoarse terrible wretchedness and praying to God
Please please O please and divers coming and the sun going away
and Huck immovable from the spot as now hard and wild and with
no mercy the rain came.

Here is the place where the ground was soft and his feet slid
down.

Here is the brown suck hole where the river comes around and
swallows itself.

Here is Aeney's rod, found in the rushes.

Here, three days later, his right sneaker.

There, my shining brother was gone.

THREE

History of the Rain

I

'There is no Heaven. How can there be? Think about it. For start-
ers, if all the good people there have ever been are already there,
how big would it have to be? Second, what a social nightmare. It'd
be like all the good characters in all the books in the ultimate
library of the world left their books, stepped out of their stories
and were told *just mingle*. Anne Archer and Jim Hawkins, Ishmael
and Emma Woodhouse. How mad would that be? Dorothea, say
hello to Mr Dedalus. What could they possibly say to one another?
It'd be excruciating.'

Vincent Cunningham just sat there looking down. His mother
died when he was eight, about six months before he proposed to
me for the first time, and, like The Monkees, he's a Believer. He
has Heaven the Standard Version that we learned in school pretty
much tattooed on his soul. It's wings and angels for him, plenty of
harps, which I personally can't stand, and those white cotton
clouds that have no rain in them but let you lay back like lounge
chairs so you can have your feet up and watch the saints come
marching in.

'Sorry, but there is no Heaven,' I whispered. I didn't want Mam
downstairs to hear. I think in a vague way Heaven sustains her and
that, although she doesn't want to consider the detail and she's too
busy just trying to keep us afloat in this world, she's sure it lies
ahead, like Labasheeda when in the river-fog the road is blind.

Vincent Cunningham said nothing.

'Okay, say there is. Tell me then, in Heaven who cooks the food?'

His hazelnut eyes came up to me. 'There's no food. You're never hungry.'

'Thirsty?'

'No.'

'That's disappointing. What's TV like?'

'Ruthie.'

'Is Heaven God's Most Boring Idea? Is that why He keeps it out of sight?'

'It's not boring.'

'So what do you *do*?'

'You don't need to do anything. You're just happy.'

'Well, I won't see you there so. I won't be going. Thank you.'

'You can't say no to Heaven.'

'I just did.'

It took him a moment. 'RLS believed in Heaven,' he said. 'You said so.'

'That was Vailima, Samoa.' It was a quote from RLS my father had written on the back of an envelope that I found inside his American copy of Jorge Luis Borges's *Labyrinths* (Book 2,999, New Directions, New York): *The endless voice of birds. I have never lived in such a heaven. RLS.* Because of its strangeness, because it was in my father's hand, and because found writing has a curious potency, I had showed it to Vincent. 'You think when we die we go to Samoa? What should I pack?'

'You're terrible.'

'Am I?'

'Yes. No. Yes.'

'Look, I have an advantage over you. I've thought it through. There is no Heaven. So, I'm just saying, if you're expecting to see me there, if you're thinking once you arrive and get over the preliminaries – Hi Peter, wings, harp and whatnot – that you'll head out and find me and propose, let me just say you'll be disappointed.'

He didn't say anything to that. The eyelashes went down. I was cruel to continue, but you already know I did. 'The tunnel of light people say they see? Just your peripheral vision shutting down. Your brain dies with floods of light. It's not a place, it's just chemistry. You're the engineer, I'm the Swain. I'm the one supposed to be partial to the outlandish. Nobody believes Milton's Heaven, nobody believes Dante's. When Dante arrived he said his vision was greater than his speech, so he stopped describing, thank you very much, which tells you he didn't believe it. Not really. Because even Dante knew, there is no Heaven.'

That, I thought, was the end of it. I'd turned my hurt around to hurt him and he looked down at his long-fingered hands and said nothing. He was wearing his socks, his wellies downstairs after crossing the flood. The socks made him look defenceless, the way they do on boys. The rain drove down on us, the skylight streaming. I wished the night hadn't been so long. I wished I'd slept.

'All right,' Vincent said, 'let's say it's just a story.'

And he'd got me there. He knew it. You could tell from the look on his face. 'It's just a story,' he said, 'but, Ruth, you believe in stories.' He smiled that smile he's planning to use on Saint Peter. 'All it takes is a leap of faith,' he said. He actually said that, knowing that if there was one thing Swains know, it was how to leap. 'Take the leap.'

Then we both heard Timmy and Packy come in downstairs. They said something about the flood and where they had had to leave the ambulance, and how now they were planning to stretcher me across the water. Mam came up the stairs. Vincent Cunningham

stood in his socks and looked that look that wanted to say *Ruth,
you won't die, you won't*, but because Mam was there it didn't come
out in words. 'Well,' he said, and then shot up his right hand, palm
out, a sort of paused wave or Stop or I Swear and I saw his eyes
were shining and knew he wanted to grab me up in his arms and
probably actually kiss me but he just said, 'I'll be seeing you.' Then
he turned and was gone and to Vincent Cunningham I did not get
to say goodbye.

After the river took him Aeney became huge. He was big as the
sky. He was in every corner of our house. He was at the kitchen
table for every meal, came and went on the stairs, blew down the
chimney in smoke, rattled the windows, and rained without end.
He kept his clothes in the chest of drawers, his mug in the press,
his wellies at the back door. He was everywhere. He was in Huck's
brown eyes looking at you with grave and patient and exhausted
asking. He was in his schoolbag thrown in the corner and gathering a pale sheen of dust, the creases first like wrinkles and then the
whole of it, solemn and undisturbed, laying on the floor and
becoming ghost. Aeney was on the road running. He was pulling
blackberries in blackberry season. He was in the *cuck-oo* of the
cuckoo that could never be seen but was somewhere on the top of
the highest tree, looking down and singing its two-note song that
could be joyous or plaintive depending. He was in *Treasure Island*.
He was at our birthday, bigger and sadder for being present but not
having presents. He was first one awake at Christmas, last one to
come inside the year it snowed. He was in the final visit of the
Aunts. He was in the fields and in the village and at the sea. He was
in the river.

The only place he was not was in Faha graveyard.

You think you won't survive it. You think there's a crack right down your face and down your body and it's so deep the pieces of you will fall apart in the street when someone says his name. You think it can't be true, you think it was a bad dream and you'll wake up any moment. You think it can't have been as simple as that. Why one day, that day, did it just *happen*?

And why is the world continuing? How can it? How can the radio be on and the kettle coming to the boil? How can the hens need to be fed?

You go to bed and you lie there and you listen across to his room for him. You listen for the way he breathes when he sleeps and you don't, the pulse and breath and clock of him, that was annoying sometimes but was just over there, had been since always, had been since before this world, and now the emptiness of it pulls at you and wants to suck you away and you think *Okay let me die tonight I don't care.*

But you don't die. You learn to sleep rocking yourself just a little, and making a little low hum no one hears but you, so that the night is never empty and like Peter Pan, un-ageing and evanescent, Aeney can come in through the skylight and you can tell him stories from the books you've read.

Your hand hurts from handshakes. Your eyes and your lips are dried out because the water has been wrung out of you and instead you've got this sour yellow anger swilling because why are all these people coming now, and why are they who never said his name before saying it now. None of them know him. None of them know his crooked smile from the inside the way you do, his yell jumping off the swing at the highest point, his crash and tumble and getting-up grin. None of them know it should have been you that drowned.

Somehow, you have no idea how, you survive.

Because you are not to die yet, because somebody needs to tell the story, somehow you survive.

We survive.

Maybe just so that we can hurt more. Maybe the finest sufferer is the winner. Maybe that was the plan for us. Maybe if we'd marched down to the river and thrown ourselves in that would have made a mess of our chapter in the Book of Swain. In my father's black rain-mottled copy of the Bible the spine is broken on the Book of Job. *Has thou not poured me out like milk and curdled me like cheese* is right there.

It became a long wet summer. I stayed indoors and saw no one but Mam and Dad and Nan. To get me out of the house Dad took me with him to town and we went to the bookshops. He did not say, 'Read this, it will help you forget your sorrow over your brother,' but he gave me books, and to avoid the eyes of others I kept mine in them.

The selfishness of children is absolute and perfect and for the progress of the world perhaps essential. I didn't really wonder how my parents carried on, didn't consider the quality of their quietness. If my mother watched over me with extra vigilance, fearful I might slip through some flaw between this world and the next, I felt it only as love.

That summer my father stopped writing. He still went to the table in the lamplight. He still sat leaned forward with his hand forking up the right side of his silver hair. But he did not pick up the pencil. From his room there came not a sound. Whether the inspiration couldn't come, whether there ever was anything that could rightly be called inspiration and sometimes descended like a tongue of fire, whether it came and out of spite or hurt or anger he denied it access or outlet, whether he had any intention of ever writing anything again and went to the table at night the same way my mother went to Lough Derg to walk barefoot over the stones and let the hurt bleed out of her, I cannot say. He stopped, that's all.

Mam was still just Mam. Yes, she'd cried, and yes she'd been wretched when the callers came and again at the time we had the Mass that Dad said he wouldn't go to and she'd shouted at him, the only time I ever heard her, and in compromise Father Tipp said he'd say the Mass here in the kitchen and Dad said all right to that, and yes, she let her hair go tangled more often, but once the worst was over she had sort of recovered, if recovered is something people ever do. What I mean I suppose is that she carried on. Women carry on. They endure the way old ships do, breasting into outrageous waters, ache and creak, hull holed and decks awash, yet find anchorage in the ordinary, in tables to be wiped down, pots to scrub, and endless ashes to be put out. The only changes in Mam were that now whenever she was in the village she went into the church to light a candle, and that since Peggy Mooney's she was continually asked for flowers for the altar, and she obliged, and in the way customs form in small parishes soon it was clear that Mam would be cutting our flowers and bringing them into Faha church until the end of time.

I had a season to grieve, and then had to go to the Tech on my own. But the fact is grief doesn't know we invented time. Grief has its own tide and comes and goes in waves. So when I went I was no more *over it* or *out of it* or any of the other absurd things whispered in my wake going down the corridors. For the first weeks I had a status above Julie Burns who had to have all her teeth removed, or Ambrose Trainer who had come from Dublin and had an infected nose piercing. My status was Half. I was The Other One. I was the one who had Half of Her Gone. In the toilets that mascara'd ghoul and Trainee Vampire Siobhan Crowley asked me, 'Can you feel him? Over there, on the other side? Can you?'

Teachers too treated me with circumspection. My story had preceded me into the staffroom, and created that space around you that stories do. I moved from The Girl Who Wears Glasses to The Girl Who Had the Brother to The Girl Who Walked On Her Own to The Girl Who Read, parts I stepped into with alacrity and relief, relishing the solitude and soon somehow proving both adages, that our natures are incontrovertible, and we become what others expect.

Stories though wear thin after a time. In this world compassion is a limited commodity, and what is first considered appropriate so soon becomes annoyance. *Why is she still like that?*

She does it for effect.

She likes the attention.

She's just so, odd.

As if wilfully, and to further confirm the indelible quirk of my own character, I loved poetry. Mrs Quinty, who was unlike Miss Jean Brodie In Her Prime in all things except seeing in some girls a flicker of intelligence, became aware of it when we read Seamus Heaney's 'Mid–Term Break', the one where his brother dies, where in the second-last line we learn *the bumper knocked him clear*, and I said I liked that *clear* because it went with the *classes to a close* in the second line and though sad somehow *clear* had hope in it. Mrs Quinty did not know then that my father had prepared the ground, that I was already hum-familiar, or that I was drawn to poetry for reasons of mystery. She gave me the anthologies the sale reps brought her and which she had told them she would consider using. Small and taut and resolute she came down the classroom, placed one on my desk and said, 'You might like to take a look in this.' Just that. She did not edit, guide or censor. She didn't go Teacher Mode, didn't ask me to tell her what I thought or to write up a report or turn the gift into an exercise. She did the most generous and implausible thing, she gave me poetry.

Note to future Swains: reading a poetry anthology in the school yard, while it now has precedent and may appear natural and unremarkable to Swain-minds, is not best equipment for the vicious nightmare that is teenagehood. Reading poetry sealed my fate. In the Tech it classified as off-the-scale weird and left me in the same company as Kiera Murphy the Crayola-eater and Canice Clohessy, The Constipated, in whose unique case shit *didn't* happen.

I lost the skill of dialogue. I was invited to no birthday party, except the time Mr Mulvihill, who had married an easterly wind called Irene, and to spite her, phoned to say he was inviting the whole year to his Sinead's fourteenth.

I didn't go, and I didn't care. When I lost my brother I lost more than half the world. I was left in somewhere narrow as the margin, and in there, parallel to the main text, I would write my marginalia.

2

There are four of us in purgatory, a concept I didn't believe in
until I was in it. I am the youngest. Eleanor Clancy is the oldest.
Like Miss Toppit in *Martin Chuzzlewit* she wears a brown wig of
uncommon size. She says *Ah pet* to me and to the nurses and
when they lift her out of bed her shins are sharp and look like
they'll snap so I look away. Mrs Merriman doesn't speak at all
now. She did when she came in, but now she's too upset. She's
too upset to be here. She wants to remain in the actual world,
where her Philip needs her and will not manage without her.
She doesn't want to be in this in-between place, which is neither
here nor there. Mrs Merriman has the side with the wall and to
it does her wailing, these high waily moans she tries to strangle
coming out and that we pretend not to hear. Jackie Fennell is
our cheerleader. She looks like one of those actresses they get
for TV hospital dramas. There can't be anything wrong with
you when you're that gorgeous. Jackie's Lucozade is white wine
smuggled in by Benny, so she can't share it. But she could get me
Green & Black's chocolate or *Glamour* or magenta nail varnish if
I wanted. We're all here for something different. There are more
things that can go wrong with you than you can shake a stick at,
Timmy said.

I've a pain in my face telling you where it hurts, Mrs Merriman
said.

My body which my dungeon is, RLS said.

The curtains are blue plastic and they come around in a single soft *swish* and when they do you know it's Business.

Mr Mackey comes with Dr Naradjan to look at my results. Mr Mackey is The Top Man; he has the world's most perfect suit and was either born in a new white shirt or can put one on without adding any human creasing. His only flaw is those ties with little symbols on them somebody pretended for a laugh would catch on. Today they are silver fishes.

'I am quite concerned about these, Ruth,' he says.

When it comes to that multitude covered by what Mina Prendergast with nineteenth-century-drawing-room manners calls *Matters of the Heart*, some women are practical. Some women see the hurt, consider the damage, and embark on a remedy right away. Some women have no hopelessness in them. They will surrender their beauty, sacrifice music dancing laughter, suffer heartache so profound there's a clean hole right through the centre of them, but still they will not be defeated. My mother is one of these.

Mam knew that Virgil had stopped writing. She knew whatever had been turned on was now turned off, and after a time it was her natural reaction to go looking for the pliers and spanners and whatever to get it going again.

Washers maybe. Aren't they a thing? I'm running a little short of time to fix my metaphors. Anyway Borges said writing is better when you leave your mistakes in. If Shakespeare had an editor we wouldn't have Shakespeare.

The remedy, she decided, was in poetry. Mam had read pieces of some of my father's poems, but they were always works-in-progress. It was always over his shoulder, bringing him a cup of tea, or telling him she was going to sleep, always just a glance and allowed always with the understanding that he was going to make them better. These were just drafts of the thing he was trying to get at. That was the thing about the poetry of Virgil Swain. You'll already know that from his Swain-ness. You'll already know a poem is the most impossible thing. It's cruel and capricious and contains within it its own guarantee of failure. What you think you've caught in the poem today is not there when you go to look at it tomorrow. Under the spell of Mrs Quinty's poetry anthologies I can admit I wrote some poems myself, and they were all brilliant until they were rubbish.

Mam had read bits, that's all, and though she's the first to say she knows one hundred per cent of precisely nothing about poetry, and considers just the fact of it, the construction, the craft, the art that has to go into it, a kind of astonishment in itself, she thought Virgil's poems marvellous.

They were not love poems in any normal sense. They were not addressed to her, but in a more profound way they were *for her*. They were for her because they had sprung out of the life she had let Virgil into. There were Aisling copies full of them. Sometimes a whole copy would be filled with different versions of the same poem. The first pages would be maybe a single phrase, a line going across the page in mouse-grey pencil. Then the same line would be written again underneath, but this time altered slightly, maybe an added comma, or a word changed or the tense of the verb or there'd be the half of a second line added and overhanging. As if he'd pulled a little too urgently at the first line and it had come bringing with it the next, but the line had snapped and he'd lost it. He'd started on a new page, written the first phrase again. There'd be nothing else on that page. You'd know he'd spent the whole night just looking at it. There'd be pages with images that came to him, ones that he'd try variants of and reject, the grey mouse scratching a line through them. Other copies might have ten, twelve poems in them, whole and clean and perfect. He liked to write a poem out neatly when it was done, a single mistake, a spelling, a smudge of the pencil, an interruption from me maybe and he turned the page and wrote it out again. It was a way of testing it, I think, and in all tests the poems failed. They were not ready.

But then Virgil had stopped trying.

A poet who can't write is a sad thing. You can see he's fallen in the pit and the sand and the grime stick to his singlet and shorts. Because it's his nature he still looks up, still sees the bar up there against the blue, but he has no way to ascend.

Mam decided the remedy was that my father needed the world to respond. He needed the living worldly equivalent of Abraham or the Reverend to read the poems and say *Not bad, not bad at all*, which would be the Swainish translation of some London editor's *Bloody marvellous*. She had heard me tell of Mrs Quinty and the gift of the poetry anthologies, and so supposed Mrs Quinty was the only one in the parish to be trusted to open my father's copies.

On Wednesday afternoons then, when my father was sent to Kilrush to get messages and the Tech took halfday to let the teachers, like warriors in the *Iliad*, bandage their wounds before the next day's assault, Mrs Quinty came to our house. She brought her typewriter with her. Typewriters were already antiques by then. (In the Tech we did have six computers in the computer room; but holes being irresistible to boys, all had pencil-tops, paperclips, chewing-gum, balls of snot and other unmentionables stuck in their drives, blinked spastically, spent a whole class saying *rebooting* and were ageing virgins who had never Gone on the Internet, so Mrs Quinty decided computers were marvels for The Next Generation.)

She came in the back door carrying her typewriter in its own case.

'Virgil is not to know,' Mam said.

Mrs Quinty had already Had Her Disappointment as far as her husband Tommy staying in Swansea was concerned and was no stranger to keeping secrets.

'Nobody can know, but us,' Mam said, when she came back down from showing Mrs Quinty where to start and the *tap tap tap ding* was already going gangbusters if gangbusters is what poems go when at last in the ecstasy of release.

I wouldn't tell. I knew this was love. I knew it was love with hurt in it and already knew that was the real kind. I knew this was Mam attempting to save Dad, and knew that in the clicking of the keys, crisp and cold and even (thank you, Wenceslas), Virgil Swain, poet, was becoming actual. In time he would come downriver into an anthology.

Except for its complications, as Barry Lillis says, the plan was simple. Mrs Quinty was to come on Wednesdays. Virgil would be sent on Messages to Brews in Kilrush, an emporium of everything, and after he could go to the library. Mrs Quinty was to work her way through the years of Aisling copies and type up only those poems that seemed to her complete. She was to put them back exactly as she found them. Before leaving she was to give Mam each Wednesday's poems. She was to make no copies. She was to be paid each week an hourly rate from the money Mam kept inside Lester the China Dog who was discovered hollow when he lost his tail in a fall.

Mrs Quinty said she would take no payment. 'It's poetry,' she said, eyes gone big behind the dust on her glasses and mouth tight and tiny.

'If you won't take payment you can't type the poems.'

She took payment. (She kept every penny of it in a brown envelope in the top drawer of her mahogany bureau. That money was

318

never spent, and later she gave it to me and I gave it to Father Tipp in Irish Christian-Pagan fashion, partly for prayers and partly for superstition.)

Mam took each Wednesday's poems and put them inside the second copy of the phonebook Pat the Post had stuck in our hedge the time the phone company were trying to prove the expansion of their customer base. She did not read the poems and she didn't let me read them. I think it was in case she had a change of heart, or in case the same thing happened to her that happened to Dad and she read them and found that after all they were not dreadful, but worse, average. She took the poems and fed them flat and singly into the phonebook. She laid them between Breens and Downes and Hehirs and O'Sheas and put the phonebook under her clothes in the bottom drawer. Each week more poems met the general alphabetised population of the County Clare, the whole enterprise taking on the timeless implausibility of fable.

The poems gathered.

When Mam went to bed at night she knew they were right there in the bedroom. She could feel them. I could feel them. If I tried hard and closed my eyes tight and listened into them beyond the rain I could *hear* them.

I know, weird. Believe what you like. (See: Religions.)

That the book would soon be real, that a slim grey volume with *by Virgil Swain* on it would come in the post, was not in doubt. Nor that it would be greeted with wonder. I of course had no idea, and still have no idea, and I expect will probably never have an idea, of how business and money works, and how it would or could work in relation to something as impossible as poetry. But it seemed a natural expectation that once the book was published things would improve for us, and something would be healed.

After six Wednesdays, Mrs Quinty came down the stairs and said, 'That's the last of it.' She stood and gave herself a little tightening tug. The poetry had kept a cold at bay for six weeks.

'There's a good-sized book,' Mam said.

'There is.'

Then Mrs Quinty wrinkled her nose to lift her glasses upward and asked, 'What will you call it?'

Mam hadn't got that far. '*Poems?*'

Mrs Quinty stood back, pressed her hands together, and allowed that suggestion to wilt in the daylight. 'Perhaps something . . . better?' she said.

They stood in the kitchen either side of the perplexity. I was at the table with the *Explorations* anthology, the one that was used before the Department became afraid of being unpopular with fourteen-year-olds, the one that set the bar high, the one that had Milton's 'L'Allegro' in it, *Hence loathed Melancholy, of Cerberus and blackest midnight born.* I looked up. 'Is there any poem longer than the others?'

'There is,' Mrs Quinty said. With her middle finger she pushed the glasses to full magnifying. 'There is one. It's about . . .'

She didn't need to say Aeney.

'It's called "History of the Rain".'

Five minutes later the complete *History of the Rain* was stacked on a sheet of white tissue paper that had come inside a cardigan box from Monica Mac's Drapery. It smelled of lilies or Monica Mac's lily spray. Mam folded the tissue paper over the poems. You could see the title through it. I held the fold closed while Mam slipped a thin green ribbon underneath and brought it up and over and tied the bundle and pressed the bow flat so it would seem less pretty.

'There now,' she said. She looked at me and smiled the sad smile of our complicity and her eyes had that look of *Please God* in them. Maybe just because these were poems, or maybe the same way chocolate grows in your mind in Lent, now that they were there in front of us we had a kind of, I don't know, reverence about them. We wrapped them again in brown paper and tied the package with string.

'You have the handwriting, Ruthie,' Mam said, showing me the publisher's address that Mrs Quinty had found for her. 'You do it.'

I wrote it careful as anything. I wrote it the way my father would have. Then Mam and I took our coats and walked to the village. I carried the poems inside my coat away from the rain.

Maureen Bowe was in Mina Prendergast's. Maureen was a woman whose range of opinion and depth of pronouncement were not, as Edith Wharton might say, encumbered by illiteracy. But I liked her. She lived in a two-room house with three fly-cemeteries hanging from the ceiling, had left school at fourteen but had Yoda-Level understanding of the world, in particular her rights and the workings of social welfare. Maureen could be fun to listen to, but we were burdened with hope and did not enjoy the delay.

'Mary. And Ruth,' she said, turning her giant self around with one elbow still holding her place on the counter.

'Maureen.'

She waited to see if we would offer anything for her to comment on.

'Will it ever stop?' she asked. The rain had almost exhausted comment. 'I have a leak. Back kitchen. Tom Keogh that built it. A flat roof about as useful as wallpaper.' For a moment she let the leak drip in her mind and then added: 'I think there's a grant out of flat roofs now.'

Mother and I said *Really? How wonderful for you*, only not in words.

Maureen swung around on the axis of her elbow. 'That grant's still on the go, is it, Mina?'

Mrs Prendergast preferred customers to conversation, and said the last post would be going shortly.

Once the door had closed and we were alone in the self-possessed but subdued majesty of Faha post office, Mam told Mina Prendergast we had a package for London.

Mrs Prendergast adhered to best practice and did not ask what it was. She took the package and weighed it. Being poetry it weighed almost nothing. That was the thing I thought of, the lightness, the non-mass of it, how the scales of the real world hardly registered it. Mam and I watched the package being ferried over, faintly regarded, and flipped back on to the counter.

Mrs Prendergast opened the stamp book, ran her fingers down the back of a sheaf before selecting The One. She tugged it free, dabbed it in the pink concave pad that looked like Aunt Daphne's powder puff, affixed it with gravity. 'To London,' she said.

And that was all. She didn't add a question mark. Mrs Prendergast wasn't asking, just stating, she would be clear on that. It was none of the Post Office's business. But because *London* was said, and because in a place like Faha in the dead middle of a wet afternoon just the fact of sending something to London had a certain gravity, and that gravity was something in which it was natural that Faha itself would like to share, because every place liked to feel it was a place that could have something important to send to London, and because the *London*, without the question mark, just sort of hung there invitational and alone and grammatically incomplete, Mam said, 'It's poetry.'

She didn't mean to. She regretted it the moment the word *poetry* was out and dragonflying around the post office. I looked to make sure the door was closed.

'I see.'

'Actually, Mrs Prendergast, I wonder if I could ask a favour?'

'Yes?'

'When a letter comes. From London.'

'Yes?'

'Could I ask you to tell Pat to hold it here for us?'

We were Swains. We were already in the embossed paisley-print parish roll-book of Odd. Mrs Prendergast pursed her postbox lips but I think Aeney and Our Grief passed through.

'I'd like it to be a surprise,' Mam said.

In the background I gave Mrs Prendergast my Forlorn Ruth, my Child of Doom, my cheeks of hollow disport and madly magnified eyes.

'I see.'

Then the door opened and Maureen Bowe was back. 'There *is* a grant,' she said, more or less exactly the way you'd say *There is a God.*

With model discretion Mrs Prendergast slid the package along the counter into Outgoing and to my mother made a nod that did not require movement of her head but happened in her eyes only.

The poems were gone.

Mam and I came out into the rain. To all appearances the world was as we had left it – in Church Street Martin Sheehan's tractor pulled over ass-out and impassable while he spoke out the window with one of the Leahys, Old Tom standing with his bicycle in the crossroad, waiting to direct the no-traffic, Centra having Centra delivery, Nuala Casey squinting out at nothing, John Paul Eustace doing his door-to-door – but we knew it was not. We walked

323

home breathing the thin air you breathe when your heart has moved up into your throat and you want to believe that maybe yes, Emily was right and Hope is a Thing with Feathers, and is flying up out of you right now. The feathers are coming out your mouth and your eyes are O's watching it rise above the hedgerows and the dripping fuchsia, above the treetops and the electricity lines and the rain, crossing Ryan's and the Major's and ours, and making its way right now to London.

'You won't tell?' Mam said. 'I know you won't,' she answered, and she looked away, both of us small and quiet, and maybe as close as we could ever be in this life.

Mrs Prendergast intended to tell no one. She only told Father Tipp because poetry seemed in the realm of prayer, and, because his heart was already at capacity with secrets, Father Tipp only told his housekeeper Orla Egan, and Orla Egan only told Mrs Daly when she was doing her floors windows and etceteras on the Tuesday afternoons because she was helpless to resist revealing her privileges within the priest's house and liked to have something to say that was not concerned with dirt Dettol Flash and Windowlene. So, because the marvellous is in short supply, because in sharing it a shine comes and reflects well on the ordinary, soon there was no one in Faha who didn't know Virgil Swain's poems had gone to London.

Except for Virgil Swain.

The way I see it, it was generous and heartfelt. As big Tom Dempsey says, Irish people are appallingly good at giving. So there was not only the first response – *A book?* – and the universal follow-up – *Am I in it?* – there was a shy pride, a prayerlike hope, and among adults a quiet but widespread gladness, as if in our parish poetry had become congregational.

3

How long does it take for someone to see your soul?

Let's say there are soul-seers. Let's say that's their business. Let's say they've been anointed-appointed for this single task. For souls they've got the Zenith Standard. They've got Paragon guidelines, Excellence Exemplars. They've got Pinnacle sunglasses, perfect vision, and those amber close-fitting 1970s Star Trek suits. Their whole reason for being is to look for these souls. They've got their instructions. They're moving out and they're all the time on Alert, Transporters set on Ready.

Dazzlement is what they're after.

Like shining, from shook foil.

They're looking for ones who have given themselves to what is most intensely seen and felt, ones who because of their natures could not see and feel it without wanting to be closer to it, whose own nature could be a kind of restless yearning, who became oddities, lived in margins, who had before them *a standard so high that a higher can be found nowhere else*, so that disappointment was keen and constant, their hair turned silver and their eyes the blue of the sea and the sky.

Let's say the soul-seers go to their work each day.

Let's say they focus their beams.

How long would it take to find him?

Because Mrs Quinty had the necessary attributes for playing a minor character, and could remove herself from scenes, my father did not notice that she had been at his table and typed his poems. In matters of his personal space he was not particular. Like Ted Hughes, for a poem he would have squeezed himself into a corner. He did not notice the copies had been touched because he was not thinking of readers. He knew the poems were so far below Readers that that never entered his head. That's what I understand now. I understand that he bore them mostly out of the spirit of chastisement, not unlike Thomas Dawes whose failings were secret until he fathered a whole family of cross-eyed sons, each one better at crashing cars than the one before, and only one of whom was sometimes sober.

Virgil still went to his table in the evenings. He still read with voracious appetite, the fat, second-hand, 1,902 pages of *The Riverside Shakespeare* (Book 1,604, Houghton Mifflin, Boston) becoming a kind of bible, but he did not pick up the pencil. He did not take-off.

Although you never really know what your parents are feeling, although you can't quite enter the world as them and see it from inside their eyes, I knew my father was lost, and like Mam I too wanted to rescue him. Maybe some part of it was that I wanted that moment in the future when Prospero says to Miranda, *Thou wast that did preserve me*, but mostly it was just love.

I thought by asking him to write me a poem whatever was stalled inside him might restart.

'Will you?'

His long body was twisted in the chair, face angular, silvery beard climbing up his cheeks. His face was composed now, but his eyebrows were these mad wispy filaments, like the way Sean Custy's fiddle strings curl off the fiddle head, or Paudie O leaves the extra bits of wires when he's wired something, as if a reminder that music and electricity were live things and could not be contained.

'Doesn't have to be a long one,' I said.

Two deep creases came either side of his mouth. 'I'm sure I can find a poem written to a Ruth.'

'That's not what I want. I want yours.'

He turned to the table covered in books, pushed a hand up the side of his beard. It made the slightest *crackle*. He pulled it down across his mouth. Beside *The Riverside Shakespeare* was Tolstoy's *Resurrection, Childhood, Boyhood, Youth* (Books 2,888 & 2,889, Penguin Classics, London) as well as the green American hard-cover of Seamus Heaney's *Poems 1965–1975* (Book 2,891 Farrar, Straus & Giroux, New York), the white paperback with the black and white photograph of Robert Lowell holding his glasses and leaning to his left beneath the scarlet title *Selected Poems* (Book 2,892 Farrar, Straus & Giroux, London), John Donne in a mad black hat and with arms folded on the cover of the fat *John Donne, The Complete English Poems* (Book 2,893, Penguin Books, London), But, besides all of these, the book my eye fell on was the small white paperback of W.B. Yeats's *Selected Poems* (Book 3,000, Pan Macmillan, London) because it was open on 'The Song of Wandering Aengus' and because across the page my father had written something in tiny black ink, as if with the poem or the poet he was in dialogue.

At last my father looked back at me. 'What would you like it to say?'

'I don't mind.' I thought I was being helpful. I didn't understand the problem, the agony and mystery of it. I didn't understand then as I do now. I didn't understand that what he wanted in his poems was Life, and that he couldn't summon it. Suddenly the air in the room was close, the rain louder, and I knew I had brought him to a naked place. I had brought him where Swains always end up, in the white glare of their own failure. But I would not stop. 'Will you?'

He turned fully towards me and he took my hands. 'Will you write one for me?' he asked.

His eyes held me. They held me in a way I will never forget, not because of the blueness or the river depth or the shine, not because of the sadness or the defeat but because it seemed right then that in his eyes was a whole history of yearning and in asking me to write he was passing it to me.

'Mine will be bad,' I said.

'But you'll write me one?'

'I will if you will. So, will you?' I shook his two hands for an answer. 'Please? Promise?'

'Do you promise?'

'I promise. Now, say "*I promise to write something for Ruth.*"'

'I promise to write something for Ruth.'

In the meantime, we waited. We waited for London to write back. Mam dropped in to the post office; Mrs Prendergast gave her 'No' with her eyes, and didn't let on that everyone in the queue knew what Mam was waiting for, and that everyone had perfect confidence the news would be good. Because Faha is like that. People like a home victory. Unlike Tommy Tuohy, who enjoys cursing Man U, the team he supports, people here are generous once something goes outside the parish. They want it to do well. They supposed that, London being London, there was a fair mountain of poems to be got through and it might take some time, but they knew. They knew because my father was Virgil Swain, and because now that they thought about it, he was more or less exactly what a man who had a book of poetry sent to London should look like.

Although no one but Mrs Quinty had read his poems, my father became *Our Poet*.

I only discovered this because Vincent Cunningham has a heart soft as cooked cabbage, and because as my serial proposer he often came to our house. He came without invitation, appeared in the kitchen, not exactly in the same way the smaller McInerneys did – eating a second dinner at our house after the free-for-all, fork-your-spuds-from-the-bowl, Go! dining chez McInerney – but quiet and courteous, as a friend of Aeney's and one familiar with loss. Mam of course loved him. All mothers did. They swam right into the place where his mother was dead, and they thought *What a nice boy* and how neat he always looked, his shirt collar just right inside his round-neck jumper and his hands always clean. Like all the best people, he only ever took tea at the third invitation.

After one such visit he asked me, 'Would you like to walk along the road, Ruth?'

'No.'

'Ruth, walk Vincent some of the way home.'

'He knows the way.'

'Air will do you good.'

'I have air. Look. Nice. Air.'

'It's all right, Mrs Swain. She's right. I know the way.'

Good people are just horrible. You just want to shoot them.

'All right, yes! I'd love to walk along the road.'

Walking Along the Road is the Faha equivalent of going to the cinema or the mall or the bowling alley in the real world. Vincent thought the road just marvellous altogether.

'I can't go any faster,' I said, 'So if you want to go ahead that's fine.'

'No, no. This is fine.'

I walked slower. But you can't lose a fellow like Vincent Cunningham, he slowed right down. The rain was not rain he took any notice of. 'Ruth,' he said, 'I'm hoping it'll be soon.'

I mistook his meaning. I was in *Middlemarch* then, maybe I was dreaming he was Mr Casaubon, whose proposal Dorothea should have stamped on. But before I could say anything, he said, 'Your dad's poems. I hope he'll hear soon.'

I did not hit him. Let me put that to bed.

I did not grab his ear and pull him to me and say 'How do you know?'

Maybe my expression did. I am not responsible for my face.

'I just wanted to say, I'm hoping it'll be soon,' he said.

4

It was not soon. Soul-seeing in London was on a go-slow. Mam and I held our breath, and although, from both sides of our family, I had advantages in holding breath underwater, most days I knew we were drowning a little bit more. One day Mrs Hanley came. She was a small brown-eyed terrier with the plainspoken forthrightness of Cork people. Mrs Hanley had buried her husband, but it had taken nothing out of her. She got on with it, she said. The exact opposite of Eileen Waters, who had so far in this life successfully avoided making a direct statement, Mrs Hanley liked to hit a nail on the head. Now she was running the FAS scheme for the unemployed, and because she knew London had still not replied, and because like everyone else she wondered how we were living, by way of asking she told my father he had to join. The scheme was for the betterment to the parish so technically anything he could offer would be eligible.

What he offered was Yeats.

It wasn't a joke.

I suppose he couldn't resist. I suppose large dreams sailed their galleons into his brain and he had that kind of brain where strange is just normal in a bit of a storm. That Mrs Hanley agreed to it was maybe the more remarkable.

I can't remember who said it, but it's true that whenever anyone reads Shakespeare they become Shakespeare. Well, the same is true for Yeats. Take an afternoon. Sit and read his poems. Any, it doesn't really matter. Spend an afternoon, read out loud. And as you do, sounding out those lines, letting the rhythms fall, following some of it and not following more of it, doesn't matter, because gradually, without your even noticing it at first, just softly softly, *you rise.*

You do. Honest. Read poetry like that and human beings become better, more complex, loving, passionate, angry, subtle and poetic, more expressive and profound, altogether more fine.

That's what I learned from my father.

He was given a room in the back of the hall. Six classes. He needed the money but expected no one to come.

When he came in the front door of the hall there were people looking to find extra chairs. They didn't say *We're here because you're the poet who has the book gone to London*, they didn't say *We're sorry your son died* or *You have to keep hope alive.* A higher form of English is practised in Ireland, and direct statement is frowned upon. Nods were passed as Virgil came in. Nobody took their eyes off him as he settled the *Collected Poems* on the desk, and in an instant, trait undiscovered until now but inescapable as his bloodstream, he lifted his chin like the Reverend, and began.

My father's teaching style was as improbable as his nature. He stood behind the desk and looked out over the faces peering up at him. He allowed a pause that felt like a prayer, that felt like he was going to attempt this and he had no idea what he was going to say or how he was going to say it or if he even could begin. Then he began. He paced, back and over in the narrow space left to him by the chairs, back and over (six steps), speaking loud and clear off the very top of his head, which was above all of ours, and which it was not difficult to believe was just then exploding. He used his hands sometimes while he read, a kind of downward cutting, sharp, a chop, like that, and sometimes he'd say a line and be taken by the quality of it. He'd repeat it in a softer voice and you knew right then, right at that moment, he was discovering newness in it, and even if you didn't know what exactly that was you knew you had arrived in a different country from the one outside that was just now discovering it was bankrupt.

The classes were theatre. They were not a one-man-show in the sense of either structure or performance, did not have any clear sense of progression, did not have pauses, did not adhere to any notion of making points or playing to the audience, but they were electric and before they were done were already becoming part of parish legend: *You won't believe it, but once in Faha.*

Even on those four times I got to go and was stacking the chairs later for Colm the caretaker – *Eight in a stack, no more no less* – I knew there would be times in the future when someone would look shyly at me and acknowledging wonder with a gentle toss-back of their head say, 'Do you know, I was at the Yeats.'

The more you hope the more you hurt. The best of us hope the most. That's God's sense of humour. Back then I hoped the soul-seers were coming to Clare. They were putting on their sunglasses, locking in the coordinates and setting out from Russell Square. Because, as Father Tipp said, there's a religious twist – which may actually be an insoluble knot – in my imagination, I lent them the mute mystique of the Three Wise Men and dreamed them arriving, if not quite on camels then certainly with amazement in their eyes.

At night I prayed one prayer: *Tomorrow.*

Tomorrow let the word come.

I prayed to God, found God unsatisfactory because He had no face, and prayed then to Aeney. There was Swain logic to it. Lying under the skylight at night I pictured the prayers of the whole world rising. (TG there were time-zones or they would all be heading up around the same time, and Prayer-Traffic Control would be . . . Sorry, fecund.) I pictured them rising off rooftops, ascending against the rain, millions of them, vague and particular, a nightly one-way traffic of human yearning, and I thought surely they couldn't all be *heard*? Surely they became just noise? How could He listen to that? Even just from Faha there would be the McCarthys, who had a Nan gone to the Regional, Mrs Reid, whose Tommy was having his heart opened, Maureen Knowles who had the bowel, Mr Curran, Sean Sugrue, Pat Crowe, all in Condition Uncertain in Galway, Patricia the Dolan's mother who was starting chemo in the Bons. And those were only the ones I had heard. So, because Aeney was that part of me that was already in the next life, because he was fair-haired and blue-eyed and generally adorable, I decided he could be our Ambassador. He could carry the word and so to him I prayed.

Come on, Aeney.

But Aeney was elsewhere, and after four months of waiting Mam had me write a letter of enquiry.

'We want something polite but firm,' she said. 'Maybe they need a slight push. We want to know if they are interested or if we should offer the book elsewhere.'

I wrote it neatly on blue letter paper. *Or we shall send the book elsewhere.* Mam signed it. When she put it in the envelope the flap wouldn't stick. We never sent letters. The envelope was probably ten years old. She put it under *The Return of the Native* and pressed down. But still the glue wouldn't hold.

Sometimes you have to defy the signs. 'Go down to Mac's and see if they have an envelope.'

Moira Mac was doing what she always did in this life, washing clothes. She had no envelopes, but took a Holy Communion card out of its white one and gave me that. I brought it back inside my cardigan. At the kitchen table I addressed it. 'Say a prayer,' Mam said.

The more you hope the more you hurt.

You drop a letter in a Holy Communion envelope in the postbox and already you are waiting for a reply. Human beings were built for response. But human nature can't tolerate too much waiting. Between the emotion and the response falls the shadow, T.S. Eliot said, and that was the principle that inspired texting, that came up with the shortest possible time, basically as fast as Sheila Geary's two thumbs could hammer ILY on a tiny keyboard and get Johnny Johnston's ILY2 back, so that between emotion and response now there wasn't all that much shadow.

All writers are waiting for replies. That's what I've learned. Maybe all human beings are.

After the Yeats classes my father returned to writing. He had been renewed. A white electric urgency flashed in him. For the first time he broke his own rule about only writing after the work on the farm was done, and now he was at his desk when I woke and there again when I came home and there when I went to not-sleep at night. It was a flood of new work. It was pouring into and out of him quickly, swift turbulent river. His pencil dashed across the paper now, worked itself down to a soft stub. When the lines were blurry as if underwater the pencil was quickly pared, soft *whoo-whoo*, the parings blown, and the writing raced on.

'Dad?'

Inside the hum he couldn't hear me.

'Dad, Mam says dinner's ready.'

He wrote faster than I had ever seen anyone.

'Dad?'

I broke the hum. He fell silent, and at last pulled back out of the poem, pencil still in his hand. I had the sense of his unplugging, and that it was both arduous and somehow regretful.

'Yes?' he said. Then again, 'Yes.' As if recollecting that Mam and I and dinner existed.

He ate little, and to remedy this Mam tried various stratagems, cooking his favourite, salmon of course, buttered & honeyed carrots with peas and potatoes, telling me a clean plate was the best way of thanking her, or announcing that she had ruined the dinner and was sorry that it was probably inedible, just to make him feel *I must try this for Mary.*

By the end of the week Mam decided it was best to keep a plate in the oven. He would come down when he was ready. We shouldn't disturb him. My mother has a natural kind of grace, which is basically wisdom.

Many plates of charred food were taken from the oven, but I never heard her complain.

We were still waiting for the reply from London, but now it seemed less vital. Aeney had done it, I decided. He'd gotten the poems turned on and now they were coming in a way that did not seem humanly possible. My father was not wrestling with these. Even though I was not getting to read them, I knew. I knew from the moments of goodnight when I stood behind him waiting for his kiss on my forehead, when I watched him, humming and rocking, pencil flashing across the page, I knew that these were different, these were his life's work. He still crossed out, wrote a line and rewrote it, sounding it that way he had where the sound and rhythm were present but you could not make out the words. He still turned the page fast and began on a fresh one.

But now there was joy in it.

As I have said, I've read every book I can find about poetry, how it's made and why it's made and what it means that men and women write it. I've read T. S. Eliot's *On Poetry and Poets* (Book 3,012, Faber & Faber, London), *Poems of John Clare's Madness* (Book 3,013, Geoffrey Grigson ed., Routledge & Kegan Paul, London), *Robert Lowell: A Biography* (Book 3,014, Ian Hamilton, Faber & Faber, London), Jeremy Reed's *Madness, the Price of Poetry* (Book 3,015, Peter Owen, London), and the basic message is, poets are different to you and me. Poets do not escape into other worlds, they go deeper into this one. And because depths are terrifying, there is a price.

The price at first was thinness. My father forgot food. In a different biography it is here that he would turn to drink. It is here he might have considered recourse to the methods of Johnny Masters who started drinking early in the day so that by evening the world became tolerable. But because at Paddy Brogan's wedding my father had drunk a glass of whiskey and shortly after thought people were trees, he knew drink would take him away and not towards the thing he wanted to capture.

He grew thin. His arms grew longer. Inside the open collar of his white shirt there were ropes and cords of tendons in his neck. His shoulders were sharp and made of the shirt a sail.

I do not mean to say he ignored us. Certainly he did not intend to, and there were moments when, like discovering a butterfly on the back of your hand, he stopped in the kitchen, looked at me the way no one else ever did. It was a look that loaned you some of what he was seeing, a look that made you feel, I don't know, transfigured.

'Hey, Ruthie.' He swept me into his embrace. I pressed myself into that shirt and held on and for those moments forgave what I didn't yet know would need forgiveness.

337

There were other times, times the suddenness in him took my hand and my mother's hand and brought us out into the garden where the rain that was not called rain was falling softly and where he said, 'I will make things better for us,' and Mam said, 'We are fine, Virgil, we are fine.' A time when he let out a roar upstairs and came bounding down and clapped his hands hard. One *clap*, like that. Then another, louder, *CLAP*, so that even Nan looked, and I said, 'Are you done?' And he smiled and his eyes were shining the way eyes only shine in love-stories and he shook his head and he laughed. He had to catch the laugh with his hand, and then he touched the top of my head. 'I am going to make things better for us, Ruthie,' he told me, and went back up the stairs again and soon was humming once more.

We had an engine, a dynamo in our house, and its output was pages and pages of poems. A week passed, then another, and another. He was still writing, and writing it seemed was not the vexing toil it was when I tried to compose my promised poem, but a wildly improbable fizz. It was giddy and swift and surprising. It was plugged in and all-powerful, a blind mad rush that came not linear nor logical nor even reasonable but with the unruly irrepressible quality of life in it, the kind of writing Gabriel García Márquez meant when he said the sheer pleasure of it may be the human condition which most resembles levitation.

And our house rose with it.

How could it not? For a time our house left behind the ordinary world. I had only a vague sense that in the news the country was actually sinking. Greece had already sunk. Spain was sinking, so was Portugal. Whole bits of Europe were returning to seaweed. Our country was on what Margaret Crowe called tender hooks, waiting to see if we'd have a Soft Landing. We would, said the Ministers, just before we didn't. But really I didn't notice. The economy, like fine weather, was something that happened in Dublin. Honestly, until the Poles left, I didn't know we had one. Gradually the Lidl and Aldi bags were coming (Mrs Prendergast called them Ly-dell and All-dee), and the croissants were departing. Shops were closing. In Ryan's Tommy McCarroll said he'd put his money in the Absolute Idiots Bank and now felt like an absolute idiot. Francie Arthur's fifty-euro notes started smelling like mattress, and then the Maguires were gone to tile Australia, Pat and Seamus and Sean Walsh to dig holes in Canada, Mona Murphy was selling her furniture in her front garden and Johnny Doyle at Doyle's Auctioneers was like Young Blight in *Our Mutual Friend*, who, to create an impression of industry, spent his days filling his appointment book with made-up names, Mr Aggs, Baggs, Caggs and yes, let me see, at two sharp, Mr Daggs.

But I was unaware of this, unaware the country was moving into a time where only story would sustain it. Our house was a house in fairy tale, unaware it was in a kingdom of disenchantment. Maybe if you could take away the front walls, maybe if you could lift off the roof of any house and see the actual life in it, the parts that are not, never were, and never will be In Recession, the parts that are people trying to live and trying to do better and be better, maybe then every house would seem magical. In our house the magic was white-hot. My father was on fire. We knew it was not normal, but normal was never a Swain consideration. Everyone adapts inside their own story. That's the world. In ours the rain fell and my father stayed up in the roof writing poems. The rain was a big part of it. In the coverless second-hand edition of *The Power and the Glory* (Book 1,113, Penguin Classics, London) that belonged once to an Isobel O'Dea, Ursuline Convent, Thurles, Graham Greene says the rain was like a curtain behind which almost anything can happen. And that's right. But if you haven't lived in it, if you haven't looked out day after day into those pale veils, haven't heard the constant whispering of the rain that you know cannot be voices, cannot be souls, sodden and summoning, then you cannot know the almost anything that can happen.

My father was filled with zeal. It is a word I have never used, *zeal*, because it sounds somehow inappropriate in ordinary life. But that's what it was. That's what the quality of animation and focus amounted to. And the zeal was this white fire coming and going on our stairs, was in the bluest eyes and the untucked white shirt and the running of hands over and back on the crown of his head, white fire.

So in a way it was no surprise when I was woken by smoke.

It was in my eyes burning, and when I turned on the light a thick grey cloud of it came across the ceiling. I couldn't move. I watched it from my pillow with perfect stillness, the way I might have watched Santa or the Tooth Fairy or God if I had caught any of them unawares when I was meant to be sleeping. The smoke travelled curiously, by which I mean it was the curious one and came across the ceiling considering the cool dark glass of the skylight and then curled to come further down into the room. I snuggled down. I breathed into the pillow. I wasn't sure if the smoke was there for me or would pass on and go out under the door. I wasn't sure if I had already died and Purgatory was as promised, only with your own pyjamas.

Nobody else was moving. From the house there was not a sound. So the fire was a dreamt one until I was choking.

The smoke descended. It came into my throat and lodged and burned. It took the walls and the ceiling and the skylight and made blind and amorphous the room so that soon there was no room. There was only smoke. My eyes stung and I closed them tight and

340

pulled up the duvet, surprised that I was to die under it and not in the river like my brother.

'Aeney?' I whispered. '*Aeney?*'

But Aeney didn't answer. The smoke was taking its time. It was letting me think *In here I will be okay* while slowly in a smoke-way it devoured the room. It found the open drawers of my dresser, found my clothes, found my go-gos and my clips-jar and my hair-brush. For a moment I pictured the floor and the walls being gone and the roof too and my bed standing alone and surrounded by flames in this ardent sky. For a moment I was thinking levitation, that the smoke was a summons only and I was in the sky and soon I would hear the Reverend.

For one perfect moment I had no fear. I was already dead.

I eased the duvet down an inch, the better to hear Him.

But the smoke that was everywhere entered me and I heard only my own gasp and ratchet and cough. I pulled back the duvet, only it didn't pull back. I got up out of the bed, but only in my mind. I felt my way through the smoke and ran out the door and called 'Dad? Dad?' and woke the house before the fire took us all, only I had passed out and discovered too late the difference between dreaming and dying.

In jump-cuts then: being borne down the stairs; my father's arms; our house in smoke-disguise; flames in the mirror leaping; Nan and Mam in the front garden in their nightdresses; *O Ruthie*; Huck lying in the grass and whimpering; cars and tractors with headlights on; Jimmy Mac, Moira Mac with blankets; the hose, the buckets, the running; the voices.

Because it was beside the river, because it was damp and soggy and owned body and soul by the rain, our house did not burn down. It smouldered.

341

The cause of the fire was not Pentecostal, it was not zeal. It was more mundane. The chimney had caught. Fire travelled in through the old stonework, eventually feeding on the ancient upper timbers until it met the resistance of the dripping slates. Before the Kilrush fire brigade got there the fire was out, but because they had come they gave the insides a thorough blast. Water went up the chimney. It dripped from the rafters after. Stubborn black pools settled on the flags and on the shelves, in the teacups and the saucers and the glasses, on the seats of our leather armchairs and under the linoleum in the bathroom, the last of the pools remaining a week and only leaving when it was certain from then on our house would be irredeemably stained and for ever smell of fire and water.

Mam and Nan and I went to Mac's. Three of their boys came out of one room so I could have it. I think I was still in shock. I was still uncertain about being saved. I lay in the bed that was warm and hollowed from McInerneys and for the umpteenth time tried to fathom why Swains were chosen for disaster.

5

It would have been easier if we had been struck by lightning. It would have made a kind of sense, would have allowed those of a certain mind to take charcoal comfort in our being singled so. It would have been easier if I wrote *My father caught fire.* Or *The poems exploded* or *What was in him reached the point of combustion.*

Because I know that is what actually happened. I know it cannot have been just random.

We want the world to have a plot.

A chimney fire is not a plot.

Your brother drowning by chance is sad, but to tell it sheds no light and lends no meaning.

What happened is what happened. Things were consequent only in the sense that they followed. Although as they did, I knew we were becoming story. I knew ours was a family waiting for a teller. But where was the meaning?

For ten days Mam and Nan and I stayed at McInerney's, and my father worked restoring the house. Faha is good in a crisis. He had help from everyone, but mostly Jimmy Mac and the Major who left aside whatever they normally did in order to carry outside the insides of our house, stack it in the haybarn, and cover it in grey canvas by night.

After a week I went back to school, and for a while added to my aura the grandeur of conflagration. I did not exploit it. A nimbus is ungainly in a classroom. In any case I had nausea, dizziness and floaters and feared a smell of singe.

Then one day, a day damp and indifferent as any other, a day without the slightest heralding, a day with nothing about it that said *This day*, I came into Mac's and asked Mam how our house was coming.

'It's coming good,' she said, 'we'll be home soon, Ruthie.'

Disbelieving, I went back to see.

My father was not in the house. The front and back doors were open. I want to say there was music playing. I want to say the tape deck was on and Mozart was playing. I want to have it blasting out, large and joyous and triumphant. I want the whole house to have been filled with music. But there was none, and I am not ready yet to go that far into story. The house was empty, the floors and all damp surfaces covered in *Clare Champions* so it seemed a place of words. I went out the back and around the haggard and up to the wall of the river meadow.

My father was down by the place where Aeney had drowned. He was standing perfectly still, Huck beside him.

'Dad?'

He only turned the second time I called. And when he did his face fell into that soft creased smile, but his eyes were the saddest I had ever seen them.

'Hey, Dad. Hi.'

Maybe we all have momentary foreknowledge, which although of little practical use seals our hearts just enough to bear what's coming. I turned to the river and saw the pages. Through the rain-mist of my glasses I saw them as white-caps. They were small, already distant, and sailing west in the swiftness of the current. I didn't believe they were pages and then knew they were the poems, and knew the answer he was going to give me when I asked why.

'They were no good, Ruth.'

I didn't say anything. A better Ruth would have gone after them, a Ruth not afraid of the river. I stood silently by. I watched the poems go, and felt a laceration, which was partly my own but partly too my father's, for I knew what throwing them into the river had cost him. I knew Abraham and the Reverend were right there. I knew he had failed the Impossible Standard and believed at that moment that everything he had done had been a failure. He had lost his son to the river, and then almost all of us in a fire that he was not even aware had been moving through the house while he had continued writing a poem he now considered useless.

I think I knew then that a letter would come from London, that Mam would open it in the corner of Faha Post Office. That I would watch her read it and hear the sharp intake of her breath and then take the letter from her and read *Dear Mrs Swain, we thank you for your letter. We are sorry to say we have no record of ever receiving* History of the Rain.

We moved back in to our house. My father was hushed, like a man with ashes in his soul.

Eloquent in his own way, Father Tipp brought a set of Yeats left to him by a cousin in Tipperary who was unaware of his taste. These were the hardcover *Mythologies, Autobiographies, Essays & Explorations* and *Collected Poems* (Books 3,330, 3,331, 3,332 & 3,333, Macmillan, London), each of which I later discovered must to my father have had an air of peculiar prompting, because though they had gone elsewhere about the world on their inside flyleaves they bore stamps in green ink that said 'Salisbury Library, Wiltshire'.

'They need a finer mind than mine,' the priest said.

My father took them with chin-tremble and head tilted to the ceiling to keep his eyes from spilling. Everything now was bigger than saying.

345

'Thank you, Father,' he said.

If wings could come they were coming then. In the three days that followed, while he sat in Aeney's sky-room and read Yeats, my father was ascending.

On the third day I came home from school into the kitchen and called 'Hello' up to him. He did not answer. I climbed the Captain's Ladder through the smells of fire and rain. I said, 'Dad, I . . .'

And that's all I said, because there, at his desk under the skylight, in the pale gleam of the rain, my father was dead.

6

Taking you down.

That's what the nurses say. *Tomorrow, Ruth, we'll be taking you down.*

Mrs Merriman was taken down but she did not come back up. I have Mr Mackey so I am In Good Hands. I have said I don't want details. I don't want medical language. I don't want a venous access device in here, or Interferon therapy or acetaminophen or arsenic trioxide or all-trans retinoic acid. I don't want them in my pages. I want mine, like Shakespeare's first folio, to be To the Great Variety of Readers, from the Most Able to Him that Can but Spell. (You kno who you ar.) I don't want mine suffocated by science. I want mine to breathe, because books are living things, they have spines and smells and length of life, and from living some of them have tears and buckles and some stains.

Mrs Quinty has come up to Dublin. I told her not to, I told her when I was leaving there was no need, and that if you believe illness is everywhere the last place you should visit is a hospital. But that woman, though small, is irrepressible. She came into the ward like a short fat bird, buttoned coat, blue handbag and tighter-than-ever hairdo. Mam hugged her and Mrs Quinty said, 'Don't, I'm all wet,' and then she looked at me and put a hand, flat, against her breastbone, pat, just like that, as though lidding what was open.

'Dear Ruth,' she said, and, after regaining herself, 'Goodness. Do they not know how to fix up a pillow?'

Mrs Quinty brought the parish with her. She brought cards and well-wishes, news of candles and prayers, and then, mindful not to burden her visit with concern, recounted stories; Danny Devlin had taken his toilet out and thrown it in his front garden ahead of the toilet tax, said he'd knock his chimney ahead of the chimney tax, and brick in his windows before they came taxing daylight. (A country that understands the potency of imagery, the memory of our bankers, Mrs Quinty said, was to be enshrined in perpetuity in septic tanks.) Kevin Keogh, though he had about as much love for her as a small donkey, had surrendered at last and married Martina Morgan. The government, believing itself attuned to the pulse of the nation, had proposed abolishing the Senate, just as the Senate, Mikey Lucy said, were about to propose abolishing the government. Sean Connors had written from Melbourne and told his father he missed being with him at the silage, and in mute desolation Matt Connors had taken a poss of it, put it in a padded envelope and brought it to Mina Prendergast for posting, silage being for the Connors what the smell of coalsmoke was to Charles Dickens, and guava to Gabriel García Márquez, the indelible imprint of home.

All paradises are lost. The Council, Mrs Quinty said, has given up the ghost. The roads are going away. The windmills are coming. In the ghost estate, in disgust at the failures of promise, two of the Latvians have constructed an artificial paradise out of drugs and alcohol and raised a flag of Germany.

The river has continued to rise. It took the graveyard, left tombstones standing upright in the Shannon, then it came up Church Street for the church, and Mary Daly, who was still kneeling praying like in T.S. Eliot to the brown God, had to be ferried out just as she was starting to levitate or drown, depending on who was telling it. Our house, home to too many metaphors, had become metaphoric and needed a bailout. The McInerneys were at it.

'You'll only hear it from others so I might as well tell you,' Mrs Quinty added, and pursed her lips and sat a little more erect to announce: 'Mr Quinty has returned.'

The way she said it you knew she was still deciding what to do with him. Mam and I looked elsewhere.

'Stomach ulcers,' she said, with not entirely disguised pleasure, and left it at that.

Mrs Quinty is the only living person who read *History of the Rain*. When it was gone, and I asked her to remember it, she could not. Because of the haste, and the need to be undiscovered, the typing not the poems had taken her attention. She would touch her lip then put her hand out in front of her as if the words were coming, as if a speech bubble was forming, but no, she'd say, she would not do my father an injustice and give me a misremembered line.

In the white paperback of Yeats's *Selected Poems*, beside 'The Song of Wandering Aengus', I read the two lines my father had written. *Why did you take him?* And *Why does everything I do fail?* And from those questions I understood Virgil Swain was applying the Impossible Standard to God.

*

I cannot say that my father had faith in God. The truth is that he had something more personal; he had a sense of Him, the Father of the Rain. The poems, the raptures and the despair I have come to think of as part of a dialogue; they were expressions of wonder and puzzlement, a longing for ascension and an attempt to make endure in this world a spirit of hope. So in my mind, day by day, the poems became greater for not existing.

This was the truth I clung to when the report into his death

349

came back, when we were told my father had had a tumour curved like a hook in the parietal lobe of his brain. The tumour was embedded, and had been growing for some time, the Doctor said. The way he said it I knew he thought it explained the raptures, the ecstasies that produced the poems. The tumour explained everything. The tumour was the whole story. And right then I knew that that was the wrong story and that I would have to write the truth.

*

That Vincent Cunningham is unreal.

Who takes a bus from Faha to Ennis — that foul fumy rattling boneshaker Dennis Darmody, who has the look and personality of a corkscrew, drives kamikaze around Blind Faith bends — who takes that, and then stands waiting for the Ennis-to-Dublin, whose passengers are all Free-Pass pensioners who go up and back not because they have business in Dublin but because they have free-passes and wiped-out pensions, who buys the Day Return when the journey is four hours each way, when they haven't ten euro to their name, when they should be studying for exams, and half the country is under water? Who brings Quality Street?

Vincent Cunningham comes squelching down the hospital corridor in wet sneakers and stands at the ward entrance with a general drowned look. If I said 'Go away' he would. He would take the bus back again, and, inconceivably but truly, he would not resent it.

'Mrs Quinty says I will not die.'

It was not my best greeting, but time was short. This is my last Aisling. I was fasting and anxious and sounds were blurry and my style was breaking up.

Vincent Cunningham sits in my visitor seat. Mam is gone downstairs with Mrs Quinty. Across the way Jackie Fennell looks at him and raises her perfectly curved perfectly plucked eyebrows and passes me the most unsubtle of nods.

'Of course you won't,' Vincent says.

'I cannot, according to Mrs Quinty, because in my writing there is such life.'

I also cannot because Alice Munro says the whole grief of life will not do in fiction. You can't have so much sorrow – readers will throw the book against the wall.

'You won't,' Vincent says again. But the way he says it sends this deep furrow down between his eyebrows and I know he's only saying it.

'But if I do.'

'You won't.'

'Vincent Cunningham.'

He swallows his objection. He is pleased and abashed to hear me say his name. 'Yes?'

'If I do, two things.'

'Two things.'

'First, you know what to do with all my pages?' Have I said, his eyes are the kindest? He has shaved for the journey, plastic blue Gillette that makes his cheeks look quite polished. Really, there's a shining in all of him. 'You remember?'

'Yes.'

'Good.'

'What's second?'

'Second is actually first. Second, is that you should kiss me.'

I may have been floating. I had the feeling I was floating.

'I do not think that if I am going to die,' I said, 'I should die without having been kissed.'

Only through story can we tolerate death.

How else can we forgive God?

I asked my father to write me a poem. He never quite did. But he left a handwritten will that was witnessed by John Paul Eustace and in it he gave the details of the life assurance he had been paying, and in it he said: 'For Ruth, my books.'

Just that. *For Ruth, my books.*

On the day I could bring myself to go in and look at them, a library of books burned and drowned but undestroyed, I saw that on his desk was *The Salmon in Ireland* and folded inside it was a page in his handwriting. On the top it said: *for Ruth Louise Swain.* And underneath, at random angles, were words and phrases, some underlined, some overwritten, and others crossed out, a scattering trying to become a gathering.

Here: *My father climbed the sky.*

Here: *from cinderway ascend.*

Salmon-ascent, struck out then written again then crossed out again.

Spire/Aspire.

Leap leap the

On the right-hand side in a pencilled circle: *Tommy okay.* Beneath it: *Morrow, Eacrett, Cheatley & Paul.*

Leap

In a small rectangle: '*We're going fishing.*'

Here: *Fish/Fly* and *Water/Sky*

Ever the light that lures and eludes/ ever the

On the left-hand side a gently curved question mark that could be a fishing line but is in fact *a bend in the river*

Leap

Only in love the light ascending/

And last, in the faintest leaden grey, his hand hardly pressing the words into the page: *I will make things better.*

And that's all. In fragments for me, the impossible poem of him.

So in a way he kept his promise.

And here, in my way, I am keeping mine.

If I am dead my pages will be put with his page and pressed inside *The Salmon in Ireland* and Vincent Cunningham will bring them to the River Shannon and throw them in.

If I am alive this is my book, and my father lives now in the afterlife that is a book, a thing not vague or virtual but something you can hold and feel and smell because to my mind heaven like life must be a thing sensual and real. And my book will be a river and have the Salmon literal and metaphoric leaping inside it and be called *History of the Rain*, so that his book did not and does not perish, and you will know my book exists because of him and because of his books and his aspiration to leap up, to rise. You will know that I found him in his books, in the covers his hands held, the pages they turned, in the paper and the print, but also in the worlds those books contained, where now I have been and you have been too. You will know the story goes from the past to the present and into the future, and like a river flows.

Because here is what I know: the rain becomes the river that goes to the sea and becomes the rain that becomes the river. Each book is the sum of all the others the writer has read. Charles Dickens was a writer because his father had a small library and because solitude was not lonely with Robinson Crusoe and Don Quixote. Each book a writer writes has all the others in it, so there's a library that's like a river and it keeps on going. My book has in it all the books my father read, and in that way his spirit survives, as mine does, because although impossible there is a communion between readers and writers, and that though writers write and fail and write and fail again the failing is what counts, being against the current and making the leap, and his leap and mine lands him impossibly here now where he walks towards a sparkling river, and where a man with flowing hair and vivid eyes comes to meet him. RLS greets him with a raised hand and welcoming expression and in softest accent calls the name Virgil. RLS has a warming smile, a quick wit and a hundred stories to tell. The ground is new grass, the air almost tender because air in the afterlife is and is so sweet and as my father breathes it in he cannot believe this place or this company, both of which are made better by being impossible. Impossible too the quicksilver brilliance, the sun-bounce and shine of the River Shannon. Impossible the birds, so many and so joyful. Impossible the sky, blue and bluer now, with butterflies, while all the time the two men bear onwards along the riverbank. Impossible that RLS hums now, humming a not-yet-line of a not-yet-poem. Impossible that my father does the same, and that to him RLS glances his shone dark eyes and in them there is such recognition and joy that both now go humming, a sound somewhere between bird and man, otherworldly in this one but natural in that, impossible too that my father looks down the bank and sees ahead of them how that place, a bend in the river, has become familiar and his breath is shortened and his heart quickened because here is Uncle Noelie in his good suit coming and he looks better than he ever looked in this life, his All-Ireland winning look, and he waves in recognition and points back along the bank where my father sees the fair head of a boy and he has to take the leap and believe in the impossible now because though he blinks and palms his forehead the boy does not go away and Aeney becomes clearer and clearer and is not yet looking but, contentedly, patiently, fishing that river in the afterlife. And RLS stops and says, 'There now,' in that softest Scottish accent, drawing back his hair with one hand, and smiling, his whole demeanour radiant from X marking the spot and treasure found. 'Your son,' he says.

And, impossibly, my father sees that it is. Aeney turns and sees too. He lays down the fishing rod. He runs the way he has always run, that way of running that seems a natural expression of human grace, and he comes to Dad who comes to him and wraps his arms around him and lowers his head into the golden hair and they hold to each other impossibly long, long, longer still, and in their embrace is all our story, past present and to come, in it is the knowledge that Mam will be all right and that though she will be lonely and sad she will take comfort in the candles where one day in Faha church she will sit up with the clear and absolute certainty her husband has found her son, in that embrace is the knowledge that I will at last go into Remission and begin to get better, that I will return home, that, impossibly, I, Ruth, will write this book, that Mrs Quinty will type my pages, that you will read them, that Vincent Cunningham will come calling, for conversation and slightly salty kisses, and that one day, impossibly, he will take me walking for my first time out the front door and I will go to the river with him and not fear water or sky, not fear failure or doom because I will know somehow we can come through, and our story is of enduring and aspiring and that it is enough to keep hoping and to keep telling stories, for each other and about each other, collaborating in the elaborate history of ourselves so that in stories we exist, knowing that in this world in this time enduring is all our victory, but victory nonetheless, and I Ruth Swain will know that love is real and forgiveness complete because, at last, unimaginably, implausibly, impossibly, the rain will have stopped.

Acknowledgements

My father believed in education, at a time when education meant books. Twice a month he took us to the library, and those visits remain among the most cherished memories of my growing up. Apart from the browsing and the borrowing, just to be for an hour in the physical company of so many books was inspiring and moving in a way that is perhaps hard to explain today, but for which I will always be grateful. When my father died, in his will he asked that his books be left to me. Among them was *The Salmon Rivers of Ireland* by Augustus Grimble.

One book inspires another. To any reader of this novel the debt I owe to so many writers will already be apparent. The debt to readers perhaps less so.

Over the five years I have been working on this book Caroline Michel achieved the impossible standard and kept believing in it, when it was still invisible. Her friendship and support has meant everything. My thanks too to Anna Jean Hughes and Rachel Mills and the whole team at Peters, Fraser & Dunlop.

Two years ago, Michael Fishwick at Bloomsbury asked me to come in and tell him about the novel I was working on. At the time I was three years in and had lost faith in it. When I walked out into Bedford Square later I had refound it. My heartfelt thanks to Michael, to Anna Simpson, Oliver Holden-Rea and copyeditor Sarah-Jane Forder, to Kathy Belden in New York and all at

Bloomsbury for their dedication and enthusiasm and generally being the kind of publisher Ruth dreamt of in Faha.

I am grateful to my brother Paul for his continued support and belief in my writing, to Deirdre Breen, Carlo Gebler, Donal Tinney, Allen Flynn, Lucy and Larry Blake, Pauline and Martin Hehir, and all the others who offered encouragement along the way; to the members of the Kiltumper Book Club, Marie O'Leary, Martin Keane, Marjorie Lynch, Dermot Mahony, Grainne Heneghan, Siobhan Phelan, Isobel O'Dea, Mary Cuffe, Jack Mannion, Carmel Mahony and Colette Keane, who have taught me so much about the pleasures of narrative and renewed my faith in stories.

Finally, to Deirdre and Joseph, and to Chris, as Virgil Swain says: 'You are the meaning.' For everything, thank you.

A Note on the Author

Niall Williams was born in Dublin in 1958. He is the author of eight novels including *John* and *Four Letters of Love* for which he has recently completed the screenplay for Element Pictures. He lives in Kiltumper in County Clare, with his wife, Christine.

niallwilliams.com

A Note on the Type

The text of this book is set in Bembo. This type was first used in 1495 by the Venetian printer Aldus Manutius for Cardinal Bembo's *De Aetna*, and was cut for Manutius by Francesco Griffo. It was one of the types used by Claude Garamond (1480–1561) as a model for his Romain de L'Université, and so it was the forerunner of what became standard European type for the following two centuries. Its modern form follows the original types and was designed for Monotype in 1929.